EPICENTRE

LEVIATHAN'S CHRONICLES 1

CHRIS ANDREWS

CREATIVE MANUSCRIPT SERVICES

For my Mother and Father

FOREWORD

This book has been a long time in coming, and couldn't have been produced without the help of some wonderful people. I would like to thank:

- The members of the Canberra Speculative Fiction Guild's Novel Critique Group
- Cover artist Les Petersen
- My beta readers Val Ackroyd and Megan Crossin

[1]

GRACE SIGHED in relief as a wave rushed up the beach and washed around her ankles, the subtle hints of lifeforce in the water making her body ache for more. As the wave slipped out, cool wet sand oozed between her toes, a pleasant distraction from her sunburn.

With her lifeforce nearly spent she couldn't afford the energy to heal. Not until she drowned someone.

Hundreds of people were bodysurfing, swimming, and jumping the waves, and she needed to drown one of them today. Grace pulled her long blond hair over her shoulders as another cool wave washed around her feet, sinking her deeper into the sand. Her claws, normally hidden when in human form, began to protrude from under her fingernails as her needs grew stronger. She had to choose a victim before she lost control and drowned someone she couldn't live with.

Hating herself just a little for giving in to her needs, she began humming, the subtle enchantment disguised by crashing waves and yelling children. She reluctantly pulled her feet from the wet sand and began meandering along the beach, determined not to let the water draw her into a killing frenzy.

Several young men eyed her as she strolled. She made herself smile at one, a tall, skinny, awkward-looking kid about sixteen or seventeen, but he turned away in embarrassment. She couldn't help her sense of relief that he didn't fall under her enchantment. Still, if she spoke to him she was sure she could easily lure him into the ocean.

A few yards ahead a boy of three or four squealed in delight as his father chased him into the waves. Grace almost swooned at the rush of the child's lifeforce when the next wave struck her feet, and not just his. Hundreds of people seemed to be begging her to drown them. She made herself continue humming, widening the effects of her enchantment. A teenage girl, maybe fourteen, quickly fell under her spell.

The girl pushed sun-bleached hair aside and bit her bottom lip invitingly as Grace strolled past. She had two friends with her though, either of which could cause a problem unless Grace took all three.

A few yards further along a toddler with brown skin and black curly hair spooned wet sand into bucket his father was holding. She felt the father's will crumble under her enchantment, but didn't dare look at him in case he left the child and tried to follow her.

A swarm of small children ran across her path to escape a wave, dodging around a tanned, muscle-bound guy carrying a boogie board into the water. The guy did a double take as he saw Grace, but made an effort to turn and follow a pre-teen girl who looked enough like him that she couldn't have been anyone else's child, his parenting instincts overriding her enchantment.

Another wave washed around her ankles, trying to tease her concentration away and draw her back to the ocean's embrace… and a killing spree. Killing indiscriminately felt so callous and inhuman, and she didn't want to forget she'd once been human herself.

Another wave struck, the lifeforce in it tingling her skin and sharpening her breath. Determined not to fall victim to her own needs, she left the water's edge for the hot sand, grimacing as her feet lost their natural toughness from exposure to the water.

Almost entirely human now, sand ground painfully into her un-calloused soles and clung to her feet and ankles, giving her a pedicure she didn't need or want.

Maintaining her enchantment, she continued to search for a victim who wouldn't weigh too heavily on her conscience. Humans ran about, lazed, read, and generally had fun. Some watched her, several young men staring openly now, but their instincts, or perhaps doubts, kept them from approaching.

Eyes followed her, heads turned, and a few mouths fell open as she meandered across the beach. She suspected that if she walked into the ocean now at least half a dozen people would follow.

An older man slathered in poorly rubbed-in sunscreen did a double take as he glanced her way. Quickly ensnared by her enchantment, his eyes wandered to her bikini-clad breasts, but then his face flushed red when he noticed her watching and he turned away, his embarrassment enough to break her hold.

Humming still, she continued her slow walk, both hoping and fearing she'd attract the right person. Many people stared openly as she strolled past, one couple even following from a distance. Grace hesitated when she saw Maria on the sand ahead. Her sister's dark hair cascaded to her waist, the light breeze moving it as she anxiously watched Grace, clearly determined to help if needed.

A toddler ran into Grace's leg and bounced off, the little girl landing on her rear in the dry sand.

Grace stopped humming. "Are you okay?" she asked as the toddler looked up with surprised blue eyes. A child of her own might have appeared much the same if Grace had had the opportunity while still human.

Sand clung to the little girl's hands and legs as she stood. "Uh-huh," she said before offering a gorgeous smile. The child's parents didn't seem to be nearby, catering to Grace's darker instincts. This close, Grace could feel the child's lifeforce emanating from her body like mist from dry ice. "You need to go," Grace whispered hoarsely.

An old, almost buried instinct to keep the toddler safe welled up in her, but it was fleeting and hard to cling to when her need to survive was growing so strong. She wanted to walk away, but her own needs ensnared her as much as her enchantments had caught the people on the beach.

Grace smiled back at the little girl, sensing herself approaching an edge she couldn't back away from. "*Hush little baby*," Grace found herself singing, the old nursery rhyme coming unbidden.

Her body ached with need and desire as her claws protruded and her serrated canines lengthened and pushed hard against the insides of her lips. Today more than any other day in the past few decades she had to kill someone. She wished it didn't have to be such a gorgeous child.

"*Mamma's going to buy you a rocking bird...*" Rocking horse? Mocking bird? She couldn't remember, not that it mattered. Slowly, deliberately, she reached for the child who watched her as if in a trance. "Are you lost?" she asked in the same sing-song voice, lifting the little girl up.

The toddler stared, wide-eyed and unblinking now, her will completely washed away by Grace's voice. "How about I help you find your mother?" Grace continued. She smiled at the little girl. "Would that be good? I saw her in the water, taking a swim."

"Uh-huh," the girl murmured, still staring.

"I think that would be best," Grace continued as she turned toward the foamy waves.

"Oh, there you are!" a young woman cried, running over to snatch the girl from Grace's arms. The woman was pregnant with her next child, at least half way there.

Grace's enchantment shattered like a stomped-on sandcastle. She clenched her fists to hide her claws as the woman became her new focus for murder, reluctantly letting the mother keep the toddler.

"She's a beautiful girl," Grace managed, clenching her teeth.

The woman smiled. "Thanks. If only she had a leash. I swear I only turned away for a second. Come on Tiani. No running off again, okay? You could have drowned and I'd never have known."

Grace's instincts made her tremble as the woman left with her victim, but she forced her needs down until her canines receded. It took a full minute more before her claws did the same.

"That was stupid," Maria said, her tone annoyed to the point of anger.

"I-"

"You could have drowned the toddler before her mother even realised she was missing." Despite centuries without seeing her homeland, Maria still retained her Italian accent.

"I was nearly there Maria."

"Two days, Grace. Just two left, including today. I can feel you slipping away." Maria touched Grace's pearl-encircled sapphire necklace with a single fingertip, the necklace similar to the one Maria wore. "You should kill more often. It makes it easier. You can't always rely on disasters to carry you through the years."

Grace tried to smile, but her charms were completely wasted on her sister.

Maria's dark brown eyes watched her, full of concern and love and fear. "You're going to have to pick someone. The less you think about it the easier it will be."

Grace watched the humans enjoying the day's warmth. "Easier? The only time it was easy was when you made me and I was in the throes of transformation. I didn't even know what I was doing."

"Pretend that's today."

Grace stared at the soft sand, a torn piece of dry seaweed crushed under someone's footstep. "Dying once was enough. It's not a memory I cherish."

Maria placed her hand on Grace's shoulder, looking up at the taller woman. "You didn't die. Of all the victims the sea should have claimed that night, I saved only you."

"I died. We can't have children Maria. Living people have children."

"*You're* my daughter! My sister. My love."

"I'm your creation."

Maria stiffened as hurt and anger collided on her features.

Grace instantly regretted the words. "You're my best friend and the person I love most in the world, but I'm not your child. My mother died in England a century ago," she said softly.

Instead of the expected outburst, Maria's eyes filled. "You're not human Grace, and neither am I. We kill humans. We have to."

"Not all Creatures kill for lifeforce. Most just take what they need to survive, like vampires."

"*Never* compare yourself to them! We're *magical*. Natural. They're… vermin. Even if there was enough magic in the world to sustain us, it'd do them no good. They're parasites by nature. They can't survive without blood. We kill only because there's not enough magic." She took a calming breath. "Never mind. You're the only thing in the world I care about Grace. The *only* thing. Don't ever belittle that. I love you more than my own life. I even defied our sisters to create you."

Grace couldn't meet Maria's eyes. "I'm sorry. It's just... I hate this part. If I didn't have to kill there'd be nothing to hate about this life." That, and her inability to have a child of her own, but she kept that to herself as she toyed with her necklace, the slight tingle of stored lifeforce it still held doing little to make her feel better.

Maria's expression softened. "Would you rather I'd let you die that day? Would you change that if you could?"

"No. I just wish…" Wish what? That she could kill without feeling guilty? Did she ever really want that? "I really hate this part."

"Sometimes you have to kill to survive, Grace. All life struggles in one way or another, and we're part of that. We keep the balance by taking the injured, the unlucky, and the stupid." She glanced around the beach. "And sometimes we take those who don't deserve it. It's how life works."

"I know."

Maria took Grace's hands. "How about I help you pick someone? That way you can blame me and you won't have to feel guilty."

"I'll still feel guilty."

"Maybe a little less guilty?"

Grace couldn't help a tiny smile. "Maybe just a little."

Maria pointed to a balding man walking toward the water. "How about him? He's old enough to have lived well, and by the look of that dark mole on his back he isn't going to survive much longer. Nothing to feel guilty about. Right?"

Grace watched the man for a moment, but he didn't go deeper than his knees. If he feared swimming beyond his depth then no enchantment would lure him further.

"A decent rip would be handy about now."

"You've got it easy little sister. In the old days we had to wait for a shipwreck or creep into a village at night and steal a child. Some of us died that way." She got a distant look in her eyes, but it disappeared almost as quickly. "Nowadays there's plenty of people in the water. Just pick someone swimming alone and drag them under. Better yet, stalk a surfer. No one will notice if they don't surface for a while after a spill, and by then you'll have another year to chance upon a disaster and top up that necklace."

Chance upon a disaster? It sounded so cold.

Maria squeezed Grace's arm. "How about that boy?" she said, pointing with her free hand. "He's out way too far, and no one's near him." She raised an eyebrow. "What kind of parent lets a kid that young swim out so deep on his own? Looks like he's getting into trouble, too."

"He's not in troub… oh."

"C'mon!" Maria began dragging Grace toward the water.

"Okay, okay!" Grace said, hating herself for listening. She could do this. It would be far too easy to drown the boy, and after that she wouldn't have to think about it again for a year. Wincing as the sand ground into her feet she walked down to the water and sighed in relief when a cool wave washed soothingly against her shins, toughening her skin.

The touch of water brought on the familiar need to change forms as well as the comforting sense of Maria's enthusiasm and love. Grace struggled to hold onto her human shape as she walked deeper into the ocean, the waves crashing into her thighs.

The beach was shallow for the first twenty steps or so, but there it dropped off. A wave crashed against her waist and it was almost too much to hold her human form. She clenched her teeth at the next wave and barely managed not to revert. She wouldn't last through another.

Looking around to be sure no one was watching too closely, she dived under and slipped off her bikini bottoms. As the ocean welcomed her, her body shuddered in near ecstasy. She held on for another second just to prove to herself that she could, but then her legs fused into a long, powerful tail.

A single flick and she was away, powering under the waves faster than any human could hope to swim, the bottom half of her body elongated and shaped like a dolphin's, the end of her tail a translucent fan over two feet wide.

Her hair washed out behind her, the golden sun-streaks tinged with green and blue now, while her skin changed to the mottled colour of the sandy bottom to help her blend in.

Better to take the boy quickly before she had time to talk herself out of it. She cleared the breaking surf and swam deeper, scaring schools of fish in all directions.

Few humans were brave enough to swim beyond the waves, but the lack of sand under their feet didn't deter them all. Only the fact they weren't the preferred prey of anything in the ocean made it even remotely safe for them. Anything except a mermaid.

Grace stopped and faced the shore as a swell moved over her, the water there almost luminescent with lifeforce. She could absorb the lifeforce, but it was like drinking from a morning mist. She needed much more than the ocean could ever give to her.

Hopefully the boy had grown some common sense and retreated into the relative safety of the group, but it only took a few seconds to find the small pair of legs pumping beyond the reach of sand, his body bobbing up and down with the surface movement.

Staying close to the sand, Grace drifted nearer, allowing her instincts to crowd her thoughts and dissolve her human desire to nurture and protect the child. If she relaxed completely she'd risk taking more than just the child though, but she couldn't do it while thinking entirely rationally either. She might drown a dozen people before regaining her senses.

She felt Maria's presence on the beach, her sister's feet in the water and her emotions calm and assured, but focused. There was no obvious danger then. Her disappearance under the waves hadn't been noticed, not that it would really matter. People would forget soon enough. Magical Creatures could never have stayed hidden otherwise.

There were no other mermaids nearby either. They all stayed clear of Grace and Maria, as Maria had been shunned since making Grace without permission, though Grace was sure there was more to the story. It would pass eventually, Maria assured her. They were all connected after all, and it hurt them as much as it hurt Maria and Grace.

Hopefully Maria had managed to collect her bikini bottoms. Clothes were hard to come by when you were naked and broke. With her tail moving up and down she eased nearer, wary of the people close enough to see the boy disappear. She didn't want searchers in the water if she lost control.

She waited until the boy drifted a few yards closer to her, and as a swell moved between the boy and the nearest person she darted in behind him, drove her shoulder against the back of his knees, grabbed his ankles and took him under.

He didn't react for a moment, but then thrashed and kicked. She dug her claws into his skin and flicked her tail, forcing him deeper.

The boy's desperation became blind panic, but she held his ankles hard against her chest.

Having drowned herself once, she hated inflicting the same fear on someone else and cursed herself for forgetting to sing, but his panic was completely beyond her enchantments now. His arms struggled wildly for the surface while he tried to kick free, but it didn't take long before his strength waned.

When it did, she loosened her grip and turned his limp form in her arms.

He seemed so small, sandy brown hair floating about his face. He blinked, smiled, and mouthed the word, 'Mum', and then his eyes rolled back.

The word felt like a knife in her stomach and Grace's instincts failed her.

Grabbing the boy by the shoulders, she shot up at an angle, breaking through the surface just beyond the breakers.

She pinched the boy's nose and blew oxygen into his mouth, but he remained limp. She flicked her tail and pushed toward shore behind a wave, and as she reached the first person she drove her tail downward and felt sand.

"Quick," she said, pushing the boy into a well-tanned woman's arms. "I think he's swallowed some water."

The woman hesitated as she came to terms with someone appearing in front of her holding a limp boy, but then she took the child. "What happened?"

"Just get him to shore! Go!"

Grace held back as the woman spun and desperately struggled toward the beach, all the while trying to keep the boy's head above water. Several people came to help and Grace took the opportunity to slip under a wave and shoot away like a terrified porpoise.

$$[\ 2\ ]$$

"STUPID, STUPID, STUPID!"

Grace swam northward toward the Tollgates just off Batemans Bay, keeping close to the reefs as she flashed through the cool salty water, scaring schools of fish. She should have drowned the boy. A few more seconds and…

"Ooh!" She drove her tail hard downward before covering her face with her hands. Water rushed around her for a few moments, but she soon began drifting with the current.

It was so much easier taking disaster victims, people who'd been swept into the ocean or lost overboard. People who would have drowned anyway. If nothing else, it was a way to justify murder to herself.

The thump of waves against a fishing boat's hull reached her and her need to kill flared again. The boat was drifting a few hundred yards away like a cork on the swell, its prow rising and dropping over waves as the propeller idled to keep it facing into the wind. Three fishing lines pierced the water, their hooks and bait taken deep on heavy sinkers.

Grace's heart began beating faster as she visualised one of the anglers falling overboard. A good shove from one side as a wave struck and she'd have a new victim. A few, maybe.

"Stop it!" she whispered to herself, tangling her claws in her hair and pulling hard to keep herself thinking straight. She turned her back on the boat despite her pounding pulse, knowing her needs would only grow worse until she killed again. Or died.

At least there'd be no grieving parents tonight, no heartache or tears because of her.

The last of the magical lifeforce she'd stored in her necklace would get used up tomorrow morning, giving her until the following evening to drown someone. She could hold a year's worth of lifeforce within her body, but any excess got wasted unless she stored it away, and it had been nearly a decade since she'd taken anyone. She'd been relying on her necklace the entire time.

She reached for her necklace, but her fingers failed to find the familiar shape.

Fear rushed through her as she checked and double checked, even running her fingers through her hair to make sure it hadn't been caught.

Never mind tomorrow, she'd die at sunset today without the lifeforce her necklace held for her. The boy must have pulled it free as he struggled, leaving it at the bottom of South Broulee Beach. Barely keeping panic at bay, Grace swam hard above reefs she'd grown intimately familiar with over the last few decades, sharks and ocean life shooting away from her in fear.

The sun was beginning to sink toward the horizon when she broke through the surface off the beach, many of the people gone already.

Fear nearly drove her to take the first life she could, but she held off in the hope she could find her necklace before sunset. Tomorrow she might chance on a fisherman washed from the rocks or a swimmer caught in a rip, someone who would die regardless of her actions, but for now she only wanted her necklace.

Diving under, her natural abilities camouflaged her skin as she ran her fingers through the soft sand, moving carefully to avoid people bodysurfing above her, a task made more difficult by the receding tide.

Nothing. Even though her necklace was attuned to her, she couldn't sense the stored lifeforce it contained.

A human must have seen her necklace and... She didn't want to consider the consequences. It could be miles away by now; a long drive up or down the coast. With luck it had tangled in the boy's fingers and been dropped in the sand. She couldn't help the hope she felt, unlikely as it was.

She was almost desperate enough ride a wave to shore and transform on the sand, ignoring the attention it would create, and not just from being naked from the waist down.

She popped her head out of the ocean just beyond the breakers, the sun barely above the distant mountains now. "Hurry Grace. Hurry," she whispered to herself.

Dropping back under the rolling surface she swam to the rocks at the north end of the beach, hoping to steal some clothes so she could search on shore. She'd only have to be within a few yards of her necklace to sense it. When she resurfaced she found nearly a dozen people fishing on the beach side of the rocks. She'd have to go further around or find a secluded spot on Broulee Island and walk back, time she may not have.

She swam around the rocks hoping the little beach there might be free of people. Maria! Her sister was sitting alone on the semi-permanent sandbar between the mainland and Broulee Island, her long dark hair playing across the sand in the breeze as she stared out over the ocean.

Grace stayed within a small wave all the way to the beach, and as the wave receded she forced the water from her skin and changed form before running to her sister.

"Maria! Where's my bikini?"

"Why do you care?" She gave Grace a look full of hurt.

"Please Maria, he was just was a little boy. A child!"

"You've drowned more than a hundred people since I made you. Do you regret their deaths?"

How could she ask that? "Of course! But most of them were going to die anyway. How could I drown that boy knowing how his parents would feel?"

Maria stood and tossed Grace's bikini to her. "You hate this life, don't you?

"Don't be melodramatic." Grace put the bikini bottoms on. "My necklace is gone. The boy must have pulled it off."

"What!" Maria's expression went to Grace's neck. "We've got maybe twenty minutes. If you don't renew your life's energy by then…"

"I know!"

Maria grabbed Grace's hand and they ran back together, stopping where the road, rocks and beach converged. "You have to drown the first person you can."

The thought terrified her. "Sometimes I hate being a mermaid, I really do," she whispered as she stared at the remaining people on the beach and in the water.

"Really?" Maria asked, devastation clear in her expression. "Do you really hate me that much?"

"You? No! Never you, only what we need to do to survive. I'll do it. For you."

"For me?" Maria replied with a whisper. "But you'd let yourself go, otherwise?"

"Stop it! I couldn't do that. I just hate… stop manipulating me! I don't want to die!"

"Then promise me you'll do everything you can to survive."

"But-"

"Promise or I won't help you! I swear I won't."

"Never make promises! You taught me that."

Maria's expression hardened. "I made you and I love you more than my own life, but it'll kill me to see you die." She took a deep breath, staring at Grace with resolve. "I promise I will not help you find your necklace unless you promise to do everything you can to survive."

"Maria, no," Grace whispered. Maria's promise was binding. Absolutely. If Grace didn't make her own promise…

Maria stared back, defiance on her face. "I'll do anything but watch you die Grace. I-"

Grace cut Maria off as she caught her sister's face in both her hands. "I promise to do everything I can to survive." She felt the essence of the oath sink into her like a chill. "Oh God. What have I done?"

Maria released her breath, her relieved expression showing how uncertain she'd actually been, which hurt Grace more than she expected. "Come on. Let's find your necklace. Tomorrow you can drown someone."

"Yay… Tomorrow I get to drown someone."

Maria gave her a look, but Grace's stomach already churned in anticipation as they ran onto the beach's cooling sand. She'd spent a century around beaches and seaside communities masquerading as a human and talking to unsuspecting people, but she was beginning to find the sensation of walking strange now. Legs felt foreign, jolting them the weirdest sensation of all.

Many mermaids never even ventured ashore, and she was beginning to understand why. Whenever she could find the money though, she loved to go to the cinema. "If I find the necklace I'll pick someone horrid-"

"Justify it any way you like," Maria said curtly. "I don't care who."

They began scouring the beach, hurriedly walking back and forth in the area the boy had come ashore. The salty breeze was rapidly cooling, most of the people coming out of the water or packing up and going home.

"Someone must have picked it up," Grace said. The compulsion of her promise was beginning to grow inside her. She had to kill, and soon. She met Maria's eyes and saw her own fears reflected.

"Do it," Maria said, nodding toward the remaining swimmers. "Do it now. You have to."

Grace wished her willpower alone could force the sun back up into the sky. Only the treetops on the nearby headland showed any direct sunlight, and they cast long shadows out across the ocean.

"Do it while there are still people out deep."

Grace avoided a dozen young men and women, probably around twenty years old, striding from the foaming waves while kicking water and laughing about their bodysurfing skills. Three girls, all carrying boogie boards, rolled their eyes at the guys.

One guy playfully shoved another out of the way and... revealed a tall guy at the back wearing her necklace! He must have found it in the surf.

Her life depending on it, Grace ran splashing into the ankle-deep water. "You!" she said, pointing at him. "That's my necklace! I need it back."

He stopped in surprise, a foamy wave striking his calves and cascading around his legs before it struck Grace's shins, enticingly full of his lifeforce. He took a step sideways, preparing to go around her. "Say again?"

"You have my necklace. I need it back." The compulsion of her promise forced her to reach for it, but he sidled another half step as his friends surrounded her.

The guy's lifeforce called to her through the water, stronger than the others. Some humans were like that. The sensation forced her claws out, making her clench her fists to hide them. "You don't understand. I lost it in the surf. I really need it back. My sister gave it to me."

"Get lost," said a busty redhead as she moved possessively close to the tall guy. "He's going to give it to me, aren't you Josh?"

Grace stiffened, sensing the redhead wasn't human. She didn't know what kind of a Creature she was, but standing in the water it was clear she was inhuman. She gave of no trace of lifeforce whatsoever. Maria jokingly called it the Great Deficit. Humans had more than they needed, whereas Creatures needed more than they had.

Despite her dubious status as a fellow Creature, the redhead must have slathered herself in sunscreen to avoid sunburn. There wasn't a freckle anywhere on her pale skin. The two friends shadowing her had picture-perfect tans though, one of Asian descent with bleached hair, and the other a plain brunette, creamy English skin and a cruel twist to her lips. Lean and hard, they both looked like athletes, while the redhead seemed more the runway-model type. The other two, at least, gave off lifeforce. There was something strange about it though, but the only reason Grace could tell was because they were standing in her element.

Grace stared at them, trying to work it out. They weren't exactly human, but she couldn't tell what they were, though the redhead definitely wasn't the same as the other two. Different Creatures banding together? She'd rarely heard of that. Unless… the other two were werewolves with a foot in both human and Creature worlds. Werewolves often served true Creatures.

The tall guy ignored the redhead. He half lifted the necklace up. "I'll give it to you for a kiss. Call it a finder's fee." He let a cheeky grin show as his mates laughed. He certainly knew how to use his looks.

On another day Grace might have accepted, but right then she had to fight the urge to drown the lot of them, particularly the redhead, though drowning another Creature wasn't always possible.

One kiss and he'd do whatever she wanted, and what she wanted right then was lifeforce. She wouldn't be able to resist luring him back into the ocean, and that wouldn't be good for anyone.

"I can't. I really can't."

Under the influence of her own promise, she couldn't help herself and stepped forward again, caught between accepting the offer of a kiss and snatching her necklace. He caught her wrist as she reached for it. She stiffened, struggling not to kill him right then.

"Kiss me and it's yours."

"Please don't ask that," she whispered. She really didn't want to kill him, but a kiss would seal his fate. Standing in the ocean she was easily ten times stronger than him. She could kill the lot of them with little trouble.

The redhead was almost imploding with impotent anger as she glared at the guy, and Grace realised what this was all about. She wanted him, and he knew it. He was teasing her, not Grace. Shit.

"You don't want a kiss from me," she whispered. "I have a cold sore coming on." A simple kiss and he'd even fight off his friends to get to her.

He released her wrist and moved around her with a shrug, walking up the beach to the dry sand. Her options fell away with every step he took.

"It was a gift," she called out desperately. She could almost feel the seconds counting down to sunset. If he didn't give it to her in the next few moments she'd have to drown the first person she could.

He paused, looking back over his shoulder with the same cocky grin. "Say please."

His friends sniggered while the bottle-blonde shoved Grace with her shoulder as she passed. One of his mates chuckled, the guy with dark skin and curly hair so thick that even the ocean couldn't pin down.

"Make her beg for it," the redhead said as she passed Grace, moving possessively close to the tall guy again. She didn't quite put her arm around him, but clearly wanted to. "Make her grovel in the sand."

"Hey Josh," said the weedy guy as he threw his boogie board on the ground. "You need your car washed, don't you? Why not trade the necklace for a carwash?

"Good call!" the dark-skinned guy said. "A hot girl in a skimpy bikini slaving over a hot car! I'd pay to see that."

"Hot girl?" the redhead asked, her voice pitched a little too high. Almost unconsciously she moved even closer to Josh, her arm brushing his.

The skinny guy laughed, himself nearly as pale as the redhead, but with sandy brown hair. There were about a dozen people still swimming out deep enough for Grace to take easily. She wouldn't have any qualms about drowning the redhead or the two extra guys facing her, but they weren't in the water anymore.

She didn't even have something she could trade. "I-"

"Not just the car!" the bottle-blonde werewolf said. "If she really wants it back, make her clean your toilet or give us all massages in between peeling our grapes."

The brunette laughed. "Totally. Make her your fucking slave," she said.

"Hell yeah. We could use a slave for the weekend," the skinny guy said, grinning.

The redhead frowned, clearly not liking the idea. "Just give her the necklace and let's go Josh."

The compulsion of her own promise rising uncompromisingly inside her, Grace couldn't help taking a step forward. If she didn't get it back now… "Fine! Just give me my necklace and I promise to be your slave for the weekend! Please."

Oh crap. That's not what she'd meant to say. She almost slapped her hand over her mouth.

He shrugged. "All you had to say was please."

He slipped it over his head and tossed it to her. As she caught it the compulsion in her promise settled over her.

Oh crap! What had she done? Slave for the weekend? She glanced at the people splashing about in the waves and hated them for their blissful ignorance. Without the necklace, one of them would have been dead within a minute.

She put her necklace back over her head, breathing a huge sigh of relief at the tingle of remaining lifeforce. She had a full day to pick a new victim whose death she could live with, which gave her enough time to honour her promise to Maria.

"Tomorrow's Saturday, isn't it?" asked the guy with dark skin.

"Yeah," said the skinny guy. "I think Josh needs his car washed first thing." There was some laughter at that.

Josh grinned. "Sounds good. Be at my place by nine, okay?" He'd decided to play along, though she could tell by the tone of his voice he wasn't serious. It made no difference. An order was an order.

Most of the boys laughed, but Grace felt the compulsion. He'd said it with sarcasm and clearly didn't expect her to turn up, but whatever else happened she would be at his house at nine tomorrow morning. She didn't know where it was yet, but compulsion was going to ensure she did everything she could to find it. She swore under her breath.

She caught Maria's eye, disbelief clear on her sister's face.

"What have you done?" Maria mouthed.

[3]

"GRACE," someone called from behind them, though Grace didn't recognise the voice. She turned to find a dark-skinned woman with long curly hair standing calf-deep in a receding wave, her expression angry as she glared at Maria.

Grace turned to her sister, only to find Maria had gone as pale as the sands of Hyams Beach. "Talithia," Maria said with a slight nod.

"Talithia?" Grace repeated in a whisper. "That's your mother?" She gave the other mermaid a second look, her dark skin set off beautifully by her white bikini. Talithia was one of the original twelve. She was also Grace's grandmother from a mermaid perspective. Technically they all considered each other sisters, but lineage still mattered and was acknowledged. Maria was Talithia's only daughter, and Grace Maria's. Although they all looked like young women barely past their teens, Talithia was rumoured to be over three thousand years old.

Grace felt her expression harden. This was the woman who'd banished Maria from all contact with other mermaids. Maria had refused to elaborate on the issue, and the other mermaids, though warm and welcoming to Grace, shunned Maria and wouldn't speak of it either.

Grace crossed her arms. "What do you want Talithia?"

Maria elbowed her. "Shut up."

Grace turned on Maria. "Why? Or she'll banish me too? I don't care. We have each other."

"Come with me Grace," Talithia said, indicating the ocean as a wave surged around her legs. She seemed reluctant to step onto the dry sand.

Maria's shoulder slumped. "Go Grace. Do as she says."

Grace stood a little taller. If she had to guess, she'd say Talithia originated somewhere in South America. Brazil perhaps, though her skin was a little darker than Grace might have expected for someone from there. "No. I'm not leaving you."

Talithia narrowed her eyes, and Grace had the impression she wasn't used to being challenged. "Maria's education efforts are severely lacking." She glanced at the people still on the beach with just the hint of a frown, most packing to go, though a few still persisted in the waves as they revelled in the last of the daylight. They had no idea how much danger they were in if Talithia turned on them. If any mermaid did for that matter, and no doubt Talithia didn't travel alone.

If Grace stepped into the water she'd be able to tell who else was nearby as well as read Talithia's emotions. Not that she needed to, judging by her expression.

Talithia pursed her lips. "Grace, I've been keeping an eye on you. Your lifeforce is almost gone. Maria should never have allowed it to get this close." She turned her dark-eyed glare on Maria. "I've given you as much leeway with your daughter as I could, but today you proved you're not worthy of raising her."

Raising? Like a frigging toddler? Grace had no intention of being intimidated, no matter their linage or Talithia's status as an original. "My situation isn't Maria's fault-"

Talithia cut her off with a glare. "Maria has been far too soft on you Grace. You need to learn-"

"Learn what? To be a murderer without pity? A brutal killer like you?"

Talithia clenched her jaw, her lips pursed as if she wanted to vent anger but was holding it back. She glared briefly as Maria as if the turn of the conversation were her fault. "Grace, you have a duty to your sisters. Your reluctance to take what you need threatens to expose us. You sympathise with humans when you shouldn't, and we need to fix that before it becomes a problem for all of us."

"But-"

"Three Creatures just walked out of the ocean with those boys you were talking to, and at least one of them is likely to have recognised you for what you are, or at least as another Creature. We leave them alone and they leave us alone, that's unspoken, but if you change the status quo we could find ourselves at war. Mermaids would die." She waved a hand toward the ocean behind her. "Would you put us at risk simply because you sympathise? Maria should have sent you to us the day she made you, or at least trained you properly. If you want to know who's to blame for this decision, it's Maria."

That wasn't fair. "I-"

"You will come with me now, Grace." Talithia didn't raise her voice, but there was no compromise either.

"I made a promise," Grace blurted out. "I can't come. Not yet."

"Shut up," Maria whispered under her breath. "Just go with her. Please. This is my fault. I thought I could do better, but I couldn't. Go."

This wasn't like her fiery sister at all. "Why are you being so submissive? What's wrong with you?"

"It's for the best," Maria said, but she wouldn't meet Grace's eyes.

Regardless, the compulsion in her promise to find out where Josh lived overrode any sense of duty she felt to Maria, Talithia or her other sisters. "I can't," she said softly. "Literally."

Talithia closed her eyes briefly. "Explain."

Embarrassment flushed Grace's cheeks and she dropped her eyes. "I made a promise in exchange for my necklace. It's only for the weekend," she added a little too quickly. "But I… need to complete my promise." She was far too embarrassed to explain it in any meaningful way.

A slight frown marred Talithia's forehead. She obviously wasn't stupid. Rather than embarrassing Grace though, she gave a slight nod. "Will you willingly come to me after your promise is resolved?"

Maria gave a nod. "She will."

Grace glared at Maria, but her sister looked so down she didn't have the heart to berate her. She sighed. "Fine. After the weekend."

"Is that a promise?" There was a slight smile on Talithia's lips, as if she'd cornered her prey. Clearly she was willing to concede the weekend for the assurance a promise would bring.

Grace, feeling as if she had no choice, nodded. "I will come to you once I've fulfilled the conditions of my promise."

"Immediately afterward? And will you stay for as long as I deem it necessary?"

Damn. She wasn't going to wriggle out of this. "Fine. I… promise." The promise settled over her like a wet blanket, claustrophobic and clinging. The sensation left her with a slightly sick feeling. In more than a century she hadn't made a single promise, and suddenly she'd made three in half an hour. "Happy?" she asked with more than a little resentment in her voice. A century with Maria was rubbing off in her attitude.

Talithia glanced at Maria and something passed between them. "Not really." She turned and strode back into the water, ignoring the few remaining people around her as she dived under a wave and never resurfaced.

"I knew this would happen eventually," Maria murmured, turning and stalking back up the beach. She appeared devastated.

"Where are you going?"

"To kill that rotten kid who caused all of this. I want you safely back in the water tonight."

Maria was taking Talithia's side on this? "Hey. That's not fair," Grace said, but Maria ignored her as she strode off.

$$[\ 4 \ ]$$

"How could you have made such a compromising promise to a human?" Maria asked as Grace caught up.

Grace put a hand on Maria's shoulder to stop her. "I panicked!" Grace said, taking a step back when she saw Maria's anger. She'd never seen Maria so mad. Her sister almost appeared ready to slap Grace, her teeth clenched and her fingers splayed as if preparing to use her claws.

After a second of impotent indecision Maria turned and strode away again. "I really am going to kill him," she said. "No one messes with my sister, and no one threatens us. Go back to the water."

Grace forced down a chill at her sister's tone as she ran and caught up to Maria again, hoping she really wasn't ready to slap her. "He didn't do anything but tease me a little. He didn't even take the promise seriously. He thought it was a joke."

Maria continued walking, leaving the beach for a sandy path between the scrub and the surf-lifesaving building. "A promise to a dead guy means nothing. After I kill him you can go to Talithia and be safe. I'm going to drown his friends too, just for good measure."

That was even less fair. "Maria-"

Maria spun, glaring. "He has control over you! I will not allow it. It's him or us."

"We're on land! We're as weak as humans. You can't do anything here."

Maria turned and began walking again. "Really?" she said over her shoulder as they found the group had delayed at the fresh-water showers outside the surf-lifesaving block. The look on Maria's face suggested a public execution was in order, and there was more than enough water coming from the shower to do it. "All I need to do is get close enough to touch the water," she said.

Grace grabbed her sister's arm, forcing it down. "Maria, don't. Please. At least, not in public." Anything to delay her. If she could get through the promise simply by washing a car and no other problems arose, everyone would survive this.

Maria frowned at all the people. It would certainly look strange if half a dozen kids suddenly drowned while showering. She tightened her jaw and kept walking past the showers, stopping at a small crafts market up the street beyond the surf-rescue building. Maria pretended to examine some hand-made gift cards featuring sketched flowers and people. Grace anxiously stepped up beside Maria, reaching for her upper arm. "Maria-"

Maria turned away, picking up a piece of amber from the next table, shaped into a dolphin. "Leave it, Grace," Maria warned, the threat in her voice clear. It was a tone Grace knew well. "I'm doing it. Would you like me to make it a promise?"

"Maria-"

"We're not discussing it." Maria moved to the next stall, faking interest in an older lady's lace craftwork, her back to Grace on purpose.

Grace clenched her fists in frustration.

"Your friend doesn't look very happy with you," said a huge biker behind a jewellery stall table. He had tattoos of skulls, death and destruction all over his arms and neck, rings in his ears and eyebrows, and long salt and pepper dreadlocks pulled in a ponytail.

He looked like he'd come straight from the set of a biker movie, not a look you'd expect from someone selling hand-made jewellery. "I like those old biker movies," Grace muttered to herself, glaring at Maria's back and hoping her sister could feel it.

"Me too," the biker said with a smile which revealed a broken front tooth. "Wish I was riding now."

"What?" Grace asked, giving the guy another look. His features were weathered, and his blue eyes... they gave Grace the shivers. Whatever the man was, he was old, and not in a human way. His eyes betrayed centuries of experience, though she couldn't figure out exactly why she thought so. He looked entirely human and even gave off lifeforce like a human. But...

"Biker movies. I like them too," he reiterated.

Was he dangerous? He had to be. What the heck was he? "Oh-kay," Grace said softly, wondering whether she should grab Maria and run for the ocean. All magical Creatures were dangerous in one way or another, though she doubted he'd be here if he was looking for trouble.

"Why are you selling hand-made jewellery? You hardly fit the stereotype."

He grinned, revealing the broken tooth as if he were proud of it. "I see my disguise doesn't fool you, but I'm not the only one with secrets here, am I, little fish? Visited the Titanic lately?"

Grace stiffened. How could the Creature have known Grace had been on the Titanic before Maria saved her? "Who are you? What are you?"

"Unique." To demonstrate, the biker ran scarred fingertips over a silver bangle without showing any pain. She held her breath in surprise. What magical Creature could tolerate silver?

The biker picked up a beautifully woven gold bracelet with five white crystals spaced around it, each crystal dangling from its own link. Each link had been woven around a pearl, which in turn had been woven into the bracelet itself. He held out the piece. "Try it on. You'll find it fits."

Grace glanced around the markets warily, sensing a trap. Everything looked normal, but that didn't mean anything. Was there some sort of enchantment on the bracelet? She didn't know of anyone who could manipulate magic in that way, but she'd seen enough to know it was possible.

"Thank you, but I've got no money," Grace said. She had to

convince Maria to go back to the ocean right now, but wasn't certain she could afford to offend the Creature. Grace and Maria were almost as vulnerable as humans on land, particularly without water nearby, and she had no idea what she faced in this man. Something powerful if he could touch silver without flinching.

"Did I ask for money?" the Creature asked. Could he be an ancient incubi? No, incubi couldn't tolerate silver any more than mermaids could. That, and he gave off lifeforce. Perhaps tolerance came with age, though even the oldest mermaids couldn't tolerate silver any more than Grace could.

"Everything has a price," Grace said softly. "Whatever it is, I can't afford it."

The biker ignored her and undid the clasp. "No price. No cost. Just a gift. You're going to need my help to save your sisters one day Grace, and this bracelet isn't a gift I offer lightly."

"What do you mean?"

The crystals dangled enticingly. Gems were often used by mermaids as repositories for magic, but Grace wasn't sure what crystals did. She'd never seen one used for anything magical. They might as well have been ordinary rocks. She eyed the gift cautiously. "What does it do?"

"It stores natural magic, or lifeforce as you prefer to call it, the sort you could feel coming from humans in the water. Not stolen." He glanced at her necklace as if to suggest he knew all her secrets. All her kind's secrets too. It chilled her. Secrets were all that kept her kind safe. All that kept any Creature safe.

She had a feeling there was very little she could say he wouldn't already know. "I can't survive on natural magic any more than a human can photosynthesise sunlight." There simply wasn't enough in the world to absorb. "And I already have a necklace that stores lifeforce."

"Stolen lifeforce." The Creature amended, and there was a predatory look in his eyes that made Grace want to back away. "Maria will be leaving soon. Better decide quickly." He held out the bracelet again.

Grace hesitated at the use of her sister's name. "What do you want? Really?"

He shrugged. "I was on the deck of the Titanic when it went down, and watched as Maria drowned you. You're younger than your sisters, the youngest of your kind on this world. I'm hoping you're open to change, unlike most of them." He glanced at the bracelet with a raised eyebrow.

"Explain it to me then. Why will that bracelet help? Why do you care?"

The Creature sighed. "The crystals attract and store natural magic, the type lost to nature when not consumed and distilled by Creatures like you." He caressed one of the crystals. "If you can find a way to access it, you'll never have to kill again."

A cold thrill of hope ran through her. "And you offer this gift without obligation?"

"Consider us allies, if it helps."

"What's your name?"

He looked away abruptly, staring westward as if seeing something far distant. He gave a slight smile. "She's here. Finally."

"Who's here?"

He focused on Grace again. "Sellendria. You may get to know her in time." He held out the bracelet. "Take it. No obligation."

Grace hesitantly held her hand out. The biker dropped the bracelet into Grace's palm and then closed her fingers over it. "Good luck Grace. You're going to need it."

"What's your name?"

He smiled, his form shifting into that of a small blonde woman wearing a plain white cotton dress that could have come from the 70s. The jewellery on the table disappeared, quickly followed by the table itself. "Kimbriel. I'll see you soon enough."

Like the table and jewellery, Kimbriel also disappeared, leaving Grace clutching a bracelet she wasn't even sure she wanted.

Kimbriel was clearly a shapeshifter, but what else? How could she disappear like that? What had Grace stumbled into?

[5]

FROM THE CORNER of her eye Grace noticed Maria moving away from the stalls, following Josh and his friends at a distance as they headed for the shops down the main road.

Clutching her new bracelet, Grace ran after Maria. The shops weren't far, but they were across the road and holiday traffic zipped past in both directions. Maria moved with a determined stride Grace knew too well. "Maria! Let it be. They're just a bunch of kids."

"Dead kids," Maria said. "Stay on the beach if you're squeamish."

The compulsion in Grace's promise forced her to do what she could to find out where Josh lived. So long as he was alive she had to fulfil her promise to him. Right now that meant following Maria. Ahead, Josh and his friends crossed the main road at the first break in traffic, heading for the shops a little further along on the opposite side.

"He didn't hurt me or even mean to do anything more than tease me a little. Let it go Maria."

Maria stopped walking, turning. "You really don't want to be a mermaid, do you?" Her expression was accusatory.

Grace stared at her sister in shock. Where had that come from? "Of course I do! I wouldn't want to be anything but your sister."

Maria gave her a flat stare. "Really?"

"Yes! I just hate having to drown people."

Maris's expression hardened. "Which is why Talithia came for you. I failed as your maker."

"Oh, come on! I'm the problem, not you."

"No," she said. "I am."

"Maria!"

Her sister's expression didn't soften. "What's your plan Grace? Drown someone tonight and then be a good little slave over the weekend? I don't know whether I'm more ashamed of myself for letting you get so desperate for lifeforce, or of you for making such a stupid promise."

Grace caught Maria's hand. "I'll find someone who's already drowning and I'll take them. We can worry about Josh tomorrow."

Maria pulled her hand free, but her expression suggested she was even more hurt by that statement. "You couldn't find anyone to drown over the last decade. Do you honestly believe it will happen tonight or tomorrow morning?" Maria watched the group of youths and the red-headed Creature enter the takeaway up the road, shaking her head. "You've saved more people from drowning than you've ever taken. If you'd sucked it up just once in the last year we wouldn't be standing here."

Grace glanced away in embarrassment, although saving people shouldn't make her feel ashamed. "Helping people… justifies… my existence, somehow. Like I'm balancing out the bad with the good."

Maria gave her a look which said she didn't understand Grace at all. "How's that philosophy working for you now, slave girl?"

Hurt flared, and Grace tried to hide it from her expression. Why wouldn't Maria see her side of it? "It's only for the weekend, and if he never finds out he has power over me there's no harm done."

"But you've still got to drown someone. Two birds…"

"Please Maria. He's a nice kid."

Maria's expression lost all enthusiasm for the hunt, replaced with disappointment. No, more than that. Disbelief, like something vital had broken inside her. She shook her head, her long damp hair sticking to her shoulders. "I should have sent you to live with our sisters. They'd have sorted you out." She stared at Grace like a lover she'd never get to see again, or perhaps never known at all. "I'm so sorry I let you down so badly."

Grace tried not to let Maria see how much that hurt her, although it felt like a full-on slap of rejection. "I promised I'd do everything I could to survive, and that promise takes precedence over the one I gave Josh. He can't harm me because of that."

Maria smiled sadly, reaching out to caress Grace's cheek. "You're too sweet, you know that? That's your problem. You're far too sweet and gentle to be a mermaid." Her fingertips trailed away. "I should never have made you. I'm so sorry for what I did to you."

"Maria," she began, not sure what to say. "Can we deal with this tomorrow please?"

Maria turned away. "The only thing I did right was force you to make that promise to me. Go to our sisters as Talithia demanded. She'll look after you." She spun and ran to follow the group of kids and Creatures, only she ran directly into the path of an oncoming car.

"Maria!" Grace screamed as a small blue hatchback smashed into Maria's legs. Maria crumpled over the bonnet and her head cracked the windscreen as she tumbled over the car, falling to the ground in a sickening heap.

"Maria!" Grace screamed, her hands going to her mouth, but otherwise unable to move.

The driver hit the brakes, screeching to a halt as Grace's immobility broke and she rushed to her sister.

"Maria?" She knelt and gently cupped Maria's bloody cheek, her hands shaking with shock as another car screeched to a stop just a few metres from them. Blood from a cut near Maria's temple trickled across her forehead while a dozen other cuts and scrapes bled as well. A massive bruise was already forming on Maria's temple.

"Is she alive?" a woman called as a car door slammed. More cars stopped around them.

"Maria?" Grace asked. "Maria?"

The woman knelt opposite Grace. She appeared around sixty years old, the grey roots of her black-dyed hair coming through. "Oh thank

God she's still breathing." The woman crossed herself as if everything were suddenly all right. Grace fought down an onslaught of murderous rage. If they'd been in the ocean Grace would have drowned the woman right then.

"Help me get her to the beach," Grace said, gripping Maria's right arm just below the shoulder.

"You mean the hospital, dear? We need to call an ambulance."

"What? No! The beach." Grace braced herself to try and haul her friend up. She probably wasn't strong enough in human form to carry Maria all that far, but she had to try.

"Stop!" the woman cried, a panicked, shrill tone in her voice.

Grace felt her claws protruding, and it was all she could do not to attack the woman right there. "Leave us alone!"

The woman didn't seem to notice her tone. "If her neck's broken or damaged, you'll kill her."

"Her neck?" Grace hesitated. She stared at Maria's bloodied body, wishing she could see the internal damage. There weren't many things that could kill a mermaid, but decapitation was one of them. A broken neck might qualify for that.

"My phone's in my handbag." The woman ran off as cars began backing up in both directions along the beach strip, someone at the rear honking.

Phone? What for? A doctor, Grace realised. The worst thing possible.

"I've already called an ambulance," said a male voice. They'd attracted a crowd of a dozen people already. "It'll be here in about ten minutes."

Grace had kept up with changes in human society, and what she'd seen was enough to know she didn't want Maria treated in a hospital. She had no idea if mermaids were even human enough on the inside to pass as one, and besides, hospitals attracted Creatures, particularly vampires for the easy access to blood.

"You don't understand. She has... special needs. She..." What? What would make sense to them and convince people to help her get Maria to the ocean? She's a mermaid? Magic's real? Water will help her heal? Maria wouldn't be the only one getting carted off. Regardless, she had to get her sister to the ocean before someone tried to stop her.

"Are you okay?" asked another woman. She was extremely pale, her voice quavering just a little.

"Maria's my best friend," Grace said, tears blurring her vision as the full extent of their predicament began to settle on her. "We've known each other for a hundred years." She gently took Maria's limp hand, hoping for a response, but her sister remained unconscious. "Get up, get up, get up," she whispered. Grace pushed her long hair back from her face. She needed a stretcher. She couldn't let them take Maria to the hospital, but had no doubt they'd try and restrain her if she tried to do anything else but wait for an ambulance.

"If everyone helps me lift her, we can get her to the beach," she said with hope, realising after she said it how irrational it would sound to a human.

"You need to leave her alone before you do more damage." The man reached for her shoulder, but she slapped his hand away with a snarl. His eyes widened and he backed away, making Grace realise her canines were showing.

Looking around, she realised no one was going to help her, and more than likely would try to stop her if she attempted to move Maria. For a long moment she didn't care, hovering on the verge wanting to murder them all just to make sure they wouldn't take Maria away, but she was little more than a human herself out of the water, and the situation was well beyond her control.

Think, she told herself, trying not to let her emotions get in the way. What could she do? She had to wait for events to settle. Later she could try to do something, probably at the hospital late tonight or early tomorrow morning. "Shit," she muttered under her breath as she wiped tears away.

What if she couldn't get Maria out of the hospital before tomorrow night? What if they took her to a bigger hospital for treatment? Grace could land in a police cell if she got caught trying to get Maria to safety, and that would end them both. She'd have to be very careful.

Someone began directing cars to pass, but it was a long while before she heard a siren in the distance. Grace held Maria's hand the entire time, wishing the crowd would leave, wishing she dared yell at them all to clear off.

"She'll be fine, dear," said the woman who'd hit Maria. She sounded as if she were trying to believe it herself. "They're almost here. The paramedics will look after her."

"Don't try to comfort me," Grace whispered with murder in her voice despite being unable to look away from Maria's broken body. "You're not helping." She didn't mean to be rude, it's just... what? She felt so helpless.

"I'm... sorry. I... feel terrible for you both."

What would the paramedics do? Was Maria's blood different to a human's? What if Grace couldn't get to her after they took her away? A single dusk and dawn was as long as a mermaid could remain out of the water. Tomorrow at dusk Maria would die unless Grace could get her back to the ocean beforehand.

As the ambulance drew closer Grace began to fret about the consequences. Maria's breathing had a raspy sound now, and she seemed paler than she had been a minute ago. Her olive skin was grey.

The ambulance dodged cars and stopped as a police vehicle pulled up from the opposite direction. Paramedics shooed Grace away while a heavy-set police officer ushered people back to the curb, Grace included.

"I need to be with her!" Grace protested, trying to see past the big man. "She's my best friend!"

"You saw the accident?" the officer asked. He was middle-aged and a little overweight, but all the more imposing for it.

"She stepped onto the road and the car hit her." She looked around for the driver, but couldn't see the woman. "Maria wasn't looking."

"So it wasn't the driver's fault?" he asked as he wrote on a notepad.

As much as she hated to admit it, Grace nodded.

"You have an English accent. Are you on holiday or do you live here?"

The question caught her off guard. She hadn't thought about her accent for a long time now. "Um, holiday. We're staying with a friend. I don't know the address. My name's Grace Harpeden."

He looked her over, his expression a little resigned at her bikini. "I'm guessing you don't have any identification on you?"

"Obviously."

"What's the name of the person you're staying with?"

This was turning into an interrogation. She should never have admitted to knowing Maria or witnessing the accident. "Um, Josh, my cousin." She pointed vaguely away from the beach and shops. "He lives that way. I don't know my way around yet."

"What can you tell me about your friend?"

Enough with the questions! She wanted to choke the voice from him, preferably with salt water, but took a deep, calming breath instead. Play the game for now. "Her name's Maria. Maria Lacopo."

"Is she from England too?"

"Italy."

"What's her address?"

She tried to see around him, but the paramedics blocked her view of Maria anyway. "I don't know. We met on a cruise ship a couple of years ago and we've been backpacking ever since. Can we do this later please? I have to get to the hospital."

He didn't seem convinced. "Sure, but you'll need to come down to the station tomorrow and answer some questions." He handed her a card with an address on it. "Are you able to get there?"

Able? Yes. Willing? No. "I'll find it," she lied.

He left her and began asking for more witnesses. His partner, a petite young woman, was interviewing the driver who'd hit Maria. Determined not to get further involved, Grace drifted back into the crowd, hugging herself as if her arms were a shield against the human world.

There was blood on her free hand where she'd been holding Maria. In her other hand she clenched the bracelet tight just to feel some physical pain. Anything. The situation didn't feel real, but the words from the market jeweller echoed in her mind. Things were about to change.

Tears brimming afresh, Grace blinked them away. Mermaid tears had strong healing powers, but with her lifeforce nearly spent they wouldn't be nearly enough to fix Maria even if she could cry a river. Screw the world. She'd drown a thousand people to keep Maria safe, and realised she may have to.

[6]

"You're staying with Josh, huh?" came a guy's voice she recognised.

Grace felt a chill as she turned and found Josh behind her. She flushed with a combination of fear and embarrassment. "A different Josh," she said lamely.

"Uh-huh. And your surname's Harpeden, like mine? How did you know that?"

She leaned away in surprise. "You're surname's Harpeden?"

"Sounds like you were lying to the cop, and eavesdropping on me and my friends." He met her gaze steadily.

Grace kept hugging herself as she watched the medics treating Maria. "My surname really is Harpeden. How could I have known yours? I…" she shrugged. "I didn't overhear anything."

His expression softened. "You must be cold," he said, an entirely different tone entering his voice. "Want to borrow my shirt?"

"Thank you, but I'm not cold." She needed to get rid of him before he inadvertently gave her an order that would have consequences.

"You're shivering."

Maybe if she was rude he'd leave her alone? "It's called shock. Research it."

He didn't react the way she'd hoped. She saw sympathy instead of offence. "I didn't see the accident, but I heard it. When I got here you looked pretty upset. Still do."

"Please leave. You're niceness is hurting me."

He chuckled, and surprisingly it made her feel slightly better. She gave him an apologetic look, marred as it was by fresh tears. "I'm sorry," she whispered. "I'm having a very bad day."

They watched in silence as the paramedics loaded Maria into the ambulance, strapped down and fully braced.

"I'm really sorry about your friend."

"Ironic, considering this is your fault."

His expression changed to surprise. "How is it my fault?"

She dropped her eyes, embarrassed she'd even made the accusation. "Never mind. It's not your fault. I'm sorry. Again. I'm not myself at the moment."

The ambulance drove off, carrying her only reason to be alive as it disappeared. Grace would have to head back to the beach and swim around to Batemans Bay to get to the hospital. At least she could walk to the hospital from there. It wasn't far, perched up the hill on the edge of a cliff just a few hundred metres from the water. "Thank you for trying to comfort me, but I have to go. Goodbye Josh." She began walking along the road as if she were going for her car.

Josh jogged and caught up with her, his sun-bleached hair bobbing slightly as he walked.

"Do you know where you're going?"

"The hospital."

His longer legs had no trouble keeping up. "I'm guessing you don't have a car?"

Oh for pity's sake, why wouldn't he leave her alone? Maybe she needed to give rudeness a proper go this time. "Can you tell that by the way I walk?"

Her anger only made him smile. "You've got no purse or car keys. No licence that I can see. How about I give you a lift?"

"Thank you, but you wouldn't give me back my necklace, so I'm not inclined to trust that your intentions are honourable."

"My intentions? Honourable? Did we just step into Jane Austen novel?"

"Yes," she said. "When you refused to give me my necklace back."

"If you'd been polite I'd have handed it straight over."

She opened her mouth to retort, but if she was being fair, he probably meant it. To be even fairer, she'd been too afraid of the consequences of not getting her necklace back to have been polite. Still, she couldn't afford to give him a chance to realise he could control her. "I'd rather not get driven into bushland and murdered."

"What if I do the murdering somewhere nice? Maybe a park? Would that be okay?"

She couldn't help herself and snorted a laugh. His smile suggested he was pleased with her reaction. She met his eyes. "Please go away Josh."

"You know, you're absolutely beautiful. I mean that respectfully. Model beautiful. You're stunning."

She took a deep breath, cringing internally as she looked up and stared at the evening sky. "Oh, for God's-"

"I don't think I've ever seen anyone with hair as long as yours. It's like, down to your thighs. Have you ever cut it?"

A mermaid? Cut her hair? Never. "All the better to strangle you with," she muttered, subverting an old fairy tale. "Please Josh, I'm sure you mean well, I really do. But if you don't mind I'd like to be alone."

"Yet you still need a lift, and I'm offering. It's a bloody long hike to the Bay from here, especially on bare feet."

Why did she have to meet the nicest guy in the world at the absolute worst time? *Suck it up*, she heard Maria say. It was either walk to the beach and let him watch her transform and swim away, or… "Fine. A lift would be wonderful. Thank you," she almost gritted her teeth while saying it.

He grinned like he'd won some sort of prize. "My car's this way."

She followed him to a side street leading away from the beach. He stopped before a beat up old ute that looked like its next adventure should be a mercy killing. "Hop in."

She looked from Josh to the wreck. "You mean push it?" she asked, staring in dismay.

He laughed. "Let's see if it starts first. You can push if it doesn't."

He unlocked her door and opened it for her, and then went around and opened his.

"You know they've got keyless entry these days?" she said as she got in. "Some cars even come without rust."

"Most have suspension too," he added.

She smiled, despite herself. Under different circumstances she might have really liked him. She wriggled on the cracked leather bench seat to get comfortable. Seeing her reaction, he reached behind the seat and handed her a towel. "Sit on that. Cracked seats are pretty uncomfortable."

She slid it underneath herself. "Better. Thanks."

She touched the dusty dashboard with two fingers. "What do you call it? Sir Rusty of the Last Legs?"

Her words produced another cheeky grin from Josh, and she began to feel justified about not drowning him. He turned the key and the car roared to life, thoroughly surprising Grace as it began to purr.

"And here I was looking for the rubber-band engine," she murmured.

Trying to distract herself, she clipped the bracelet Kimbriel had given her around her right wrist. There was a little of Maria's blood on the gold, which she rubbed off with her thumb, fighting off fresh tears.

"It might look like crap, but I've totally rebuilt the engine and replaced almost everything under the hood. So, what do you do for a living?" he asked.

The question caught her by surprise. "Professional athlete," she said, hoping he'd buy it.

"Really? What sport?"

"Swimming. Long distance."

"So you're pretty fit then? You look it. I'm a mechanic. Looking for a new job."

How old did that make him? Early twenties? "Where are your friends from the beach?"

"The guys are going to a party. The girls had to go to work."

He turned right onto a parallel back street, and then back down to the main road before heading out of Broulee.

"So," she began a little hesitantly, compulsion forcing her to find out where he lived. "I take it Sir Rusty's not your mobile home?"

"I live pretty close to the hospital, actually. Just across the golf course. So, Grace Harpeden? Is that seriously your name? What's your real surname? Where did you hear mine?"

She gave him a sidelong look, wondering where this was leading. She hadn't thought about her surname since she'd drowned her husband, and didn't particularly want to remember the incident. "I lost my real surname in the ocean."

"Stranger danger, huh? Here you are in a car with some guy you've never known, and you're worried I might stalk you in the future?"

What could she say to that? At least talking was distracting her from dark thoughts about Maria. "I... I was married for about six months. Painful memories, to be honest, or at least how it ended was very upsetting. My married surname really was Harpeden."

He looked a little surprised. "How old are you? I mean, you don't look like you're old enough to be married... Maybe nineteen or twenty at most. Younger than me, surely?"

Give or take a century. "Something like that."

"So what was the story with the marriage? Older guy? Daddy syndrome?" He had that cheeky grin back.

She couldn't help but respond in kind. "No," she said, looking down as if that would help her avoid the memories. "He had prospects I didn't think I had. It doesn't matter. What about you? Single?"

It took him a moment to answer. "Yeah, though plenty of girls keep trying to hook up with me." Somehow it didn't come across as conceited. More like it embarrassed him, which was odd. She expected a pretty big ego. Quite clearly he preferred to do the chasing than be chased. No wonder the redhead had no chance.

It was really hard not to like him. "Adding to the size of your swollen head, no doubt?"

He laughed. "No doubt. Fortunately my Mum keeps me grounded," he said as they turned onto the highway.

"Keep talking Josh. I need the distraction. You got a dream? Something you want to achieve in life?"

"Oh yeah. One of these days I'm going to get myself a really big fishing boat and take people out on charters. You like fishing, Grace?"

"Fish pretty much make up my entire day." Grabbing an angler's hook and swimming off with it before snapping the line was one of her favourite pastimes, and usually provided something for the angler to boast about too. It was petty, but it amused her every single time.

They eventually entered the Bay area, and after a couple of sets of traffic lights he turned off the main road and up a steep hill, and from there drove into the little hospital's car park. She still found herself surprised that the building was perched on the edge of a cliff, of all places.

He pointed. "Entrance is just there. Would you like me to come in? You could be waiting a while. Maybe all night."

She was tempted to say yes as she was beginning to like him, but that was a bad thing if he got in her way and she had to drown him. "No, but I might need a place to crash later, if you don't mind?" She still needed his address.

"Um, I guess that would be okay, as long as you're quiet. My Mum's pretty sick. Today's one of my rare child-free days out with friends."

Her jaw literally dropped. "You have a child?" she asked in surprise.

Now it was his turn to look down, slightly embarrassed. "Yeah. Was a bit like your marriage, I guess. Met a girl when I was about fifteen. She got pregnant and chose to go through with it."

"And?" she prompted, intrigued.

He hesitated. "She died during the delivery. It wasn't a good time. Her Mum had died a few years before that, but her father's a really good guy. Mum's looking after Mikey, my boy, this afternoon, but Greg's going to take him for the weekend while I do a couple of casual jobs. If it wasn't for Greg and Mum I'd never have gotten through my apprenticeship."

"Oh," she whispered. "That's very good of them."

He grabbed a pen and notepad from the glove compartment and jotted his address down. "If there's no lights on, knock on the window to the right of the front door." He touched the car's dashboard. "That is, assuming Sir Rusty's in the driveway. Otherwise you'll have to try somewhere else. Please don't knock on the door otherwise. My mother really is sick."

"Thank you Josh," she said as she left the car. "I really appreciate it."

"No probs. Be safe."

She held the slip of paper up to a street light. She could see in total darkness in the ocean, but in this form her eyesight was as limited as any other human. "Josh Harpeden." She stared through the car's open window. "Perhaps your family's related to my former husband's?" If anything could help her to dislike him, that would be it.

"He must have been an awesome guy," he said with enough sarcasm to ensure she knew he didn't mean it.

She stared at the hospital's entrance. "He was, right up until he left me for dead so he could try and save his own life."

For once, Josh didn't have a ready smile or even a comeback. "I'm really sorry Grace," he said.

"So was he."

[7]

GRACE MEMORISED the address Josh had given her and dropped the slip of paper into a bin as she approached the hospital entrance. The walkway was a little steep, but in moments she entered the hospital's overly-warm reception area. The place smelled of antiseptics and sterility, and everything echoed. Worse, it was like walking into a void without lifeforce. There was none. Traces of lifeforce were normally everywhere, on the air, in the water, and radiating from humans. Here it was parched. A desert.

The place had to be full of Creatures. Nothing else could absorb the ambient lifeforce in the air. She glanced around nervously. It was impossible to tell the difference between humans and Creatures unless she got close enough, as humans radiated lifeforce while Creatures absorbed it. She should have realised that when coming here. Hospitals were the perfect place for Creatures. People regularly died in hospitals, which made stealing lifeforce easier.

She remained on the threshold, uncertain how to proceed, but Maria was in there among Creatures who would probably do her harm if the opportunity arose. More than likely she was being treated by humans, but that was no measure of safety. While there was normally an uneasy truce between Creatures, they'd kill Grace and Maria just to get rid of the competition for lifeforce.

Vampires were particularly common in hospitals, especially in pathology labs where blood was literally on tap.

When no one threatened her or even took any real notice, she cautiously walked to reception, waiting as the women behind the counter consoled an old lady who didn't seem to understand the meaning of 'waiting for results'. She eventually turned to Grace when the woman left. "How can I help?" Nothing in her expression suggested she recognised Grace as anything but human herself, and she gave off a feint whiff of lifeforce, implying she wasn't a Creature.

"I'm looking for a friend who just came in. Her name's Maria Lacopo. She was hit by a car." She had to fight down fears once again. Was Maria's life in more danger from being treated as if she were a human, or from the Creatures who might recognise her for what she was?

"Oh yes." The woman pulled up the details on her computer. "She has head trauma and possible spinal injuries, a broken leg, and they're checking for internal injuries. You're not going to be able to see her tonight."

Grace quelled her disappointment though she should have expected it. "Has, um…" What was she supposed to say? Does Maria show any mermaid traits? A tail? "What are they doing to her? For her, I mean," she quickly amended.

The woman glanced at the screen again. "She's listed as critical and scheduled for more scans. It's never good when someone needs help to save their life. Are you related?"

Hardly daring to voice the words, Grace cleared her throat. "She might die, you mean?" Was the trauma enough to kill a mermaid?

"You'll have to ask the doctor. Perhaps one of the nurses will be able to tell you more. There's a waiting room down there." She pointed. "I doubt there'll be any news for a while yet."

Grace followed the directions, the lack of lifeforce in the air making her skin crawl. She'd never been in a place so… dry. So devoid of natural energy. Every other person here must have been a Creature to cause this.

She'd frequently been in human buildings over the past few decades, including huge shopping malls and even an office, but never a hospital. She didn't like the chemical smell either, the heat, or the general aura of tragedy. She caused enough tragedy herself and this place only contributed to that feeling. Her instincts told her to get out as quickly as she could.

In the waiting room she found a nurse talking to a young man about another patient. Grace waited for them to finish, trying not to fidget.

"Excuse me," Grace asked a little too quickly when the man walked off, determined to catch the nurse's attention. Judging by the faint hint of lifeforce in the air around her, she was human. It was reassuring.

"Yes?" the nurse asked, her lined face care-worn and patient. She seemed to be genuinely interested in helping.

"Maria Lacopo. How is she?"

"Are you family?"

"I'm all she's got. When can I see her?"

The nurse gave her a sympathetic look. "A while. The doctors suspect she's fractured one of the vertebrae in her neck or at least ruptured a couple of disks. That's bad enough without anything else, and we're trying to confirm the extent of her injuries before we determine treatment. Dr Lemier is talking to a specialist in Sydney right now. We'll know more in the morning."

Fractured a vertebrae? That could lead to a broken neck, and a broken neck would kill her. "But she's going to be okay, right?" Long forgotten human traits crowded in on her and she felt her palms sweating with fear and worry.

The nurse gave her what appeared to be a well-practiced smile. "She's critical. Can you give me some details about Maria? I've got some forms I need to fill in."

Another interrogation, and she hated lying. "Um. Sure. We're on holiday here together."

"I'm going to need specific details. I assume she's got travel insurance? There would be details with her bags. Are you staying in the same place?"

"I could check them when I get back. Would it be okay if I brought in the details tomorrow, assuming I can find them?"

The nurse took Grace's hand. "Don't worry for now. Come back in the morning and we'll sort it all out. There's nothing you can do now anyway."

"So I can see her in the morning?" A surge of hope rushed through her, flooding her with premature relief.

"I doubt she'll be conscious. There'll be lots of tubes and… well, just prepare yourself, that's all."

The thought of Maria in such a vulnerable position made Grace feel sick, particularly when surrounded by Creatures who may see her as another competitor for the limited amounts of lifeforce available to them all. She glanced at the clock on the wall. She had less than a day to get Maria back in the water.

"And tomorrow I'm on slave duties." Crap.

She left the waiting room, trying to figure out how to get Maria out of the hospital without landing in a police cell. Ideally she'd simply sneak back when the hospital's shifts changed and push Maria's bed down the hill to the water, though as practical as that seemed it wasn't likely to succeed. Her stomach twisted as she mulled the problem over.

She still had no idea how she might get Maria out when she realised she'd taken the wrong turn. She looked around.

She was near the hospital's small chapel. She walked in, feeling the presence of something greater than herself as she did, and more lifeforce than anywhere else in the hospital. Creatures never entered holy ground as far as she could tell. It had the same presence and barrier that prevented Creatures entering homes. Grace had been raised a Catholic though, and despite everything that had happened to her, she still went to church every Sunday unhindered. She couldn't remember being invited into a church, but she must have been at some point in order to be able to enter.

Taking a seat near the front, she knelt and said a prayer for Maria, letting the place's calm wash over her. She took a few minutes to gather herself, and even though she still had no plan to help Maria, she stood and left, blessing herself after touching her fingertips into the font of holy water near the door.

Forgetting which way she'd came from, she went left and soon found herself in a small cafeteria. The reek of coffee and hot food made her nauseous. She was fine with most unprocessed foods, but couldn't stand the smell of most cafeterias. Maria, on the other hand, loved deep fried food.

Doing her best to hold her breath so she wouldn't dry retch, Grace hurried toward the opposite door. Someone bumped into her and cried out as scalding coffee splashed across her arm and chest.

"Hey! Be careful!" they said.

She recognised that voice. Her heart skipped a beat. The redhead who'd been with Josh at the beach glared at her.

"You!" The redhead was displaying more cleavage than physics suggested was possible for such a low-cut top. She narrowed her eyes, clearly recognising another Creature in Grace. "You spilled my coffee."

Grace backed a step in surprise. "You ran into me."

The redhead glared, too much eye liner and makeup giving her the appearance of a prostitute looking for clientele. "Buy me another coffee. Now."

"Do I look like I've got a stash of coins in my bikini?"

"Your problem, not mine."

So it was going to be like that, huh? "I accept your apology," Grace said to annoy the Creature, her own anger rising.

"How about I cut your hair and sell it for a wig? Should be enough for a coffee or to in that."

"You want money?" Grace purposely asked a little too loudly. "You're more likely to find clients on the main street."

The redhead's expression went from anger to rage. She shoved Grace with more strength than a human should have.

Grace cried out as she stumbled backwards over a chair, her upper left arm clipping a table as she crashed to the ground.

"Ahh!" Grace cried, pain shooting all the way up to her shoulder. She tried to move her arm, but pain kept her still. "You broke my arm!"

"Serves you right," said the bottle-blond crony, walking up to stand beside the redhead.

"What'd you expect?" said the third girl, her makeup applied with a spatula. "This ain't your turf. Clear out."

The redhead gave Grace a vicious smile as a big-built guy in a security uniform approached. Looking him over, Grace was certain he was another Creature. Shit. The three girls laughed and walked away as if they'd accomplished everything they'd come to do.

The security guard stopped at Grace's feet and crossed his arms. "Get out before I call the police."

"What?"

"I've known Abbey for three years. If there's trouble here, it's from you. Out."

Holding her arm, Grace awkwardly got to her feet. Three people at another table looked on without trying to be subtle about it.

"Any of you want to tell him what happened?" she asked a little belligerently, daring any of them to meet her eyes. None did. It wouldn't do any good anyway. The security guard raised an eyebrow, apparently both amused and a little surprised she was arguing the point on his turf.

Being in public was all the protection she had. Considering she wasn't human and had no identification, no one would miss her except her sisters if he wanted to take it that way. She was certain he would if she made any more trouble, but for now he seemed happy to kick her out. With the security guard shadowing her, she left the cafeteria. As she strode through the doors beyond reception she wished they'd would slam behind her so she could make her feelings known.

They closed politely.

"That was stupid," she muttered to herself. She'd allowed her feelings to get the best of her, which meant it would be even harder to get Maria out now. Angry with herself, she stalked down the steep hill toward the ocean, her arm aching, but as long as she held it still it wasn't too bad.

If that security guard had been human he'd probably have ushered her in to see a doctor, but he'd known what she was just as she'd known he wasn't human either. She was the one trespassing and upsetting the status quo, so she considered herself lucky she'd only been kicked out and nothing more.

The soles of her feet were hurting and a small cut under her big toe bled by the time she arrived at the rock wall along this part of the Bay, the little waves splashing noisily against the oyster-clad stones. Her arm sported a huge bruise already, ensuring she moved gingerly as she sat on a rock by the water. She looked around to be sure she wasn't seen as she removed her bikini bottoms, and clambered down the last couple of rocks, almost cutting her foot on an oyster shell.

"Never return to the water angry," she whispered to herself and took a long calming breath. Maria had said that to her once. It was better to shake negative emotions than share them with her sisters around the world. She didn't need curious mermaids coming by to ask about her problems.

After about a minute she felt calm enough to return to the water. Trying not to jolt her arm too much, she stood and jumped into its darkness.

Relief flooded her as the joy of her tail replaced her aching feet. Her arm instantly felt better too. She focused on the water and manipulated it to flow over her body, and with a couple of kicks she shot away from the shore. To her, it felt like she was flying, her body designed to slip through the water like a bird through air, only she could float and they couldn't. It didn't take her long to cross the bar and head out past the Tollgates and into deeper water.

She sensed some night-time divers near a small reef about a mile off the headland and stayed well clear of them, even though it was unlikely they'd see her at night. With her promise to survive she didn't want to risk killing anyone without making the choice herself.

As long as she was at Josh's place by nine, it didn't matter what she did in between. She considered returning to the divers and picking one to drown, but she wasn't desperate enough to take a completely innocent human. More than that, divers tended to be friendly toward the ocean and its creatures. There were better options.

After luxuriating in the depths and simply enjoying the distant feel of her mermaid sisters' comforting emotions, she eventually sought out the underwater cavern she shared with Maria. Lonely and empty, she rested among her collected trinkets on the sandy floor and tried not to think about Maria, still in hospital and plugged into machines and tubes. Exhaustion eventually forced her to sleep, at least for a little while.

She woke well before dawn, but it wasn't fear or tension that drove her from sleep. It was the urge to kill. The coming day represented her last unless she drowned someone, and her body knew it like an insidious cancer growing inside her.

She fought it down despite the urge to rush to a beach and take a pre-dawn swimmer, or to lure a lone angler into the water. Right now she'd almost be prepared to burst from the water, grab someone in a small boat, and drag them back over the side. Finding someone to kill wasn't the problem. Choosing the right person was the problem.

"I hate my life," she whispered to the empty cavern. It really would be best to let herself go, and Maria along with her. Even if she hadn't promised Maria she'd do everything she could to survive, she didn't want to die, and she didn't want Maria to die either.

Without any desire to return to land she procrastinated among her small collection of memories. There wasn't much. She'd kept her wedding and engagement rings, simple designs that reminded her of her happiest days as a human. And then there was her husband's wedding ring, a reminder of the worst of it. She wasn't sure why she hadn't taken it out to the middle of the Pacific Ocean to drop into the deepest trench she could find, or simply pawned it somewhere for a few dollars.

Maria had saved it for her while she was still in the thrall of being a newly-born mermaid, though she'd never said why. She'd never really discussed her own past either, not in any meaningful way, but Grace's husband's wedding ring clearly meant more to Maria than it did to Grace.

She half wished she'd saved a trinket from the Titanic, though she could go there at any time and retrieve whatever she liked. There were bound to be plenty of jewels and other items that wouldn't have corroded or rotted away, but she didn't like the thought of disturbing the dead, particularly people she might have known.

She polished her rings with her fingers and put them back in their nook beside a baby's plastic doll and a glass cube with a three-dimensional image of a family etched within the centre, a mother, father, and two children. They looked happy, particularly the children. Someone had thrown it into the ocean. She guessed they didn't want to be reminded of what had once been, but for Grace it represented everything she wished for and didn't want to forget.

Compulsion and a growing need to kill eventually forced her from the cavern, her bikini bottoms in one hand, though she suspected Josh wouldn't object if she turned up without them.

"Another day, another twenty-five cents," she muttered, although even that was more than a slave earned.

[8]

GRACE BURST from the waves like a dolphin, transformed in the air and dropped to the wet rocky shelf, the impact jolting her newly-formed legs. She straightened, wincing. Thanks to the gloom of dawn she'd avoided being seen by some anglers further along the rocks, one of them reeling a fish in.

She stretched, her arm barely sore now, and tried not to let her fears take hold. She had to renew her lifeforce today, her promise to Maria taking precedence above all others, even her instincts, yet they aligned like an insidious claw in her gut. It made her fear for Josh and what she might do to him if she couldn't find someone else to drown. With trepidation she touched her necklace, wishing yet again... "Don't think about it," she said aloud.

She put on her bikini bottoms and picked her way over the rocks to follow a path around the headland, pilfering a damp sarong left overnight on a clothes line to give her a slightly more modest appearance. It was gloomy enough for the outside sensor light to come on, but nobody woke to find her in their backyard as she wrapped the sarong around her waist.

She followed the footpath to the hospital, the street lights turning off as the sun rose. She didn't have to be at Josh's house until nine, but her fears for Maria's survival caught her again and she procrastinated outside the hospital for nearly an hour, fearing what she might discover if she entered. Eventually the compulsion of her promise became a chain threatening to drag her away if she didn't go willingly.

She reluctantly walked over the hill and down to the golf course, dodging early players as she crossed the fairways to the homes on the other side.

Her feet were sore again by the time she stopped before Josh's house, the sun making the day surprisingly humid. The house was an old weatherboard in need of fresh paint and a new roof, and although the front lawn had been mowed recently the fresh clippings were only just beginning to dry.

Sir Rusty of the Last Legs guarded the driveway before a single garage at the side of the house. The car was so old it didn't even have a clock on the dash, and although Josh had modified the engine he hadn't done anything to the interior. Most of Rusty needed as much work as the motor had probably received.

She crossed to the single tree in the front yard and sat in the shade with her back to the rough bark. She'd barely gotten comfortable when Josh came out of the front door with his keys in hand and a child's backpack slung across his left shoulder, a boy of about five on his right arm. Mikey. His son. A bright red singlet showed off Josh's well-toned biceps and chest. He paused when he saw her, surprise on his face, clearly trying to work out why she was sitting under his tree. "Your hair's messy," he said.

She fingered some of the sun-bleached strands and held them away from her face, her heart pounding with... what? Fear? Anticipation? "Lost my brush."

He studied her expression, this time with some concern. "You didn't stay out here all night, did you?"

She couldn't help a smile. "No Josh." She glanced at Rusty. "I'm here to wash The Beast." She held up her necklace. "For returning this, remember?"

He raised his eyebrows. "Really? Um, well, I'm dropping Mikey off and then going to the gym. You're going to have to wait a while." The little boy regarded her solemnly, his eyes so different to his father's he must have inherited them from his mother.

Wait? Oh crap. She felt the compulsion in the words. He stared as if expecting a reaction, for her to tell him she was not going to wait around and was going to leave. She opened her mouth to say exactly that, but compulsion forced her to silence. She was going to have to wait around for a while. Genuine fear gripped her then. Fear she might have to wait all day and wouldn't be able to get to Maria. She swallowed bile. "I'm a girl of my word, Josh. Enjoy the gym and try not to make the newbies feel jealous. I'll wash Rusty when you get back."

By the expression on his face that was clearly not the answer he'd expected. "You're seriously going to wait?" His smile was easy if a little uncertain. "Yeah, well, Sir Rusty's only held together by dirt and grease anyway. You could probably forget the wash."

Damn, so close to a dismissal she could almost taste it on the breeze tickling the leaves above her. Almost. Mikey, still in Josh's arms, wriggled to get free. "Settle down," Josh said. He gave the boy the keys to the car. "Go hop in, okay? I'll only be a second." Without a glance at Grace who was clearly an adult and therefore not of interest, he ran to the car and shoved the key into the lock, well-practiced. In a moment he was inside, bouncing over the front seat to the booster in the back before putting his belt on.

Grace stared at the car, trying to remember if she'd seen the booster seat last night. She really didn't remember it, but it must have been there. "So you don't want me to wash Rusty then?" she said hopefully.

"Um, yeah. No need. Hey, you hungry?"

Thank God! The compulsion dissipated like an ocean mist breaking against trees. "I'm good." She stood to leave. "Thanks anyway. Goodbye."

"When was the last time you ate? Honestly?"

"I'm fine Josh," she said over her shoulder without stopping. Any further conversation could lead to her being forced into something else she couldn't afford the time for.

"That's not an answer. Did you eat today or not? C'mon. Tell me."

The command wrapped around her and squeezed the answer out. "No," she squeaked, but she continued walking. She felt like a genie in a bottle bound to grant wishes. She was almost to the edge of his property. Would it be rude to run?

"Thought so. Hold on. Mum's cooking bacon and eggs." As commanded, she stopped, and before she could protest he opened the door again. "Mum! You got any spare eggs?"

"Of course dear. Always extra when you're in the house."

"Great!" he called back. "Come on," he said to Grace, nodding toward the front door.

She glanced apprehensively at the house, uncertain if she'd just been given an invitation or not. Like any other magical Creature she couldn't enter uninvited no matter the compulsion, and it would look very awkward if she got to the front door and some magical field prevented her from going in. Worse, she felt sick at the thought of bacon and eggs, though Maria would have been delighted at the prospect.

"Go inside and eat up."

Invitation granted and order confirmed, and now she'd have to eat bacon and eggs. Ugh. Why hadn't she sprinted away when she'd had the opportunity? With her stomach turning at the thought of the greasy bacon, she moved toward the door before the compulsion could force her. "I'm really not hungry," she said as she passed him. Please, please, change your mind, she pleaded silently.

"Sure you're not. Mum! This is Grace, a friend of mine. She hasn't had breakfast. Would you mind feeding her up?" God, he was so frigging nice. Why couldn't she have gotten an asshole?

"Of course not hon. Send her in." There was no hesitation, as if his mother had been eavesdropping.

"Make sure you get some scrambled eggs. Mum cooks the best eggs. Trust me."

Another command. She groaned.

"Kitchen's straight through the hallway and to the left."

"Thanks," she said, wishing he'd hurry up and drive off. What she'd hoped would be a simple car wash before escaping to the hospital was turning into a nightmare, and she wasn't entirely sure she wouldn't drown his mother in the kitchen sink at the first opportunity.

Grace followed the horrible smell of cooked bacon and scrambled eggs to the kitchen and found Josh's reed-thin mother at the stove, apron on and busily stirring the eggs around the frypan. Her hair was short as if it had recently been clipped, and she was gaunt to the point of starvation, her hollow cheeks making her look a decade older than what she probably was.

She smelled… sick. Dying sick. A chill went through Grace. It was the perfect opportunity to take a life… and the place was full of lifeforce. There was an energy she found very appealing for all the wrong reasons. The entire family was strong with it.

"Come in, sit," the sickly woman said as she used a spatula to flip some of the scrambled eggs over. After a moment she grabbed a plate and emptied the lot onto it. "There's enough for both me and Josh, and a dozen more starving people." She smiled. "Or just Josh."

"He'd really eat all that?" Grace asked, staring at the pile of eggs. There must have been a dozen in it.

The woman shrugged. "Josh did his usual trick and crammed down a handful of bacon before leaving me with the rest. He'll finish it when he gets back from the gym."

She turned with the plate in hand and stopped, staring at Grace. "My, you're gorgeous, aren't you?"

Grace blushed, her looks more due to her magical heritage than her human one. "Um, Josh told me to tell you that your scrambled eggs are the best, and I should ask for some." If she didn't actually ask by herself compulsion would make her. "May I take that to the table for you? I'd love some, if you're sure Josh won't want it all when he gets home." Anything for an out.

The woman handed the heaped plate to Grace. "Thanks. Have as much as you like. I'll just put some water in the pan to help lift the eggs that are stuck."

Water blasted and Grace could smell it like longing. She put the eggs on the table next to a pile of bacon. The woman could run a restaurant with that much food. "Thank you for sharing, uh, Mrs…"

The woman waved the words away. "Call me Sandra. You know, you're the first girl Josh has actually invited here in years. He must really like you."

"Um, we only met last night, so he could hardly *like* me. I'm only here to return a favour."

Sandra sat and indicated the seat opposite. Grace sat, determined to eat and get through the latest compulsion keeping her here.

"He mentioned you."

Grace glanced at the gaunt woman in surprise. "He told you about me?" The situation was embarrassing enough without having to deal with an inquiring mother less than half her own age.

Sandra spooned scrambled eggs onto a plate and handed the pile over, and then served herself less than half of what she'd given Grace. "Help yourself to the bacon." She sighed, as if remembering something. "Toast. Would you like some toast?"

Grace had rarely eaten since becoming a mermaid, and the thought brought back fond memories of mornings with her family. It was far more appealing than the bacon and eggs she smelled. Still, she wanted to leave and it would be another delay. "Um, no thanks. I'll stick with the bacon and eggs." There was the equivalent of at least three eggs in front of her, and her stomach was already turning at the smell. She'd be lucky to keep what she had down, toast or not.

"Don't be silly. I'll make you some."

"No! Please don't. I have a gluten intolerance." It was a good thing she spent so much time on land reading whatever she could get her hands on. "And besides, I rarely eat processed foods. Fresh is best and all that."

Sandra looked relieved not to have to stand. "Smart girl. So, tell me about yourself, Grace. You're English?"

And now for the inquisition. She did her best to smile pleasantly while avoiding glancing at the sink and a steady supply of water she could use to drown Sandra. "Born and bred. I've been travelling with a friend for a while though. Backpacking. Figured we'd find some sun."

"It's nice here in summer, but winter's a bit cool."

Grace speared a glob of eggs and tried it. She almost vomited. "This is really good," she said with as much enthusiasm as she could find. She nearly choked swallowing it.

Sandra watched her, and then grinned. "Don't like eggs, huh?"

Grace tried to look apologetic. "I'm more of a sushi girl. I hope you don't mind?"

"Leave it. Josh will knock it off. They reheat pretty well."

Her stomach did a slow roll, but she managed to keep the eggs in. "So, Sandra, you're not married?" Her duties to eat eggs fulfilled, she snagged a tiny bit of bacon and chewed it just to make sure the compulsion to eat wouldn't hold her. She needed to get back to the hospital. A moment of polite conversation to avoid rudeness and then she'd say goodbye forever. She doubted that even if she returned Sandra would still be alive, she looked that sick.

"I'm a single Mum these days. Josh said you were married briefly?"

Caught off guard by the painful memory, Grace looked down at her eggs, tempted to eat some so she'd feel more nauseous than hurt. In her last days as a human she'd discovered she was pregnant. She was planning on surprising Will when the ship hit the iceberg. Becoming a mermaid had ended her pregnancy and her human life at the same time.

"Painful memories?" Sandra asked.

God, the woman was perceptive. "There were… issues." For the first time in a century she wanted to open up to someone besides Maria, but even if she did Sandra wouldn't remember Grace. A week from now she may not even remember having had breakfast with her, assuming she lived that long.

"None of my business. Would you mind if I asked why you came to see Josh?"

"He found my necklace on the beach. I promised to wash his car in return."

Sandra laughed. "He keeps it looking trashed on purpose. No one's likely to steal a wreck, but he's got more security under the hood than you'd expect to see in a brand new car. He plans to give it a full makeover eventually. Wants a show car, but for now he's happy to drive it without attracting too much attention. It's a passion project."

Grace noticed that Sandra had barely touched her eggs as well. "Not a fan of eggs either?" she asked, hoping to find a way to end the conversation so she could get on her way. "I take it you only make them for Josh?"

Sandra smiled. "We're both full of wrong assumptions. No dear, I've got cancer. Riddled with it. A mouthful or two at a time is all I can stomach on my medication."

"I'm sorry. I really am," Grace said, although she'd suspected that's what it was. "I figured… I didn't want to be rude and mention it, but you do appear a little tired."

"Oh, come on!" Sandra said with a laugh. "I look great this morning."

Grace couldn't help but smile. Sandra had a similar personality to Josh, and it was contagious.

"So, you're keen on my Josh, huh?"

"What? No!" She felt herself blushing again.

"You're braving his mother's company. Says something to me."

Stupid promise. "It's… he gave me a lift to the hospital last night, so I thought I'd better make good on my promise to wash his car. That's all."

Sandra hid a smile that said she believed differently. "He is a catch, you know."

Grace had to laugh at that. "So am I," she replied, knowing the irony was completely lost on Sandra.

"And neither of us are biased, of course. I don't mean to impose on you, but would you mind helping me clean up? I don't like to let onto Josh, but I'm a lot sicker than he realises."

"You look fitter than me."

Sandra forced another laugh, but there was a hollow sound to it. "They're trying to give me morphine for the pain, Grace, and they only do that when you're on the downhill rush. At best I've got a few more weeks with Josh and Mikey. I'll pretend things are still normal until I can't any longer, but the next time I'm admitted to hospital I doubt I'll come home. I can feel it pulling me down. Every day gets a little harder."

Guilt trip. The woman was either a skilled manipulator or genuinely exhausted and really needed the help. Grace sighed and gave her the benefit of the doubt. "You rest, Sandra. I'll clean up." Maria would have to wait just a little bit longer. And besides, she still didn't have a plan to get her sister out of the hospital.

[9]

GRACE FINISHED DRYING the pan before putting it in the bottom cupboard beside the stove, growing more restless to get out of Sandra's home. Hurrying now, she grabbed the dishcloth and quickly wiped down the kitchen bench and table. It had taken longer than she'd expected. The dishwasher was broken and there'd been pots, cutlery and plates from several meals.

She could have controlled the water to make it scour everything for her, but dipping a pot into the sink and having it come out clean would have raised questions she didn't want to dodge, and that was only half the issue.

Her promise to Maria was beginning to push at her. She had promised to do everything she could to survive, and right now the most likely way for that to happen was do take Sandra's lifeforce.

As she rinsed the dishcloth under the tap she shuddered with need once again, the water driving her hands to clench around the cloth, claws protruding. She had everything she needed to meet her promise; water and a dying woman so full of lifeforce it was probably the only thing keeping her alive. A near-perfect combination.

"Not now," she whispered to herself. "Not her."

It wouldn't take any effort to get Sandra over to the sink and… she took a deep breath as she broke out in a sweat, struggling not to let her instincts take.

"Think about her family," she whispered. "Josh and Mikey." She couldn't imagine the devastation Josh would feel at finding his mother dead on the kitchen floor, drowned in her own sink.

"Done," she said, forcing the words out. "I have to go now." She said it a little too loudly as she shook her hair back from her face. The words seemed to help ease her nerves. "Sandra?" Grace turned.

Sandra started as if she'd been dozing. When she saw the kitchen was clean she smiled tiredly, her expression full of appreciation. "Oh Grace, you're wonderful. Thank you. I just haven't had the energy lately."

It wasn't just the kitchen that needed cleaning, but Grace had no intention of doing the entire house. "I have to go, Sandra. I've got a very sick friend at the hospital."

"Would you like to stay for a cup of tea? It won't delay you all that long." It sounded like genuine offer, not just polite words.

She hadn't had a cup of tea in… she didn't know how long. Decades. Tea and honey. She'd barely known the woman an hour and already she felt like she had more in common with her than Maria.

"I'd love a cup of tea Sandra, but… I'm sorry. I have to go." The woman's expression, which had filled with hope at the first words, fell at the rejection. Despite Sandra's illness and clear need to rest, Grace had the feeling she was quite lonely. She sighed. Maybe just one cup then.

The doorbell whined like a dog too lazy to move off a nail, suggesting the batteries, like almost everything else around the house, needed replacing. Sandra began pushing herself to her feet, but Grace left the sink to put her hand on the sick woman's shoulder. "Rest. I'll get it."

The front door was the old fashioned heavy wood type, and needed a paint. She pulled it open with horror movie sound effects.

"You!" It was Abbey, the red-headed Creature who'd assaulted her last night.

Grace stepped back as Abbey took half a threatening step forward.

"Bitch," Abbey added. "How dare you try and steal Josh! What do you want him for?"

"Steal?" Grace asked, a little taken back. Abbey was a Creature and Josh was human, so unless she planned to turn him, what could she possibly want other than his lifeforce?

Abbey's two friends stood in the front yard, neither looking surprised to see Grace, but they clearly didn't care nearly as much as Abbey did. Abbey, she realised, was more infuriated than surprised too. She'd known Grace was inside, but hadn't wanted to believe it.

Abbey narrowed her eyes, looking Grace over as if studying a maggot. "What are you doing here?" Her tone was dangerous, but a lot quieter now. "This is my turf."

"Breakfast, if you must know."

Abbey narrowed her eyes as if that were exactly what she thought, though it was clear she read a lot more into it.

Grace tried to remember that sane people didn't normally hurt each other, except that Abbey was a Creature of some kind, and probably a lot less sane than the average psych-ward patient.

"Josh is fine," Grace said, needing an excuse to divert the Creature. If Abbey found out Josh could control Grace, Abbey might be able to use Josh against her. "I merely slept with him," Grace added, giving voice to the first distraction that occurred to her. Shit. That's not what she meant to say.

Abbey's face flushed nearly as red as her hair and Grace realised it really wasn't Josh's lifeforce she wanted at all, or at least not exclusively. Abbey began to move forward, but stopped as if held back. For a moment she seemed confused, but then she glared at Grace as if prepared to murder her right then. Like Grace, she couldn't enter the building without an invitation. Thankfully.

Even so, Grace fought down a rare desire to turn and run for the rear door. In the ocean she was the apex predator, but on land she was little more than a young woman, and right now she was outnumbered three to one. Her heart rate would have betrayed her fears to anyone capable of listening, and by the look of Abbey's cronies, they may have been capable. Werewolves, both, she was sure of it.

Abbey angrily pushed forward again, but it was as if she'd walked into a wall of clear plastic film stretched across the door. She glared at Grace, fists clenching and unclenching. "You are going to pay," she whispered. "I know where your friend is. It won't take any effort to suck her lifeforce dry."

Grace nearly stepped through the doorway, ready to murder the Creature for that. Nobody threatened her sister. Her fingernails hardened into claws. Three against one seemed like good odds right then.

"Abbey!" Sandra said from the end of the hall. "How nice to see you."

Grace hid her claws and Abbey's posture instantly changed. A smile replaced the glaring hatred as she glanced past Grace. "Hi Sandra. I was hoping to catch Josh," she said lightly, as if she and Grace had been having a pleasant conversation. She backed half a step. "Would you mind if I came in?"

Sanity returned, and Grace's stomach twisted with a desire to lose what little breakfast she'd eaten. Abbey had wanted her to charge out, and Grace had nearly fallen for it. Now she was trying to get in.

Sandra, being the polite woman she was, would most likely fall for it, and Grace had no way to intervene. Worse, she still had no idea what sort of Creature Abbey was, or what she was capable of. Vampires didn't like sunlight, but they tolerated it well enough despite movies depicting them bursting into flame. Still, the sunlight didn't seem to bother her at all.

"He went to the gym, Abbey. He'll probably be there another hour or two. Are you a member?"

Thank God that wasn't an invitation, but it didn't mean one wasn't coming.

"I'm not a gym type," Abbey said.

"You're not a beach babe either," Grace said under her breath, just loud enough to make sure Abbey heard. It produced a fresh flush of anger on Abbey's cheeks. She definitely wasn't an ocean Creature such as a selkie or siren, both often mistaken for mermaids, but that didn't tell Grace what she might be.

Grace narrowed her eyes, trying to puzzle it out. Abbey had only been at the beach because she'd been trailing Josh, which meant she could be any kind of land Creature. What then? She was unlikely to be a dryad. Dryads didn't wander far from their trees.

If Grace didn't figure it out quickly there was a good chance it could cost her life. Abbey certainly wasn't a werewolf. Werewolves were only affected by the protection keeping magical Creatures out of homes on the full moon. What else had she met in the region? A harpie?

Abbey lost her fake smile. "I'm leaving for the hospital so I can kill your friend. I hope you've got a car."

Was that another ploy to get Grace to rush through the door? Grace buried her misgivings and smiled sweetly as she glanced at Abbey's friends, still seeking information. "I thought all the lunatics were supposed to wait for the full moon before venturing out."

Her two friends stiffened, but not Abbey. She'd hit a mark, at least. Definitely werewolves.

The blonde girl hopped onto the porch close to Abbey. "Want us to drag her out?" she asked softly.

Grace stiffened. Two to one odds were better than three to one, but still not good. If they came in she'd rush for the sink. With water she could defend herself, at least.

Abbey began smiling at Grace as if the idea hadn't occurred to her. Grace held her breath and readied to defend herself, but Abbey finally shook her head, her smile turning vindictive. "I'll see you at the hospital in about fifteen minutes, or your friend will see me instead." In a louder voice, she called, "I might try the gym, Sandra. Perhaps I'll see you later?"

"Good luck," Sandra called.

Grace couldn't close the door fast enough. She turned her back and leaned against it, uncertain about what to do. How had she managed to make a Creature her enemy? She had to be a harpy. Harpies liked coastal areas, but weren't of the ocean. It fit.

If she was, it meant Abbey would be able to control winds, just as a mermaid was incredibly powerful in the water, or a dryad inherently dangerous with earth, particularly if her tree was threatened. For the moment though, neither Grace nor Abbey had a significant advantage. Even old, powerful harpies couldn't do more than take advantage of windy conditions to shove someone off balance or flick dirt and stand at someone. The werewolves would be a little stronger than regular girls, but not much stronger until night-time, and then they'd come into their own. The full moon was both their greatest weakness and strength, depending on how you looked at it. Few Creatures would go up against a werewolf on a full moon.

How was she going to get Maria out of the hospital now?

$$[\ 10\ ]$$

"I TAKE it you two have met?"

Grace jumped. She released her breath, not realising she'd been holding it. She found Sandra watching her with genuine concern. So, Josh's mother didn't trust Abbey either. Good to know. "Met, as in 'did she break my arm over a spilled coffee'? Yes."

Sandra seemed a little surprised at that. "I see. I can't say I've ever liked that one, and I doubt Josh does either, but she's been sniffing around for months now." By the tone she was more than a little unhappy about that, but clearly wise enough not to mention it to Josh. If Sandra had told Josh he couldn't have something… "She seems to be the complete opposite of you Grace, to tell the truth."

Sandra's approval to date her son was not what Grace needed, but having a friend couldn't hurt.

What did Abbey really want with Josh though? She clearly had emotional attachments to him, but it had to be more than that. His lifeforce *was* strong. Was it that simple? She was attracted to him because his lifeforce was strong?

Grace would love to get Abbey into the ocean. If she could, there'd be one less Creature to worry about. "If you think Josh's after me Sandra, he's going to have to do plenty of chasing." And more than a little swimming. At Sandra's look of disappointment Grace tried a friendly smile. "I'm sorry. I'm just… not over my last relationship."

So far she'd done everything Josh had told her to do, even wait. Fortunately, he hadn't specified for how long. It was well past time she left for the hospital.

Sandra raised her eyes, meeting Grace's. "You're quite perceptive for such a young woman."

Grace smiled. "I'm a lot older than I look."

"Really?" Sandra asked, giving Grace a speculative look. "I've got a feeling Josh just might give you a shot." She hesitated, wincing as if a pain shot through her chest. After a moment she took a shallow breath and continued. "Grace, would you mind terribly if I went for a rest? You can stay if you like, but I need a good half hour to myself."

In seconds Sandra had gone from unwell but okay to clearly exhausted, almost appearing to age a decade. There was an anxious look about her too, as if she'd made an offer she really wished she hadn't.

Seeing the woman so vulnerable, Grace's murderous instincts rose up again. She could drag the woman to the bathroom and drown her without any real effort, and it might even be a kindness. She took a step toward Sandra without even thinking it through.

She bit her lip hard enough to hurt, stepped back again to close her eyes, leaning her shoulders and head against the door in an effort to get herself under control. After a moment she unclenched her fists. "In all honesty Sandra, I wouldn't feel comfortable staying. Tell Josh I'll talk to him later."

"Are you sure? I really don't want to seem like I'm forcing you out."

"I really have to get to the hospital." Before Abbey did, though that was another problem.

"Well, you're welcome in my home anytime."

Grace froze. It was an invitation she honestly didn't want, but desired in the worst possible way. The words felt like a net had been pulled off her, an open invitation to do murder. Sandra had just given her complete access to her home. The woman had no idea how much danger she'd put herself in, along with Josh and Mikey.

"I... appreciate it. Thanks."

After checking the front of the house, she left. The hospital wasn't all that far, but with her bare feet already sore Grace was wincing within a minute, and every pebble on the hot road felt like a personal insult as she jogged. She couldn't regret releasing that boy yesterday, but her life would have been so much easier if she hadn't. Hers and Maria's.

She cursed under her breath at the chain of events consuming her. If she couldn't sort things out soon, the world would be down two mermaids by dusk. And if she did find a way to save herself and Maria, next she was going to find a way to rid the world of one vindictive redhead. Except for werewolves, Creatures were immortal, and there was only two real ways to end a vendetta; forgive and forget or finish it the hard way. She guessed Abbey was a hard way kind of girl.

She winced as she nearly crippled herself on a rusty bottle lid. She stopped, rubbing the bottom of her foot, but fortunately the lid hadn't cut her. She tapped it into the gutter with the edge of her foot and was about to cross the road when she noticed a red convertible idling up the street. It had three girls in it; a redhead, brunette and blonde. It was like a bad bar joke.

"Shit." If she turned and ran they'd come after her, but going forward didn't seem better. At least going forward took her closer to the hospital and might buy her some time. If Abbey wanted to do something, Grace's only chance was to run.

Grace continued walking until she came level with the car on the opposite side of the street.

Abbey glanced her way, a huge grin on her face. She'd clearly been waiting, knowing this was the fastest way to the hospital. Grace's stomach did a sickly turn. She was a couple of streets from the golf course and a sizeable water hazard she could use to defend herself. She looked around for water, any source, but there was nothing nearby, not even a bird bath.

There was an open park on her side of the street, but no drinking fountain or tap she could get to. Homes lined the opposite side of the street where Abbey was parked, but she doubted she'd get to a tap before they could get to her, and Abbey was just as likely to run her over as chase her down.

One of Abbey's stooges, the blonde, got out of the car and began walking along the opposite side of the street, staying level with Grace.

Trying for a nearby yard meant running the gauntlet of werewolves and whatever Abbey was, or sprinting ahead, crossing the street a hundred metres away and finding a house's tap there. With water she'd be deadly. Without it…

"Hey slut! I see Sandra kicked you out," she called.

It may have been the worst thing she could do, but Grace panicked and ran, the werewolf breaking into run a moment later.

Grace surprised herself by outdistancing the werewolf, her longer legs paying off for once. She hit the corner of the road half a dozen yards ahead of the werewolf.

Tires screeched just as she made it to the opposite side, the convertible sliding sideways around the corner and barely missing Grace. The blonde jumped and slid across Abbey's hood without missing her stride, still chasing.

Grace ran at a rusting metal gate taller than she was, jumped and caught the top to pull herself up, but the werewolf grabbed her ankle.

Grace kicked, heart pounding in fear, but the girl reefed her back and Grace's hands slipped. She felt a moment of panic before she face-planted the concrete. Bright light exploded and she cried out in pain. The taste of blood filled her mouth as the centre of her face became a region of agony.

One of them kicked her side and she doubled up, gasping. Another kick caught her thigh. She curled into a ball to try and protect herself as dozen more kicks thumped into her legs, arms and back.

"Do it now, Abs. Go on. Suck the lifeforce out of her."

"Yeah. No one's around," the other werewolf said.

"Shut up. Grab her. Well take her back. It's too public here."

Grace moaned, spitting blood as hands grabbed her and hauled her to upright. "Get away," Grace hissed. Her lip was cut and a tooth broken, judging by the pain which shot through her head with every breath. She spat, blood and saliva dribbling down her chin.

"Shit Abs, I don't think she'll last till later. We messed her up pretty bad."

Everything hurt. One eye was already swollen closed and the other blurry. She must have fractured her cheekbone.

"I'm going to hurt you dogs real bad," Grace slurred, talking with more bravado than conviction. "That's a promise." She felt the promise settle on her, but it was a promise she knew she wasn't likely to be able to keep despite the magic that would hold her to it. She spat more blood, tried to fend one of the werewolves away, but got a punch in the stomach for it. She doubled up again, gasping.

"Hurry up you two!"

"She's heavy, Abs. Heavier than she looks, and she's a dead weight too."

The rough driveway scraped the tops of her feet like a cheese grater as they half carried, half dragged her. One of them tripped on a broken piece of concrete and it was enough to throw Grace off balance and send her sprawling to the hot driveway. "Ahh," she cried out with fresh pain.

So this was how she was going to die? Shit.

"Just do it now Abs," the brunette said, sounding a little desperate. They were in a public place after all, and bundling a beaten-up girl into the back of a registered vehicle was likely to draw notice and a future visit from the police. Who knew how many nearby homes had security cameras as well.

Grace tried to push the werewolf away, but didn't have the strength. She distended her claws and with what little strength she had left, punched them through the girl's calf instead.

The girl screamed, reefing her leg away. After taking a second to stare at the wound the werewolf kicked out, the heel of her foot catching Grace's hand. Grace barely felt it amid all her other hurts.

"Okay, hold her down," Abbey said.

Grace's fear for her life rose up. Not now. Not now. She still had to help Maria, and there was a thousand other things she wanted to do with her life. When you don't age though, it seems as if you can put those things off indefinitely.

She struggled, but the two werewolves held Grace by the arms, forcing her onto her back and pinning her to the hot concrete. Abbey dropped a heavy knee on Grace's stomach and Grace gasped, wriggling to try and force her aside. "Get off me!" she said weakly, wishing she had the breath to scream as one of the werewolves slammed the heel of her palm against Grace's temple.

Dizziness hit her and she almost lost consciousness, only fear keeping her from going dark. She struggled as Abbey grabbed her jaw to hold her head still. "You're going to enjoy this far more than I'd like," Abbey said. "That really sucks."

"Piss off."

Excitement filled Abbey's eyes as she leaned close, her lips almost touching Grace's. "I'll take as long as I can," she whispered sadistically. "I want to see desperate love for me in your eyes before I wrench it away. I want you to remember what's happening before I drain the rest."

"You're a succubus?" Grace whispered, finally understanding. She hadn't even considered that.

Abbey smiled, and it was a wicked smile full of anticipation. She opened her mouth and drew in a deep breath, and Grace felt her lifeforce obey the other being, leaving her body as Abbey drew it out. "No, no. Please…" Grace whispered, tears and pain blurring her vision. "Please." She bucked as hard as she could, tried to turn her head, but nothing helped. Worse, Abbey's enchantment didn't take hold. Grace didn't fall under the Creature's spell, and she felt vile fear instead of the obsessive lust and desire a human would feel.

Abbey abruptly fell back, dry retching.

"What the hell?" the bottle blonde werewolf said, leaving Grace and going to her mistress.

Abbey shrugged her off while Grace tried to fight off the brunette. With one hand free she swiped with her claws, but the girl blocked her while the other turned and kicked Grace hard in the side. Grace doubled up as the werewolf raised her leg to stomp.

"Hey, what are you girls doing!" a male voice demanded. Grace tried to look up but couldn't uncurl, the pain in her side too much.

"We found her like this." That was the brunette's voice. "We're taking her to the hospital."

"You found her like that after you chased her down and kicked the shit out of her? I saw from across the park." His dogs barked, one of them snarling. Grace finally managed to uncurl enough to see. He had two dogs on leads. Big dogs too, and though he was lean, it was a muscled kind of lean a fit runner would have.

One of the girls swore, but Grace couldn't tell which one. "If you're so concerned, take her to the hospital yourself. We were just trying to help."

"I'm calling the cops."

Grace heard footsteps and laughter as the girls helped Abbey into the convertible. The succubus was still dry retching. The man got to Grace and crouched beside her as the car's engine kicked into life and tires screeched. The man's dogs sniffed her, but neither tried to lick while one of them actually whined and backed away. Smart dogs.

"You okay to stand?"

Grace tried to speak, but it was more of a moan. "I just need water," she whispered. An ocean of water.

"Water? Sure, but first the hospital." He helped her up with a grunt, barely keeping her upright. "Crap you're heavy for such a slight-looking thing," he muttered. "You're all muscle, that's for sure."

Pain shot through Grace's chest as she shifted her weight. She probably had a cracked rib from one of the kicks. Maybe several.

"I'm calling an ambulance," her rescuer said as he pulled out his phone, and Grace didn't have the strength to stop him.

$$[\ 11 \ ]$$

GRACE STRUGGLED FOR CONSCIOUSNESS, but something kept pulling her under. It was painful to breathe, difficult to think, and her temples pounded in time with her pulse.

As the pain became more real she finally recognised the sterile smell of a hospital. She tried to open her eyes, but only one would work. She squinted at the brightness streaming in from the window, trying to make sense of the patterns.

Everything ached and she felt groggy. They must have given her medication for the pain then. Apparently drugs affected mermaids as well as humans. Who knew?

"Where's Maria?" she whispered in the hope someone was nearby, her throat raspy.

"You shouldn't be awake for hours yet," said a familiar voice she couldn't place. Her heart raced in fear when she remembered Abbey's attack, but the voice wasn't Abbey's.

"Maria?" she asked uncertainly, but it hadn't sounded like Maria either. The voice was older. Turning her head set off a ricochet of pain from the back of her skull to her chest. She moaned. "Who's that?"

"It's Sandra. Sandra and Josh."

"Sandra and Josh?" The names meant nothing for a moment, but memories returned with a slap of fear. Josh was here? She had to get rid of him before he inadvertently gave her an order, like telling her to stay in bed until she was better. "What are you doing here Sandra?"

"Abbey and her friends came by, waiting for Josh. They were boasting about what they'd done to you and didn't realise I could hear them from inside. I called the police."

Concern came on strong. "You shouldn't antagonise a succubus," she said.

She heard Josh laugh. "Succubus. Yeah, that fits perfectly."

Grace opened her good eye again and looked around, careful this time when she moved her head. Sandra was sitting beside her bed next to a drawn blue curtain, Josh standing by her side. His sandy, sun-bleached hair was tousled in a sweaty kind of way, instead of water-kissed as it had been yesterday.

"You don't need to be here. Why don't you both come back tomorrow when I'm back to fighting sharks for sport?" How was she going to find Maria if she had two people constantly watching her? How was she going to get out of bed?

Sandra shook her head with a slight smile, amusement in her bruised-looking, sunken eyes. "You took a bit of cleaning up, you know?"

The fear they might ignore her and stay by her bedside ate at her. "I feel fine. Please don't feel obligated to stay." Annoyed she couldn't open her other eye to see them, she reached up and found bandages there. She couldn't remember getting hit there.

Josh laughed, and even Sandra smiled. "Fine? Aren't we counting the twisted knee, sprained wrist, broken ribs and nose, cuts, scrapes and bruises anymore?"

Grace sighed. "Don't forget the broken tooth." She could feel it with her tongue, though whatever they'd given her for the pain wasn't entirely helping. It was already beginning to ache and probing it sent a sharp stab of pain through her. She wasn't going to look her best before it grew back, assuming she lived long enough.

Sandra took Grace's hand. "I've got some bad news about your left eye. They're not sure if you'll regain sight in it. There's a lot of swelling. I'm really sorry. I feel like this is my fault."

Grace's mouth ached, and the gum around the stub of her broken tooth was very tender, despite the painkillers. At least they hadn't tried to do anything about that. Yet. The thought of them trying to rip the stub out scared her more than being in hospital. She'd had a couple of decayed teeth removed as a child, and the trauma still haunted her.

Josh crossed his arms, clearly uncomfortable. "Don't worry about Abbey. The police are looking for her. I doubt she'll give you any more trouble."

"I need to get out of here." She tried to sit up, but pain lanced through her chest and she let out a soft cry. "God that hurts."

What was she going to do now? She was helpless, and the hospital hid Creatures, most of which would probably see her as a threat.

Sandra put a hand on her shoulder. "Rest. Trust me, it's the only thing that will help now."

The truth of it forced a laugh. "Rest will kill me."

"I hate to ask you this," Sandra continued as if Grace hadn't spoken, "But do you have insurance?"

Grace laughed, and then winced. "Ow, ow," she whispered. Everything really did hurt, from her head to her legs. "Not even when the Titanic sunk."

They both looked confused. "I assume that means you don't?"

"I don't mind racking up a few debts." No one was ever going to collect.

"Any kind of treatment is expensive, and if you're from another country you could be returning home with a very large bill."

Another country? Ah, her accent. "Bills aren't a concern." Josh's jaw dropped, no doubt thinking she must be filthy rich, but Sandra frowned.

"I doubt you'll be doing a runner in your condition," Sandra said, interpreting her intentions correctly.

"I really have to see Maria. I need to know how she is." Once she found Maria she could figure out how to get them both back in the ocean. Drowning a human or two would speed up Maria's healing process considerably, though taking someone's life was far more of a necessity for Grace. And she'd promised.

She tried to move again and found she wasn't even close to being up to it. Illness and injury were almost new concepts to her. She hadn't experienced either in any significant way since she'd become a mermaid, and she didn't like it.

"You need to stay where you are until you're healed," Josh said.

Grace froze, her heart almost skipping a beat. It was far too close to a command. "I understand you're concerned. If it makes you feel better I'll listen to the doctor's advice and do everything I can to heal as fast as possible. Okay?"

"You better. You need to live so you can spread the word about how much of a chick magnet Rusty is," he said with a lopsided grin, his face flushing at the attempted humour. "Otherwise people might think we're together."

She couldn't help returning a grin, though it hurt her face. "Would you do me a favour please Josh? Visit Maria for me? Make sure she's okay? Spend a bit of time with her if they'll let you. I don't want her to be alone." She wouldn't be surprised if the local Creatures had already killed her. Devastated, but not surprised.

Josh glanced at his mother, who nodded. He returned his gaze to Grace. "Yeah, sure. You right for a while Mum?"

"Of course."

Grace sighed in relief. With Josh by Maria's bedside, it wasn't likely a Creature would try something. "Her surname's Lacopo."

He nodded and pushed through the curtain barrier, his joggers making very little noise as he left the room. Grace closed her good eye. She had to figure out how to get rid of him for good, get rid of them both. In a nice way, of course.

When she opened her eyes again she found Sandra looking at her in an unnerving way. "What?" she asked the dying woman.

Sandra kept her eyes on Grace. "I used to be a nurse," she said. "Before I got sick and had to give up work." She'd clearly been holding onto this while Josh was in the room.

Grace knew that look. It was a look she'd seen in only a few people, and it was going to be a problem if she couldn't do something about it. "You must miss nursing."

Sandra smiled slightly, but her expression didn't change and the attempted diversion didn't work. "Which is why I know the sedatives they gave you should have kept you unconscious for a day or more, and even then you'd have been groggy. I wouldn't have been surprised if you'd slept until tomorrow afternoon."

"I have a fast metabolism."

"Faster than anyone I've ever met." There was a question in that, almost an accusation.

A shiver of inspiration came over Grace. Perhaps if she played this well… What did she have to lose anyway? If she couldn't get out of this bed she was going to die anyway, and Maria along with her. Time to roll the dice and gamble.

"Let me guess what you're thinking. I'm different? You feel it more than know it, and it's something akin to the feeling you get around Abbey and her friends? Not the same, but similar?"

Sandra raised her chin slightly as if she'd been caught doing something she shouldn't have. "There's other things, like no identification or local records matching your name and age. The police are doing a background check to see if you came through customs. Someone plans to talk to you about that later, you might like to know."

Grace really didn't like the tone Sandra had used at the end. "Is that all?"

"I've always had a sixth sense about these things, like some of the staff in this hospital. They're… different too, not all, but enough. What it comes down to right now is that you've been lying to me and Josh. Your charts don't make sense, yet nobody here has commented, like something's being covered up. I've seen it before, but never had the courage to say anything about it."

"Your Spidey Sense is tingling then, right?"

Sandra frowned, but nodded. "That's as good an explanation as any."

What Sandra said explained a few things. The hospital didn't just have Creatures working among the staff, it was controlled by one. As soon as Grace and Maria became yesterday's news they were likely to face... issues. Death probably. The first problem she needed to sort out wasn't that Sandra recognised her as different, but that it didn't seem to bother her. The fact she was speaking about it with Grace suggested it was more of a trust issue. Sandra had trusted Grace, and that trust was under question now, but she was giving her the benefit of the doubt. If that was all it was there was a simple solution. Grace smiled and winced in pain, which produced a deeper frown from Sandra.

"What?" Sandra asked.

"There's a truth to all your suspicions, that's all."

Sandra's expression changed slightly, but there was no less hardness or determination. "I don't understand."

Grace sighed. Either the woman would help, or Grace and Maria were dead anyway. Grace didn't have much of a choice. "Sane people usually come up with a logical explanation for the things that don't make sense to them, but few question those things." Sandra's ability to notice beyond casual curiosity must be due to her strong lifeforce, probably the only thing keeping her alive when her body clearly wanted to shut down. "Care to guess?"

Sandra looked Grace over as if wondering if she were serious. "You don't seem concerned. You could be deported, you know?"

And there is was, rational logic trying to overrule what the woman knew she felt. "I'll be dead by dusk unless I can get out of here." One mess at a time. "Care to guess?"

Sandra raised her chin, clearly surprised and apparently concerned, which was something of a slight relief to Grace. "Is someone else after you?"

Grace took as deep a breath as her pains would allow, and released it slowly. "Maria and I are mermaids. If we don't get back into the ocean before sunset we'll die."

Sandra crossed her arms over her wasted body, her frown deepening. "You know, I was going to offer to help you, but-"

"But you do know I'm not lying, don't you?"

Sandra narrowed her eyes and opened her mouth to speak, but

didn't seem to be able to say it. Doubt crowded her eyes, and she merely stared.

"I can prove it," Grace said softly. "If you like." The dying woman seemed to be on the verge of speaking again, but hesitated. Grace nodded toward the pitcher of water beside her bed. "Can you please pour me a glass?"

Sandra kept up the stare for a long moment, but more than doubt and distrust, there was curiosity in her expression, as if she'd suspected such things her entire life but had never given them credit. After a moment she did as asked, passing the glass to Grace.

Grace splashed a few drops on her arm above her bandaged wrist and spread it out with her fingertips. "Do you notice anything strange?" she asked.

Sandra raised an eyebrow. "You're arm's wet? What am I supposed to be looking for?"

"Where did the hair go?" There was none at all where the water touched her.

Sandra glanced at the wet skin and then back to Grace. "It was never there to start with."

"That's your mind tricking you." She put the water on the side table and used a bedsheet to dry her arm. "Look again."

Sandra looked, and then leaned closer, her expression changing. "There's fine blonde hair there. I could have sworn..." Sandra drew back a little, a slightly worried look on her face. "That's a very impressive trick." She was still trying to rationalise it.

Grace dribbled more water on her arm. "Touch it. Tell me what my skin feels like where it's wet."

Almost gingerly, Sandra reached out and touched Grace's arm with her fingertips, and just as quickly pulled back. She stared, but curiosity got the better of her and she tried touching it again.

"What's it feel like?" Grace asked.

Sandra swallowed, taking several seconds to think about it. Rather than speaking, she touched a dry part of Grace's arm, and surprise crossed her face. "Rubbery, but soft like a boiled egg with the shell removed. The rest of your skin's normal."

Grace concentrated and the water sheeted down her arm to the back of her hand, and from there she made it dribble back into the glass. "I'm a mermaid, Sandra."

Sandra swallowed, looking from the water to Grace and back again. "Why tell me?" She didn't sound like she believed it despite the evidence.

"Because I need your help. I have to get back to the ocean this afternoon or I'll die."

"And if I tell someone? A mermaid would be worth quite a bit."

Grace raised an eyebrow, but quickly realised that despite the words there was no real threat in Sandra's voice, though there was concern. Concern for Grace, as if someone else might use that knowledge.

"A pool won't trap me. Water is both my salvation and my weapon. Put me in that much water and I could do a lot of damage. You can't trap a mermaid with water."

Something seemed to occur to Sandra. "It's not just mermaids, is it?" There was certainty in her voice.

"No. There's faeries, sprites, pixies, and all manner of other magical and fey Creatures. We're all around you, but you don't notice or remember. All you have are the myths written down and repeated as fiction, tall tales and fantastic stories. Your mind understands fiction and can relate to it, but genuine magic defies human thought for some reason. Only the crazies believe for longer than a few weeks, and a few rare individuals with exceptionally strong lifeforce if they pay attention."

Sandra watched Grace's eyes as if looking for lies. "So when you said Abbey was a succubus, you meant it?" It was ironic how she associated a succubus with danger, but not a mermaid. Mermaids were far deadlier in their element.

"Yes. It's almost as hard for us to recognise another supernatural Creature when in human form as is it for you. It was also rather stupid of me to piss her off while I was away from the ocean, but I didn't realise how psychotic she was. Maybe she's newly made and still on a power trip." She reached out and gently took Sandra's hand, and was pleasantly surprised when the woman didn't withdraw it. "I'd strongly suggest you don't invite her into your home." She vaguely remembered her promise to make Abbey's werewolves pay, which she didn't really want to do anymore. Another stupid promise. At least she hadn't put a time limit on it.

"Thanks for the unnecessary tip."

She gave Sandra's bony hand a gentle squeeze. "I need your help, Sandra."

"I'm struggling to believe this."

"Few do."

Sandra gave a subtle nod. "Okay, I'll help, but you're going to owe me big."

"Doesn't cleaning up your kitchen count?"

Sandra smiled, but her eyes remained serious. "I want you to keep an eye on Josh for me after I pass. That's my price."

That was something she could agree on. "It would be my genuine pleasure. I mean, not in a sexual way…"

Sandra seemed far more relieved than Grace had expected. "Deal. What do you need me to do?"

Grace's tension eased until she remembered Abbey worked at the hospital. Abbey was probably waiting for the commotion to die down, and then she'd make a move. But for that to happen she must have other accomplices here. "Get me into a bath or a pool. The ocean would be better. I heal much faster in my natural form." It added another dimension to her need to get out of the place.

"We'll need a wheelchair. Most rooms have showers. Will that do?"

"It'll help, but I'd rather be fully submerged. The greater the volume, the better. A bath will do in a pinch, but to fully recover I'll need a couple of days in the ocean where I can sense other mermaids."

Sandra almost did a double take when Grace mentioned other mermaids, as if she hadn't considered that Grace and Maria weren't unique. "I'll go see if I can rustle up a wheelchair. There's a spa bath in one of the birthing suites."

[12]

A FLASH of guilt made Grace look down when she heard Sandra returning, breathing hard. If she could have, Grace would have ordered the woman into the chair she was pushing. Frustration with her own weakness made her feel even guiltier. Sandra was sweating, with little but willpower keeping her moving.

"Why don't you sit? Rest." She pointed to the wheelchair.

Her hands shaking, Sandra dug into her purse and took a tablet from a plastic container, washing it down with some of the water from the jug. "When they wheel me around, I'll be on a gurney to the morgue, not a wheelchair."

Grace smiled at the woman's determination. "No doubt you'll be trying to remove the wheels while arguing that you're not dead."

That got a smile from Sandra. "Stop lazing around. We've got an appointment to make, and you're not helping. Literally."

With her twisted knee and broken ribs, Grace struggled to get out of bed. Every movement, no matter how small, sent jabs of pain through her.

Sandra took a step forward to help, one hand on the back of the wheelchair.

"Rest," Grace said, not wanting to push the woman into a coma.

"You've done enough, and then some. You keep trying to do too much and you'll end up on that gurney well ahead of schedule."

"Said the invalid who can't stand up. A hundred bucks says I can beat you to the ocean and back."

Clutching her ribs, Grace carefully manoeuvred out of bed and placed her good leg on the floor to take her weight. Sandra manoeuvred the wheelchair behind her, a foot bracing one of the rear wheels to help keep it from shifting. Gripping an arm rest for added stability and taking her weight on her good leg, Grace gingerly lowered herself into it.

Sitting hurt her ribs, but it was better than standing.

"Okay?" Sandra asked, still a little out of breath.

"Totally," Grace lied. "Having doubts?"

"Plenty, but I'll get you to that spa."

The curtain pulled back and a dishevelled nurse who easily outweighed Grace and Sandra combined stared at them in surprise. "What's going on?" The woman's grey hair was starting to come loose and her cheeks were slightly flushed.

"Grace needs to go to the toilet," Sandra said before Grace could respond.

The nurse glanced at Grace, but returned her attention to Sandra as if Grace was the least responsible for her being out of bed. "I was coming to insert a catheter. It should have been done earlier but we've been busy." She held up the catheter still inside its sterile packaging. "Holiday season's always crazy."

Grace cringed away from the device. "I'll use the toilet thanks, even if I've got to crawl."

The woman gave a half smile as if she wasn't surprised by the reaction. "I'm impressed you're awake young lady, let alone speaking. How about I help you back into the bed and get the catheter sorted?"

Grace leaned away. "I'd prefer it if you'd shoot me."

The nurse turned to Sandra, hands on her ample hips. "I don't want you to take this unkindly Sandra, but you should have asked for help." Of course the nurse would know Sandra.

"It's just a wheelchair Patricia. I'm okay to push."

The nurse gave the wheelchair a glance, eyed the catheter she held, and then focused on Grace. "Okay, you can use the toilet, but then straight back to bed. You took a very serious beating."

Grace released her breath. She hadn't realised she was holding it.

Sandra touched Patricia's arm. "As she'll already be out of bed and in the chair, I was thinking of taking her for a coffee. Shouldn't be any more than half an hour. Is that okay?"

The nurse's frown deepened. She looked Grace over again, assessing. She reached out and placed a hand on Grace's forehead. "You're a little on the cool side. Are you warm enough?"

"I'm fine." What if Patricia didn't allow her to leave the room? She tried to think of an alternative excuse but came up blank.

Patricia's expression held doubts, but she nodded after a moment. "Okay, but if you experience any pain, nausea or light-headedness, come straight back here or call for a nurse, okay?"

Grace forced a smile, trying not to let her tension show. "Okay."

"I'll be back in an hour to check on you, which reminds me, I'll need you to fill out some admission forms and other documentation. Why don't you pick them up from the nurse's station on the way back from the cafeteria?"

Everyone wanted her to fill out forms it seemed, as if the world couldn't turn without them.

"We'll do that, thanks Patricia," Sandra said. When the nurse left, Sandra pushed Grace toward the room's door and past the bathroom on the left. There were only two beds in the room, and sitting in the second one was an old woman watching Grace suspiciously. Grace's intuition told her the stickybeak had been listening to everything.

"Was there anything you missed?" Grace asked the old woman. "I can provide a recap, if you like."

"You know young girl, that's-" she began in a completely condescending way.

"Young girl?" Grace asked. "I was a married woman before *you* were born. Why don't you tell the nurse everything you overheard? You might score an entirely new set of medications."

The old buzzard shut her mouth and turned away.

"Thought so."

"You really aren't the most polite person in the world," Sandra remarked as she pushed Grace out of the room.

Grace couldn't help a smile. "I've met my share of people wanting to put their fingers in my life. Magic or some higher power keeps our secret from reaching the world, but it doesn't prevent the odd person catching a glimpse of us as we really are. I had a stalker decades ago in South Africa, one of those 'not quite wired up properly' people, and he wouldn't forget. Nobody believed him of course, but he purchased a camera in the hope of catching me emerging from the water."

"I take it you haven't been to South Africa lately?"

"Frequently."

"You're not concerned about him?"

"Maria lured him into the water and drowned him for me. Never kiss a mermaid. Just saying."

"What? That's... horrid!"

She supposed it was.

Somewhere ahead a woman screamed, the sound followed by exhausted breathing. Seconds later she gave another cry. Grace tried to ignore the unwanted maternal feelings the cries generated. It seemed almost sacrilegious to talk about murdering people in a place where new life was being born. "Mermaids aren't quite the lovely Creatures of legend we're often portrayed as, Sandra."

Sandra paused, taking short, shallow breaths.

"You okay?"

"I think I'll need a nap while you're splashing about."

No one questioned them as they moved to the delivery suite at the far end of the ward. After checking it was unused, Sandra wheeled Grace in and shut the door behind them, and then took her into the bathroom where a large triangular spa sat in the corner.

The room smelled of cleaning agents and water, the water arousing Grace's murderous instincts. Her nails began growing into claws almost immediately, and she had to force herself to remain calm. Sandra turned the taps on, the water pounding against the bottom of the bath. The smell of it raised Grace's killer instincts to a new level, and it was only willpower that stopped her from lunging at Sandra. At least the water would give Grace half a chance if Abbey ventured in.

"Sandra," Grace said, catching the sick woman's attention. "Once I'm in the water, I want you to leave the bathroom. Before I get in, actually. I've almost no lifeforce left and my body's desperate for more. I'll drown you before I even know what I've done, and I don't want to risk that."

"You… take lifeforce from people? By drowning them?"

She nodded, looking down and unable to meet the woman's eyes as she continued. "It's like food or warmth to you, I guess, and humans are the only creatures that generate enough to make it worthwhile taking. Without people, we'd die."

Sandra's expression turned speculative, though oddly not fearful. "I'll stand well clear."

Her tone was enough to raise Grace's suspicious. "Don't even make eye contact, and plug your ears if you hear me singing. I'm so weak I won't have any self-control."

"Sure. No eye contact. Fingers in ears. Can I at least sing along?" Sandra asked, eyebrow raised.

"I'm serious Sandra. I'll charm you into the water and drown you while you're still smiling if you're not careful. I really won't have any control, and may not even remember doing it afterward. Close the door and stay on the other side until I've drained the bath and you're sure I'm dry. I was desperate for life's energy before I got injured. In water and injured... I won't be myself. Please, I really don't want to hurt you."

Sandra sat on the edge of the bath, folding her skinny arms across her chest. She met Grace's eyes. "I hear drowning's a relatively pleasant way to go."

Suspicions confirmed. Grace wasn't surprised. "I drowned once. I can promise you it wasn't pleasant."

Sandra's expression only slipped a little. "I'm thinking that maybe now's my time. Here. You said you could charm me so I die with a smile?"

The woman had a death wish. "It doesn't always work, and

knowing about it means you have a fighting chance of not succumbing."

"If that's what I wanted. I don't. It makes sense, don't you think? You get my life energy or whatever you call it, while I get freedom from this horrible wasting disease and pain. Josh won't have to suffer through my final days either, watching me die in agony. You've got no idea how often I've thought of overdosing. You'll be doing me and everyone else a favour."

Grace tried not to let the appeal in Sandra's suggestion get to her, though her instincts desperately wanted to force her to push Sandra into the bath and hold her under until that moment of death when she could take everything she needed. "Josh won't have a chance to say goodbye Sandra, and from what you've said he's not prepared. I couldn't do that to him. How would he explain it to Mikey?"

Sandra dropped her eyes. "I still think it would be better for him."

Grace held up her hands, showing Sandra her hardening claws at the thought of taking her lifeforce. Sandra's eyes widened. Grace tried again. "Please Sandra. I can't take a friend, so don't tempt me. Please promise me you'll stay away."

The woman raised her eyes, determination there. "My only choice right now is how I go, and if I wait much longer I'll lose that too."

Grace closed her eyes, the scent of the water almost compelling her to take Sandra up on her offer. Her canines were distending, serrated against her tongue to help her catch prey, and her sharp claws already out. She let her teeth show, and got another frightened reaction from Sandra, but it didn't make her back down. "How about I make you a promise if you make me one? My promises are binding."

Sandra cocked her head. "I'm listening."

"Promise me you'll stay out of here while I'm in the water, and I'll promise you I'll help you to die once you've sorted things with Josh. If it's what you really want, and you don't resist, you won't even realise you're drowning."

"What if you're not around? What if I forget from that magic thing you mentioned?"

"I won't let you forget. If I'm in the ocean when you make your decision, just stand ankle-deep in the surf and call my name. I'll hear."

Sandra checked the bath water. "It's deep enough to cover your legs now." Droplets splashed enticingly from the tap. "Okay. That works for me, but if it gets to the point where I can no longer make the decision myself I want you to make it for me. Fair?"

Helping Sandra to end her life on her own terms was a better option than causing her death now, although Grace's promise to Maria was a bigger issue. It was taking all her willpower not to drown Sandra. "Fair. I promise not to let you forget and to help you die once you've sorted through the issue with Josh. I also promise to make the decision for you if you're no longer capable." She felt the binding magic in the words. It was a promise she could live with, at least.

Sandra held out her hand to shake on it, but Grace leaned away. "You're hand's wet and there's a large volume of water behind you. You better move. My body can sense the water and you're between it and me."

As Sandra stood Grace shifted her weight to the front of the wheelchair and managed to stand on her good leg, nevertheless biting her lip in pain. Sandra moved to help. "No! Stay back. Go around me."

Grace hobbled to the spa bath and sat on the edge as Sandra walked around her to the door. Despite her body aching for the water, Grace carefully removed the hospital gown to reveal her heavily bandaged chest and leg.

"Do you want me to help?"

With so much water sharpening her senses, Grace keenly sensed Sandra's lifeforce, rich and vital despite the decaying state of the woman's body. She wanted it. Needed it. The woman had a strong will to live, no matter her talk of death.

"No, thank you," she said, her need to kill making her terse. Her claws were showing as she removed the bandages. "Really Sandra, you have to stay away now. Please take another step back." She unwound the chest bandages, letting them fall to the floor beside the bath, leaning over to begin working on the bandaged leg before she realised her necklace was missing. "My necklace. Do you know where they'd have put it?"

"The gaudy thing with the pearls?" Sandra didn't sound very impressed. "Probably in the drawer next to your bed, or at the nurse's station."

"Would you mind checking? It's got a lot of sentimental value."

"Sure. I'll take my time." Sandra left, shutting the bathroom door. A moment later the door to the birthing suite closed as well.

Grace finished unwrapping the bandages on her bruised and twisted knee and then removed the dressings on her feet where the werewolves had dragged her across the concrete. Her feet were a mess.

She dipped a finger into the warm water, moaning with pleasure. She couldn't have left the bath had she wanted to, and it was all she could do gently lower herself into it. She barely held off her change until she was in.

The pain in her leg flared and then drained away as if the water were drawing an infection out. Breathing a sigh of relief, she removed the taped-on dressings from her damaged eye and dropped them over the side of the bath. Her entire face throbbed.

The bath was deep and wide enough for her to hide from view if someone casually glanced into the room. She turned the hot water off and let the bath fill with cold water, relaxing in the joy of it.

The change of form would heal her leg so she could walk on it, but the pain in her chest remained as she sunk to her chin. She didn't have enough residual life force to heal, and so only the natural change of form was responsible for repairing her leg.

Regardless, the longer she remained submersed the faster her damaged body would heal.

When the spa was full enough, Grace turned the water off and sunk under the surface, finally opening her painful eye. She jerked as the water stung it, but like her leg, the pain quickly leached away. It was hardly the peace or freedom of the ocean, and lacked her sisters' empathic presence, but it would do for now.

For the first time in what seemed like weeks, she relaxed.

[13]

Grace dreamed...

Her hand was white as she gripped her husband's, her fingernails digging in.

The Titanic was dipping toward the bow and the steward wasn't waiting for stragglers as he led Grace, her husband and the other steerage passengers through the gloomy maze of corridors and stairs, the corridor sloped. It took far longer than it should have due to blocked corridors and stairwells, and they'd already been kept below for hours.

They finally made it to the icy air, the cold a slap to her exposed face. Grace hunched as her breath fogged under the ship's external lights, shivering with fear more than the temperature. The cold made her throat ache, quickly penetrating her clothes. Her other hand held her suitcase, all the possessions she had.

"Hurry now. There's a lifeboat waiting for you," the steward said as the last of the group exited the door. "The ship's in no danger of sinking, but it's best to be safe."

She could feel the deck tilting further, but Grace ignored the blatant lie, still hopeful he might be right. It felt better to believe the lie than accept what she knew. Her knuckles whitened further as her grip on

Will's hand was tested by the throng merging with a group of women and children, and a few of the younger married men. One of the men carried a boy about three or four while his wife held a younger girl.

Grace shivered with cold now, her teeth chattering. Her best and only cloak wasn't thick enough to keep the chill away as they began toward the lifeboats. They followed the lean steward along the dipping hardwood deck, careful of stumbling over dropped and shifted items.

The ship's tilt seemed worse.

Will squeezed her hand, his other holding his own hefty suitcase, his reddish hair a beacon under his woollen newsboy cap. The suitcases were gifts they'd received on their wedding night in preparation of this journey. They were supposed to be starting a new life across the ocean in America, with Will being offered a foreman's job in a new factory.

"We'll be fine," Will said, probably sensing the tension she transferred through their grip. His calloused hand held hers too tightly, as if he too were scared. "You heard the steward. The ship won't sink.

The ship's band was playing somewhere, an odd thing considering their circumstances. It gave the misguided impression that everything was in order. Despite their being so many people crowding the deck, the crew seemed to have everything well in hand.

As they neared the lifeboats the officer in charge yelled, "That's it! There's no more room on this one."

"What do you mean?" yelled a hysterical woman. "There's only one more life boat on this side."

The deck shuddered. It felt as if something below decks had given way. Will pulled her closer. "We'll be fine," he said.

A tall woman, Grace stood on her toes and to see over the heads of the men and women waiting to board. "There's got to be a hundred people waiting, Will. More. We'll never get a place."

He shifted his balance in response to the dipping deck. "We should head for the stern. I think the bow's going to go under soon. Perhaps help will arrive soon."

He pulled her through the group, several of the passengers beginning to cry as they came to the same realisation Grace had. She couldn't help thinking of the newly created life in her womb, a secret she'd planned to tell Will the following night at dinner. "Will, I need to tell you something," she said.

"Not now!" he almost dragged her along.

The steward caught Grace's wrist as she passed, stopping them both. "I wouldn't go that way," he said. "When the ship goes down you'll be sucked under. You'd be better off near the side and jumping for the water to get clear. They're already signalling the other lifeboats to return and pick up more passengers. If you can get to one you'll be safe."

"I can't swim," Grace said, feeling panic stirring now. She could hear the despair in her own voice.

"Then hang onto those suitcases. They'll float. They'll do a better job of it if you empty them."

Someone slipped over and landed hard on her back as Will took the man's advice and pulled Grace toward the railing. She didn't resist. What choice did they have? There were people at the railing already, some preparing to jump overboard, but it was still a long drop to the water. "We're too high," she whispered as he dropped her hand. Her hand went protectively to her stomach. "Will, I really need to-"

He gave her a look, though there was just as much fear on his face as she felt. "Later. We have to get into the water and swim to a boat. The water's closer than it was a few hours ago, and if we don't get to a lifeboat first there won't be room when everyone else gets into the water. They'll get terribly overcrowded in short order."

Grace tried to stay strong. "Darling, I'll drown!"

He put his suitcase on the deck against his leg so it wouldn't slide away, and then took hers, laid it flat and undid the clips. "We'll empty them and you can use one to float. All you'll have to do is kick toward a lifeboat."

She glanced over the side, unable to see far in the gloom. There was only one lifeboat nearby, and that was full and rowing away. "Will, I'm really scared." Her hands were trembling, a combination of cold and fear.

He upended her suitcase on the deck, her spare clothes a wasted pile of cloth now. She had little else. "Here," he said, locking the clasps and handing the suitcase back.

She took it with shaking arms, holding it with trembling arms close to her chest to keep from dropping it. It gave her a measure of comfort, but not much. People were either moving to the stern or grabbing hold of something. "Come on," he said. "We'll throw the suitcases first, and all you have to do is jump next to yours, grab onto it and kick toward a lifeboat." He dumped the contents of his own suitcase and relatched it. "Ready?"

"Are you sure they'll float?" What if they didn't? She'd drown.

"Of course." He didn't look as confident as he sounded, his trimmed red beard and the gloom obscuring his expression, but his eyes betrayed his fears. "We need to get to a lifeboat. Now."

He took her suitcase and helped her mount the railing in a most undignified way, but without his help she doubted she'd make it. Her legs finally over the other side, she clung tightly to the railing with both hands, facing outward.

"I can't," she whispered. There was nothing but the black ocean below. The lower port holes had already disappeared under the dark water while the stern of the ship was almost out entirely.

Will dropped her suitcase overboard, and then his own. They seemed to fall for ages before hitting the water. They landed a few yards apart, slightly away from the sinking ship. They were dim spots against the dark water. "Jump Grace. You have to jump," he said as he climbed the rail.

"What if I can't get to the suitcase?"

He pried one of her hands free of the railing and held it, a little warmth still in his own. "We'll jump together, okay? One, two, three."

"No. No!"

He jumped and she screamed as his weight pulled her from the railing. She fell awkwardly and plunged headfirst into the freezing water. She hit hard, holding her breath, but the cold almost shocked her senseless.

She twisted, turning in the water and trying to kick, her skirts hindering her. She couldn't tell up from down and flailed wildly. Her lungs demanded air and her whole body was aching with cold and pain.

Flailing and kicking, she twisted wildly about without any idea of what direction she needed to go. Struggling, flailing and kicking in any direction, hoping the surface was near as the air in her lungs burned up. The cold sunk deep into her body, making it hard to kick or try and swim.

Within moments her lungs were burning, salty water horrid-tasting in her mouth. She needed to breathe. Had to breathe. She opened her mouth, desperate, and broke through the surface like a moth escaping a cocoon.

She sucked in frigid icy air, but air nevertheless, but then went under again. Panicking, she splashed and struggled, burst through and saw her suitcase a few yards away.

Thrashing her arms and legs through the water with all her strength and fear combined, she splashed toward it, and just as she thought she was going to go under again her hand touched it. She went under anyway, but broke the surface once more and her suitcase was right beside her. She grabbed a hold and clung to it, coughing and spitting horrible-tasting salty water back into the ocean.

"Will!" she cried, shivering. "Will! Help me Will."

Someone landed in the water maybe thirty yards away, and then another nearer to her. The stern was completely out of the water now, and despite the darkness she realised even the massive propellers were exposed to the frigid air.

"Will!" she called again, her breath frosting in front of her face and her body shaking terribly. Her teeth chattered.

Her suitcase was getting lower in the water and she realised with absolute dread that it was filling up. "Will!" she screamed in panic, twisting about to try and find him.

She saw him twenty yards away, kicking hard, his suitcase out in front to help him stay afloat. "Will," she screamed. "Will. Please!"

He glanced back, met her eyes, and turned away. He was abandoning her to try and save his own life. The devastation she felt crushed her. He hadn't even tried to help her get to her own suitcase.

She doubted he'd had any intention of helping her once off the ship and away from the eyes of people who might judge him. He'd only wanted to make sure he put on a good show for the other passengers. Still in shock at his betrayal, she watched him continue kicking toward the distant lifeboat, leaving her behind. "Will!" she called in denial and panic. "Will! I'm pregnant!"

He didn't glance back.

Teeth chattering painfully and the weight of her clothes beginning to drag her under, she was so cold she could barely feel her hands. She desperately shrugged her cloak off her shoulders in the hope it might give her more precious time, but it made little difference. Her suitcase was almost entirely under.

She clung to it regardless as an almighty tearing sound shattered the night, metal ripping, followed by a huge splash. "God help me," she whispered, panic rising. A wave washed over her and the suitcase went under, taking her with it.

She clung to it for desperate seconds before letting go and kicking. Her legs caught in her skirts as her clothes conspired against her, but she reached the surface again. She choked on salty water and coughed it out, desperately kicking her legs to stay on the surface. "Will!" she cried, barely aware of other screams and cries for help. She paddled as best she could, her ice-cold hands plunging into the water as if she could claw her way on top of it. "Help! Someone please help me!"

With her body aching and desperately cold, she slipped under the surface again. The cold was the only thing giving her an indication she was alive. Pressure began building in her ears as she struggled, her lungs aching.

She was going to drown. She had no strength left. Despite trying to move her arms and legs, she couldn't. Oh God, she really was going to die, her baby along with her.

Like a miracle, something caught her and pushed her upward. She broke the surface with a cry of relief, followed by a desperately in-taken breath and coughing.

Teeth chattering, she spat icy seawater. Somebody supported her weight, holding her around her waist to keep her head above the surface.

"Do you want to live?" It was a female voice with a foreign accent. European. Italian, maybe.

Grace barely managed a nod. "Of c-c-course!"

Strong hands turned Grace in the water. She could barely make out the woman's face, but surprisingly her arms and shoulders were bare. Her skin was as cold as the water, but then so was Grace's.

The woman smiled as if delighted by the response. "Good. Then let's go find someone to help you stay alive."

Without any apparent effort the woman lifted Grace tighter and began pushing her through the water as if the two of them were holding a towed rope. A ripple washed from them, but the ride was short.

"Help!" someone cried as they stopped almost within touching distance of a man struggling to stay afloat. "Please, help me."

With the loss of momentum, Grace and the strange woman sunk deeper, but the woman had no trouble keeping Grace's head above the water. Clinging tight to her, Grace barely noticed the woman's skin was oddly soft and rubbery, and she had no clothes on her upper body at all.

"W-who… ar… are… yo-you?"

"Your only friend, it seems," the dark-haired woman said.

The man frantically paddled toward them, and Grace felt a renewed burst of fear. He'd drag them under. Grace clung even more desperately to the woman.

With one arm wrapping protectively around Grace's waist, the woman caught the splashing man by his throat. His eyes bulged in surprise as his big hands caught her forearm in what must have been a painful grip, but it didn't show on the woman's face. It was only then that Grace noticed the woman had claws for fingernails. Long, sharp, dangerous-looking claws.

The woman smiled, revealing canines long and sharp enough to put fear into a lion. She glanced quizzically at Grace. "What's your name?"

Not sure whether to panic and try to get away or to cling tighter, Grace chose the second option. "G-Grace."

Almost passionately, the woman, or whatever Creature she was, pressed her icy lips to Grace's. A pleasant, warm sensation spread from the kiss. The woman pulled back and smiled. "I'm Maria. Welcome to the sea, my darling daughter." The warmth stayed with Grace, filling her. Her shivering eased and the water began to feel almost pleasant, like a bath.

"What's happening?" Grace asked as her teeth stopped chattering. She didn't feel the cold anymore. "What did you do?"

Maria smiled, but there was something deadly in it. Dangerous, but not, somehow, directed at Grace. Maria turned to the man who was still struggling with her grip, both hands pulling desperately at Maria's wrist and trying to break her hold. Her claws had punctured his neck.

As if speaking a ritual, Maria spoke. "We offer you thanks for your sacrifice." The man's eyes widened as Maria shoved him under the water.

"What are you doing? Let him up!" Grace cried in shock.

One of his hands reached through the surface, splashing, but Maria held him under. The surface roiled as his hands broke through in a panic. Maria met Grace's eyes. "I'm sorry you have to go through this, but it will be over quickly."

The woman pulled Grace close and they slipped under the water. In a fresh panic, Grace barely managed one final breath before her head went under. She struggled with all her strength as they went so deep her ears hurt and complete darkness enfolded her.

Although she had been disorientated before, she wasn't this time. She could feel the water now, even the depth. Ten yards, fifteen, twenty. Thirty now. Forty. Her lungs burned and the wonder of it got lost in fear. She was so deep she would never be able to reach the surface, and she desperately needed air as she tried to push away from Maria.

Maria only held her tighter. She struggled frantically, desperately hoping for something that might help, a piece of flotsam she could jab at Maria to make her let go, but she couldn't feel anything but water. Even the starlight didn't penetrate this deep. She needed air, her mouth opening and closing as if in a heartbeat she'd discover air instead of water. She tried one final desperate push, trying to escape Maria's grip, and failed.

Her heart pounded insanely as Maria held her like she was a child needing comfort, much too strong for Grace to fight off.

She was dying. She could feel it. Her lungs burned, and there was nothing but the warm salty ocean surrounding her.

She sensed the man Maria held lose his own fight for life, his flailing stopping. Her own thoughts grew faint as she weakened, and without thinking she took a breath.

Salty water burned her throat and she choked on it. She jerked as her body finally remembered to fight, panicking anew, and for a few seconds more she fought for the surface, desperately sucking in more water as she did so. Choking on it. Dying from it. She would never become a mother. Never know old age. Never have grandchildren.

With one hand outstretched for the surface well above her, the last moments of her human life passed and her eyes rolled back.

Energy rushed into her.

She took a deep breath, desperately filling her lungs like she'd never breathed before.

Vitality filled her, crushed her legs and made her strong. She needed more. Much, much more. Looking around, the water was no longer dark, but strangely luminous and filled with beauty. She could see the currents, the microscopic life within. It enfolded her like a long lost lover eager to have her back in his arms. The ocean was alive with beauty, and she felt as if she were flying high over the ground, which was an impossible distance below her.

"Welcome, sister," Maria said, releasing her grip on Grace.

For the first time Grace could see Maria had a tail like a dolphin, but longer and more elegant, the end spreading into gentle fan-like wisps. Grace couldn't tell where the tail ended and water began. Grace had a tail to match; a little longer, yet just as elegant, and if she hadn't been so desperate for more of the energy that had just rushed into her she might have cried out in shock. The man Maria had dragged into the depths was only a few feet away, sinking, his lifeforce spent to transform Grace and bring her into this new life.

And she needed more. It was as strong as her desire to breathe.

"What have you done?" she asked, trying to resist the urge to shoot toward the surface and grab someone and suck their vitality from their body. Anyone. She needed that lifeforce, and could sense it in the people above them. She should have been surprised she could speak under water, but it felt natural now. Her fingernails had become claws too, and she could feel her canines were long and sharp and serrated.

"You said you wanted to live, and there's far too many people here for me to take alone." The dark-haired mermaid held out a necklace to Grace. It had a pearl-encrusted sapphire dangling on a golden chain. "This will help in the lean times. Take your husband first. He gave you up for dead. It's only fair that he be the one to deliver to you the essential lifeforce to ensure your survival."

As soon as the woman, no mermaid, said it, Grace knew exactly what she meant. Anger and bitter hatred filled her. Will. The coward. She'd drag him down into the depths so no one would ever find his body.

She could sense Will's lifeforce through the water and see him still struggling to reach a distant lifeboat, his suitcase gone now and the lifeboat moving further away. He swam awkwardly. Even if she left him be he'd never make it.

She smiled, her canines lengthening in response to her murderous new mood. It was time to get her revenge…

[14]

Grace jolted to full consciousness as something jabbed her forehead. She surfaced, snarling and ready to kill, but stopped as a body slid from the edge of the bath to the floor.

Shock rushed through her and she hesitated, an altogether unexpected feeling of wellness warring with fear and dread. Sandra stood near the door, a broom in her hand, the end of it wet.

"What did I do?" Grace asked. Sandra shuffled back a couple of steps, eyes studying Grace in revulsion and fear, and more than a little betrayal.

The woman's expression told Grace everything that had happened.

"What did I do?" Grace asked again as she stared at the sick woman. Sandra looked ready to scream or run away in fear. "I told you not to come in until I was out of the bath," she said a little too harshly, and regretted the words as soon as she saw Sandra back a little further away. Grace wanted to put her hands up, to implore her to be calm, but didn't dare in case the movement was enough to tip the balance. "Sandra?" she asked gently. "I… I'm so sorry if I scared you. I told you I was dangerous when I'm like this."

She didn't dare glance over the side of the spa bath at the woman she'd drowned without even realising it. Did she have a family? Did

Sandra know her? Of course she did. Grace could tell by her expression.

Sandra, pale and tense, just stared at Grace's mermaid body. The claws. The elongated canines. The lean hard muscle. Taking a risk, Grace glanced over the side of the bath as guilt began gnawing at her. She closed her eyes in regret when she saw it was a female nurse, soaked and bleeding from Grace's claws. Guilt deepened, welling up despite not knowing the woman. Puncture wounds seeped blood from the woman's neck, creating thin rivulets down her neck to the floor.

"Sandra?" How would Grace survive if the woman ran or called for help? "I'm sorry Sandra. Do you know her?"

"You killed Bec," Sandra whispered, fear and more than a little anger in her voice.

Pained by Sandra's expression as much as her own actions, Grace closed her eyes. She wanted to pretend it had never happened, but only a coward would embrace that kind of a reaction, and she'd never been a coward.

Hoping that if she kept talking, she might reach Sandra. "I was dreaming..." she said softly, remembering her husband's panicked kicking and fighting as she'd dragged him under. She'd thrilled in her own strength. She'd been so strong. Far too strong. And she'd played with him until he'd had absolutely no strength left.

Bile rose as she remembered the joy and satisfaction she'd felt when he realised who was murdering him. How many times had she bought him to the surface, only to let him catch his breath and drag him under again? She was sure shame flushed her cheeks. She hoped she'd been kinder to the nurse.

There was nothing she could say to Sandra about the murder she'd just committed, but she had to try. "I'm so sorry."

Sandra took a shuddering breath. "Bec delivered Josh," she finally said. "We were best friends for nearly thirty years. She was my mentor when I first started nursing."

"I wish I could undo it," Grace said softly. And she did.

Sandra took a long, deep breath and let it out slowly. She met Grace's eyes, resolution there. "I made a mistake in helping you."

Grace's stomach filled with acid at the words. She had no one to help her save Maria now. Hoping she'd misheard, Grace studied Sandra's eyes and the resolution there, but only saw her own self-loathing reflected back to her. "Maybe you're right," Grace whispered. "I should never have burdened you."

Being forced to take lives just to stay alive had to be the cruellest punishment she could think of, at least for anyone who wasn't a psychopath. As her shock began to recede memories encroached of her moments with Bec, even as she wished she could keep the memories buried forever.

She wanted to talk about it with someone sympathetic, but Sandra would do. "I'd drifted to sleep," she began softly. "But even in the dream I sensed someone's presence. I was so far gone I acted like a wild animal the way I had when I'd first been turned, murderous instincts overriding my thoughts and emotions. Maybe Bec noticed the water in the bath or heard me splash, but by the time she came close enough I was ready."

Grace couldn't meet Sandra's eyes and stared at the surface of the water. Like a shark she could smell Bec's blood from where her claws had punctured her skin to ensure she couldn't escape, and to help her drain her lifeforce.

"She had no chance. Even if I wasn't half mad with old memories and need, I was still too desperate." There'd been no guilt when she'd drowned Bec, only desire and the lust. Her fresh guilt surpassed the old but fierce pleasure she'd felt when she'd drowned Will. It had been sweet revenge then. Now it made her feel sick.

Perhaps sensing it was safe to approach, Sandra took a step closer to the nurse's body, though she kept her eyes on Grace. "Can we… resuscitate her?" Sandra asked, as if the evidence before her weren't enough.

Grace wanted to drop back below the surface of the water until all her problems went away. "No." How could she explain it in a way Sandra might understand? "When you drain someone's lifeforce, it's like dissolving the glue that holds their soul to their body. Nothing can bring them back."

Almost too softly to hear, Sandra whispered the next question. "Was she scared? Did she suffer?"

More guilt etched at the barriers Grace wanted to build between herself and the memories of what she'd done. She'd hummed a soft and subtle enchantment to attract the nurse, but merely grabbed her throat and held her head under the water while she'd kicked and thrashed and drowned.

"I enchanted her. It would have been very peaceful for her. Joyful, even," she lied, not wanting to add to Sandra's pain.

Grace shivered with remembered ecstasy as she drew the woman's face into the water, and hated herself a little more for feeling so... predatory. Drowning someone always felt like lust, desire and sex all combined. It felt so good she didn't dare try to explain it to Sandra.

"You liked it, didn't you?" Sandra asked as she picked up on Grace's tone, a sharpness in her expression. She seemed to be trying not to vomit as she rolled Bec to her side and examined her pale, age-lined face. Expressionless.

In movies when people died from fear or joy, it stayed on their faces. In reality, emotions during death left no expression as the muscles relaxed. Only the physical marks of Bec's struggles remained, the puncture wounds and the soaked uniform.

Grace didn't want to lie to anyone, let alone Sandra. "Drowning someone can be addictive. There's a sensual sensation that comes over us the moment someone realises they're not going to survive. Our, I don't know, lust perhaps rises in equal proportions to the victim's absolute panic and fear." Grace shuddered. "That's why I prefer to charm people if I can, so it's peaceful and intimate, but not sexual. I'm just left with the guilt."

Sandra had gone paler than she normally seemed. "You're-"

Grace cut her off. "Yes, mermaids are monsters. I'm so sorry, Sandra. I never wanted you to see this side of me."

Sandra looked from Grace's tail to her face. It was clear she didn't want to believe any of it despite the evidence. "You warned me. I just didn't... I..."

Grace hauled herself up to the side of the bath and forced the water to sheet off her body, transforming back into a human. Sandra flinched away in fear, taking a half step back as if Grace were about to drown her too. Grace tried not to let her hurt feelings show, wishing she didn't miss Sandra's friendship already. Sandra's eyes were hard now. Fearful. There was a barrier between them. The friendship was lost. "I'm sorry Sandra, but I can't dwell on Bec. It'll drive me mad if I do."

Sandra gripped the broom as Grace stood, her knuckles white. The lifeforce she'd stolen had reinvigorated her body, healing her, but it came at a cost. She would have to kill again sooner than normal. The damage had been too great to allow herself the time she needed to heal.

Surprisingly, Sandra stood her ground beside her unconscious friend, holding the broom handle like a weapon. "You should have taken me when I asked you to. Bec was a good woman. She had a life. I've only got days, weeks at best."

"Sandra-"

"How is this going to affect her family? Her husband and children? Her grandchildren?"

Grace forced herself to look at Bec's prone form, wet hair plastered to her face and the ground. "Sandra," she whispered, hoping the woman wouldn't run screaming for help. "Neither of us can afford to be here when they find Bec. There are other Creatures in this hospital and they'll recognise the signs. I'd like to give you time to deal with this, I honestly would, and I'd like to do the same, but it's not possible right now."

What she really wanted to do was swim down to the bottom of the Pacific Ocean and sulk in the darkness where no one save her mermaid sisters could ever find her. If Maria had told her about the costs of becoming a mermaid before changing her, Grace might have refused. Then again, Grace had been drowning and desperate, and would have taken any offer that didn't involve a direct journey to Hell. She still wasn't sure she hadn't signed up for one despite being able to enter holy ground.

Sandra took a moment before she nodded. Judging by the way she blinked, she was struggling not to cry. "I've seen bodies before," she said. "Lots of them. It's just so much harder when it's a friend. I need a moment or two."

"You hate me, don't you?" Grace asked, the weight of it in her voice. Saying the words hurt, so they had to be true. Her newfound vitality warred with self-hatred, the negative emotions winning the battle.

The heartbreaking guilt would hit her later. It always did. She'd been depressed for years after she'd taken all those lives after the Titanic, but at least the lifeforce she'd unknowingly stored in the necklace Maria gave her had ensured she didn't have to do so again for a long time. That, perhaps, made it worse, as Maria kept insisting.

Grace touched her face, feeling no bruising. Her eye was healed as well. She seemed to be entirely back to normal, and even her broken tooth had regrown. As Sandra watched nervously Grace put the hospital gown back on. "I'm not going to hurt you," Grace said gently, trying to break through the anger and fear in Sandra's expression. "Please don't look at me that way Sandra. Most of the time I'm just… well, a girl. A girl with a tail sometimes."

"I don't hate you," Sandra said softly. "I pity you. How can you live like this?"

A cavern full of emotions threatened to collapse and drown her, or drag her into the depths of self-loathing. "I've been asking myself the same question for a century," Grace said quietly.

She glanced at the doorway, doing her best to focus on her problems instead of regrets. They had to leave as soon as they could.

"You should go home before anyone discovers what I've done. Take Josh with you and pretend you were never here."

Sandra took a deep breath, but didn't say whatever was on her mind. For a moment she seemed on the verge of losing it, but after a couple more deep breaths she nodded to herself. "I said I'd help you, and I will, but you're right about Josh. I don't want him involved in any of this. If they pin Bec's death on me, fine, I'll be dead soon anyway, but I can't have this come back on Josh in any way."

"We leave him out of it," Grace agreed, a little tension releasing from her shoulders. The further she stayed away from Josh the better. She picked up her bandages to throw them in the room's yellow bin.

"You should probably take them with you," Sandra said, clearly beginning to think properly again. "We can put them with the other medical wastes which will be properly disposed of. No one's likely to go through all that."

Grace held onto her bandages. "Do you think you're up to pushing me in the chair again? It'll look better if you can."

Sandra hesitated, but nodded. "I think I'll need something to lean on anyway."

"It'll only be until I can find some spare clothes." Grace turned the chair around and got into it, allowing Sandra to get behind her in the small room. "Shouldn't we let the water out?" Sandra asked.

Grace glanced at the bath.

"No. They'll know it wasn't an accident or suicide. It'll take them longer to figure out what happened." She got out of the chair and despite her misgivings, touched the water, commanding it.

The water flowed out, lifting Bec's body up and carrying her back into the bath. Sandra looked on, struggling with fascination and disgust and... Grace couldn't help a frown when she saw more than a little envy in Sandra's eyes.

Grace touched the woman's shoulder and was grateful when Sandra didn't flinch. "You okay?" she asked.

"Certainly not."

"Good. You don't want to get comfortable around a mermaid."

BACK IN THE WHEELCHAIR, Grace put her bare feet on the rests as Sandra began pushing her from the room. They were barely one door down the corridor when a young nurse in a crisp white uniform approached, her determined gaze focused on Sandra. Probably still learning her job, she hurried over on a mission. Escaped blond locks drifted near her temples in defiance of the rest of her hair, which was bound at the back of her head.

"Sandra, have you seen Bec?" the young woman asked. "She's supposed to be on duty."

Grace's heart did a flip and she almost had to pin herself to the chair to stop herself from running. The young nurse had one of those overly-keen faces that spoke of efficiency and a fanatical devotion to her job, but with a horrible feeling coming over her, Grace detected no discernible lifeforce. She had to be a Creature, though what she was Grace had no idea. Hopefully Sandra's proximity and strong lifeforce hid the same truth about Grace, and the Creature wouldn't notice. Grace wished she dared turn around to see Sandra's reaction, but instead had to endure long, nervous moments of silence.

"Sorry Catherina. I was just giving a friend a tour. She's thinking of having a baby when she gets well."

Catherina smiled without giving Grace a glance. "Babies are the only things that matter, right? You'll never regret it." Even then she kept her eyes on Sandra, as if Grace was of absolutely no interest. Despite some relief at the casual lack of acknowledgement, Grace hid a familiar hurt at the topic.

"Bec?" Catherina asked with zealot-like intensity.

"Um, sorry Cat. I haven't seen her."

Catherina was clearly far too uptight for her own good, Creature or not. "Uh, okay. Thanks. Maybe she's helping someone. Oh, and you look well, Sandra."

Grace wished she could see Sandra's expression at that.

"Tell everyone I said hello," Sandra said.

"Sure will," Catherina said, hesitating in the act of leaving. "And stop by later if you can. Maybe have a coffee?"

"If I get the time I will," Sandra said as she began pushing Grace. Catherina didn't watch them go, already seeking someone else to pounce on.

They saw several more people in the corridor, two of them Creatures by Grace's best guess, but no one questioned them. Sandra took Grace to a room where waste was kept prior to disposal, and she dropped the small bundle of bandages into a marked bin for contaminated waste to be properly disposed of before continuing.

"Oh," Sandra said, handing Grace her necklace. "Forgot." She dug around in a pocket, removing more jewellery. "And this was with it too. You didn't mention it. Is it yours?" Sandra handed Grace the crystal bracelet Kimbriel had given her at the markets near South Broulee Beach.

"Yes, thanks," Grace said gratefully as she put the necklace on, and then the bracelet. Her necklace was empty, but ready to store any excess lifeforce she couldn't hold herself, but from the bracelet she still sensed nothing. Whatever it was, it wasn't anything she could use or control.

"Can we go to Maria now?"

"She's still in intensive care, though she's out of immediate danger. We'll drop this wheelchair off, rustle up some clothes for you and then I'll take you there."

Dropping off the wheelchair posed no problems, but finding unattended clothes in her size was nearly impossible. Grace was just about to resign herself the hospital gown when they chanced on a patient's empty room with clothes in her size. By the time Grace changed, the sunset was only a few hours away.

"You look like a grandmother," Sandra said, eyeing off Grace's beige skirt and white blouse. "Here," she said, holding out a pair of slip-ons.

Grace tried them, and winced. "Too small." Her toes were painfully crammed.

Sandra didn't look in the least bit sympathetic. "You need shoes."

"I have nerves in my feet too, you know?" Grace said, but kept the shoes on.

"So, you weren't always a mermaid?" Sandra asked as they walked, keeping her voice quiet as they passed a family carrying flowers. Sandra's words sounded casual, but there was an element of true curiosity there. "You said something about drowning."

Grace wondered how long Sandra had practiced that line before finding the courage to speak it. She made sure there was disapproval in her voice. "You looking to join Murder Club?"

Sandra flushed and dropped her eyes. "I… Just curious."

"You've seen what I have to do to survive, Sandra. Is that what you want?"

Sandra bit the inside of her hollow cheek, almost slowing to a stop. "No."

But she was almost certainly thinking of Josh and Mikey, and wondering if the cost was worth it. "Then how about we don't discuss it?"

"I thought… I mean, nobody wants to die, but-"

"Bec included." Grace said as harshly as she dared. "Maria tells me you get used to killing, and the guilt goes away. I can see how it could. Killing's a thrill, sensual, sexual, even if you try not to let it be." She caught Sandra's eyes and held them. "But I don't ever want to begin looking forward to that. I've drowned a lot of people and every one of them was someone's child, parent, lover or friend. Like Bec. I wouldn't curse you like that."

"I didn't mean it that way," Sandra said a little too softly.

Grace put a hand on Sandra's arm for comfort. "I know, but I really want you to understand. I'm told there was magic in the world where mermaids originally came from, and they didn't have to kill to survive. It's different here."

Sandra caught Grace's eye with a raised eyebrow. "Other worlds?"

Grace dodged a human. "That's what I've been told. Never seen any evidence though."

Sandra watched her for a moment, breaking into a tentative grin. "Seriously? You believe it?"

"We had to have come from somewhere."

The grin disappeared, replaced by genuine interest and curiosity. "Can you… go to other places? Can a human?"

Grace shrugged. "I don't know, but I think it's mostly bad luck, like stumbling into a sinkhole and not being able to climb out. That's probably a bad analogy. One water sprite told me she met a Creature who said it was like stumbling through a cave without light, and when you emerge everything's different. I think it's why people sometimes disappear and never show up again. They've stumbled between worlds."

As they were passing a bin, Grace kicked off the horribly tight shoes and dumped them in. If people noticed her walking barefoot, too bad. "Where's Maria's room?"

"Just up here. It's not a big hospital." They continued in a slightly uncomfortable silence. "So, you were married?"

Grace supposed she did owe Sandra a few answers. "I was a passenger on the Titanic."

"Really?" There was genuine surprise and even a little delight in the sound.

The memories were bitter. Painful even. "The day the ship sank was the worst day of my life."

"Because you became a mermaid?"

Grace shook her head. "Because I'd recently become sure I was pregnant. I was bursting to break the news to my husband, but didn't want to do it at any silly moment. I'd organised to tell him over a special dinner, but my plans hit an iceberg."

"Oh. That must have been terrible," Sandra said. "I'm so sorry."

Grace stared ahead, afraid to meet Sandra's eyes. "My husband was the first person I drowned."

Sandra's jaw dropped. "What?"

"And your baby?" Sandra asked, obviously trying to change the topic. "Were you forced to give it up? I mean? Was it human or a mermaid?"

Grace wished she could suppress the hurt and sorrow that swelled up and took her breath away. After a moment she steadied herself with a deep breath. "Mermaids, Creatures, can't have babies Sandra. We… procreate by… turning humans into our kind." The words came out flat, but even a century later she couldn't hide the raw emotion from her loss and how much it still pained her.

"Oh. When you were talking about price, I didn't realise that was a part of it. I'm truly sorry Grace."

"When we get Maria back to the water I'd advise you to stay clear. She might just do what I did to Bec, and I really don't want to see you… hurt. I promised to help you, and I don't want Maria denying you that chance, even unintentionally."

$$[\ 15 \ ]$$

Grace fidgeted with her necklace, the hardness of the sapphire, gold and pearls a counterpoint to her soft, human skin. Casually glancing along the corridor, she realised her sister's room was distressingly close to the empty nurse's station, which wouldn't be unattended for long.

"Sandra?" someone called.

Grace jumped as an older nurse left an open storage room across the hall and crossed the corridor to wrap Sandra in a bear hug. The nurse stepped back and gave the bone-thin woman a penetrating stare. "How are you doing honey?" There was genuine concern there, and her eyes didn't waver as she stared into Sandra's.

Even from a distance she stank of cigarettes, while her eyes were bloodshot with dark circles under them. What was it with nurses? They should be the healthiest group of people anyone would be likely to come across, but this lot certainly weren't. Maybe they all turned to drinking and food to cope with the proximity of too many Creatures and the unanswerable questions they raised.

"I'm fine Jane," Sandra said. "Honestly."

"Bullshit. How are you really love? Be honest." She gripped Sandra by the shoulders, keeping eye contact.

Sandra gave a grudging smile. "I'm still breathing."

The expression on the nurse's face softened. "Nothing a huge bowl of chips and gravy couldn't fix, huh?" Jane laughed, sun-lines crinkling the corners of her tired eyes. "Who's your friend?" She looked Grace over as if trying to figure out a puzzle Grace had no intentions of helping with.

"I'm Grace. I met Josh recently." Grace smiled, hoping she didn't look as uncomfortable as she felt. No doubt Jane had seen Grace as an injured patient, only now she wasn't injured and there was a dead nurse not too many rooms away, waiting to be discovered. The alarm could be raised at any moment, making her fidget. She met Sandra's eyes, trying to give her a *hurry up* look.

"Grace! What a lovely name. We've got a patient here called Grace. Fancy that?" She gave the mermaid another once-over. "You look a bit like her, actually."

Grace's stomach did a slow backflip as Jane gave her another puzzled look before returning her attention to Sandra, speaking conspiratorially. "You didn't tell me Josh had a girlfriend."

Sandra's eyes widened at that. "I think they're more friends than *together*."

"Really? She looks like his type. Tall and beautiful in an untouchable way. I hate her already." She laughed.

"Untouchable?" Grace repeated. "Me?"

A smirk played at the corners of Sandra's mouth. "She's a bit spiky too."

Grace felt a touch of hurt for no reason she could identify, though she suspected it was because Sandra actually meant it. "I'm a teddy bear," she said softly.

Sandra heard and raised an eyebrow. "A prickly teddy bear."

Jane chuckled. "So why the visit Sandra? You seem to have done your best to avoid the place since you quit work, not that I blame you. Too many sick people around here." She winked.

Grace moved forward, hoping to get things moving ahead. "We're here to see Maria Lacopo. Is that possible?"

"Maria? Oh yes, poor girl. Doesn't remember a thing, not even her name. Took a serious blow to the head."

"She's awake?" Grace couldn't hide her relief. She wanted to run into Maria's room.

"Yeah, but she's not with it. I'm genuinely surprised she's even conscious."

"She'll remember me."

"To be honest, the drugs should have kept her in a coma for a while yet, but she fought her way out of it. Really tough girl, that one." The nurse shrugged as if she'd seen far stranger things. She probably had.

"I'm positive she'll remember me. Can I see her?"

Jane gave Grace a look which said it was unlikely. "It might help, although her memory loss isn't the worst of it. Her neck was badly hurt and she may never walk again. We're preparing to take her to Sydney for further assessment. We're not properly equipped to deal with her injuries."

Nervous tension began gnawing at Grace again and she shifted her feet, trying not to fidget with her necklace. "When?"

Jane gave her another quizzical look. "Say, you wouldn't be the girl who was with Maria when she got hit, would you?"

"No," Grace said a little too quickly. She couldn't help nervously grasping her necklace. She was telling too many lies and was sure to be caught out if she didn't find a way out of this mess soon.

"That girl seems to have disappeared and Maria has no identification. Perhaps you could give us some details like her address, family info, things like that?"

"I don't know much. I met her at the beach."

"So how did you find out she was in hospital?" Jane had an intense look which made Grace wish the woman wasn't so intelligent. It seemed as if she was on the edge of seeing the truth, despite the influence that hid magical Creatures from humans.

"Josh saw the accident. When Maria didn't turn up for lunch today I figured it out."

Jane smiled, her second chin jiggling slightly. Despite her run-down appearance, her faculties weren't slow. "Why don't you go in then, Grace? But be aware, she's in a bad way. When you're done I'd like you to help me figure out some details."

A fate best avoided. "I'll do what I can."

"Sandra, would you mind staying a moment?"

"Sure. Grace, you go ahead. I'll be in soon."

Leaving them, Grace entered Maria's room with kamikaze butterflies threatening to explode at any moment. If she didn't get Maria out of the hospital now she wouldn't get another chance.

The room had two beds, one empty, the other with a figure Grace almost didn't recognise. Maria's eyes were closed and her head was bandaged, her face bruised and swollen, and she had a hard brace around her neck and upper body. Maria's legs seemed to be free of any sort of bracing or other hindrance, at least. A drip in her arm kept her hydrated and probably medicated, while monitors advised of her precarious state.

"Oh Maria," Grace whispered, desperately wanting to hold her sister. It would take her weeks in the ocean to recover unless Grace helped her take a life to speed up the healing.

Not wishing to disturb Maria just yet, Grace opened the bedside drawer. Maria's necklace was in it, three pearls set into gold surrounding a thumbnail-sized sapphire. Grace put it around her own neck for safekeeping, sensing the lifeforce trapped within. It wasn't hers and didn't attune itself to her, but it was familiar, like wearing someone else's shoes.

If Grace got desperate she could access it, but she'd waste at least half of anything she took. She gently placed her hand on Maria's right forearm. Her sister stirred and groggily opened her eyes, blinking until she focused on Grace.

"Maria?"

There was absolutely no recognition in Maria's eyes. ·

"Maria, it's me." Grace wanted to cup Maria's bruised and swollen face, but feared hurting her. "Maria?"

The blank stare continued. "Chi sei?" Maria finally whispered in Italian, her voice raspy. She closed her eyes, swallowing with a wince.

There were ice cubes in a glass beside Maria's bed, beginning to melt. Grace switched to Italian too. "Hai sete?" Grace asked, desperate to help. She took an ice cube and held it where Maria could see it, but her sister's eyes remained closed.

"Sì."

"Here," she said in English, putting the cube to Maria's lips. Maria opened her mouth just enough to accept the cube. "We've had tougher times than this," Grace lied, trying to keep the heartbreak from her voice. "You'll remember soon enough."

"Who are you?" Maria asked around the ice.

Grace almost lost her battle with grief. "Oh Maria. We're sisters. We met in the ocean. Remember?"

"The ocean?" A flicker of recognition passed her eyes. "Swimming."

"Of course."

She frowned. "People drowning. Is that why I'm here? Did I nearly drown?"

"What else do you remember?"

"A woman."

Grace almost laughed with relief. "That would be me."

"Not you. She had dark hair. I think I loved her."

Grace's chest compressed with hurt. She blinked tears of anguish at the thought of Maria loving someone else. It could be any one of a thousand memories, a thousand other mermaids. "Would you like me to take you to the ocean, Maria? We could go swimming together."

"I can't feel my legs," she said, her voice a whisper. Tears escaped her eyes and ran.

"I know sweetie, but you'll get better soon."

Maria let out a long sigh. "No I won't. They told me."

"Yes, you will."

More tears.

Grace took Maria's feverishly warm hand, wrapping it in both of her own. She didn't squeeze back. "What if I can help you get well again?" This wasn't the happy, emotional, beautiful sister she loved. "Maria?"

Maria turned her eyes away. "You should leave. I want to be alone."

Grace squeezed Maria's hand. "You need me."

"I want you to leave."

The words hurt Grace more than she'd ever realised they could have. Her own tears ran down her cheek. She quickly caught one before it could fall to the floor, hoping to try something. Still holding Maria's unresponsive hand with her free one, she held the teardrop on the end of her finger. It glistened in the downlights, radiating just a little more life than a drop of moisture should.

"You've forgotten, but there's magic in our tears," she whispered. "Only a little, but perhaps enough to help you remember."

Grace held the teardrop out so Maria could see it, but her sister stared at the roof. "Go away."

Before Maria could protest, Grace touched the tear to her sister's lips.

"Eww!" Maria rasped. "Get out."

Shocked by the reaction, Grace held still.

"I said get out!"

Sandra shuffled into the room, a grimace on her face as if she were in pain. She seemed to be having trouble walking. She glanced at Grace, then Maria. "They've found Bec. We need to leave. Now."

"Maria, can you feel anything?" Grace asked, speaking softly. "Are your lips tingling? Perhaps there's a tiny rush of energy or strength? Do you feel any better?"

"Nurse!" She tried to call loudly, but there wasn't much volume fortunately.

"Maria, don't do this! I'm here to help you."

"Nurse!"

Grace clamped her free hand over Maria's mouth. "I'm trying to help you!"

"What's going on?" Jane said as she barged into the room. She took the scene in and outrage flushed her face. "Get away from her now!" She strode toward Grace. She was easily twice Grace's weight, and physically imposing. There was plenty of fat there, but she was used to manhandling patients.

Grace let go of Maria's mouth and snatched the cup of ice, the only source of water nearby, but Jane shoved Grace aside using her bodyweight alone.

Grace stumbled. She caught herself and took a handful of ice and reformed it into water, spreading it all over her hands and forearms. It tingled as her skin changed, and with a sense of desperation she forced her claws out. She'd kill if she had to in order to save Maria.

Grace grasped Jane's wrist as she checked on Maria, and as Jane turned, outraged, Grace gripped her throat, claws biting but not quite drawing blood. Jane stiffened but held still as Grace's grip tightened.

"Grace! No," Sandra cried.

Using the supernatural strength the water gave her, Grace held up the woman's other arm so she could see the sharp claws.

"Wha… What are you?"

"Look at me. Look at me!"

"Help!" Maria cried.

Grace glared at her sister. "Maria, Zitto. Zitto o io ucciderla!"

Maria went silent.

"Jane, look at me," Grace said. Jane's eyes lifted from the sharp claws encircling her wrist to Grace's eyes. "You're going to do exactly as I say. Understand?"

The big woman trembled, but gave a slight nod.

"Grace," Sandra said, distress making her sound almost as desperate as Jane. "Please don't hurt her. She's just doing her job."

"I have no intention of hurting her, but I value my sister far more than anything else in this world. Jane, I'm taking Maria out of here. Got it?"

"You can't," Jane whispered.

"You see the claws?"

She nodded slightly. "I do."

"We're not getting married Jane. *Yes* is fine. Now, you're going to help us or I'm going to use these claws on you. Okay?

A slight jiggle of her head.

"Good." The woman was trembling in Grace's grip, although there was an edge creeping back into her expression. Jane was going to cause trouble if Grace didn't do something to control her. "Is there a gurney or something we can use to transport Maria out of here?"

"Yes. Behind the nurse's station."

"Sandra, can you get the gurney please?"

Sandra left.

"Now Jane, you're going to unplug Maria from all this equipment. Do it now."

"You drowned Bec, didn't you? Why?"

Again, the woman's insight surprised Grace. "It was an accident. I'm very sorry. Honestly." She tried to put as much truth in that statement as she could.

"Are you going to kill me?"

"Of course not, not unless I have to. Unhook her."

Grace kept her claws on Jane's skin as the nurse prepared Maria to be moved. Maria looked terrified and kept glancing at Grace's claws. Grace tried smiling, but only received abject fear in return. A century of memories gone in a single blow. Jane was done before Sandra returned with the gurney.

"You're going to help me get her onto the gurney, understand?"

"Moving her like this could make her a quadriplegic if she isn't already."

"Please don't move me!" Maria said, this time in English. "Please, I can feel my legs. Really, I can."

Grace pulled Jane aside as Sandra returned and manoeuvred the gurney up beside the bed.

Sandra nodded to Grace. "The best way to do this is to grab the sheet at both ends and slide her as gently as you can."

Jane glared at Sandra. "Why are you helping her?"

"Have you forgotten her claws already? She's not human. Neither is Maria."

Jane glanced at Grace's hands and her eyes widened slightly as if only just remembering. "How...?"

"Demonic possession," Grace muttered. "I slept with the Devil. Let's move her. Jane, take the other end."

Grace's claws punched through the sheet like tissue paper as she grabbed the end near Maria's feet. Jane took the other end while Sandra held the gurney steady.

"One, two, three!"

She heaved, lifting and sliding at the same time. Maria cried out, and by the time she was safely on the gurney she'd passed out.

"I told you!" Jane said, furious. "You may have killed her."

"She's breathing," Grace said, more relieved than she wanted to show. If Jane saw weakness or doubt she might act on it. Claws still extended, she moved to the end of the gurney near Jane and grabbed the half-full glass of ice. "Now, we're all going to calmly walk out of here. I assume you have a car, Jane?"

Jane shook her head as if the thought were ridiculous. "I catch the bus."

She couldn't catch a break. "Really?" Grace stared in frustration. "You're going to help us steal an ambulance then."

"I have Josh's spare car keys," Sandra said. "We can lay Maria across the back seat."

Jane glared at Sandra, but Grace put her hand on Jane's shoulder and let her claws bite in just a little. "I want you to push the gurney, Jane. I'll be behind you. Take it nice and slow for Sandra's sake. She's sick, remember? Sandra, you lead the way. If anyone asks questions, Jane can put them off. Can you do that Jane? I really don't want to have to push a claw between any of your vertebrae."

Jane belligerently grabbed the drip that was still running into Maria's arm and hooked it onto the gurney's stand so it could continue to function. "You've got no idea how much harm you're doing to this poor girl."

"She's not a girl."

"She's my patient."

Grace ground her teeth. "Do you have children, Jane?"

"Yes. A daughter and two sons. Two granddaughters as well."

"Good, I'm very happy for you, but right now I want you to

consider they'll never see you again if you screw this up for me. Do we understand each other?"

The woman stiffened, but nodded slightly. "Yes."

"Good. Let's go." Sandra caught her eye, disbelief in her expression. Grace shook her head in the negative. She would have to apologise to Sandra later for making the threat.

[16]

THEY WERE BARELY OUT of the room when a young male nurse rounded the corner and saw Jane. He hurried over, caught her arm in a friendly but urgent way, and steered her a few feet to the side. Grace had no choice but to let her go or cause a scene, but stayed as close as she could. At least she could sense his lifeforce, marking him as human. In the desert this place was, it wasn't difficult to detect.

"Have you heard about Bec? How could she have just fallen into a bath and drowned?"

Grace watched Jane's body stiffen, but she didn't glance at Grace or Sandra. If the woman gave them away now Grace would have no choice but to try and rush Maria out the hospital and push the gurney downhill toward the Bay, hoping she'd get there before she got caught and dragged her off to a police cell somewhere. That would end both their lives.

Growing more and more tense with every heartbeat, she glared murder at the man holding Jane up. Grace's insubstantial threat certainly wouldn't hold given the circumstances. Nearly panicking, Grace caught Jane's eye and indicated she should get back to pushing Maria. She extended a claw so only Jane could see, and mouthed the word 'grandchildren'.

Jane's eyes immediately focused on the man. "Yes Dave, I've heard. Can we discuss it later? I've got to transfer this patient and it's rather urgent. Give me half an hour, okay?"

"Uh, yeah, sure," he replied, following her eyes to Grace and the gurney Maria lay on. "Maybe after your shift." He clearly had questions, but before he could voice them Jane came back and began pushing Maria again, Grace close behind. The young man looked disappointed by the lack of gossip, but turned and walked in the opposite direction.

"Thank you Jane."

"You know, one day you're going to pay for all this, and I hope I'm there to see it."

"This is happening because I couldn't bring myself to drown an innocent child, so don't talk to me about karma. Just do what I asked. Please. All I want to do is save my sister."

Jane glanced over her shoulder quizzically as if checking to see if Grace was serious. "You're going to kill Maria, you know."

"Have you already forgotten? *Maria's not human*?" Sometimes the magic that kept them hidden could really work against them.

Jane straightened slightly. "She's not... Oh... I thought you were threatening my patient with a knife."

Grace wasn't sure whether to feel relief or to explode with exasperation. "Your mind tries to make sense of things. It twists the truth to suit the circumstances. I don't know why, but if I ever figure it out I'll be sure to tell you." She glanced at Sandra. "Where's Josh's car?"

"On the street out the front," Sandra said.

"You okay to guide us there Sandra? You look tired."

"Nothing a month of rest won't fix."

She didn't look like she'd survive another day. Life was so unfair.

As they neared reception, the sliding doors opened and Grace's heart stopped. Two police officers walked into the building, both young men, one of them eyeing the small group and Maria's gurney. The other ignored them completely. Grace held her breath, but fortunately Jane didn't give them away. Grace glanced at Jane for any other sign of betrayal, some hidden signal perhaps, but although she looked like she wanted to call for help, she didn't say anything.

"Thank you again," Grace said once the police were out of earshot and they were moving. "That could have been... troublesome."

Jane gave her a cold look over her shoulder. "Have you got any idea how little I care about your thanks? You're threatening me, my family, and my patient, human or not."

"Mum!"

Grace's heart almost stopped at the sound of Josh's voice. She glanced back to find him hurrying toward them, looking a little stressed.

"Where have you been?" he asked as he neared them, and then stopped dead when he saw Grace standing there. "How the...?" He was seeing the impossible, Grace walking and healthy. "You're hurt..." He looked her over again, apparently unwilling to believe the truth. "You are Grace, right?"

"We have to go," Grace said to Sandra, who was leaning on the gurney now Jane had stopped pushing it thanks to Josh's delaying presence. "Go, Jane."

"Wait!" Josh said, and Grace stiffened as the compulsion in her promise froze her in place. She stared pitifully at the entrance, so close yet entirely beyond her capabilities to reach right then. She wasn't even sure the command was directed at her and not the group, but it had the same effect.

How could she convince him to leave? She resorted to anger, hoping he'd back off if it was clear she didn't want him around. "What?" she asked acerbically.

He looked her over again, disbelief on his face. "You're really Grace, aren't you? But... you were injured. How?"

"My name's Florence," she lied, speaking the first name that came to her. "I assume you're talking about my twin sister, Grace?"

His disbelief rapidly changed to surprise, and then relief as the higher power keeping Creatures hidden worked for her for a change. "Florence?" he asked. "I, I'm sorry. I didn't know Grace had a sister.

She's not in her bed. Do you know if she's been transferred? The nurses didn't seem to know either."

Confounded, she didn't know what to say.

"She's in surgery," Sandra said, coming to her rescue. "The paperwork probably isn't through yet."

Grace noticed Jane shifting her feet restlessly. "Don't try it," she whispered, putting a hand on the woman's shoulder. She allowed her claws to press a little, just enough to remind the woman. Her forearms were still wet enough to permit it, though the water was evaporating rapidly despite Grace's best efforts at controlling it.

"Josh," Sandra continued. "I'll meet you in the cafeteria in about half an hour. Okay?"

"Go," prompted Grace, giving Jane a very slight shove. She'd done as Josh had commanded and waited, but he hadn't specified for how long. Every moment of delay was a risk to Maria, and the sun wasn't going to delay setting for them either.

Jane pushed, but Josh ran to catch up. "Hey, this is the way to the car park. Why you going outside? Who's this? Isn't that Grace's friend Maria?" He leaned over the gurney, eyes widening. "It is Maria. I was just in her room before I went looking for you."

"No," Grace lied.

"Where are you taking her?" He glanced out the glass doors, an ambulance near the front of the building.

Grace glanced heavenward and asked for the strength to avoid a killing spree, starting with Josh. She glanced at the building's doors and the receptionist at the desk, but the woman had her attention on a computer monitor. She wasn't looking at them, but any more commotion and she might.

"Josh," Sandra said, her tone demanding he drop the subject. "Meet me in the cafeteria. Please."

"Not until you tell me what's going on."

Oh for pity's sake. "Let him come," Grace muttered. They could probably use his strength to move Maria into the car anyway, and it was better than causing an incident that might get noticed.

"I don't want him caught up in this," Sandra said. She focused on Josh. "Cafeteria, now!" she said as if talking to a ten-year-old.

"No. What's going on?"

Why did he have to choose right now to get all defiant? Grace wanted to scream at the world. Maria, still unconscious and her entire motivation for being here, didn't move, though Grace wished she'd wake up and take command as she always did.

The doors were just ahead, but they seemed a mile away and Grace felt helpless to reach them. They opened to let a mother and child walk in holding flowers. Fresh ocean air and fake perfume washed in, making Grace more and more edgy to get outside. Every second they delayed was another moment hospital security might intervene.

"Josh?"

Grace turned, and her heart pounded with a newfound fear. One of the werewolves who'd beaten her up stood there. The bottle-blond. She saw Grace and her eyes widened. "Oh shit," the werewolf said. She turned and ran.

"Looks like the situation's snowballing," Jane commented dryly.

Grace flushed before glancing down the corridor where the werewolf had run. "You better let him come Sandra. He'll be safer with us."

"Maybe you're right," Sandra said, eyes following Grace's. "Hurry up then Josh, and no questions. Not yet, anyway."

Finally! They hurried out the front doors as the receptionist looked up, but with the expression of someone too new to the position to know what to do. It was a break, if only a small one. They went down the ramp to the street, following the footpath to Josh's car as curious visitors gave them more than a once-over. Josh's car was dwarfed between two huge four-wheel-drives, both black and shiny.

"I'm worried about that receptionist," Grace said. She had a feeling she was already calling security, and once that happened they'd be out of time and luck.

"We need to get Maria across the back seat," Sandra said. "Feet first to avoid jostling her neck."

"Are you insane?" Josh asked. "You can't put her in my car."

"We're trying to save her life," Sandra said. "Please Josh, no questions. Just help."

He shook his head in disbelief but did as asked, trusting his mother by opening both back doors so whoever had Maria's feet could crawl right through without hindrance. Heat billowed out like he'd opened an oven. Jane moved the gurney close, ready to shift Maria. Grace caught movement from the direction of the hospital and noticed the blond werewolf watching again, a phone to her ear.

"Hurry," Grace said. "Abbey might be along soon."

"Abbey? How do you know Abbey?" Josh asked.

Grace growled in frustration.

"She beat Grace up, remember?" Sandra pointed at the blonde, but the girl ducked back behind a wall. "Her friends are keeping watch."

"I don't see anyone," he said, shading his eyes with a hand.

"Just help us get Maria into the back," Grace said tersely, riding nervous tension like a cowboy on a mechanical bull a heartbeat away from losing it.

She doubted there was more than an hour until sunset, and they were about to be pursued by Abbey and hospital security. Probably the police too. "Jane, if you could lift her upper body as you know what you're doing. Josh, her legs, I'll try and support her middle."

Jane shook her head in disbelief or disgust, but did as asked, while Josh nodded. Together they lifted Maria by the sheet and managed to manoeuvre her into the back seat without too much jostling, Josh crawling backwards and out the door on the road side.

"So where are we going?" Josh asked.

Grace glanced at the hospital. "You drive Josh, I'll direct. Jane, thank you very much for your help. Please, and I'm asking now, not threatening, please don't say anything to anyone for at least fifteen minutes. Tell them I had a knife. After that, do whatever you need to do to protect yourself."

"That's my patient," Jane said, pointing at Maria. "I'm coming."

Grace stared. "What? No you're not!"

She glared at Grace, hands on hips as if a hurricane couldn't move her. "I'm coming."

Grace stared for a heartbeat longer, but couldn't afford the time to argue. "Fine, but you'll have to ride on the roof. I hope you're good at holding on. Josh, Sandra, get in. We need to go."

Josh got into the driver's seat while his mother took shotgun. Grace clambered into the back beside Maria, trying not to jostle. She had nowhere to sit and ended up crammed on the floor with her side pushed against the seat, but at least she was close to Maria.

The car rocked and she looked up in alarm, to find Jane squeezing in beside Maria's bent legs and sitting herself half on the seat.

"Oh, fantastic," Grace said. "Perhaps we could find a scout troupe to take with us too?"

"I'm not driving with you lot like that. I'll get booked," Josh said, twisting around so he could see them.

"Just go!" Grace said. "You've got no idea how… Please, drive. Head for a beach. Somewhere secluded if possible."

"A beach?" he asked, staring down at her over the bench seat. "Why the hell do you want to go to the beach?"

"Oh, for God's sake! Just go!"

"Josh," Sandra said. "Just do as she says. I'll explain on the way."

He shook his head in disbelief but turned the car over at his mother's urging, the engine roaring before settling back into a rumbling purr. "Why is it I'm the only one with any common sense today?" he muttered. He put the car in gear and eased out from between the bigger vehicles, trusting his mother if no one else.

"Try not to jostle us," Grace said as she wound the window down to release some of the heat. They took off up the street, directly away from the beach. "Nice and easy."

"That *was* nice and easy!"

"Toward the ocean would be better too."

"Fine, but someone better start explaining things," he said.

"I will," Jane volunteered. "Grace murdered a nurse called Bec, threatened to kill me and my family if I didn't help, kidnapped Maria and is now trying to avoid the authorities. That about sum it up, Grace?" She raised an eyebrow.

Grace frowned, wanting to put her hands around the self-righteous woman's neck and squeeze until she squeaked. "You forgot to mention that Abbey's a succubus, her friends are werewolves, and they're trying to kill me because they think I'm into Josh," Grace responded.

The car swerving. "You're into me?" Josh asked.

"What? No, I'm not! Focus on the road!"

He turned left before glancing over his shoulder. "You know, if you don't start levelling with me I'm going to pull over and you can all walk."

"You're going to make me walk?" Sandra asked her son acerbically.

"I didn't mean you Mum," he said, his expression apologetic.

"What about Maria?" Grace asked. "Are you suggesting I drag her by the hair?" Her sarcasm was enough to make Josh focus on his driving. "Please Josh, just take us to the beach."

Grace watched as Jane, cramped as she was, did her best to check on Maria while holding up the drip at the same time. The nurse met Grace's eyes. "You know, she doesn't look like a monster."

"Neither do the two werewolf bitches that tried to drag me into a car so a succubus could suck me dry."

Jane rolled her eyes.

"What?" Grace asked. "You think mermaids are the only supernatural Creatures in the world?"

"You think you're a mermaid?" Jane frowned as if trying to figure out why they were even talking about something so stupid. "I thought mermaids were supposed to be nice."

"We are. Kind of. We're just… Shut up. Look after Maria."

"You know," began Josh as he changed gears. "You can joke around all you like some other time, but I *really* want to know what's going on considering we just kidnapped a patient from a hospital. I'm pretty sure that's a crime in this country." He sounded calm, but there was an edge of panic to it.

Grace wished she'd drowned that kid at the beach yesterday. None of this would be happening otherwise. "We're trying to save Maria's life, Josh. All of us, believe it or not."

"So what's wrong with the hospital?"

She was getting sick of lies. Worse. How was she going to keep him out of Abbey's clutches once she got Maria back in the water? "She has a rare condition that can't be treated there."

"But a good suntan by the ocean will do it?"

Clearly the talk of mermaids and other Creatures wasn't going to convince him of anything. "There's a rare plant that grows near the beach. It contains a chemical she needs, but it's only good for about a minute after it's picked as it oxidises fast." Shit, she probably wouldn't believe that herself.

Even from her position in the back she could see the disbelief on his face. "Didn't you just tell me to find a secluded beach? Any secluded beach?"

Jane raised an eyebrow, clearly enjoying Grace's flustered state judging by the slightly amused expression. Revenge suited her.

"The fewer the people around, the more likely we'll be to find it."

"Josh!" Sandra said with finality. "Let it go."

They were heading out of the Bay now, but despite the calm way Josh drove, Grace pushed herself up high enough to see out the back. No obvious pursuit, but the sun was low and the shadows growing steadily longer. How long before sunset? She sunk back down, gently touching Maria's unconscious face. It was a face she knew better than her own.

"Plenty of time, Grace," said Sandra, trying to comfort her.

"I thought her name was Florence?" Josh said, a hardness in his voice again.

Jane smirked. Sandra put the back of her head against the headrest and let out a deep sigh. "I meant Florence," she amended. "They look alike."

"Yeah, well things aren't adding up. I want some real explanations. Now."

Josh pulled the car to the side and stopped, turning to look back at Grace crammed in next to Maria. "What's going on?"

"Please Josh. Just drive."

"Answers." There was no compromise in his expression, and it could have been taken as a command she didn't want to test.

She sighed. "I'm a mermaid. So is Maria. If I don't get her into the ocean by sunset she'll die." She met his eyes, meeting them like he'd declared a challenge.

He gave her a look that said he was really getting annoyed. "Next."

The truth never worked anyway. "Okay, my name's Grace, I accidently drowned a nurse and now I'm making my escape with Maria. Because… she's my evil overlord and I have to protect her."

He gave her a long hard stare before turning to his mother. "What's going on, Mum?"

Sandra must have been drifting off to sleep, but she roused with a deep breath. "It's all true, Josh. Mostly."

"Mum!"

"Have I ever lied to you Josh?"

He turned around again and glared at Grace. "Last chance to come clean. Tell me the truth or get out."

She definitely felt the compulsion in the words, but without water she had no way to prove anything. She'd left the glass of ice on the gurney. "I'm a mermaid. So is Maria. Get me to the ocean and I'll prove it."

Jane, who'd remained silent, gave Grace a self-satisfied smile. Grace ignored it as Josh spoke again, his voice too soft. "That you're a mermaid?"

Jane put a hand on his shoulder, and shocked Grace by agreeing with her. "Her fingernails do turn to claws when they're wet." Grace could see the calculation in Jane's eyes, but the woman looked away before any clear plans seemed to have formed. What was she up to?

"You've got grandchildren," Grace whispered to the nurse. "And I've got sisters. Thousands of them. Whatever you're planning, it isn't going to work. Okay?"

Jane paled. What was she planning? Did she hope to capture a mermaid for study or sell to the highest bidder?

Josh turned to his mother. "This is ridiculous," he muttered to her before he checked the rear view mirror. He put the car in gear and drove off. "The sooner this is done the better. I'm over this shit."

"Head past Surf Beach, and turn left onto Denise Drive. It's secluded down there," Grace said.

They'd been driving for about five minutes when Maria stirred.

"Maria?" Grace asked. "How are you?"

"She shouldn't be alive considering what you've put her through," Jane said.

"Maria?" Grace asked again. "How are you?"

Maria winced. "Bit of a headache."

Grace felt her heart thump with hope. That sounded like the Maria she loved. "You remember me?"

"No."

The momentary euphoria vanished, replaced with a sickly feeling. "Oh God," Grace whispered in despair.

"Like you believe in God," Jane said with derision.

Grace glared at the nurse. "I go to church every Sunday."

Jane's did a double take. "What? Really?"

"Yes." Grace turned her attention back to her sister. "How you doing, Maria?"

Her eyes lost focus, and then suddenly returned to Grace's face. A smile spread across her lips. "Grace?"

Grace almost cried, her eyes blurring with joy. "Yes."

"Did I swim into a warship's propeller? I feel like crap."

Blinking tears, Grace nodded. "Near enough. A car. What do you remember?"

"I guess I should have chosen a bigger one."

That didn't make any sense, but then a cold feeling swept through Grace's heart like a hand of ice clenching it. "Chosen?" Grace asked. "Tell me you're joking."

Maria met Grace's eyes. "Do you honestly think I didn't see the car?"

For a long moment, Grace didn't know what to say as Maria's words crushed the life from her. Devastation overcame shock, like the world was trying to shove her off the edge. "You... You tried to commit suicide?"

Maria closed her eyes. "I did it for you. I love you so much."

$$[\ \ 17\ \ ]$$

"WHAT DO you mean you did it for me?"

Maria looked away, though with the brace holding her neck still she was unable to turn her head. "Forget it."

"No!" Grace said. "Tell me!"

"I… Thought you'd be better off without me."

Grace tried to get the words to work logically, but they became chaotic and unknowable. "But… You're my sister!" There wasn't a universe where her logic made sense.

Maria closed her eyes. "You deserve better than me."

There was simply no way to express her fears that she might have lost Maria forever. "How could you say that? I love you." She wanted to say more, so much more, but she felt empty inside. Devastated. "How could you abandon me?"

The sense of betrayal she'd felt when her husband turned his back on her and swam away revisited her, and it was all she could do not to cringe away from Maria. It had happened again, and by the person she loved most in the world.

"I should never have told you." Maria whispered.

"But… We're *sisters*! Why? Answer me Maria!"

"Because you don't want to be here, and the only thing holding you here is me. You could have made your own choices."

Grace waited for the words to fall into some sort of patters that made sense. "You think killing yourself is the answer to my moment of weakness?" Hurt, rage and anger were building somewhere deep within. She might hate killing, but she'd never wanted to end her life or see Maria do the same.

"You're missing out on so much. Our sisters shun me, but not you. You could-"

"Maria! I could never be better off without you. Never!" Grace wanted to slap the stupid out of her.

"When you stand on a beach, the waves lapping your ankles, what do you feel?" Maria asked, her voice soft.

"The ocean. Our sisters. Perfection."

"And when you leave the water?"

"Nothing of course. We're only connected when we're touching the same body of water."

"You're the only one I feel now, Grace, the only one of all our sisters. The others not only shun me, but since I made you without permission they don't even let me sense them anymore."

"What?" Grace asked, shocked. "But we're connected. Intimately. We can't be separated. It would kill..." Grace sat back, suddenly understanding. It's why Maria had been so desperate to make sure Grace lived. It was the certainty that Grace was everything to her. Losing Grace would have killed Maria, so she was pre-empting that. She really thought she'd lose Grace sooner or later.

Maria sniffed, a weak sound. "When I made you it was out of loneliness, not compassion. I could feel our sisters then, but I was still alone. I needed someone, and with every year that passed my longing grew worse. It's in our nature to be together, but I was alone. They all hate me Grace, and I hate some of them back. I don't know why none of them ever told you, but despite my hurt and anger I thanked them every day for that simple mercy."

"Maria-"

"Let me finish," she whispered. "I want you to leave me and go to our sisters. They'll welcome you. Go to them and be happy."

"And you believed killing yourself would force that?"

"Yes."

"Oh Maria." She took her sister's hand and squeezed it. "It's their loss. You're enough for me."

Maria swallowed hard. "You haven't even asked why they shun me."

"I don't care."

"You should."

"I don't understand."

"I made you a mermaid for my own needs. But when they made me a mermaid, that was the punishment."

Grace stared. "I… still don't understand. How could giving you the greatest gift of all be a punishment?"

The car suddenly swerved, throwing Grace sideways. Her head thumped against the door. "Ow! What are you doing Josh?"

"Abbey tried to cut me off!" he said as the car accelerated. "Hold on."

The car swerved hard around a corner, throwing Grace off balance while Jane almost fell across Maria.

"Don't be so bloody reckless!" Jane called.

"She has a gun!"

"What?" Jane squealed.

"Slow down!" Sandra yelled in the same tone.

"A handgun!" He turned hard, throwing Grace toward Jane. "Where the hell does anyone get a handgun in this country?"

"What is she doing now?" Grace yelled.

"Chasing us. Everybody brace yourselves."

Grace held onto Maria while he accelerated away, turning hard several times. Other cars blared horns as tyres screeched. Grace used all her strength to brace Maria against the jolts and swerves.

"Bloody hell," Josh said. "She's a frigging maniac. What does she want?"

"What does any Creature on a power trip want?" Grace asked.

"Don't start that shit again," he muttered as he took them around another corner, the tires screeching.

"Slow down!" Grace said. "You're going to kill us."

"I'm not the one with the gun!" He took another corner hard enough to throw her against the door. "Hold onto something. I'm going to hit the brakes hard."

"What?" Grace cried.

"She'll hit us!" Sandra cried.

"I'm counting on it Mum! This thing's made of steel and I've got a heavy-duty towbar on the back. If she hits us it'll cripple her car."

"It'll cripple us!" said Jane.

"She'll cripple us with the bloody gun if she starts shooting. Her friends have got guns too. Brace yourselves. One, two, three!"

The force of the brakes threw Grace off Maria and against the front seat, but it was the jolt from behind that threw her back onto Maria. By the time she recovered she found herself on the floor with Jane crushing her. They were barely righting themselves as Josh accelerated again.

"What the hell have you done Grace?" Josh yelled at Grace. "Sane people don't come after you with guns."

"*Sane* people, Josh. Figure it out!" she yelled back.

Once Jane righted herself, Grace got off the floor and helped Maria back to a better position, but her sister was unconscious now. Grace checked her pulse, relieved when she found it. Jane clambered back to a half-sitting position and made sure the drip was still in Maria's arm before putting the bag back above the seat under the rear window.

"Her car's still running, but it's pretty badly damaged," Josh said, looking in the rear view mirror.

"Josh, is there anywhere nearby that's close to the water?"

"What?"

"Mermaid stuff! The less distance we have to carry Maria the better. Abbey probably knows we're heading for a beach. You need to find us a place where they won't expect."

"There's a few boat ramps, and there's jetties in some of the creeks," Sandra said helpfully.

"Something like that will do. Please, take us to a boat ramp and get as close to the water as you can, Josh."

"This is insane," he said, twisting around to stare briefly at her and Maria before turning back to the road. "Maria should be in the hospital!"

"I know it's insane," Sandra said, "But she's also telling the truth Josh. Trust me if not her."

"Fine! There's a boat ramp just past Lilli Pilli," Josh said. "It's not far."

He pulled up at the ramp a few minutes afterward, but someone was there trying to get their boat onto a trailer, making it impossible to take Maria straight to the water without being obvious about it. It would look like they were trying to drown an invalid. The beach to the right side of the boat ramp was too exposed as well.

"What about Mossy Point?" Grace asked. "There's plenty of little jetties on Tomaga River. You could drive pretty close to one."

"There's a lot of houses around there too," Sandra said.

"I don't care if we're seen from a distance, as long as nobody tries to stop us. Humans forget quickly enough. Josh, please. Take us to Mossy Point."

It was a little longer before Josh parked in the nearest spot he could find to one of the river's many private piers. It was rapidly closing on sunset and few people were about, although several homes had lights on and cars were parked nearby.

Grace opened her door and clambered unsteadily out, the rush of salt air lifting her spirits a little. "Nearly there," she said to Maria, gently caressing her sister's forehead as everyone else got out.

Grace met Josh's eyes. He didn't look happy.

She tried to look contrite. "I'm sorry about your car," she said.

He frowned as if he hadn't even considered it. "Abbey will be too when I get a hold of her."

Panic gnawed at her at the thought of Josh confronting Abbey. She gripped his muscle-hard forearm. "Stay away from her," she said. "You've got no idea how dangerous she is."

He rolled his eyes at the reference to magical Creatures. "You were going to prove you're a mermaid once we got to the water."

At least he hadn't forgotten that, and it was something she could prove. "I will, just as soon as we get Maria to the landing at the end of the pier."

"No," he said. "Now."

She felt the compulsion settle over her. "But," was all she could manage before she turned and marched down to the rocks and water. Crabs scuttled away she stopped at a small rock pool where several anemones had made their home. Resenting the fact she had no control over her actions, she tensed to dive in.

"Stop," he said.

She stopped, slowly turning with fear on her face. Oh crap. He'd worked it out. "Josh-" she began, but he held up his hand to cut her off. It was as good as a verbal command.

He eyed her speculatively. "You've done everything I've told you to do since we met on Broulee Beach, haven't you?"

"Don't be ridiculous."

"Stand on one foot."

"Josh-" she stood on one foot. Her heart thumped with anxiety. "Josh, I-"

"Shush."

She stopped talking, fear clenching her heart. She couldn't help herself. All she could do was plead with her eyes.

He pushed his sun-kissed hair from his face, disbelief in his expression. "You promised to be my slave for the weekend, and now… you have to keep that promise, don't you?"

She nodded. If she touched the ocean she could command it to rise up and drag him out to sea. Did she really want to though? Could she really drown him even to save her own life, and Maria's?

The command to shush had ran its course now, at least, as well as the command to stand on one foot. "Please don't give me another command," she whispered. "I promised Maria I'd do everything I could to survive, and that promise overrides yours. Please be very careful what you say." There had to be sway out of the situation. "If I die now, you won't be safe. Ever. Mermaids don't forgive the death of a sister."

"Are you threatening me?"

"No! But there would be consequences completely beyond my wishes. Josh, please. Maria's going to die if she's not in the water before sunset, and our sisters won't let it pass unavenged. It's about group survival. Please let me get her into the water."

The sun was rapidly heading for the horizon now and she wasn't sure how long they had. Ten minutes, maybe. Perhaps just a few. He still seemed undecided.

"Yes, I have to obey you Josh, but there's wriggle room in every command. Push me too far and you'll regret it, and not because of my intentions. I promised Maria I'd survive, and that could very easily mean killing you and anyone else who tries to prevent me keeping the promise."

He stared at her, his expression half way between anger and fear and a dozen other emotions. She couldn't tell which way he was leaning. "Are you threatening Mum? Mikey?"

"No!" She tried one last time. "I'm not threatening anyone. Josh, Maria needs us or she'll die soon, and I'm not strong enough to carry her down to the pier on my own. Please help us carry her down here. I'm begging you."

He held a hand over his mouth as he came to some sort of decision. "Uh, yeah, okay," he whispered. "Of course. Come on." His unintended command had her moving before she could speak.

When they arrived back at the car, Sandra had slumped back to her seat, grey with exhaustion. She smiled at her son, but didn't seem to have the energy for anything more. "Stay here and rest up," Grace said to Sandra. "We can take care of Maria."

Sandra sighed. "And miss the greatest thing I'm ever likely to see?" She raised her hand toward Grace. "All I need is a shoulder to lean on."

"But..." Clearly there was no stopping the woman once she'd made a decision. "Of course." Grace smiled, but her stomach was still in knots thanks to Josh's new knowledge.

While Jane helped Josh manoeuvre Maria out of the car and into

Josh's arms, Grace helped Sandra to stand. It took Grace longer to get Sandra out of the car than it took the other two to collect Maria. "You weigh next to nothing," Grace whispered to Sandra so Josh wouldn't hear. "If I weren't afraid of snapping you, I could pick you up as easily as a child."

"I had a choice between wasting away and retaining my gorgeous looks," Sandra said with a half-hearted smile. "I was a little tipsy when I made that call."

The joke didn't lift Grace's spirits, but she decided to play along for the dying woman's sake. Her conversation with Josh was still twisting her stomach, as were the consequences of what her sisters might do to him if he prevented her and Maria from returning to the ocean. They didn't get along, but they weren't likely to let it pass, either. "Aren't you supposed to be making life difficult for everyone?" Grace asked.

"Never my greatest strength, but I'll try harder tomorrow."

"Works for me," Grace said, following Josh as he carried Maria, with Jane just behind, still holding the drip high. Grace didn't have the heart to tell the woman it wasn't necessary. "You know, I'm beginning to suspect that your son's a pretty decent guy."

That made her smile. "He turns a few heads, and some of them aren't even human," she said as they walked down the hill toward the water.

"I guess he does. He seems to have it together for someone so young."

"He had to grow up fast. It's why I've been trying to make these last few months easy on him. His dad ran off when he was six, while the next guy I married used to hit both of us, and I even found the bruises on his legs and arms where the bastard didn't think I'd notice."

"Poor kid," Grace muttered.

"He isn't one to hold a grudge, fortunately. I never thought I'd say this, but he's a really great father. He loves Mikey like crazy."

They were falling behind a little, but Grace didn't mind. Sandra had obviously been hiding just how sick she was not only from Josh, but from Grace too.

"Can I ask you a favour?" Sandra asked after a few steps. "Just a small one?"

"Anything."

"Josh's pretty tough, but he's still a kid at heart and I really hate the thought of leaving him on his own. Would you... I don't know? Try to keep him out of trouble, or at least ensure he doesn't make a mess of things when I'm gone?"

"Does that mean I can't drown him if he annoys me?"

Sandra gave Grace a long look. "Sometimes I can't tell when you're joking."

Grace smiled. "Me either. Of course I'll look after him. I think we covered that at the hospital anyway. Whatever it takes."

Long shadows were moving ahead of them as they stepped onto the heavy wood of the pier. Quite a few piers jutted out onto the water along the shore, some with little dinghy's roped to them. The tide was quickly going out.

"He's got plenty of friends, and I do too, so he'll have more than a few people looking out for him, but one more won't hurt. Besides, I think he likes you."

"He could do far better than a mermaid who could never be what he needs. I'll look out for him Sandra, but don't try and push me into anything."

"I wasn't-"

Grace smiled. "Yes, you were, but I don't mind. I'm sure he'll find someone who deserves him, but it won't be me."

Sandra sighed. "I want him to be happy."

"He deserves someone he can grow old with and start a proper family with. I can't be either."

Ahead, Josh was carefully laying Maria on the end of the jetty, the width of the walkway just wide enough so her feet didn't hang over the edge. Jane crouched beside Maria. Whatever the woman's reasons for hanging around, at least she wasn't causing trouble, and she'd had plenty of opportunities. Professional curiosity, she guessed.

"I keep forgetting you're not as young as you look," Sandra said when they arrived.

It took Grace a moment to remember what the conversation was about. "And I keep forgetting you're much younger than you look." She softened the words with a smile.

"Thanks," Sandra said sarcastically.

Grace was more than happy to offload Sandra to Josh, who helped her to sit on the thick hardwood planks. The river was calm except for the rush of water toward the nearby ocean, which was just around the bend. Only small waves lapped against the wooden posts.

"We need to hurry," Grace said. "I can sense the approach of dusk. Let's get this brace off her."

"But-" Jane began.

"Just take the brace off," Grace told Jane. "I assume it's valuable and you'll want to return it to the hospital?"

Jane stared at Grace. "Prove she's like you first." She put the saline drip on Maria's chest, the tube still running to the back of her hand.

"Jane, all I have to do is roll her into the water and she'll rip the brace and everything else off and leave it at the bottom. Take it now or lose it."

"Grace?" Sandra asked.

Grace turned. "Yes? Sandra?"

"You know that favour you owe me?"

Grace suddenly felt herself go cold. "You haven't met the conditions."

"I don't care. I want you to do it here. Tonight."

Grace couldn't help a glance at Josh, his curiosity clearly piqued. "What's she talking about Grace?" His sun-bleached hair half fell across his eyes.

It was a question, not a command. Grace focused on Sandra. "Not until you've squared it with Josh. That was the deal."

"Mum, what are you talking about?" By his tone she suspected he already knew.

Jane frowned back at Sandra. "I'm guessing Sandra's got a death wish?"

Sandra ignored the comment. "You know he'll never accept it Grace. I want you to do it tonight."

"Sandra-"

"Grace. Please!"

"Mum! What did she promise you?" The tone of his voice was rising.

Sandra put a hand on Josh's. "You've got to know how sick I am. They tried to give me morphine tablets. The next step's a morphine drip and higher and higher doses until it kills me. I can't do that to you."

He pulled away. "No, Mum." His voice cracked. "Just... No! You're not doing this." He glanced at Grace. "You will not kill her. You got that? I said no."

Grace stiffened as the command tool hold. Shit. The promise she'd made to Josh came before the promise she'd made to Sandra. No matter what, she couldn't do it, at least not this weekend.

Sandra reached out but Josh pulled away. "I love you Josh. You've got no idea how much. Let me choose my own passing."

"I love you too Mum, but it's not happening like this. You can fight this. I know you can."

"Grace promised it will be painless. That's the best offer I've had in a long while."

Grace turned away, determined to let them have as much privacy as she could allow. She helped Jane as she began to unfasten the brace, tears in Jane's eyes from the conversation behind them. "You guessed this might happen, didn't you? Sandra wanting to die, I mean. That's why you're really here."

"You never get used to it," Jane whispered as she pulled a Velcro strap aside with a rip. "People dying, that is. Friends dying."

"I know that better than most."

Jane paused, meeting Grace's eyes. "If you could be human, would you want to be?"

"In a heartbeat." She touched Maria's face. "If it wouldn't break Maria's heart, that is. It's not possible though. It's a one way trip from human to Creature. Come on, remove the drip and we'll get her into the water."

Jane put a hand on Grace's wrist. "Can... I want to be like you."

Grace shook her head, trying to pretend she hadn't seen it coming. She'd almost convinced herself. "Never."

"Why?"

"It takes… a death. After that, mermaids have to kill roughly one person a year to survive. Do you really want an existence like that?"

Jane turned her attention to the drip in Maria's arm. She removed the tape and withdrew it. "I… Maybe. Logically no, but-"

"The fine print's not as much fun as the glossy brochure."

Grace heard fresh footsteps on the pier and almost swore under her breath. Someone must have seen or heard something and come to investigate.

"What do you know? Trapped on a pier," Abbey's said. Her blond crony chuckled from the water's edge, the brunette further up the bank.

"Get Maria into the water!" Grace spun.

A bullet hit the wood by Grace's hand and sent splinters into her skin, the shot echoing like thunder. Abbey stood a metre along the pier, the handgun pointed at Grace's heart. Grace glanced up the hill. Surely someone would have heard. There were too many homes nearby for the shot to go unnoticed.

"Vivisection would improve your looks considerably," Abbey said with a wicked smile. "Come along."

[18]

SHADOWS COVERED the water and the other side of the river, and Grace could almost feel the sunset in her bones. They had maybe a minute if she were being optimistic, and Maria still remained out of the water, unconscious. She couldn't even help herself.

Abbey's third crony revealed a sawn-off shotgun, pointed at the ground for now. The blonde's matching weapon rested causally against her shoulder. If only she'd slip and blow off her own head.

"Call me curious," Abbey said, but her eyes betrayed a glance at Josh. "What do you want with him?"

Grace slowly stood, trying to think of some way to shove Maria into the water without drawing a bullet or getting anyone else hurt. There was about two feet between Maria and the end of the jetty, and the water was out of Grace's reach below her.

"Nothing, Curious." It was a lame dad joke, but she wasn't up to being wittier. "I'm just here for Maria. Let us go and you'll never have to see me again."

"Oh, very mature." Abbey aimed the gun at Grace's head. "Do you think a silver bullet will put you down for good?"

Grace stiffened. Silver would kill her the way a normal bullet would kill a human. All Creatures reacted badly to silver at the best of times. "Why do you care, Abbey?" Grace asked. Only the tops of the trees on the headland caught any sun now, and that was almost gone.

Abbey betrayed another glance at Josh. "I'm drawing all sorts of assumptions which suggest you're intentionally sticking your nose in my business."

"Pure coincidence," Grace responded. "Maria got hit by a car. Josh offered me a ride to the hospital." She gave Josh a warning glance. If he told Abbey about the promise and she forced him to use it against her, she and Maria were as good as dead.

"But you can see why I'm interested, right? I don't even know what you are. Siren? If you were a harpy you'd have been airborne long ago, so I'm ruling that out."

"Now you're the nosy one."

"I'm just protecting my business interests. I consider Josh and his family a big part of that, and I won't have you interfering."

What the hell did that mean? What could she possibly want from Josh that didn't involve killing him for his lifeforce?

Josh crossed his arms. "That kind of puts you in the stalker category, doesn't it?"

Abbey lost her smug look, and for half a second Grace thought she was going to turn the gun on him. Grace braced herself to grab Maria and throw her into the water, but after a tense few seconds Abbey relaxed slightly.

Abbey returned her attention to Grace. "You've got no idea how dangerous I'm going to be in a minute or so, do you?" Without looking, she indicated the horizon behind her. Sunset. Succubi, like vampires and similar Creatures, were far more dangerous at night.

"Piss off," Josh said.

"You should watch what you say Josh. I'm the only person who's got your back here," Abbey said. "If it wasn't for me you'd have been dead a year ago."

So it really was about Josh then. What exactly did she want with him? Why not Sandra too? Her lifeforce was just as strong, and she guessed Mikey's was as well. Grace took a half step back, disguising it by shifting her weight. She felt Maria's arm against her heel, fear pre-empting her choices. She doubted she had any time to spare to get Maria into the water now.

"No moving," Abbey said, swinging the gun back on Grace.

Grace's heart thumped as she realised she was perspiring like a human. She needed a weapon. Preferably a tank-mounted machine gun.

"Why did you drown that human nurse? Even water sprites have no need to drown people, and you're not a sprite. Are you?"

"It's a psychopath thing, Abbey. You'll understand if you look in the mirror."

Abbey gave her murderous smile, partly lost in the gloom. "Now you're testing my good nature." Abbey put both hands on her gun to hold it steady at Grace's head. "Kelly, why don't you blow some of her toes off for me? See if you can take the shine off that attitude?"

The blonde squealed with delight and jumped onto the pier, walking past Abbey and then Josh, her shotgun raised at Grace.

Jane cringed aside as Kelly stopped a foot away. The water was lapping gently just a couple of feet below Grace, but with Kelly's gun trained on her she couldn't even jump in without getting hit.

"I just want to get my sister back into the water," Grace said, swallowing nervously. Sunset was far too close and she could feel the pressure.

"Which foot do you want to lose?" Kelly asked. "I'll pick if you don't," Kelly said with a nasty grin, pointing the weapon at Grace's feet. "But I'm always happy to take requests."

Grace didn't doubt her. She shifted aside, caught and turned the shotgun with one hand and grabbed the werewolf by the shirt. Kelly squealed as Grace head-butted her. The werewolf cried out and staggered back as Abbey shot, but it struck Kelly in the shoulder. Kelly cried out and dropped her shotgun to the timber where it triggered, the noise deafening.

Grace spun and grasped Maria's hospital smock as she cartwheeled over her. A bullet grazed her leg as she used Maria's mass to swing her legs back down with a thump just behind her sister. Grace hauled backwards, using her momentum to drag Maria into the water on top of her.

As they plunged under Grace felt her own body transform, just as Maria's did.

"Go!" she cried as Maria's eyes opened. A bullet hit the water above them. "Go!"

Maria twisted in the water and shot away, much slower than normal but fast enough for now. As she sunk deeper and moved further into the creek, she felt the sun set, a subtle tingle that seemed to reverberate throughout the ocean like a wave crashing on the shore. They'd barely made it. Unfortunately, it meant that Abbey was also much stronger than she had been a moment before, and Josh, Sandra and Jane were up there with her.

On land it would be no contest, but she couldn't let her friends take the brunt of Abbey's anger. She focused on the water around her to purge the salt from it so she could freeze it into a shield several inches thick. She rose to the surface behind it. A bullet chipped ice away and put a big crack in it, and a moment later a shotgun spray slammed into it, splintering the shield and pushing Grace back slightly.

Heart pounding with fear for Josh and Sandra, and even Jane, Grace drew more water from the ocean to strengthen and repair the ice, and then made it as clear as glass.

Abbey stood on the edge of the landing, gun pointed at her, but she didn't shoot again.

"What the crap are you?" she asked. The concept of mermaids obviously hadn't crossed her mind yet, and it was probably too dark under the water to see. Mermaids rarely revealed themselves to other Creatures for good reason - they didn't want the attention.

Grace formed a ball of ice in her hand, and then used the water to propel it hard at Abbey. It wasn't fast enough to do any real damage, but the ice smashed into the gun, knocking it from Abbey's hands.

The Creature cried out in surprise and staggered back. Grace formed another ice missile and propelled it at Kelly, the werewolf's shoulder dripping blood all the way down to her hand.

"Ahhh!" Kelly cried, staggering back. The other werewolf girl was already at the edge of the pier, her shotgun levelled.

"Grace!" Josh called. She found him cradling his mother's body. "My Mum's been shot! Help!"

Sandra's leg was bloody, and a good number of shotgun pellets had hit her foot. Grace swore as compulsion overcame her, but she was already helping and her own survival was also at stake. She formed another ball of ice and propelled it at the werewolf at the edge of the pier.

The girl wasn't expecting it and it smashed her in the face. She fell back and dropped her shotgun, the weapon striking the edge of the pier and dropping into the water without discharging.

Grace formed another ball of ice, but Abbey moved faster than any human could. With incredible strength she grabbed Josh, pulling him away from his mother like he was a toddler. He yelled and fought, but he might as well have fought a gorilla. Abbey pulled him close to her and pressed sharp claws against his neck.

"Keep it up, Ariel. I see what you are now. I didn't think your kind were real."

"Let him go."

"Crap I will! I can't wait to tell everyone about you. You lot keep yourselves very well hidden."

Grace propelled a new ice ball at Kelly, striking the girl's shoulder again, but it failed to knock her into the water.

"Abbey," Josh said, but Abbey pressed her claws harder against his neck. Blood welled.

"Sorry Josh. You're valuable, but not as valuable as my own life. I'll tear your throat out before I give Ariel a chance at me."

"I never figured succubi were such cowards," Grace said, hoping Abbey would take the bait.

"Try again, little mermaid."

"Sure. Come and get me and we'll see how you fare."

"I have a nasty suspicion I'd be at a serious disadvantage in the water. Why don't you have a go at me up the hill? We'll discuss the terms of Josh's continuing existence there."

Kelly picked up her gun and fired another shell at Grace, the pellets smashing into her shield but doing no harm. It was a standoff.

"It's night Abbey. You've got the advantage with your strength. Jump in. If you take a mermaid out in the water you'd get some serious bragging rights."

"Probably would," Abbey said, "But not today." Keeping a hold of Josh, she backed toward the stairs up to the road, dragging him with her like he was a big teddy bear. "I'm calling this a draw, unless you want to duke it out up on the road?"

Grace moved toward the shore, but it only forced Abbey to retreat faster. Kelly moved with Abbey, her nose bloody and her arm dripping blood.

"Grace," Josh cried, still struggling. "Help Mum! She's hurt real bad. She needs an ambulance. Don't let her die!"

A more powerful form of compulsion caught her and twisted her into action. She commanded water and used it to lift herself up to the height of the pier. Kelly shot at her again, the pellets cracking into her shield.

Grace commanded more water again, this time shooting a blinding spray at the werewolf and Abbey. They ducked it and backed up the hill, and when they seemed sure they were out of her range they all began running away, Abbey dragging Josh with her.

Grace sheeted water from her body as she dropped to the timber, her legs forming as she touched it. The compulsion still holding her, she rushed to Sandra and found the woman bleeding profusely. There was blood all over the pier, dripping into the water below.

Jane tried to staunch the bleeding with her hands. "This is very bad. She's lost way too much blood." She met Grace's eyes. "She won't last long enough to call an ambulance, let alone for help to arrive."

Sandra's breathing was shallow and ragged as Grace raised her eyes to Jane. There had to be another way. Had to be.

"I'm sorry," Jane said. "But there's nothing I can do."

With those words the compulsion in Josh's last words forced the only option left to Grace. There was no way he could have understood the consequences of what she was about to do, but she couldn't help herself either. She'd promised...

"You shouldn't have said that Jane," Grace said. "If you'd have lied for a little while longer, and made me believe it... I'm so sorry."

"What?" Jane asked, seeing something deadly and dangerous in Grace's eyes. Grace leaned close and kissed Sandra tenderly on the lips, imparting a little of her own lifeforce into the woman, an enchantment as old as mermaids themselves.

"I'm so sorry Jane. I don't have a choice." She'd rather have carried Sandra into the water to ease her passing with dignity and love. Not now though. Her body still partially wet so she could retain the strength it gave her, she grabbed the nurse by her uniform.

"Grace?"

"I really am sorry Jane." Grace shoved the woman off the pier. The big woman cried out before water engulfed her with a splash. As she made the surface Grace caught Sandra under the shoulders and legs and jumped into the water after Jane.

Grace's body transformed immediately.

Holding Sandra close so her head stayed above the surface, she followed the current toward the ocean and caught Jane by the throat, using the tidal waters to propel the three of them beyond the narrow opening and into the ocean.

"Please," Jane said, sensing Grace's intentions. She held Grace's arm with both of hers, trying to force her to let her go, but she wasn't nearly strong enough. "Grace, please," she said, struggling for breath as Grace half choked her.

"There's nothing I can do," Grace said. "I made Josh a promise, and he's collecting." Even singing wouldn't ease the woman's fears now. Reluctantly, she let her claws sink into Jane's flesh, sealing the connection.

Jane struggled as the water deepened and Grace forced the nurse under. Jane's grip loosened and she began splashing for the surface, fighting hard. The poor woman didn't deserve this, but Grace couldn't help herself. She held off taking Sandra under, making sure she didn't drown before Grace had the chance to steal Jane's lifeforce and transform her.

Jane gave a violent kick in a valiant effort to free herself, catching Grace's tail, but it did nothing. She tried again to pry Grace's fingers from her neck, but she might as well have tried fighting off a gorilla on steroids. Grace closed her eyes, not wanting to see the fear and devastation on the woman's face. The drowning nurse began to panic, forcing Grace to bring her tail up and slam it into the old nurse's stomach to get the ordeal over quicker.

Jane let out a burst of bubbles, sucked in, and began choking, her body spasming. Trying not to think, Grace took Sandra below the surface then, counting the seconds before Jane's body went limp and she stopped struggling.

Close to the sandy bottom, Grace finally felt the woman's lifeforce release. It flowed though Grace, but rather than topping up her own lifeforce, she used the connection to Sandra through her kiss and channelled the lifeforce into Josh's mother.

The woman jerked as if electrified. Her body spasmed almost as Jane's had, and just like Grace had done herself more than a century ago, she fought it with everything she had, right up until she took in a lungful of water. Her mouth opened and closed several times, her eyes wide and panicked, but with her lungs full of water already, her life was soon over. Briefly.

Everything that remained human inside her burned away under the onslaught of magic. "Sandra, I'm so sorry," Grace whispered.

Grace released her hold and let Sandra float free, her human essence leaching from her skin as she became as translucent as water itself. A fresh spasm racked her body, and then she changed in a flash of blinding energy, her new body tearing her jeans apart.

Sandra sucked in another lungful of water, but now it was like air to her.

Colour returned to her skin, leaving her as young and healthy and as beautiful as she must have been in her youth, more so, only now her legs were fused into a long, powerful tail, her hair a yard long.

No trace of the ravages of cancer remained, leaving her extraordinarily beautiful, her rich brown hair floating free around her.

"Sandra? Are you okay?"

Sandra's wide, surprised eyes went to Jane's body, and she moaned. "I'm hungry," Sandra said, and no doubt it drove her thoughts. Grace knew that hunger.

Sandra looked Grace up and down with a mixture of fear, disgust and love, seeing her new sister for only the second time in her natural shape, but this time with new eyes.

Grace tried to smile and found it hard. "You'll have to take someone's lifeforce very soon to complete the transformation. If you don't it will drive you insane and you'll wake up having killed far too many."

Sandra glanced around as if only just realising she was under the water. "You killed her?"

"Josh commanded me to keep you alive. I had no choice."

"You should have taken me, not her!"

Grace caught Sandra by the shoulders, sensing the curiosity of other mermaids around the world reacting to the presence of a new sister. "You have to take someone, Sandra. I'm sorry, but you won't be able to stop yourself once you begin. Go. Try to make it someone who's alone."

There was fear on her face. "I can't do that. If you knew me at all you'd know I can't."

"You'll have no choice if you fight it. I'll take Jane's body to the beach and leave her there so it looks like misadventure, but you need to do something about your needs before they consume you. Go."

"But I have to find Josh! Abbey took him!" Sandra's protective instincts where clearly overriding her need to attain more lifeforce. She darted past Grace and swam for the river's opening.

Grace swore and went after her, but Sandra reached the pier first and burst out of the water, landing hard on the wood in her new form. Grace landed beside her in human form. Sandra still had her tail, and now she was choking on air.

"You can't transform yet! You can't even breathe air until your body finishes transitioning. It'll take a year before you can walk on land again."

Sandra flopped around like a landed fish, choking on the air. Half a dozen people who'd come out to investigate the gunshots milled about on the shore, staring at them, stunned looks on their faces.

"Great." Grace grabbed Sandra's tail and shoved her over the side of the little pier with a splash. Half naked herself, she gave a brief curtsy. "That concludes tonight's show. Have a good evening." She dived, transforming as the water welcomed her back, and quickly caught up to Sandra who was now swimming deep into the ocean.

"Don't touch me!" Sandra yelled over her shoulder. The rejection hurt, but against Grace's better instincts she kept her distance.

"I can't even breathe air!" Sandra cried. "How am I supposed to help Josh when I can't breathe or get rid of this ridiculous tail?"

"Sandra, calm down!"

"My boy is in danger and I can't help him!"

"Then let me help him! He's your son, Sandra. That means you've now got thousands of sisters who will do anything for you. Let us help!"

"But-"

"You need to look after yourself, and that means taking lifeforce. The transformation depleted everything you had and everything I took from Jane. You have to renew your lifeforce. Go! I'll help Josh."

"Grace-"

"Go! Before your needs consume you and you drown dozens of people. Please Sandra, take my advice. Don't carry the same regrets I do."

"I can feel it growing inside me Grace, like I'm a starving predator. I'm so hungry, but not for food…"

Grace caught Sandra and hugged her tight. "Go while you're still thinking clearly." She gave Sandra a tiny push toward the beach where people may still be swimming. After a moment's hesitation, Sandra did as she was told.

Grace turned, slipping through the current until she found Jane's limp body near the sandy bottom.

She'd been a good woman. A very good woman, and was now dead because Grace had made a stupid promise to a boy over a necklace.

She towed Jane's body around the headland to Candlagan Creek at the end of North Broulee beach, and then used the water to carry the nurse to the high tide mark. Grace transformed herself as she left the water, turning Jane onto her side before giving her a gentle kiss on the woman's water-chilled cheek. "I'm so sorry," she whispered. "You deserve more dignity than this."

She returned to the water and swam away from the beach, wishing she'd never survived the night the Titanic sank.

Whatever else happened, she was going to make Abbey pay for Jane's death.

[19]

GRACE LET HER SENSES ROAM. She found her newest sister's presence a few miles away in a northerly direction.

Sandra was a long way short of being able to control and mute her emotions, and at the moment she was a mix of need, self-loathing and fear. She'd killed, and needed someone with her to soothe her emotions and hold her close.

Scattered throughout the ocean, Grace sensed her sisters' curiosity. It wouldn't be polite for them to come and see exactly what had happened to create a new sister, but at some point Sandra would need to be introduced. And Grace, no doubt, would have to face them, along with whatever consequences they chose. For now though, they were prepared to wait.

It might as well be now. She'd told Talithia she'd go to her, after all. She might as well face both issues at once.

Not quite ready to disturb the newest mermaid, Grace slowly made her way north, giving Sandra time to recognise her approach and hopefully prepare herself for company. Surprising Sandra could be dangerous if she reacted poorly. Grace considered kicking her skirt off and discarding her blouse, but she'd need them again when she left the water, at least until she could get something less grandmotherly.

She intended to go after Josh, but not before dawn. Chasing down a Creature that thrived during the night was suicide for the human she might as well be. At least during the day she had a chance, if not an advantage. The Creature had guns and werewolves to protect her too, and they'd be waiting for her. She would need more than cutting sarcasm and bad puns to help Josh. She needed a plan.

She found Sandra curled up on a sandy patch of ocean floor, crying softly to herself.

Grace hesitated when she saw her, but there was no point in putting it off. She swam down to her sister, surprising herself again at how different Sandra's transformation made her appear. She was a young, vivacious mermaid now. Her claws and tail looked a little out of place, but it wouldn't take long and she'd expect nothing else.

"Sandra?" she asked gently.

Sandra jerked and kicked back with her tail, looking around in fear as the sand she stirred up began to settle.

"Stay away from me Grace!"

Grace did as asked. "I never wanted this for you Sandra. I'm sorry. I wanted to help you die peacefully."

"Then why didn't you? I just murdered three men because of you. Three! One of them was barely Josh's age. I couldn't help myself."

"And I murdered Jane to make you this. I couldn't help myself either."

She glared. "Why? Why would you do this to me? I was ready to die. I'd come to terms with it!"

"Because our promises are binding, and I made a promise to Josh. You bore the brunt of the consequences, intended or not."

"Leave me alone!" Sandra turned and swam off as fast as she could.

Far more at home in the ocean than Sandra, Grace controlled the water around herself and caught up in seconds. Sandra's motions were almost awkward to watch. There was no skill or finesse at all.

"Where are you going?" Grace asked.

"I'm going home. I'm going to find my son, and I'm going to help him."

"Land is that way," Grace said, pointing.

Sandra paused, and then changed direction. "Go away."

"Do you have any friends on land that can help you?" Grace asked.

"What do I need help for?" She turned aside slightly, though still angling for the shore.

"You'll need help getting home," Grace said gently. "You can't breathe air. Your friends will need a big tank."

Sandra stopped swimming, as if she hadn't quite mastered swimming and talking at the same time. "I'm feeling pretty energetic just now. I'll figure something out."

"Like walk on your tail while you choke on air?"

"Get stuffed!"

"You can't transform, Sandra. Not yet. It could take as much as a year."

Sandra glared. "I'll find a way, even if I have to drag myself."

Grace put her hands on Sandra's shoulders. Sandra stiffened, but didn't fight as Grace gently drew her closer. "Once you learn to transform your body you'll be able to go ashore and see Josh, but for now you can breathe only water. You won't even be able to speak to a human."

Sandra became deadly calm. "Undo it. Make me human again."

Grace dropped her eyes. "I can't."

Sandra flicked her tail and swam toward land again, but Grace caught up in moments.

"Where are you going?"

"I told you, to find Josh and get him away from that psycho succubus."

"Did you miss the part about breathing air? Everything about you has to settle. It's like pouring metal into a mould, it has to cool down before you can do anything with it."

"You should have let me die! You promised!"

"I made another promise first, and it took priority."

Sandra stopped again, and if she weren't under water Grace was certain tears would be flowing down her cheeks. "I don't want to be like this, Grace."

Grace tried not to let the new mermaid's sorrow get to her, though her emotions were like a knife to her chest. "You've got no idea how many people would kill for this."

Her expression changed from devastation to anger. "I did kill for this!" Sandra looked like she was about to say more, but her bottom lip quivered and she turned away.

Gently, Grace took Sandra in her arms again. Her new sister tried to struggle free, but only for a moment before she went limp and shuddered, letting out a sob.

"I'll help you through this. It happens to us all," Grace said soothingly.

Sandra's sobs only grew stronger, becoming a torrent of anguish. Grace held her for a long time, the two of them floating together just under the surface. She closed her own eyes, remembering Maria holding her just as close, just as tightly, and just as lovingly, so long ago.

Eventually Sandra pulled away.

"Feeling better?" Grace asked.

"No. I'm a fish."

Grace laughed, to Sandra's chagrin. "You're *so* much more than a fish. You're a pink-faced fish with red puffy eyes."

"Oh shut up!" she said. She began to wipe her eyes, but stopped as she realised the ocean had washed them away. "What now?"

Grace reached for Sandra's hands, her nails as long and sharp as her own. "How about I take you to my home? I can sense Maria there already."

"A home? In the ocean? I... thought you swam around all the time."

"We've got the cheapest beach-front property around. Great views of the local reef. It's not exactly the Great Barrier Reef, but it'll do."

Sandra hesitated, but finally sighed. "Ok. I ... I don't want to be alone Grace. I'm very scared." She looked around. "What if there's a shark?"

"Sharks are scared of us, and I won't abandon you Sandra. Soon, as your new body settles down, you'll begin to sense our sisters all over the world. Without them I'd never have gotten through the first year either."

Sandra seemed surprised. "You can really sense other mermaids?"

"Of course, so long as I'm touching the same body of water as they are. I can even sense Maria if she's close to the water and we're not too far apart. You'll never be lonely Sandra, and you'll never be lost. What's more, you'll always be loved. I can feel them now, all curious about you. You're the first new mermaid to be created since the Titanic sunk."

"Which was you?"

Grace nodded. "We have to regulate our numbers, so consider this a once in a generation gift. Once in many generations, actually. Come on. Let's go home. Home's not much, but we don't need much."

Grace kept the pace slow for Sandra's benefit, although her skirt and top didn't help. Sandra hesitated when she saw the narrow entrance to the mostly-hidden cavern, but followed Grace in anyway.

"I can see in the dark!" Sandra said. She looked around in surprise. "I mean, it's not light in here, is it?"

"No. It's not light out there either. Sunset was a while ago. Only works when you're in water, though. We lose most of our special abilities when in human form."

"Oh."

"Maria?" Grace called. She could sense her sister in a small side-room they'd carved from the stone.

It took her a moment, but Maria finally emerged, looking unhappy. "You should have let me die," she said, ignoring Sandra completely.

Despite the words, Grace could sense Maria's curiosity. "Why does everyone seem to have a death wish today?"

"I should go," Sandra said softly to Grace. "She doesn't want me here."

Grace grabbed Sandra's hand. "You've got no idea how desperately she needs you."

Maria moved awkwardly, her body still recovering. "There are rules, Grace. Rules about creating Creatures." Her eyes flicked to Sandra and back. "They may not let her live."

"What?" Grace pulled away slightly, as if distance would allow her to see better. She'd never heard of a mermaid being killed by other mermaids. The idea was abhorrent.

"I'm still surprised they let you live, to be honest."

Grace felt herself go cold. There was absolutely no hiding the truth in Maria's voice. "Why didn't you tell me?"

"We can't allow our numbers to grow, Grace. You know that. We have to kill to survive, and if too many people start drowning the humans will begin asking questions, and no matter how careful we are or the strength of the magic that keeps us hidden, something will go wrong. You know it as well as I do. Some of us would die. Many of us, potentially. There's an order to things, and all three of us sit outside that order. They're going to take action. Maybe not immediately, but you can be certain it won't be long."

"I've always felt welcomed. Loved," Grace said. Even now she felt that way. There was absolutely no threat directed at her in the emotions of the other mermaids. She glanced at Sandra and opened her senses fully. She felt her newest sister's fear, but beyond the cave there was anger too, but it was all directed at Maria.

"Why are they so angry with you?" Grace asked. "I've never felt such animosity until now."

"They were going to kill you, Grace, after I made you. To punish me for doing it."

Grace tried to read her sister's eyes, her emotions, but she kept them tightly to herself. "Why didn't they?" she finally asked.

"Could you kill one of our sisters?"

"Of course not!"

"They promised to let you live if I promised never to make another."

"But-"

"I was lonely. So lonely. For two hundred years all I'd felt was their anger. I needed a friend and you were drowning. By that point I didn't care if they killed me. I figured a few more days of life with a friend was better than none. For you, I'd have been happy to let them kill me."

"What did you do? What was so horrible they'd kill me to punish you?"

Maria glanced at Sandra. "You should go. This doesn't involve anyone but Grace."

Grace caught Sandra's hand and stared defiantly at Maria. Her sister sighed, realising there was no way Grace was going to force Sandra from the cave.

Maria let herself drift to the sandy bottom of the cave, her shoulders slumping. "You're my only child, Grace, the only one I can ever have. You're their insurance policy against me."

"But... they love me. I can feel it!"

Anger crossed Maria's features then. "It's in our nature to love each other! They can't help it any more than you can."

"But-"

"Grace, you should go to them before they come here. Take Sandra with you. Explain what happened. They'll forgive you, I'm sure of it."

"Forgive me for what? I didn't do anything wrong!"

"You made a Creature! We're immortal, Grace. We're only allowed to make more of our kind when one of us dies, and that's rare." She closed her eyes and sighed.

"You're blaming yourself for all of this?" Grace let the water take her to Maria so she could wrap her sister in her arms. "This is not your fault!"

Maria gently disentangled herself. "You need to go. Sandra too. If I remain here they might show restraint. Kindness even."

"What did you do to make them so angry with you, Maria? Tell me, please."

Maria took Grace's cheeks in her hands and kissed her forehead. "Please don't return."

"Maria, I'll always return."

"Maria isn't even my real name," she whispered. "Go. Please, just go. And no matter what they tell you, I'll always love you even if you no longer love me."

How could that even be possible? Not love Maria? What possible crime could she have committed? "I'll return soon," she whispered. She pulled her human clothes free and dropped them on the cavern's sandy floor. "Sandra, you'll probably want to take your top off. It's much easier to swim without clothes, and we've got a long way to go tonight."

Hesitantly Sandra complied, removing her top and bra. She looked slightly embarrassed.

"You'll get used to it."

Before they left, Grace turned to Maria. "What is your real name?"

She appeared vaguely embarrassed, dropping her eyes to the sand below them. "Antonio."

[20]

Maria had once been a man? Antonio? Nothing made sense, even her own knowledge.

"Are you okay?" Sandra asked.

"No," Grace replied softly. The world had done a backflip and she hadn't had time to brace herself.

"You want to talk about it?" Sandra asked.

"No."

She had to focus on the roiling emotions that thousands of mermaids were generating throughout the ocean. Curiosity. Fear. Shock. There was a new mermaid, and it was clear to Grace there would be consequences.

"Conserve your energy. We'll be swimming most of the night." She controlled the water around them to act as a personalised current, easing their way.

They were a long way into the Pacific Ocean when she sensed dozens of their sisters gathering deep, far deeper than any creature but the most specialised sea life could survive. Her sisters were mostly curious, but some were furious.

"You look worried," Sandra said.

They were only a few feet under the surface as they drifted to a stop. A storm raged overhead and fat drops peppered the waves and whitecaps, but below the surface everything remained ominously calm. Lightning flashed and Grace squinted at the brightness. All they needed to do now was dive, and dive deep, yet Grace hesitated.

"Should I be worried?" Sandra asked.

Should she? Grace didn't know. "I'm just... I've never met more than a few of our sisters together before, and mostly only in passing." Other mermaids had always avoided Maria, which by default meant they avoided Grace, but none had ever been less than welcoming when she'd met them. That feeling had changed. Animosity had built in a select group as she and Sandra drew nearer, and it seemed to be feeding the others. What emotions one felt they all experienced, and it was hard not to get caught up in it.

"I think I know how you feel," Sandra said blithely, at least several months from being able to sense the emotions of other mermaids. "How much further? I'm exhausted."

A safe topic, sort of. "If you draw on your lifeforce you can ignore sleep at will. You can also use it to restore your energy, and heal. Of course, you'll have to kill sooner if you do."

Sandra leaned away as if the thought were abhorrent, her long brown hair streaming about her. "No, thank you." She said softly as she met Grace's eyes. "Can you still sense them? Your, our sisters?"

"Always. I feel their love," she said more than a little cautiously, but hiding the truth wasn't a good way to start a relationship that could last forever. "I can sense them all around the world. Most are curious. Quite a few though, the oldest, aren't happy." She measured the uncertainty in Sandra's eyes. "I really don't know what's going to happen," she admitted.

Another flash of lightning illuminated the dimpled, roiling surface, the calm water they drifted in a counterpoint to the raging storm above. Grace's thoughts returned to Maria. "Antonio," she whispered in disbelief. She'd never heard of a man being changed, and hadn't known it was possible. It was a punishment of some sort. For what, though? At least it explained why there were no mermen. Grace had made some very poor assumptions about that.

"Aren't you afraid of sharks?" Sandra said as if she couldn't let the thought drop. "There's got to be big sharks this far out. Really big."

"I've never met a shark that didn't fear a mermaid. Trust me, we're the scariest creatures in the ocean."

Sandra didn't look convinced. "I'm more scared than scary."

Grace took Sandra's hands. They'd delayed long enough. "We need to dive. If you're lucky we might even see a giant squid on the way down."

Sandra blanched. "A what?"

"Giant squid. Whales eat them."

That seemed to worry Sandra more than sharks. "How deep do we need to go?"

"A mile or so."

"Won't that crush us?"

"It might crush a nasty little minx like Abbey." Grace savoured the idea until she realised Sandra had gone quiet at the mention of the succubus's name. Grace took Sandra's shoulders. "If Abbey wanted to harm Josh it would have happened long before I met you or him. She's playing a different game, and it involves Josh being alive. We can figure out why later." She squeezed Sandra's shoulders, took her left hand and began diving, drawing Sandra down with her. All sight of the storm-tossed surface soon disappeared.

"I'm pretty sure there shouldn't be light this deep," Sandra said after a minute. "Why can I see you just as well now as I could near the surface?"

"You're not human anymore."

"Yeah, but... shouldn't the water at least be cold? It feels like I'm swimming in the tropics."

"It's cold."

"And how is it we can talk as if the water's air? It even feels like we're flying, not swimming."

Grace slowed, certain she was going to be inundated with a lot more questions over the coming months. "It's... I don't know. Magic."

"But-"

Grace caught Sandra's hands. "Later. Our sisters have convened, a good three dozen of them. Shush from now on, and show respect when we arrive. Some are thousands of years old."

Sandra's eyes widened. "Thousands? Really?"

Grace led her down. It wasn't long before a large group of their sisters came into view, waiting expectantly in a rough sphere. Grace had never seen so many mermaids in one place, and they were just a small representation.

Other than Talithia, she only recognised three. Blonde Gwyn, the dark-skinned Tse, and a mermaid who'd once been a Japanese princess, Shakiko. The rest came from all over the world as well, including a gorgeous pink-eyed albino with African features who smiled readily when she saw Grace and Sandra. It didn't make Grace feel any better. There was still too much animosity hidden within the group.

Sandra gripped Grace's hand tighter as they descended into the middle, the circle enclosing around them as if to prevent them escaping. "I feel like we've stumbled into a porn movie. There's tits everywhere," Sandra whispered.

"Are you a teenage boy?" Grace asked with just a hint of annoyance.

Talithia drifted forward with no discernible effort. "Why didn't Maria come?" she asked without acknowledging Sandra.

Slightly taken aback at the tone, it put Grace on the defensive. "She's recovering from an injury."

Talithia acknowledged Sandra with narrowed eyes. Sandra gripped Grace's hand tighter. "Hi," Sandra said with a tenuous smile.

Talithia turned back to Grace, no friendliness in her expression. "You made this Creature?"

Grace stiffened. "Sandra. Her name's Sandra." She was tempted to leave with her new daughter right then, not that she was sure they'd let her.

The speaker gave Sandra another glance, the mood among their other sisters tense. None spoke.

"I lead this Council," Talithia said. "You will speak only to me unless invited to do otherwise."

Grace inclined her head at the group of mermaids with a respect she didn't entirely feel, and no doubt Talithia sensed it. "Thank you for seeing us," Grace said, doing her best not to cause more tension.

Talithia's expression mirrored her emotions, hard and uncompromising. "The Council has made its decision."

"What? Without even asking what happened?"

Talithia gave a single nod of her head. "Sandra cannot be allowed to exist. Our numbers are already too great."

Grace automatically forced Sandra behind her. "This isn't Sandra's fault!"

Talithia pursed her lips. "Grace," she said in a patronising tone. "You were allowed to exist for Maria's sake, but we have to police our numbers." She pointed to Sandra. "Your daughter must leave the oceans."

"That will kill her!"

Talithia raised a clawed hand, her nails much longer and sharper than Grace's. Her canines were showing in anger as well. "Would you take Sandra's place and suffer this Council's decision on her behalf? That option is open to you."

It was a vendetta then. Nothing more or less, and it chilled her to see the hatred in Talithia's eyes and feel it emanating from her emotions. "This is about Maria, isn't it?" she said so softly only Talithia might hear.

The ancient mermaid's eyes narrowed.

Sending Grace to her death would devastate Maria, just as sending Sandra to hers would devastate Grace, and through her Maria. The problem was, even if Grace wanted to accept something like that she'd promised Maria she'd do everything possible to survive. No matter what, she couldn't take Sandra's place if the order was upheld.

"Talithia," Grace began, desperate to find some compromise or a way to acknowledge the problem she'd caused and make amends. "I was ignorant about the rules when I made Sandra."

"So Maria is to blame then?" Although she kept her emotions tightly controlled, Talithia's expression showed triumph.

"What? No! Maria had nothing to do with this." Talithia clearly wanted to hurt Maria, and Sandra was her excuse.

"Yet she failed to guide you properly, judging by this Creature's... Sandra's creation. Responsibility must be taken, Grace. Is that yours, Maria's or Sandra's?"

"How could you ask that?" Despite the newness of their relationship with her daughter, there was no possible way Grace could sacrifice either Sandra or Maria. "Are you that vindictive?"

Fury crossed Talithia's face and she opened her hand to strike with her claws.

Sandra pushed her way around Grace. "It wasn't her fault!"

Talithia barely held onto her anger. Ignoring Sandra as inconsequential, she glared at Grace. "Then the punishment is death. I'll leave it to you to choose which of the three of you takes it."

Grace went cold all over. "You can't do that," she whispered.

Talithia ignored her protest. "One of you will return to shore and walk as far inland as you can. You will not return to the ocean." There was a general murmuring from the other mermaids, some in agreement, most in protest.

Sandra let go of Grace's hand and glared at Talithai. "Screw you and your vindictive ruling. I might be new, but you're more disgusting than those stinking werewolves and their succubi mistress who took my son. I think I might actually prefer the succubus's company."

"Sandra!" Grace said, hauling Sandra back, but the newest mermaid didn't back down, struggling against Grace's grip. "How could you be so cruel?" she yelled over Grace's shoulder.

Clearly unthreatened by Sandra's anger, Talithia glared until Sandra calmed down, but there was no compromise in her posture. "We made a mistake allowing you to live after Maria made you. The fact we're allowing two of the three of you to survive is generous."

"Your intentions are obvious," Grace said, fury growing so strong she wanted to strike out. Once she was certain Sandra wouldn't try to get past her again, she drifted forward until her nose was an inch away from Talithia's face. "But if you want one or any of us dead, you'll have to do it yourself." Her heart pumped with adrenaline and fear, but she had to call the bluff or all three would likely die.

"Don't tempt me." Talithia raised a clawed hand.

Grace glared with just as much venom as Talithia. "And yet we both know you can't." She really hoped she was right as she spread her arms wide, opening herself to the strike. "Do it, if you can."

The surrounding mermaids began whispering as Talithia's face flushed with fury. Her hand trembled, but no matter how much she wanted to hurt Maria by killing Grace, she couldn't. After several more seconds she let her hand drop. "We should never have left you with your maker. Her loneliness was supposed to be her punishment, and you destroyed that."

"Neither Sandra, Maria nor I will be leaving the ocean. Ostracise us if you wish, but that's your only weapon. Goodbye Talithia. My promise to come to you is fulfilled. Don't trouble us again."

Talithia raised her chin with impotent rage. "Never forget that it was our compassion alone that allowed you to remain with Maria."

Grace hesitated. "Compassion had nothing to do with it. I'm guessing you couldn't stand the feeling of Maria's loneliness? It hurt you and every other mermaid just as much as it hurt Maria. Your punishment, whatever it was for, hurt you just as much as it hurt Maria." Grace felt her claws growing as long as Talithia's, and for the first time in her life she wanted to use them against another mermaid.

"It's what she deserved," Talithia said in the same dangerous tones. "We should never have permitted her to keep you."

"Deserves? For what? For loving me the way you're supposed to love her? What did she do? You're ruled by spite, not compassion. Whatever it is between you and Maria, it's clear that you're the problem, not her."

One of the mermaids swam to them, a blonde with European features, perhaps Scandinavian. She put her arms protectively around Talithia. "I need to speak to you," she said softly, and gently drew the ancient mermaid away. Although reluctantly, Talithia allowed it. Grace watched suspiciously as the blonde whispered something to Talithia, and then returned to her place.

Talithia returned, no less angry, but it was clear she had other matters to consider now. "Come to me, Sandra."

Grace put her arm between Sandra and Talithia, keeping Sandra where she was. "Why?" she asked Talithia.

Talithia gave Grace a dangerously measured look before returning her attention to Sandra. "I'm not going to harm you. Even Grace knows that's impossible." She gave Grace a murderous glare though.

Regardless of the insult and the response Grace wanted to give, she let it pass. They really couldn't harm each other, at least not directly. Mermaids hardly acted with a hive mind, but they really were connected on an emotional level. She knew, without doubt, that Talithia wasn't about to try and hurt Sandra. Grace gave her daughter a slight nod, letting her pass.

"Relax," Talithia said as Sandra apprehensively swam forward, stopping just short of Talithia. The older mermaid reached out and placed clawed fingertips against Sandra's temples. Sandra stiffened at the touch, but allowed it.

The onlooking mermaids drifted forward slightly in anticipation, but Grace had no idea what to expect, and not knowing concerned her as much as Sandra's proximity to Talithia.

Talithia gently bent her head and touched her forehead to Sandra's. To outward appearances nothing happened. It didn't calm Grace, however. Sandra was her daughter, and she didn't trust Talithia. She'd emotionally tortured Maria for centuries and had shown she was capable of transferring her hatred to Grace and Sandra.

Despite Grace's concerns, they stayed like that for minutes, unmoving, and when Talithia raised her head Sandra seemed dazed.

"What happened?" Grace asked Sandra, pulling her back and holding her close.

"Memories," Sandra whispered. "Just memories. I'm okay."

Talithia's expression became dangerously cold, only now it didn't seem directed toward Grace or Sandra, which only gave Grace slight comfort. "Your turn," Talithia said to Grace.

Grace looked around the circle at her sisters, but neither saw or felt any sign of conflict or danger. "What is this? Mindreading?"

Talithia merely held her hands out, anger still in her eyes, but it no longer seemed to be focused on Grace. Considering Sandra seemed unharmed, Grace pushed her feelings of dread aside and complied. If it changed the outcome of the decisions the Council wanted to make, she was willing to try. She felt a slight pressure when Talithia placed her fingertips against her temples, and then their foreheads touched.

"Relax. Let it flow."

It took her a moment to comply with the command, and when she did the past few days flashed through her mind in a heartbeat. It took her a moment to realise Talithia's fingertips no longer pressed against her temples or that their foreheads no longer touched, but Sandra's arms were around her. Judging by the expressions of all the other mermaids, Grace suspected it had taken much longer than seconds.

Talithia drifted a few feet away, fear in her expression now. "That was… I must discuss this with our sisters." She turned and swam to the nearest mermaids. Several others, curiosity clear within their emotions, encircled Grace and Sandra.

"What's happening?" Sandra asked apprehensively.

"Our elders are convening," the albino said, looking Sandra over with pure curiosity. The others schooled around them with similar inquisitiveness.

"Who were you when you were human? Were you young or old when Grace changed you?" the Albino asked.

"Um-"

"Did you know Grace beforehand?" said another, a beautiful dark-haired Caucasian with the longest hair Grace had ever seen. It almost reached the tip of her translucent tail.

"Were you friends on land?" said a mermaid with long red hair and a greenish tinge to the tip of her tail. "How did it happen?"

"Where did you live on land? You sound Australian," said a mermaid with an Italian accent and tone eerily similar to Maria's. Grace had met her and the redhead years ago. Carmen. The redhead was known as Strawberry, though Grace didn't know her real name. Along with an American mermaid who went by the name of Tink who wasn't here, they lived off the north-east coast of Australia.

"What did you do as a human?" said another that Grace guessed was Egyptian. "I haven't been on land in decades. What's it like now?"

Grace raised her hands. "Please, not so many questions," she said as Sandra began pressing up against her, clearly overwhelmed. "She's new, remember?"

The mermaids stopped the barrage, some a little petulantly. "We're sorry," the albino said.

"Thank you," Grace said. "Are you okay Sandra?"

"Yeah." She looked at the mermaids surrounding her. "It's all so surreal. I keep thinking I'll wake up soon, a morphine drip in my arm and..." She took a deep calming breath, releasing it slowly as if she were still breathing air.

The albino took Sandra's hands before Grace could stop her. "We're just curious. There hasn't been a new mermaid since Grace, and we've been forbidden to approach her because of Maria.

"Forbidden?" Grace asked. "I didn't realise you were actually forbidden-"

"We were allowed to speak with you, but only when we chanced upon you while you were alone." She smiled at Sandra. "Which was rare."

"Sisters!" Talithia called.

The albino sighed, and with a flick of her tail shot back into her place in the circle. The others did the same.

"We've come to a decision," Talithia said. "Those who wish to vote independently may remain. Those who leave must designate their vote to another."

"Vote over what, exactly?" Grace asked.

Most of the mermaids scattered in all directions after touching Talithia's arm, signifying they trusted her with their vote. The albino, Carmen, Strawberry and a handful of others stayed. Grace wished she'd asked the albino's name.

"Why are they leaving?" Sandra asked. "Don't they want to cast their own votes or even hear what the vote is going to be for?"

"I left my mermaid behavioural manual at home," Grace muttered. They clearly trusted Talithia too much.

"I've got no idea what Josh sees in you," Sandra replied. "Honestly."

"I'm only sarcastic when I'm nervous. Or tense. Or uncertain. Or facing death." She squeezed Sandra's hand and got an answering squeeze in reply.

A stern glance from Talithia sent Grace's stomach into turns. "Everything's going to be fine," Grace lied, but something told her it wasn't.

Talithia smiled warmly at Sandra, but there was an edge to it that Grace didn't like. "We have decided to welcome Sandra as our sister. As I have the majority of votes, the decision is final. It wasn't your fault you became one of us, and neither was it your desire. You remain blameless." She came forward and pulled the newest mermaid into a hug, though Sandra remained stiff. "Welcome Sandra. We're not the family you had, but you'll grow to love us as much."

Somehow Grace doubted that.

"Um, thank you," Sandra said as she caught Grace's eyes. Grace wasn't sure what to say, so gave a brief nod despite the subtle feeling of dread she harboured. That seemed to be enough for Sandra.

Talithia released Sandra from the hug and moved back. Her smile disappeared as she turned her attention to Grace. "Grace, as you've broken the rules, you are forbidden to speak with Sandra or Maria. You shall remain in the deep with your other sisters and have no further contact with either."

"What?" Sandra cried.

Grace caught Sandra's hand protectively, anger rising. It was clear the vindictive streak hadn't abated. "You said this wasn't Sandra's fault, or Maria's! Why punish them for what I did?"

Anger returned to Talithia's face. "You're missing the point!"

"I understand the point! You're hurting Sandra and me, which will in turn hurt Maria." She glared Talithia down. "Well? What kind of a sister would do that?"

Talithia crossed her arms, eyes narrowed, but she refused to respond. "The punishment stands."

Grace had had enough. "You can shove your punishment. Cast us out if you wish, but the three of us don't need you. We have each other. Come on Sandra. Let's go."

Talithia and the remaining mermaids moved as one to prevent Grace from swimming off. "I haven't finished," Talithia said dangerously.

There was something in her tone that gave Grace pause, and she was sure it had nothing to do with Grace or Sandra. She needed to get to the bottom of it if she were to ever have a chance of unwinding the tangled emotions between Talithia and Maria. "What exactly did Maria do to you? What could be so terrible she's been shunned for hundreds of years, and even now you'd hurt me to hurt her? You've been waiting for an excuse for centuries, haven't you?"

Talithia glanced at the dozen or so mermaids remaining. After a long moment, one of them nodded. Talithia showed her canines in anger, clenching her fists, but finally spoke in a quiet voice. "She murdered my daughter."

Grace felt her heart twist with shock. Maria murdered a mermaid? "I don't believe you. That's impossible." She couldn't even conceive of violence against another mermaid.

"Maria was human at the time, so we made her a mermaid to ensure she understood exactly how we felt."

Grace's jaw dropped, and for a moment she was completely speechless. And then her anger returned. "Oh, great job. How'd that work out for you?"

Talithia pursed her lips. The anger was still there, but it was clear she regretted what had happened. "It was a mistake. We should have drowned her and been done with it, but I was so distraught..." She took a deep breath, slowly releasing it as if she were breathing air, not water. "Drowning wasn't good enough for her, so I made sure she would always know my pain."

Sandra gently gripped Grace's shoulders to lend her support. "That's cruel," Sandra said to Talithia. "You should be ashamed of yourself."

Talithia glared at Sandra, clearly annoyed she'd spoken. Talithia may have regretted turning Maria into a mermaid, but she certainly hadn't forgotten the feelings that led to it. There was a vindictiveness in her tone as she went on. "While Maria was still in the thrall of change we set her loose on her own human children. She drowned them all without even realising what she was doing, just as Sandra drowned three fishermen recently. Afterward we cast Maria from our midst and shunned her."

"You're horrid," Sandra whispered, echoing Grace's thoughts.

"And you don't understand yet. You will, eventually."

"How could a human even kill a mermaid?" Grace asked. "We're far too powerful…" and then she put the pieces together. Maria did it on land.

Talithia raised her chin. "It doesn't matter how. Maria murdered my daughter and I'll never forgive her."

Maria had mentioned the old days occasionally, but Grace had never connected it to the reason she was a mermaid. She closed her eyes, trying to visualise how everything fit together. "Your daughter went on land to entice a victim into the ocean, only it didn't go well for her, did it?"

"Maria is still to blame."

"Yet it's the risk every one of us takes when we leave the water." Grace couldn't hold back her anger. She met Talithia's eye with new understanding, but no sympathy. "You need to make peace with Maria before it destroys us all."

"Maria's-"

Grace cut her off. "I no longer recognise your authority Talithia. Shun us if you will, but there's nothing more you can you do to us."

Talithia motioned to their other sisters. They swam forward, surrounding her and Sandra. "Harm my daughter and you'll know true wrath," Grace said softly.

"Hold onto that anger Grace, you're going to need it."

"Let us go!" Did she dare try and fight through them? The two youngest, and probably weakest mermaids in all the ocean? What chance did they really have if it came to a struggle.

Talithia caught Grace by the throat, claws biting but not enough to pierce her skin. Despite her instincts to defend herself, Grace refused to sink to the same level.

"I'll forget this entire issue on one condition."

Grace met the South American beauty's eyes. She may not be able to harm either her or Sandra physically, but she had the numbers to do whatever else she liked. It was likely the best offer she was going to get if she ever hoped life would get back to normal. "What?"

"Tell her to shove it, Grace," Sandra said.

Grace gave Sandra a look and her daughter calmed down. "What are you offering Talithia?"

Talithia smiled wickedly. "Kill the succubus, Abbey, and make sure our secrets are safe. We can't permit threats to our kind. She knows too much already."

Grace hesitated, knowing it was most likely a suicide mission. "You want me to kill a succubus on land? Her turf, no less. Really? How?"

"I don't know yet, but I'll be coming with you to make sure it's done."

Grace stared at the ancient mermaid, shocked. Talithia was going to shadow her? "I hope you're packing your bazooka."

Talithia gave her an inquisitive look. "My what?"

[21]

"PLEASE," Sandra said. "I don't want you to leave me." She glanced at the other mermaids, all as unfamiliar to Sandra as they were to Grace, and Sandra couldn't yet feel their emotions. All she'd feel was the hurt of being forced apart when Grace left the ocean, the only person she knew she could trust. "They can't expect me to stay here. In the ocean. Alone."

Grace took Sandra's hands. "They can't force you to do anything Sandra, not really, but there are consequences if we defy them. We all share the world's oceans, and like the oceans, we're connected to each other. Until you can breathe air and follow, we need to…" To what? Comply? Like a couple of submissive slaves? Grace clenched her fists in frustration, her claws biting. "We need to try and stay on good terms. Conflicts can last centuries." She knew that for sure.

"It's cruel!" Sandra's face betrayed devastation.

Grace squeezed Sandra's hands in sympathy. "Once you begin to sense the presence of our sisters, you'll sense that they don't mean to hurt you. They just… there are old scores to settle and you and I are caught in them. Even so, I couldn't live without them now. I literally couldn't." It was like they were all part of a single organism, each as precious as any part of her own body despite the fact she'd like to punch Talithia in the face.

"Then why are they punishing me? I can't do this Grace. I really can't."

"I'll ask Carmen, Strawberry and Tink to stay with you. They're lovely. In a few weeks you'll start to develop a sense of our sisters, and that sense will grow stronger over the coming year. We'll all support you and love you no matter any differences, even Talithia. I'm pretty sure she'd give her life to save even Maria's, despite the fact she'd love to shove Maria under a bus if she could. It's how we are. Sisters always come first, even if we have issues. Even Maria and Talithia would rather put distance between each other than come into direct conflict. Let them love you first, and let yourself love them back. It's the first step."

Sandra closed her eyes. Grace knew what she wasn't saying. A year before she could see Josh, and in that time he would entirely forget what had happened to her. Sandra may have found a new family, but she couldn't sense that yet, and it would never quite replace her son and grandson. "A year before I can walk on land again."

"Puberty takes longer, but at least this time you won't have to do it alone."

Sandra sighed. "Okay, I'll try. Just don't take too long, and watch your back."

Grace smiled. "Despite our differences, I'd trust Talithia over Abbey any day." Grace drew Sandra into a hug, feeling for her. "I'll do everything I can, but at least succubi don't need to kill to draw lifeforce from a person. Some Creatures do, like dryads and us, but not succubi. If she wanted him dead she'd have killed him long ago."

Sandra seemed a little relieved. "I know this seems selfish, but I think I'm starting to develop separation anxiety."

Grace smiled. "I'm leaving my only daughter for the first time too. We're social creatures and incapable of surviving in true isolation. You're just starting to feel that."

Sandra looked away. "Is the bond between you and Maria really so strong? And the other mermaids?"

There was no way to explain it. "Why else would Talithia hold a grudge for three hundred years? It'd be like you losing Josh and Mikey, only worse. We're a part of each other." If Grace and Maria wanted some sort of peace between themselves and the other mermaids, Grace needed to do what Talithia wanted, at least for now. "Stay strong."

After organising Carmen to stay with Sandra, returning to Maria took longer than reaching the Council, mainly because Grace was so tired and didn't want to burn lifeforce to counteract it. It was close to evening when she arrived at her underwater home, and she dreaded the news she needed to break to Maria.

Grace found Maria asleep on her sandy bed, looking much better than she had a couple of days ago. She wanted to wake her but couldn't find the will. Grace settled in behind her and held Maria close, falling asleep.

It was well past dawn when Maria finally jerked awake in Grace's arms, waking Grace too. She seemed somewhat surprised to find Grace there. She produced a glorious smile at the sight of her sister and daughter, but something in Grace's mood must have told her everything wasn't as well as it seemed.

"They took her from you, didn't they?" Her big brown eyes expressed the hurt and pain Grace felt.

"Not quite."

"I thought they'd take you from me too."

"They almost did." She took a long, deep breath, struggling to ask the question she'd buried for days now. "I need to know… that you're okay now." She closed her eyes, remembering the impact of the car hitting Maria, and the consequences.

Maria looked away, clearly catching the intention. "I wouldn't do that to you again Grace."

"Promise?" she asked hopefully. Desperately.

After a moment's hesitation Maria conceded a small nod. "I promise. I really thought you'd be better off without me. I'm *so* sorry."

Grace grinned, changing the subject before they both cried. "So… Antonio, huh?"

Maria raised her eyebrows, a coy smile spreading across her lips. "Is it so hard to believe I once grew hair on my chest?"

"Eww! I should slap you for that." They were quiet for a long time, merely revelling in each other's company. Finally Grace found the courage to ask the question she wanted to know, despite the trepidation she felt. "What happened, Maria? I mean, I know what happened, but… Why? How?"

Maria's smile quickly disappeared. "If a human today discovered a mermaid was preying on their community, drowning friends and threating their family, what do you think the consequences would be?"

Grace closed her eyes. "I understand," she whispered. It was why they had to be so cautious when taking lives. Humans forgot quickly, but whatever caused that may not hold forever, particularly in the face of indisputable evidence which could be gained with current technology. "How about we go mete out some punishment to a certain red-headed succubus?"

Maria seemed relieved by the change in topic. "Deal. Anyone who threatens you threatens me."

"Threatens all of us," said a third voice.

Grace and Maria spun. Talithia floated at the entrance to their home, dark eyes watching them carefully. Her emotions were carefully controlled, otherwise Grace would have sensed her approach. Talithia glanced at Maria, and there was a coldness there that even three hundred years couldn't thaw. "Maria deserves everything she's been forced to endure."

"And so do you," Grace replied.

Talithia flinched as if slapped. It really was hurting her to hold onto her grudge. For a moment Grace thought Talithia might relent, at least a little, but then her face hardened again. "I should have drowned Maria while she was still human."

Maria narrowed her eyes. "I wish you had."

Hatred shattered Talithia's composure. "She was my sister!"

"And you murdered my family!"

Grace backed away as if punched, the emotions hurting her nearly as much as they seemed to hurt Talithia, but Maria moved forward as if she had nothing to lose. "For three centuries you've made me suffer, and I swear you'll ask for *my* forgiveness before I apologise to you."

Faces barely inches away, Talithia opened her hands, claws ready to strike. "I will never!"

"Please!" Grace cut in. "Neither of you can change the past. It's done."

The two of them glared at each other.

"Please," Grace whispered again, distressed more than she could convey. Their anger at each other felt physical. Despite their posturing she had no doubt they'd never come to blows, but the anger and resentment cut into her like thousands of paper cuts. "Please stop fighting."

Seeing the pain they were causing, Maria and Talithia backed away from each other.

"I'm sorry, Grace," Maria said.

"As am I."

Neither apologised to the other, however.

"Why are you here?" Maria coldly asked Talithia after an awkward silence.

It took Talithia a moment to gather herself and respond civilly. "Abbey. I'm here to ensure Grace ends the problem."

"We don't want your help," Maria said, moving close to Grace and putting an arm around her back. Maria's presence was comforting despite the hostile feelings coming from her, mostly because they weren't directed at Grace.

"You don't need my knowledge? My experience? My assistance? Shall I leave?"

"We do need it," Grace said before Maria could intervene. They really were in territory nether she or Maria understood well. "What do you know about succubi?"

"Are you begging for my assistance then?"

Begging? Grace bit back the response she wanted to deliver. "Any help you can offer would be appreciated."

"No," Maria said. "We're not."

Grace touched Maria's cheek. "What do you know about succubi, sis?"

Maria shrugged. "Not much, but it won't stop me figuring things out."

For Josh and Sandra's sake she had to get Maria and Talithia on terms where they could at least work together. "She has supernatural strength at night, can draw lifeforce without killing her victims, and can't enter homes without permission. That's about the sum of my knowledge," Grace said.

"Some Creatures are a hell of a lot harder to kill than we are," Talithia said. "They also integrate better into human society. All share our problems when it comes to making promises though. None except werewolves can enter homes uninvited, and werewolves can only do it in human form. There's a few other things you might like to know."

"I know you'd speak nicer to a vampire than to me," said Maria.

Talithia's expression changed to contempt. "Most vampires I've met are pretty nice people. None of them have killed any of my sisters, at least."

"They must have thought you were a harpy then."

[22]

IT WAS WELL past dawn when the three of them found a secluded place to emerge from the water, a craggy headland between wave washed rocks. Surfacing on a gentle swell a few dozen yards from shore, Grace studied a few fishing boats and a larger luxury yacht bobbing on the waves further out, but none of their occupants were paying attention and she couldn't see anyone on shore.

Grace gripped the stolen clothes she'd worn from the hospital and held them tightly as she darted into shore hidden within a wave, caught the rock with the sharp claws of her free hand as the wave receded, and forced the water to sheet from her body at the same time, transforming. As quickly as she could she scrambled up the crevice, and once safe from being dragged back into the ocean she focused on the water within her sopping clothes and forced it out of them, leaving her with a slightly damp skirt and blouse. They were horrible-looking clothes, but she put them on anyway.

"Hi there grandma," Maria said from behind her.

Grace raised an eyebrow. "Yet only one of us is likely to get arrested for indecency today."

Maria winced as she stood on a broken shell.

Talithia surfaced as the next wave washed her up, and as the water receded she got her legs underneath her and walked up, still entirely wet. Grace stared in shock. "How do you maintain form like that?"

"I'm old, Grace. We gain more control as we age." Her tone was patronising, and Grace felt like she'd just been bitch-slapped.

"I guess I'll need to steal some clothes for you both," she said.

"Shoes would be nice too," Maria said. "Ooh, and a burger, with wedges on the side. Don't forget the chilli sauce and sour cream to dip the wedges in."

She had to deny the urge to give Maria the finger. "Why don't you two braid each other's hair while I bring the ride around?"

They glared at each other, and in unison said, "She's not touching my hair."

Grace smiled wickedly to herself.

It was getting blowy as she got to the nearby beach, so there weren't too many people about. A handful of keen surfers were in the water, but there were few unattended piles of clothes she could pilfer from. She managed to steal a towel and a tiny, almost child-sized t-shirt and high-cut shorts, but that was it from the beach.

Maria, being small, took the clothes while Talithia was forced to wrap the towel around herself until they could find something better.

Talithia glanced at Grace's long skirt and blouse, and raised an eyebrow. "I think I prefer the towel."

Grace sighed. "I'm old enough to be a grandma, so I guess I shouldn't complain."

"You're only as old as the man you feel," Talithia said. "When was the last time you felt Maria? Oh yes, last night. How old are you, Maria?"

Maria glared. "That towel looks pretty loose. I hope it doesn't fall off in front of a cop. I'd hate to see you explaining your way out of an arrest."

"Please," Grace said, exasperated already. "Any idea where to start looking for Abbey?"

"Josh's house," Maria suggested.

"The hospital," Talithia ventured.

"The hospital? Good call, Talithia," Maria said with heavy sarcasm.

"Nobody will recognise us there. Unless, of course, they've seen the security footage of Grace kidnapping a nurse and a patient."

"Oh crap," Grace said. Footage would probably exist, and being a mermaid wouldn't make people forget the incident, only that she was a Creature if they saw something that didn't fit 'normal'. All they'd see would be a human girl, and that was hard to forget. "I'm probably wanted for murder as well as kidnapping, and a whole bunch of other offences." If it wasn't for Josh she'd return into the ocean for a few decades.

Maria's expression reflected her concern. "You need new clothes, and a haircut."

Grace felt herself go pale at the thought. She stroked her long sun-bleached locks. "No one's touching my hair."

"Tell that to the cops. Pixie cut, I think," Maria suggested.

"What?" Grace asked, horrified. "Why don't you just give me a nose-job while you're at it?"

"Perhaps a perm," Maria said, "And maybe some pink streaks."

Maria and Talithia looked at each other grinning, and then realised they were agreeing on something and glared in unison. They crossed their arms and turned to Grace. "We do need to do something with your clothes and hair. You're far too recognisable as you are," Talithia said.

"No one touches my hair," Grace said, putting her hands on her hips. The two of them stared back, challenging her. She'd lost the fight already, it seemed. "Let's go," she muttered.

Once they left the beach and entered the suburbs, they kept a close eye out for clothes drying on backyard clotheslines.

"That's a car," Maria said to Talithia. "They're like carriages, without the horses."

Talithia glared. "I'm not stupid. It's my job to make sure I know everything I can that's happening in the human world. I have three homes, two Ferraris and more computer equipment than you've probably ever seen."

Maria held Talithia's eyes for a long moment, then looked away. "Touché," she muttered.

Grace found a flowery two-piece bikini and short blue cotton skirt on a clothes line at one home, while two streets over Talithia stole a red summer dress that fit as if it had been made for her. It was a pity Grace didn't still have the sarong she'd stolen the other day. She really liked it.

"You look like a whore," Maria said to Talithia as they left the yard.

"Could be worse. I could look like a man."

Maria clenched her fists. "I dare you to say that again." Her voice was cold and flat, and the look in her eyes suggested she was a single breath away from clawing Talithia's eyes out.

"Please!" Grace interrupted, stepping between them. "How about you agree to not talk to each other? We can't fight like this." And not just because it would draw attention. They just… couldn't. It was eating Grace up from the inside.

"She started it," Maria said.

Grace turned on her. "Are you six years old?" Still, she was right. Of all the things Grace didn't need right now. "And no, you started it. Regardless Talithia, that *was* uncalled for."

Talithia's eyes went from Maria to Grace, and there must have been something in Grace's expression because Talithia looked away. Although she had a look that said she'd rather slit her own throat than apologise, she nodded. "You're right, Grace. I should never have said it. My apologies Maria."

Grace's feet were killing her by the time they arrived at Josh's house, her skin so roughed-up she wasn't sure why they weren't bleeding. Maria and Talithia weren't in any better shape, the softness of newly-created skin working against them all. Josh's house was closed up, no doors or windows open, and everything was locked. His car wasn't in the driveway either.

"Better to be sure it's empty," Grace said crossing the lawn to the porch. With Maria standing beside her, she knocked.

"Sounds… empty," Maria said. "I sense no fresh lifeforce around the place."

Grace concentrated and found the same absence.

Talithia moved up behind them. "If only we knew where the spare key was kept. Oh wait, we do." There was a pot plant beside the door, and after scraping away some of the chunky pine mulch on the near side, she held up a key. "Sandra invited me in and told me where the key was. How about you, Maria? You get an invite?"

A look from Grace stopped any comment.

Grace took the key and opened the door, entering. Her footsteps creaked on the bare wooden floor, but no answering response came from within. The house had a musty closed-up smell as if no one had been inside in a few days.

She turned to find both Maria and Talithia still on the porch, Maria looking incredibly annoyed, and Talithia surprised. "Coming?" Grace asked the South American beauty.

Talithia glanced at Maria, somewhat embarrassed. "No."

"Why not?"

"This is Josh's place now. I can't enter without his permission."

"Then why can I still enter?"

"He was living here when you got your invite. They're blood. It holds."

It sounded like a loophole to Grace, but she'd take it.

"See if you can find some hair dye," Maria said.

A chill turned her stomach at the thought. "You're kidding, right?"

"You want to be recognised? Go find some dye."

"I'd rather return to the ocean."

"Suits me," Maria said. "I already have more revenge standing at my side than I want."

"You think I'm here for revenge?" Grace asked with more than a little hurt.

"You've been a mermaid for over a century now Grace, and you can't help your nature, so yes, I think you want revenge on your daughter's behalf. It may not be a conscious decision, but anything that threatens you, me or any other mermaid is something that needs to be dealt with. That about what you're thinking?"

"No," Grace said. "Not exactly." But it really would be nice if she could put that nasty succubus in her place. An active volcano, for instance.

"Good then. Now, either you find some way to disguise yourself, or

I'm going to find a way to get in there, hold you down and cut your hair myself."

"Okay, okay!" As bad luck would have it, she found hair dye in the bathroom's cabinet, the edges of the mirror badly corroded under the glass. She held the packet up and felt her stomach sink. Black. She was going to look horrible. Like any mermaid, she loved her hair. It was a weakness they all seemed to share.

"This is going to take a while," she called as she read the instructions. "Why don't you two set up shop under the sprinkler out back?" She heard muttering, but they went through the side gate to the backyard. She glared at the dye pack as if just by willpower she could make it disappear. It was going to take forever to get it out of her hair.

She pressed her forehead against the mirror, already mourning her long, golden, sun-streaked locks. "If the first words Josh speaks to me are anything but how gorgeous I look after this, I'm going to make him eat the empty packet." She thumped the box on the basin and opened it, pulling out the protective gloves before staring at the detailed instructions in dismay. There was a whole page of steps to go through.

When she finally emerged from the house a couple of hours later, her hair dyed, washed and conditioned, she found Maria and Talithia sitting on hard plastic chairs in the shade under the house's sad-looking pergola. The corrugated plastic sheeting on the roof was yellowed and dirty with moss growing in patches, and the wood supporting it needed to be replaced in more than a few places.

Maria stared at Grace for several seconds, as if struggling to come up with something to say. "Oh merda," Maria said under her breath in Italian. "I mean, gorgeous," she added quickly with a rictus of a smile, but then her face split in a genuine grin. "The Goth look goes wonderfully with your peaches-and-cream skin."

More than a little hurt, Grace frowned. "This was your idea," she murmured. She ran her fingers through her horribly jet-black hair. Why couldn't there have been a shade of brown? Any shade of brown.

"You look like a vampire," Talithia added.

Grace clenched her fists.

"I hate to say it Grace, but you're going to have to find yourself a good dog collar and a bunch of nose rings. That's really horrible."

"Maria!" Grace said, shocked her sister would say something so mean. It made her feel strangely vulnerable. At least it wasn't red. Abbey would probably take it as a compliment.

Maria stood up and gave her a conciliatory hug. "I'm sorry," she said. "I'm just jealous. You're hair's darker than mine now."

"Maria," Grace whispered. "Please don't jest. It's my *hair*."

"Come on," Maria said gently. "I've always been jealous of your hair. So, why don't you go inside and grab some dark robes and blood capsules?"

Talithia looked just as self-satisfied. If there was one flaw common to all mermaids, it was vanity.

The doorbell rang.

All three stopped talking. Grace turned toward the house with a brand new feeling of dread. What if it was Abbey, with a gun? Worse, what if she'd somehow made Josh invite her in? They were a long way from the ocean.

"Don't answer it," Maria said.

"Hello!" a male voice called out. "Josh?"

"It must be one of his friends," Talithia said softly. "Perhaps he'll go away."

"I know someone's home," the male voice called again. "The front door's open."

Maria grabbed Grace's hand. "C'mon. Let's run for it."

"Where?" Grace asked. "Over the fence?" They all glanced at the back fence. It was taller than any of them and made of cream-coloured metal. There was no telling what was on the other side.

"I doubt we could sneak out the front without being noticed," Talithia said.

The doorbell rang again. "C'mon Josh! Open up. Is everything all right?"

"Better do something," Maria said. "Go tell him you're busy having sex. That should convince him to come back later."

"What?" Grace asked. "Don't be rude."

"Then make something up! We can't enter the house. You'll have to do it."

"Fine." She went to the front door to find a young man about Josh's age and height standing outside the screen door. He wore a faded yellow t-shirt and shorts, and his hair was a little too long, but like Josh it suited him.

She stopped at the screen door. "What do you want?" she asked the guy. "We're busy."

He looked her up and down, eyebrows raised in surprise. "Who are you?"

"Would you mind going away please?" Grace said, intentionally keeping her voice low. With a deep flush she took Maria's advice. "Josh's about to go for a shower and I'm hoping to get lucky while he's in there." Even though standards were different these days, she still felt awkward saying it.

The young man stared as if he couldn't believe what he'd just heard. "You, um, I mean, Josh is..."

"Josh is going for a shower, yes," Grace repeated. "Were you hoping to join us?"

He almost backed away at that. "No! No. I just, I need to talk to him."

"I'll pass on a message. What is it?"

He eyed her without any trust whatsoever. Smart guy. "I think I should tell him myself."

Before she could stop him, he pulled open the screen door and stepped through. Grace backed up, wishing she'd had the foresight to lock the door. It'd been a century since she'd had one of her own, but still.

"Excuse me!" she managed to say, only just realising just how big he was. Like Josh, he was a little over six foot tall, although more wiry. "Get out!"

He ignored her. "Josh!" he called. "Josh?" He shoved past her and stomped down the hallway toward the bathroom. "Josh?"

Grace backed toward the kitchen and rear door. Like many old houses, the back door had once been through the laundry, but an internal modification at some point had added another exit via a glass sliding door in the meals area.

"He's not here!" the young man called in annoyance, an edge to his tone suggesting he knew something wasn't right.

"Oh crap," Grace muttered. She turned and ran, darted into the meals area and tumbled over a chair. She hit the floor with enough impact to bruise her hip and elbows. She clambered to her feet, but the guy grabbed her from behind and shoved her against the wall.

"What's going on? Who are you and where's Josh?" He held her by the shoulders.

"You're hurting me!" she cried just as Maria and Talithia stopped outside the door, powerless to enter.

He noticed them. "Who the hell are you two?" he asked. "I'm calling the cops."

[23]

"GET THE HOSE," Maria yelled at Talithia, who darted away.

The guy wasn't stupid. While holding Grace with one hand, he grabbed the sliding door's handle and shoved it closed, flicking the lock. Maria banged uselessly on the toughened glass, but even if she'd been strong enough to break it there was no way she could enter.

Grace used the moment of distraction to try and get away, but he held on tight, his fingers digging painfully into her shoulder. He twisted her around and shoved her hard against the wall again, thumping the back of her head far too hard. She felt her legs give way, but he held her up.

"Are you here to steal stuff? Where's Josh and Sandra?"

It took her a moment to get her feet back under her while she blinked him back into focus. "I don't know." The back of her head hurt.

"What are you doing here then?"

"I'm looking for him too! I'm a friend."

He leaned in close, pinning her tight. "I've been friends with Josh since our first day of school, and I've never seen you. The cops came to my place last night asking all sorts of questions." He fingered her newly-dyed black hair, his eyes narrowing. He pulled his phone out with his free hand. "I'm calling the cops."

"No! Please don't! You'll put Josh in even more danger."

"Where's Josh? What have you done with him?"

Talithia stopped outside the door beside Maria, the hose in her hand gushing water. With that water they could do some serious damage, regardless of whether they were stuck outside the house. This kid was in a lot more trouble than he understood. Afraid for him more than herself now, Grace put her hand out toward her sisters, telling them to stop. Talithia already had a hand in the water, but she hesitated. Despite Grace and Maria's issues with Talithia, the mermaid would kill the kid without remorse if she thought Grace was in danger, and that would lead to more complications.

"Let me go and I'll explain it all. I promise." Oh crap. She shouldn't have said that. How could she have been so stupid to make a promise again? She felt it bind her to her word. If he released her she'd have no choice.

Some of the fury went out of his expression, but he held her pinned for a few more seconds before removing his hands from her shoulders. He looked out the glass door and frowned. "Do your friends think I'm the Wicked Witch of the West?"

"Just don't provoke them. I'm serious. Touch me again and they'll kill you. They really will."

He frowned. "With a squirt of water? Are you stupid?"

"Please, you've got no idea how much danger you're in."

"From two girls locked out side with a hose?"

"I need to show you something, okay? Please. Let me go to the sink." Cautiously, he released her, shadowing her to the sink.

"Holy shit!" he said a minute later as she formed water into the shape of a mermaid and froze it solid. "How did you do that?"

"Here," she said, holding out the ice. "Take it."

He backed another half step. "I don't think so."

At least he had enough intelligence to be scared. "What you need to think about right now is that my sisters are outside and have access to a whole lot of water, and they're a lot more powerful and experienced than I am. If you threaten me again they will kill you. They really will.

Understand?" She hoped he did, because she really didn't want to see him dead.

He glanced at the glass door and back, but his expression was still uncertain.

"You're obviously a nice guy just looking out for a friend, but that won't matter to them if they believe I'm in danger. Can we agree on that?"

He glanced at the hose still bubbling water onto the ground. "Ah, yeah. Okay."

"How about we sit down at the table and have a chat?"

"I don't think so." He took a step toward the front door.

She moved forward, reaching out but not touching. He hesitated, obviously seeing the move as a threat. "Please don't run," she said. "If you run they'll assume you're going for help. Please, sit down at the table and we'll talk. That's all. Josh is in trouble and we need to help him. Do you want to help Josh or not?"

He glanced nervously at the water still running out of the tap and into the sink, and then at Talithia and Maria and the growing puddle under their feet. "How about you tell your friends to turn the tap off. Then we'll talk."

"They won't. Not while there's any risk to me. How about I turn the sink tap off and we'll talk here?"

He glanced at the water again. "Okay. Sure." She noticed his hands were shaking as he crossed his arms over his chest.

"What's your name?" she asked as she turned the tap off. "I'm Grace. Grace, Harpeden."

"Harpeden?" he asked, a single eyebrow raised. "Really?"

"Really," she said. "No relation to Josh though."

He stared at her, obviously wondering what to believe. "How'd you do that trick with the ice?" he asked.

"Would you like to see it again?"

His face paled. "No."

If she could convince him not to run to the police they had a better chance of helping Josh. "So, you going to tell me your name?"

"Rick."

"Okay, Rick, I'm going to tell you a secret. Are you ready for it?"

He nodded, though he didn't look like he wanted to hear it.

"I'm not human, Rick. And neither are my two sisters out there."

He seemed to take it at face value. "So what are you then? Water sprites?"

It caught her by surprise and she almost laughed. "Close. Let's just say that there's more than one type of magical Creature in the world, and I'm the kind that likes water. I could make water dance on the counter if you like."

He looked slightly more nervous. "Thanks, but no. What's this got to do with Josh?"

"Another magical Creature has taken him."

"Why?"

She wasn't sure exactly how to answer that one. "Because Sandra is now our sister, and sisters look out for each other. They'll know we'll come for him."

His expression dropped at Sandra's name, like it hurt him nearly as much as it hurt Josh. He'd probably known Sandra his entire life, so it was reasonable. "Sandra has cancer. She's dying."

"No longer. Sandra's alive and healthy and she'll never get sick again. Josh, however, is in a lot of danger."

He kept glancing through the glass door, at the water still flowing freely. Both Talithia and Maria glared at him, neither softening their expressions. "Let's pretend I believe you."

Pretend? She could see he believed her. He just didn't want to admit it. "Do you know Abbey?"

"Psycho Abbey? Yeah. There's something about her that's not quite..." he trailed off, focusing on Grace's eyes. "She's like you, isn't she?"

Grace grimaced, but tried to look as friendly as possible. "She's not human, if that's what you mean."

"So what is she then?"

"You really want to know?"

He stared at her for such a long time she wasn't sure he was going to answer. He eventually nodded.

"She's a succubus."

He stared blankly. "Like a vampire?"

"No. What do you know about her?"

"Not much. We met her a few months ago. She's been hanging around ever since. Every now and again Josh and Abbey will disappear for a day or two, but then they'd be back pretending they were never gone." He frowned at Grace. "If Abbey's a vampire, what are you?"

"Abbey's a succubus, not a vampire. I'm a mermaid," she said, the compulsion from her promise making her say it before she could think to say anything else. She felt slightly hurt when he looked disappointed. She supposed in popular culture almost every magical Creature was way cooler than mermaids. Even Aquaman had been considered lame until Jason Mamoa's version gave him a new look. "You going to help me find Josh?" she asked.

He gave her a steady look as if considering it, but not sure whether to commit. "What does Abbey want with Josh? Is she going to kill him?"

She shook her head. "Succubi don't kill. I mean it's unlikely as they don't need to kill to survive. I don't know what she's after though. Perhaps she's got a crush on him." Nothing else made sense. Regardless of anything else Abbey might want, she was fairly sure that was part of it.

He looked worried. "So he's a succubus now?"

"Incubus. And no. Well, hopefully not. I doubt making more of her kind is as easy as a werewolf's bite." She needed to kill this conversation and get on with finding Josh.

"Werewolves," he repeated staring at her as if she'd said something even crazier than before. "So if she doesn't want to kill him or make him into a succubus, then she must want something else, right? Why Josh? Couldn't she get what she needs from anyone?"

She'd been grappling with the same question. "Probably."

"And mermaids? What do your kind want?"

The conversation was getting into dangerous ground. "To be left alone, mostly."

"So mermaids are... nice then? You don't... hurt people?" He glanced at Maria and Talithia who were watching quietly, the hose still bubbling water with muffled splashing sounds through the glass door. Judging by his expression, the water took on a whole new meaning, and rightly so.

"Not by choice. How about we focus on helping Josh?"

A frown crossed his face. "The nurse who drowned in the bath at the hospital? Was that one of you?"

Reluctantly, Grace nodded. "Me," she whispered, feeling her face flush with guilt and regret. A completely innocent woman who probably had a couple of decades of life left. She desperately caught his hands, holding tight. "It was an accident."

"You accidentally murdered someone?"

"Yes." Memories rushed back, memories she wished she didn't have. "I was badly hurt. I didn't even know I'd drowned her until afterward."

"She was my great aunty." The words were soft, but unforgiving.

Grace's stomach knotted. "Rick, I'm so sorry. I never intended to hurt her. She was in the wrong place at the wrong time and I was so banged up…"

He sighed, his expression still flat. "I heard she was a good nurse, but she hated children, probably because she couldn't have any herself. She might have been my aunty, but she was always nasty to me."

So… what did that mean? "Once it's dark Abbey will be gorilla strong. In the daytime though, she's pretty much human. Do you have any idea where she might be?"

He shook his head. "She turns up randomly. I've never seen her place, only that red car of hers."

"What about her two friends? Any idea where they live?"

"None. I've seen her at pubs and the beach, but only when Josh is about. Frigging stalker. I think the first time we met her was at the hospital. Josh was taking Sandra in for a check-up."

"The hospital." It was their only lead and full of Abbey's allies. Grace might have slipped their notice before, but she doubted she'd be able to sneak around without drawing attention this time. "I bumped into her there too."

"She after blood?" Rick asked.

She gave him a look at the fixation on vampires. "No, but we need to check it out."

She moved, but he stepped in her way. Both Maria and Talithia tensed dangerously. Grace held up her hand, forestalling any action. "Getting in my way looks threatening, probably not a good idea Rick."

He followed her gaze, paled and immediately stepped back. "I was just going to say that the hospital's probably a bad plan. The police are looking for you."

"They're looking for a girl with sun-streaked, light-coloured hair."

He frowned at her as if she were an idiot. "Are you really that naive? You stand out even more now. It doesn't look the least bit natural."

She tried not to react. She didn't like the colour either, but there was little she could do about it. "People won't recognise me. Do you?"

"I've never met you before. With hair that dark and long though, you'll stand out. Maybe if you cut it-"

She backed a step, heart racing at the thought. "Nobody touches my hair," she said. "Not ever. No way. Never going to happen." Not even if it meant she could walk around the hospital without being noticed. She'd rather drown a shipload of people than cut her hair. Okay, maybe one or two people. One. Definitely one.

$$[\ 24\ ]$$

GRACE FELT sick as she held the small mirror up before her. The glass door to the house was open now, but Maria and Talithia were still forced to remain outside. Talithia had turned the tap off, at least.

Neither of them seemed to be able to look Grace in the eyes.

Her hair was horribly black and short. Devastation pulled at her heart. Surely Sandra's happiness wasn't worth what she'd done to her hair. She'd understand, wouldn't she? Josh couldn't mean more to her than Grace's hair? She had to force down the need to vomit. "My hair," she whispered as if her distress wasn't apparent, fingering what was left.

Her neck felt cool and her head too light. It was horrible. Every time she turned, nothing happened. No gentle pull as her hair moved across her shoulders and back. Only a gentle tickle across her forehead and eyebrows and the back of her neck. Thanks to Rick she had a thick fringe now, almost long enough to reach her eyes.

She glanced at her sisters. Maria and Talithia both looked away as if their necks were synchronised. Even Rick, who still held the scissors, was wise enough to keep silent. "Not one word," she said through the back door.

Grace figured it must be biological. Long hair appealed to men of any age, making it very handy when trying to lure a guy into the water. Whatever it was about her hair, she'd inherited some sort of biological response to wanting it long and sun-kissed.

Her exposed neck, combined with the black hair, made her look like a Goth giraffe. She felt naked in a way she hadn't for a century. "What have I done?" she whispered, pulling a short strand through her fingers. It quickly slipped free and fell back. It would take years to regrow.

"I think it looks good," Rick said.

She glanced at him in horror, but he genuinely seemed to like his handiwork. "It feels wrong," Grace whispered. A couple of unnaturally dark strands Rick had missed fell across her eyes and tickled her nose. "I'm going to have to kill myself." She was breathing fast, as if something constricted her chest. She glanced at Maria. "Tell me it's not so bad."

Maria tried to smile encouragingly. "It looks great," she said, gritting her teeth in her best attempt at an encouraging smile, and failing. Talithia's expression was as devastated as Grace felt.

Grace covered her face with her hands. "I want to die."

It was just hair. It would grow back. And yet, she really did want to go and hide at the bottom of the ocean for the next decade or ten. She felt her cheeks flush at the thought of other mermaids seeing her like this. Even Sandra would feel ashamed to have her as a mother and sister, looking like this.

"Nothing's worth that," Talithia said. "You should never have done this."

"What is it about you lot and hair?" Rick asked, genuinely puzzled.

Grace looked to Maria for support, but Maria held up her hands. "I'm happy to give Josh and our secrets up and call it even."

And have her daughter hate her for abandoning her son? "No. We have to get to the hospital. The day's half gone already."

Grace took the scissors and brush from Rick and with trembling hands found the courage to snip away the strands he'd missed. She stomped off to the bathroom to get a better look in the big mirror. She wished she hadn't. Straight, black and obviously unnatural, she looked like a poster-girl for a vampire movie.

"Grace?" Rick stood just outside the bathroom, apparently uncertain whether to come in or protect himself from abuse. The room was small, but that didn't seem to be the issue. "This really is a big deal for you, isn't? The hair, I mean?"

She nodded, so close to crying it was ridiculous.

"You know, Sandra had a really nice leather jacket that'd go well with that haircut. Why don't you put some makeup on while I go see if I can find it?" He didn't wait for a reply, but turned and left.

She stared at herself in the mirror. The haircut really did cry out for accompanying makeup. Problem was, she hadn't worn makeup in a century. She couldn't guess what half of Sandra's makeup was for.

When Rick returned, he held not only a cropped leather jacket, but a short black leather skirt and some strappy sandals that looked like they might fit. "I feel like a thief," he said. "But I guess Sandra's not returning for them, is she?" He held the skirt up. "I doubt she's worn this in years anyway.

Grace shook her head. "Even if she could return for clothes, it would be a year from now."

Rick put the clothes on the side of the bath. "I'll leave you to it."

"Wait a sec," she said. "I know this is a long shot, but do you know anything about makeup?"

He studied her face for a moment before coming to the right conclusion. "Not much call for it in the deep blue, is there?"

She shook her head. "It's not like I have an office job."

"My mother was in a car accident a few years ago and badly hurt her neck. My sister had already married and had moved out, and Dad… never mind. Mum couldn't do much for herself for a while, still can't do what she used to do, and though my sister helps as much as she can she's got two kids and a job. I help Mum do everything, sometimes even her makeup when she's having a bad day."

Grace looked down, thinking about how Maria and Talithia had come so very close to killing him. She couldn't imagine the consequences that would have caused, or how many other lives she'd damaged in similar ways. "Would you mind helping me?" she asked. "I'd really appreciate it."

"Sure," he said. "Do you have a particular clown face you like?"

She narrowed her eyes. "I will seriously drown you if you try," she said, but made sure she was smiling so he knew she wasn't serious. Well, not all that serious. Maybe she'd just hold him under for a while. Several times, until he begged.

"Here," he said, and began rummaging through the makeup drawer. "I'll make you look like you just walked out of a photo shoot. I promise."

"There's plenty of women on magazine covers I wouldn't want to emulate."

"You want to look hot, or what?" He raised an eyebrow.

"Hot, as in a teenage boy's wet dream?"

He shrugged. "I'm sure there's a few older men who'd also appreciate that look."

"Just… make it fit with the hair."

It took about fifteen minutes, but the change was so dramatic she didn't recognise herself. And he was right, once dressed in the leather jacket and skirt she really did look like she was ready to shoot a magazine cover. It was the heavy eye liner that did it, she decided. That and the cherry-red lipstick. She wasn't sure whether to feel impressed or shocked at her own appearance. She doubted even Maria would recognise her.

"My sisters are going to laugh their…" she hesitated. "Bits off," she finished lamely. The beach babe she knew was totally gone, replaced with an urban assassin who carried several guns under her jacket along with some high-kicking moves. Grace wouldn't look at all out of place in a Ferrari or a penthouse now.

"Only one way to find out." He handed her a small black leather handbag after putting some of the makeup he'd used into it. "Maintenance."

"Thanks. I can handle the lipstick and eyeliner." She'd watched everything he did via the mirror and was reasonably confident she could replicate most of what he'd done.

She nervously followed him out into the dining room. Both her sisters were comfortably seated in their plastic chairs outside, but it was the body language that caught Grace's attention. Both stiffened and sat up straighter, staring.

"Holy crap!" Maria finally whispered. "I wouldn't recognise you if we butted heads. You look awesome!"

Grace paused, uncertain. "Really?"

"Oh yeah," said Talithia. "You've no idea."

She offered them a tentative smile. "You really like it?"

"Hate it," said Maria. "It's not you at all, but you do look awesome. You're about the hottest thing on the planet right now." She looked at Rick. "Good job. Better than the dye-wreck she was. How'd you like to help *me* with some makeup?" She gave him a smile that made Grace thoroughly nervous.

Grace cleared her throat. "Another day. Let's go."

"What's the plan?" Maria asked. "Storm the castle walls and hope for the best? I don't suppose you've got a big water tank in your pocket?" she asked Rick.

He stared at her as if he couldn't tell if she was serious.

"Shank's pony for now," Grace said. "Plan on the way." Finding water at the hospital shouldn't be a problem, and with water they were nearly invincible.

THEY WERE hot and tired by the time they made it to the hospital, though only Rick was sweating. He wasn't in the best shape, unlike Josh and the other guys she'd seen at the beach.

"Are you sure no one will recognise me?" Grace asked.

"They'd be more likely to recognise me," Maria said.

"I think I'll be fine," Talithia said sarcastically. "We go in, look around, and get out as soon as we can. No one's expecting us, and no one will recognise us as anything other than Creatures, and perhaps not even then. We're here to find Abbey. That's all."

"They'll still be expecting us," Grace said. "Abbey would have said something. Our only advantage is anonymity. And plumbing, but that means finding a tap to turn on." If only they could control water without having to touch it. "We'll follow them to Josh."

"Josh is not my concern," Talithia said. "Keeping our secrets is."

Grace glared at the older mermaid, but Talithia stared back flatly, without compromise.

"How do we follow them?" Rick asked. "We don't have a car."

Grace broke her stare-off with Talithia. "Taxi?"

He gave her a long look. "I could call a friend and have him pick us up, I guess."

It was much cooler inside, but as refreshing as it was, Grace still felt nervous. People stared as her. She was attracting notice for all the wrong reasons now.

"Stop fidgeting," Maria said.

"Everyone's looking at me."

"Only the guys and their jealous wives. Hey, that rhymed!" Maria grinned.

"Ugh," Talithia said, pushing past them both.

If Grace got recognised she'd be a dead body in a police cell by tomorrow night. Despite their assurances, she still felt nervous.

"Why don't we split up?" Maria said. "Cover more ground?"

"Have you never seen a horror movie?" Rick asked.

"I don't like scary movies," Maria said.

Rick rolled his eyes. "Splitting up's the worst thing we could do."

Talithia shrugged. "Hospitals get lots of visitors. We're visitors."

"And this isn't a haunted house," Maria added. "Just avoid going through any doors that say *Secret Lair*."

"It's mid-afternoon already," Grace said, feeling the stress of inactivity. The longer they talked the more likely they were to attract attention. "We need to find Abbey before it gets dark and she gets much stronger. How about I go with Maria?" Grace suggested, pointing to a corridor. "We'll search physio and rehabilitation. You two go down there and we'll meet in the cafeteria in fifteen minutes. Rick, I assume you remember what Abbey looks like?"

"A big ego with a 'full-of-herself' complex?" he asked dryly.

Maria smiled. "I like him."

Grace sighed, too nervous to appreciate the humour. "Don't go near Abbey or her friends, and try not to be noticed. Last time we met she tried to shoot me."

Rick's jaw dropped. "What? You never said anything about guns."

"Go home if you like." It came out harsher than she'd intended. "I'm sorry, that was rude. I meant… I just don't want to see you get hurt and this isn't your fight. No obligations."

Rick shook his head. "Whatever. If I'm going to get shot, a hospital's about the best place it could happen."

After three full searches of the hospital and more time in the cafeteria than any of them liked, they'd found no leads, and evening was approaching. Grace's feet were aching by the time she returned to the cafeteria with Maria the fourth time, the place now closed for business.

"Hungry?" Maria asked. "I could really chow down on a flounder about now. Let's go back to the ocean," she said hopefully.

Grace glanced at the clock above the shuttered canteen. "Shouldn't Talithia and Rick be back?"

"Which section were they checking?"

"Maternity wing. Isn't all that big."

"Give them a few more minutes. With luck, Talithia will have been mistaken for an expectant mother and been forced to watch gory videos of babies being born."

"No. Something's wrong." Grace took Maria's hand. "This place is full of Creatures. We made a mistake in coming here. Come on."

They made their way to the maternity ward and dodged a sleep-deprived new mother who was walking the corridors and trying to get her newborn crying baby to sleep in an ancient-looking pram. The pram had probably done the rounds of the maternity wing for a generation. Catching a glimpse of the crying baby's face in the pram brought on the familiar pangs of regret. Red-faced and looking like the babe still needed its first bath, the young mother didn't seem to know what to do next and the nurses weren't offering any assistance.

Where would her descendants be now if she'd had them?

"Come on!" Maria said, tugging on Grace's hand. "They're not handing out babies tonight."

They did a lap of the maternity wing with no success, returned to the empty cafeteria and found it still empty.

"I know it's a cliché, but I've got a horrible feeling right now," Grace said.

"Let's talk to a nurse. Someone's got to have seen them."

Maria all but dragged Grace to the nurse's station. "Excuse me," Maria asked, "But have you seen a tall guy, about twenty, bit overweight, and a girl with long dark hair? South American looks."

The nurse smiled. "Yes. They were with Catherina."

"The young nurse?" Grace asked, her stomach churning. Catherina was a Creature. Vampires were rife in many hospitals, so there was a good chance she was one. "Any idea where she was heading?"

"She was restocking our supplies earlier. Catherina needed some fresh towels. Perhaps your friends offered to help?"

Grace and Maria locked eyes, a feeling of dread passing between them.

"Thanks," said Maria. "Which way?"

The nurse pointed.

"Trap?" Maria asked once they'd gotten better directions.

Grace nodded. "We need a plan."

[25]

"THIS IS A STUPID PLAN," Maria said. "Abbey will shoot us before we can get close enough to do anything with this little bit of water."

They stood in the overly-clean ladies toilets holding large disposable soft-drink cups filled with water.

"Well, I'm out of ideas," Grace said. "It's not like we can bring the ocean to us, and we can't bust open the walls and wreck the plumbing."

"Well this is hardly going to help."

"You haven't come up with any other ideas, so unless you fancy running down to the nearest knife shop, stealing some weapons and coming back all army-style, this is it." She held up her drink cup. That, or admit defeat and go back to the ocean without Talithia, something neither she nor Maria were capable of despite all their differences.

"There's barely enough to drown a rat," Maria muttered, her dark mood showing on her face. "The best I could do is freeze it and thump Abbey over the head. I couldn't even use it to chill her temper. She's a *succubus*, Grace, and it's dusk. She's at least ten times stronger than us now and mostly invulnerable to any mundane weapons. What good is a cup of water going to do us?"

"I don't know!" Grace felt her protests splitting like a paper bag full of mud. "It's not like we can… fire hoses." She glanced about, and then at the roof. "Or we could set off the sprinkler system." There wasn't one in the bathroom, but that didn't mean the rest of the building wouldn't be protected that way.

Maria shook he head. "We don't even know if there's a fire sprinkler system in the basement, and even if there was we'd be hard pressed not to transform and flop around like beached fish."

"But-"

Maria wrapped an arm around Grace's shoulders, though being half a head shorter it was mostly around her back. "Hey, we're not here looking for a fight. We're here to find Josh and Rick and go home."

"Talithia's looking for a fight."

"And I'm happy to leave her to it."

Grace pulled away. "We'll find a fire hose." She picked up her cup of water and straightened her shoulders. A little bit of water was better than none until she found something better. "Unless you've got a better idea, let's go."

"Scalpels!" Maria said. "This is a hospital. There's got to be scalpels and all sorts of nasty things."

The thought of threatening someone with a scalpel had about as much appeal as getting shot at.

"What about the morgue? There'd be power tools there. Cordless." Maria looked surprisingly enthusiastic about hunting a succubus with a drill.

"You want to attack her with a cordless power tool?"

"Maybe she's vulnerable to blood loss?"

Grace gave her a look. "She's got a gun. And besides, she's stronger and faster than us. She'd just take our weapons and use them on us. At least water can't harm us."

Maria shook her head. "Then we need more. Fire hose it is unless you want to wait until dawn and mess up her advantage."

"That's too long."

Maria's mood seemed to darken further. "If it wasn't for Rick, I'd gift-wrap Talithia and personally hand her over to Abbey with some very specific instructions."

Grace gave her a look. "No you wouldn't."

"Oh come on. She hates me!"

"You killed her sister. What do you expect?"

"She murdered my family, yet you expect me to forgive her?"

They both had points. "Maybe you need to forgive each other."

Maria pursed her lips. "And maybe she could drive a scalpel into her own eye while I eat popcorn."

Grace put a hand on Maria's shoulder. "Not now," Grace said.

Maria met Grace's eyes. "She isolated me from all our sisters. Half the reason I walked in front of that car is because I know that no matter how much she hates me, losing any of us would hurt her. The thought of her suffering because of my death... well, it was appealing in a petulant way."

Grace caught Maria's chin with a fingertip and tilted her face up until they were looking at each other. "Even if I were to walk away, you'd still try to save Talithia alone, wouldn't you? Admit it."

Maria sighed. "You know I would. I'd hate it, but I would."

"And you know she'd do the same for you, just as she's here for me and Sandra right now, even if she's using other excuses. You need to end this feud, Maria. It's hurting everyone. Do whatever it takes."

Maria took a deep non-committal breath, releasing it slowly. She dumped the cup in the sink. "Let's not be stupid and rush into whatever trap they've planned for us. We need go back to the ocean and get help. Let's see them deal with a hundred mermaids and a dozen fire hoses."

Grace glanced at her cup of water. "Okay. We go back, call for help, and come up with a real plan."

"Deal," Grace said. It was their best chance to help Talithia, Josh and Rick.

She opened the toilet door and found Abbey standing there.

She never saw the punch, but she felt it as her head snapped back. She hit the ground hard.

"Maria?" she whispered, struggling to get up, but another blow knocked her flat.

GRACE WOKE TO A HEADACHE, something she hadn't experienced in a century or more except for her previous hospital stay. Her nose hurt from being hit, and she couldn't move her arms or legs.

She tried to swallow and realised her mouth was stuffed with a rag held in place with tape. She found Maria on a gurney beside her, her wrists roped to side rails, her ankles tied together and half a dozen lengths of rope holding her to the gurney.

She struggled with her own bonds as she realised their predicament. Not ready to give up, Grace strained, but couldn't get any slack from the ropes. "Hmph!" she called to Maria. "Hmmmph!"

Maria opened her eyes, but it took her a moment to focus. When she found herself bound to the gurney she panicked and struggled.

After thrashing futilely, Maria dropped her head back against the metal gurney, breathing hard through her nose as she stared at the roof. When she turned her head and met Grace's eyes, she moaned.

They were in a musty, windowless room. The only door was to just past Maria's feet, and it was solid-looking with a dead bolt to lock it, but only a flimsy handle to pull it open. The handle would break long before the deadbolt gave.

Cursing the gag, she considered her options. She'd been out of the water for a long time, maybe a full day. She could feel it, though her body wasn't desperate to return to the water yet. It was probably after dawn, which gave her until sunset to get back to the ocean.

A key slid into the dead bolt and turned before the door opened inward. Grace stiffened and tried to see, expecting Abbey or one of her psychotic cronies. Instead, the nurse they'd spoken to from the maternity ward last night walked in, her eyes widening at the sight of them.

"Oh my!" she said in shock. She immediately came over and removed the gag from Maria's mouth. "Are you okay?"

"No! Get us out of here."

The nurse hurried around Maria and removed Grace's gag out of her mouth, and then pulled uselessly at the ropes. "Who did this to you?"

"Genie?" someone called from the corridor outside. "You okay?"

"In here Catherina!" Genie called, and a moment later the young nurse came in.

Oh crap. Catherina stared at Maria and Grace. "Genie! What have you done?"

Genie spun, shock and anger on her face. "I found them here you silly girl! Help me get them out or go and get help. I'll see if I can find a knife to cut the ropes."

Catherina took a couple of steps into the room and punched Genie in the face. With a startled noise the older nurse fell back, hitting the ground without trying to break her fall. She didn't move.

That punch had been far too strong for a human girl Catherina's size. Catherina put her hands on her hips and stared at Maria. "Mermaids, huh?" She looked over Grace's face. "Can't say I know much about mermaids. You keep to yourselves pretty well."

A sickly feeling came over Grace. "What did you do to Talithia?"

"Let us go," Maria said, straining at the ropes.

"You know what, I'm actually inclined to do that," Catherina said. "Your flesh smells like salted shit, truly horrible, so you're otherwise useless to me. I really don't want the hassle of disposing of your bodies either."

"We're good with that," Maria said, still struggling with her ropes.

"Whatever scam or gig you've got here, we don't care," Grace added a little desperately. "Let us all go and we'll call it even."

"Scam?" Catherina asked with disdain. "No scam, just convenience. Most hospitals are riddled with vampires, but not this one. We play the middle role in supplying the local population, which takes the hassle out of it for the vamps and we get the body parts uncontested. You've got no idea how much good flesh and blood would get wasted without Creatures."

"Great," Maria said with heavy sarcasm. "So you're selling blood to the vamps. Good for you. Unbind us and we're gone."

"And Talithia," Grace added. "Rick and Josh too."

"Sure," Catherina said, but she didn't move. "First though, explain what you're doing on my turf."

"Why don't you-"

"Maria!" Grace said, cutting her off. They couldn't afford to antagonise the Creature, especially as they still didn't know what she was. Not a vampire. Possibly a succubus then, but the reference to flesh didn't fit. Not knowing how much the Creature knew, she decided to play it as straight as she could. "Maria got hit by a car, and I got beat up by Abbey's cronies. We both wound up here. Abbey kidnapped a human friend, and we just want to help him."

Catherina met her eyes. "You mean Josh?"

"Yeah, Josh."

"Josh won't be harmed. Abbey may play with him for a while but she'll let him go. She knows how important he is to us."

Important? Grace pulled at the ropes. "And us?"

"You'll be released tonight on condition you never return."

"We'll be dead by tonight," Grace said. "We've been out of the water too long already." She met the Creature's eyes. "We're mermaids, remember? Water is a thing."

Catherina gave her a wicked smile. "Not my problem, 'maids. I can't have you running around on my turf when I'm not at my strongest."

"Please," Grace said. "We're not going to do anything! We're practically human when we're out of the water."

"And I am not letting you go before sunset, water *thing* or not. Tough it out." Grace struggled as Catherina forced the tape back over her mouth, but at least she hadn't bothered with the rag. What she wouldn't have done for a bucket of water just then. When Catherina finished with Maria's gag she grasped the older nurse by the front of her uniform and dragged her to the door. "Bloody shame, this," she said, shaking her head as if she really did pity the unconscious nurse.

Grace yelled into the gag, drawing the Creature's attention. Catherina closed her eyes, dropped the nurse and came back to remove the gag. "Well?"

"If you let us die, you'll be starting a war. We're bound to our sisters. They'll know."

Catherina raised an eyebrow. And then she shrugged. "Whatever."

As Grace opened her mouth to yell for help, Catherina put the tape back on. She blew Grace a kiss, smiled wickedly, and then left the room with the unconscious nurse, locking the door.

Grace let her head fall back against the gurney. Maria wriggled as best she could, and with a little work she managed to lengthen her serrated canines and shred the tape holding the rag in, spitting the bits out. Grace quickly did likewise.

"Creatures infiltrating hospitals," Maria muttered sarcastically. "Who'd have known?"

"They obviously don't have to limit their numbers nearly as much as we do. They survive without killing."

There wasn't enough slack in the ropes to get her hands near enough to cut anything. Or more to the point, her claws. It'd take a bit of effort to get them to harden and become sharp, but if she could use them on the ropes it'd be worth it. She struggled briefly with her bindings, but it did no good.

"We're dead," Maria said softly. "God, I won't even get the chance to kick Talithia's arse now. I so want to shove that bitch's vindictive smile so far down her throat-"

Grace snorted. "You couldn't harm her if you tried."

"I can hurt her pretty bad with foul language, and she has it coming, trust me."

"Let's focus on escaping."

Maria glanced at the roof. "Plumbing in the walls and roof?"

"Out of reach. The gurney's on wheels, though." She experimented by throwing her weight about as much as the ropes would allow, but the wheels must have been locked.

"I'm guessing they use these things for moving patients around."

"Ready to give up?"

"Hell no! Start screaming sister."

AN HOUR later neither of them could shout anymore. Grace lay back on her steel gurney, wishing her throat wasn't so dry. What she wouldn't do for a glass of water, or an ocean of it.

"So," Grace began. "You used to be a guy, huh? What was that like?"

Maria shrugged. "It's been three centuries. Can't remember."

"Bullshit! Why didn't you tell me?"

She heard Maria sigh. "Painful memories. I had a wife and three gorgeous daughters. When Talithia made me, she did it out of hate. She and a few others entered our house at night and clubbed my wife and I unconscious, and dragged us to the water. It wasn't far. Then she woke my daughters. One was four, the second nearly three, and the youngest almost old enough to walk, and brought them down to the water."

"Oh God, I don't think I want to know," Grace said. She faced her sister, but Maria was staring into memory.

"Good, because I don't want to talk about it."

They were silent for a while. Grace was trying to summon the courage to ask her to continue when Maria sighed, as if she couldn't hold the pain in any longer. "She made me into a mermaid using my youngest daughter. I found her body floating face-down beside me when I woke as... I am now."

"I'm so sorry," Grace whispered.

A tiny frown marred Maria's pretty Italian features. "You know what it's like just after you're made, the need for lifeforce rising inside you, consuming you? Your thoughts are clear for all of a few minutes, and then the desire to kill takes over. They held me back for hours, watching as the need rose in me. The moment I sensed a human in the water I didn't hesitate. I was beyond it. You lose yourself in that need, and nothing else matters when you get that desperate. You'll kill anyone without even seeing their faces."

"Until later," Grace whispered, staring at the roof. "You remember later."

"Until later," Maria echoed softly. "I remember my children screaming as Talithia stood on the shore, holding them up, but I didn't recognise them. She'd kept me away from humans for so long I was almost insane with the need for lifeforce. She knew I wouldn't be able to control myself when she and her closest sisters let me loose."

Grace blinked tears away, unable to look at her sister. "Maria..."

"She threw my daughters to me, one at a time, and I couldn't help myself." She paused, sniffling. "When they were dead, she forced my wife into the water too. I'll never forget her confused expression as she saw me. I looked different, obviously, but even so she recognised me. As with my daughters, I couldn't stop myself." Maria took a deep shuddering breath, a tear running down the side of her face. "Do you honestly think that, despite the fact that our nature forces me to love her, that I couldn't hate her as well?"

"I'm sorry," Grace whispered. "What was your wife's name?"

Maria smiled. A pain-filled smile. "Maria. Of course?"

Grace desperately wanted to fold her sister in her arms. "It's a beautiful name."

[26]

"HELLO!" came a muffled shout from outside the door.

Relief rushed through Grace. "Talithia?" she called as she reflexively strained at the ropes. "Help. Get us out of here!"

Talithia spoke with someone outside, Rick she guessed, and then something hard slammed into the door, making it rattle. It smashed into it again and Grace flinched away as an axe-head burst through.

"Great," Maria muttered. "Rescued by the one person I despise. If there's a God, he must truly hate me."

"Really?" Grace asked. "You care who rescues us?"

The door splintered with the next hit, the axe lodged where the lock had been. The lock itself hung by a long strip of plywood.

"Took your time," Maria said acerbically. Talithia stood with one of Abbey's werewolf cronies held by a knife at her neck. The dark-haired one. The werewolf didn't look worried, so either she was stupid or overconfident. The knife certainly couldn't kill her unless they used it to hack off her head, but it'd do a lot of damage. While it wasn't silver, it could still put her down for days.

"Had to convince our dog here to tell us where you were, and then we had to move through this maze of a hospital without being seen," Rick said.

"We can talk later," Grace said. "Get us free before someone comes to investigate."

Rick pulled the axe from the splintered door and leaned it against the wall as he untied Maria.

The werewolf laughed, caught Talithia's wrist with her hands, pulled her arm forward, and then flipped Talithia to the ground. Talithia hit with a solid thump and a muffled cry of pain. Grace heard a bone break. Talithia opened her mouth to cry out but no sound came.

"Get out," Grace said to Rick. "Go get help. The police. Anyone." Despite their differences in size, she wouldn't like to take odds on him taking down a trained werewolf, even with an axe. Without the full moon the werewolf would still be stronger than she looked, and probably able to take a considerable amount of pain and bruising before going down.

The werewolf gave Rick a cocky smile. "Wanna try me, Rick? Pick up the axe and we'll see how tough you are. Come on, smash my head in if you can."

Rick glanced nervously at Talithia's unmoving form as he picked up the axe. It was clear he wasn't a fighter. "How about you back off Brenda. We'll clear out and everyone wins."

"Oh, come on. Have a go. You turned me down twice when I wanted to date you, so now its payback." She punched a palm with her hand. "I'm just a little girl after all, half your size. All I've got are my good looks and ten years of ju-jitsu training. You can take me."

"That's enough, Brenda," said a new voice. Catherina entered the room behind the werewolf, and Brenda immediately lost her fighting stance. She stepped to the side and deferred to the Creature like the well-trained pet she was.

"Aren't you going to give her a doggy treat?" Maria asked.

Catherina focused on Grace, her demeanour entirely different compared to when she'd first met her. No longer did she seem to be the overly-efficient young nurse. Now she was cold and in charge. Her gaze was enough to make Grace shiver.

"Brenda is not a pet, she's a guardian."

Grace met Brenda's eyes. "I'll triple whatever she's paying you,

Brenda," Grace said. "You've got no idea how many treasures lay at the bottom of the ocean. I could make you filthy rich." How had she never considered that before? She could be filthy rich herself if she wanted to be.

Catherina stepped between Brenda and Grace. "Brenda's been assigned to look after Abbey, who does quite a bit of valuable work for us in identifying..." she hesitated, glancing at Rick before smirking. "Candidates. Last night she was asked to distract your friends." She nodded toward the prone form of Talithia before frowning at Rick. "We let it play out because we wanted to see what you lot were capable of while out of water. Not much, apparently. Couldn't even slip the ropes."

Maria pulled free of the last rope Rick had untied. "This was a test?" she asked, getting off the gurney, her fists clenched. What she could do without water was a mystery though.

"Why not just let us go," Grace said, a hint of pleading in her voice. "We only wanted to make sure Josh was all right. We could be allies. Friends. We don't want trouble with your kind." Whatever her kind was.

Catherina pursed her lips, eyes cold. "You drowned two nurses," Catherina said. "Two. Do you know how much trouble that causes in a hospital? Police everywhere, extra shifts to cover, rooms out of use. It's a nightmare, not to mention the fact that those two nurses were bloody good at their jobs. It's surprisingly difficult to replace good nurses these days. Just one is worth at least ten doctors."

Grace was momentarily lost for words. "You're a bureaucrat?"

Catherina gave her a steady look, sighing in disappointment. "We live within human society Grace, not alongside it like your lot. I'm being practical."

She glanced at Brenda and then Rick, who kept a hold of his axe but still looked like he had no idea how to use it. He didn't even have it raised.

She had to keep her talking in the hopes Maria would come up with a plan. "And Josh? What's he to you?"

Catherina glanced at Maria before turning back to Grace, almost as if she could read Grace's mind and didn't care that she was trying to delay. "We might allow Brenda to bite him so he can enter the ranks of our guardians one day."

"Otherwise?"

Catherina began to look amused. She was teasing Grace now, and probably playing along to see what Grace revealed. She clearly didn't care what Grace learned, which meant she intended to kill them. "He's human, stupid, just like Rick. He'll forget all about us soon enough, at least consciously. Maybe he'll develop a fetish for vampire television shows or tacky werewolf movies, but that's the natural order of things. You three though, now there's a challenge. It'll be interesting to see what mermaids are capable of."

"Better be quick," Maria said with a glare. "We're dead come sunset."

"Thanks for the tip, but I'm inclined to keep you lot in water tanks to prolong the experience."

Grace met Maria's eyes with a surge of hope. Catherina really didn't know anything about mermaids then. "Our sisters will know what happened when we don't return. You're starting a war." Grace strained at the ropes again, a less-than-subtle hint to her sister.

Maria put a hand on Rick's bicep to get his attention, but she spoke to Catherina. "How about we promise to tell you everything you want to know, and you promise to get us back into the ocean before sunset? Promises can't be broken," Maria said, an undercurrent of stress in her voice. Catherina probably didn't notice, but Grace did. It wasn't herself or even Talithia that Maria was concerned for. It was Grace.

"You lot don't want to give up your secrets any more than we do, and I don't trust you not to work around any promise you make. I'll take the scientific approach, thanks. You," Catherina said to Rick. "Can help Brenda wheel Grace and Maria down to the room at the end of the hall. Come back for this one, and after that you're free to go home."

He seemed surprised by that. "You expect me to work for you?" He raised the axe as if thrusting it would work.

"It's a hacking tool you idiot," Maria said, failing to push him back. "Not a sword."

"Do you mind?" he asked, pointedly looking at her hand on his arm.

It was all the opening Brenda needed. She moved and had the axe out of Rick's hands before he could swing it, and a moment later she clubbed him with the blunt end. He dropped, unconscious before he hit the ground.

Maria stepped back from the threatening werewolf, but it was Catherina she glared at. There was no way out but past the two of them, and with Grace still restrained Maria didn't have a chance. She must have realised the same thing, and didn't like her odds. Although Brenda stood between Maria and Catherina, it was the nurse she spoke to. "I swear if the opportunity presents itself I'm going to drown you and drag your corpse to the bottom of the ocean."

"I'm a ghoul you stupid mermaid. I can't be drowned."

Ghoul?

Brenda slammed the axe haft into Maria's thigh. Maria cried out and grasped the leg just as Brenda swung again, cracking it against her temple and knocking Maria to the floor. With both Maria and Rick down, Brenda threw the axe to the floor where it slid and hit the wall.

Grace pulled hard at the ropes in a final attempt to get free, but it did nothing but cause an abrasion. Hopefully she might get a chance to do something later. "You're not going to hurt them, are you?" Grace asked as Brenda began wheeling Grace out. "You'll let Rick go at least, won't you? He's just looking out for his friend."

Catherina shook her head as if she pitied Grace's naivety. "He'll make a nice meal once his body begins to rot. You should be more concerned for your mermaid friends."

THE ROOM BRENDA wheeled her into was large enough to house several cars end to end, and maybe four wide. Bright recessed lights in the roof shone down on long benches bolted against the back wall, including two with a sink. Grace could smell the water, her body beginning to crave it as she'd been out of water for so long. Big cabinets lined the walls at each end. Grace and Maria were pushed together near the middle of the long wall opposite the benches, not far from the door. There was only one way in and out, and the floor and roof were concrete.

When Brenda returned with Talithia, she dumped the unconscious mermaid on a spare gurney and tied her down.

"We're going to die because of a stupid human," Maria muttered as she stared at the roof, a welt already forming on her temple where she'd been hit. At least she was conscious again. She hadn't been out for long.

Grace glanced at her sister. "He's Sandra's son. She'd do the same for you."

"Sandra can't even leave the ocean." Maria didn't even bother looking at her.

Grace shook her head. "Maybe not yet, but soon enough."

Maria pressed her lips tight. Grace could have sworn she saw jealousy.

Catherina entered the room and put her hands on her hips. "I'm assuming you can't change form just because you want to, otherwise I'm sure you'd have done so to escape the ropes. That right girls?"

"Girls? I'm three hundred years old," Maria muttered.

Catherina smiled thinly. "I know the feeling. Would you prefer *old maid*?"

"Shove it, hyena." Maria pulled her ropes, doing little more than bruising her wrists.

Catherina turned to Brenda. "Move that one away from the other two." She pointed at Talithia. "Let's see if water makes them change form or if it's a conscious decision."

They splashed just a few drops at first, and then more and more until Talithia was completely soaked. Only then did she shift form, the rope binding her ankles snapping like a vine to allow for the thicker tail. Unfortunately she didn't wake up. With all that water she'd have been able to do a lot of damage.

"I can't hold human form much past half wet," Maria whispered to Grace. She sounded impressed.

"Me either."

Brenda mopped up the water and used a hair dryer to remove the rest, even meticulously wiping the gurney underneath Talithia. They weren't stupid then. Shame.

Catherina examined Talithia. "The bruising around her hip faded since she shifted form." She made some notes on a clip-board as if discussing a specimen instead of a person. "Water appears to heal them. Let's see what else they can do." She tried ice next, but that had no effect, even when Brenda dumped buckets of it all over Talithia. The smell of water heightened Grace's killer instincts, but it wasn't close enough to touch and control.

After that they tried steam under pressure from a small steam cleaner. "Remarkable," Catherina said, examining Talithia's skin. "Doesn't even scald her."

"I could have told you that," Maria said. "Why don't you ask?"

Catherina crossed the room and patted Maria's leg. "Because if I were you I'd be lying. Let's see what else your kind can do."

She wheeled Talithia next to Grace and pushed Maria across the room to the benches. The separation made Grace nervous.

"I'll show you what I can do-"

Brenda punched Maria in the face, snapping her head to the side.

"Maria!" Grace screamed. Maria moaned, her lip split and bleeding.

Brenda attached a cable to Maria's foot while the ghoul picked up a rubber-handled clamp connected to a small transformer sitting on the bench.

Electrocution? "No. Please don't do that," Grace said urgently.

Catherina ignored her. "Tell me Maria, do you change form when in pain or threatened?" She touched the clamp to Maria's leg.

Maria cried out and jerked, thrashing so hard Catherina pulled the clamp back. Maria took a strained breath and then let out a soft cry of pain, almost a whimper.

"Please don't hurt her anymore," Grace pleaded. "Ask me anything. I'll tell you."

Brenda barely glanced her way. "Is that a promise?" She raised an eyebrow, and Grace was tempted to comply to spare Maria. When she hesitated, Catherina turned away and made several notes before readying the clamp again.

"Go eat a maggot," Maria whispered.

Catherina touched the clamp to Maria's arm this time, and the reaction was the same. Grace squeezed her eyes shut, unable to watch. In the disturbing silence that followed she dared to open an eye. Maria was unconscious.

"Well," said Catherina. "That was about as much as a human could take too."

Brenda wheeled Maria back and pulled Grace into the middle of the room. "What are you going to do to me?" Grace asked.

"Nothing you wouldn't do to me."

"Thank God," Grace said. "You're going to try and drown me? I thought you were going to try something nasty." She'd love the chance to drag the ghoul into the ocean and hold her under forever.

Catherina, her beguilingly youthful face belying the cruelty behind her eyes, smiled. "I'm getting to like you, Grace. I really am." Catherina picked up a large syringe. "Let's start with some bloodwork. There's got to be a reason your bodies smell like salted crap."

Grace stared at the syringe. It looked like it could suck half a litre out of her. "Come near me with that and I'll verbally abuse you."

Catherina paused, meeting Grace's eyes with a smile playing at the corner of her mouth. "I really do like you. It's a shame you're not a ghoul. I think we'd get on great."

Grace barely felt pain as the syringe plunged into the vein at her elbow.

"Results will take a while," Catherina said as she withdrew the syringe.

Grace really was going to die, she realised. With both Maria and

Talithia unconscious, and no help coming, she couldn't see a way out. For a moment her fear took her back to the ocean and Sandra's waiting presence, her daughter still hoping for news Josh was safe. She'd be waiting forever now.

The ghoul left with her blood while Brenda sat on one of the benches opposite them, watching.

"How come you got babysitting duties?" Grace asked. "Not respected enough to play with the big dogs?"

Brenda narrowed her eyes, picked up a scalpel, hopped off the bench and walked over to Grace. She stabbed the scalpel into Grace's leg.

"Ahh!" Grace cried out. "Shit, shit, shit!"

"At least Abbey was fun." Brenda twisted the scalpel and Grace screamed and strained at the ropes, struggling to breathe through the pain.

Brenda pulled the scalpel free, pushed Grace's head to one side and put the edge of the scalpel against her cheek just below her eye. "Say something else I don't like," she murmured. "Go on, please. I want to see if you can regrow an eye."

Grace squeezed her eyes shut and held still, certain the sadistic werewolf would follow through with the threat if she provoked her again.

"Thought so." She shoved Grace's head hard, but walked away. She threw the scalpel onto the bench and left the room.

"Oh shit!" Grace whimpered again. Her leg ached abominably. "I'm going to kill her," she whispered. "And it's going to be painful."

"I'll hold her down while you dig out her heart with your claws," Maria replied, filling Grace with relief that she was awake.

"If you don't," Talithia said. "I'll do it for you."

Grace stared in surprise at the sound of Talithia's voice. "You're awake too?" Grace whispered, not daring to raise her voice in case the werewolf returned. Just knowing the older mermaid was back with them was a comfort, even if she didn't like Talithia much.

Talithia glanced at Grace's necklace. "How much lifeforce do you have stored?" she asked.

"Nothing," Grace said with regret. "Why?"

"You could have drawn on the stored lifeforce to heal yourself. Maria should never have allowed it to get so low."

Maria glared at the older mermaid. "This is my fault now?" Maria asked acerbically. "You know, that werewolf's a sadistic bitch, but at least she's honest. I'd rather spend time with her."

Talithia returned the glare. "Do you honestly expect compassion from me?"

"I am your sister! I'm also your bloody daughter! And besides, you've got no idea what happened that night your other daughter died. None whatsoever!"

"No idea? You murdered her while she was weak and injured."

Maria turned away from her. "Like I said. No frigging idea."

Talithia's face darkened with rage. "She was defenceless!"

Maria kept staring at the roof. "It was a mercy," she said softly.

"I wish I'd killed you."

Maria sighed, and it sounded as if the fight had gone out of her. "You want to know what happened that night? She came ashore looking to lure a victim into the water, but someone recognised her. For three years in a row she'd come ashore, been seen with someone, and for three years in a row that person's body had been washed up on the rocks near the village, drowned."

"Yet it was you who killed her," Talithia said, murder in her tone.

Maria snorted. "They caught her, and fuelled by alcohol and violence, they hurt her so badly she couldn't even crawl. After that they tied her to a post and whipped her until her back was bloody and she couldn't even raise her head, and left her there so they could do worse later. Late that night I cut the ropes and tried to carry her away from our village, but someone saw. I didn't know she was a mermaid, just a girl, and figured she'd been through enough. Rather than let them keep torturing her, I cut her throat. It was the only mercy I could give her."

"I..."

Maria glared at the roof as if she could bore holes through it. "And for that you murdered my wife and daughters and shunned me for three hundred years. I don't want your forgiveness Talithia. I never did, so don't expect mine."

"I never thought-"

"Of course you never thought! You've never asked or even gave me the opportunity to explain."

The door opened and Catherina walked in. She didn't look happy.

[27]

"Why?" Catherina asked, glaring at the bloody scalpel.

Brenda cringed near the door. "She pissed me off," she said petulantly with a brief glance at Grace. There was no arrogance or even defiance in the words. Just fear.

"Do it again and I'll toss you into the ocean with one of *them*. You could have opened an artery and she'd be dead now."

Brenda glared at Grace as if it were entirely her fault.

"Oh yeah, blame the girl tied to a gurney," Grace muttered, grasping at any opportunity to sow discord.

Catherina gave Grace a look which suggested she knew exactly how far she could trust Brenda. She examined Grace's wound, fingertips probing. Grace stiffened in pain. She didn't have enough lifeforce to heal at a faster-than-human rate.

"You need water to heal?" Catherina asked.

Grace considered the wisdom of saying nothing. "It'd help."

Catherina raised an eyebrow. "How much water do you need to stay alive beyond the sunset?"

Blood seeped from the wound, her leg throbbing and blood pooling under her thigh. What would Catherina do if Grace didn't tell her? She signed. "A lake the size of a harbour big enough for warships," she whispered. "With at least three or four other mermaids. We can't survive alone for long."

Catherina seemed genuinely curious. "Why so much water?"

"How the hell should we know? Just because!"

Maria cut in before Grace could say more. "We need water like humans need air. A little isn't enough."

Catherina ignored Maria. She ran a fingertip over Grace's bracelet, the one Kimbriel had given her, glancing at Maria and Talithia's wrists. "Cheap trinket," she said as she reached up and delicately touched Grace's necklace. "But you all wear these. Why?"

"Because they're pretty," Grace muttered.

The ghoul squeezed Grace's thigh. She cried out and gritted her teeth, thrashing until Catherina released the pressure.

"Again. Why the necklaces?"

"None of your business."

The ghoul squeezed again and Grace arched in pain. "Oh shit! Stop, stop, stop!"

Catherina let go. "Last try. Next time I open a new hole in your leg."

Grace squeezed her eyes shut, determined not to give in. "I've got a spare."

She screamed as Catherina not only squeezed, but forced her thumb into the wound. She couldn't breathe as she thrashed until the ghoul withdrew her hand, her entire leg aching with a pain she doubted she'd ever forget. Tears ran down her cheeks, healing tears she was unable to use.

"I'll tell you," Maria said, shared pain in her tone. "But only if you don't hurt her again." When Catherina nodded, Maria continued. "We can store excess lifeforce in them so it doesn't go to waste when we gain more than we can hold ourselves. It saves us from killing when we don't have to."

Catherina took Grace's necklace in one hand, painfully gripped her hair and lifted her head to pull the necklace free.

"I wonder if ghouls could benefit from something like this?" she mused aloud. She eyed Grace speculatively. "I guess we do in a way.

Dead bodies hold residual lifeforce, distilled into their flesh. As they decompose we access it. How do I use this?"

"It's attuned to me," Grace whispered, sweating from the pain. "You can't.

Catherina dangled the necklace before her face, examining the jewel. Looking thoughtful, she placed it on one of the stainless steel benches.

"How do you make them?" she asked without turning around. "Sapphire, pearls, gold. What's the connection?"

The door to the room opened and Abbey strode in like she'd purchased the place. Kylie, the blonde werewolf, followed after her.

Abbey caught sight of Grace's bleeding leg, and grimaced. "Their blood smells like shit," she muttered to Catherina.

Catherina tossed Grace's necklace to Abbey. "Tell me what you sense."

Grace felt a sickly fear as Abbey fingered it, frowning. "A hint of lifeforce, but it's wrong somehow." Rather than play with the necklace, she strode to Maria and grasped her necklace. Her expression immediately changed. "Woah, this one's got much more, but there's still something wrong with it." She took Maria's necklace from her and handed it to Catherina.

The ghoul raised an eyebrow as she touched it. "I see. I'll need to study these."

"Can we use them?" Abbey asked. "If other Creatures could draw that much lifeforce into themselves, they'd be very powerful. I can see why mermaids wouldn't want to let the secret out."

"It's even got the potential to put your little project out of business," Catherina said with a smirk.

Abbey frowned, but then her expression rapidly brightened. "Or complement it."

Catherina gave her a steady look. "Possibly," she conceded.

Grace tried to sound nonchalant. "What's Josh to you?" Grace asked.

Abbey's expression darkened as if she'd slipped up on some great secret. "We need to capture more mermaids."

Ghouls hunting mermaids? It would ignite a war if it hadn't already.

Catherina nodded. "Definitely. Apparently they don't last long out of water. I need to discover how they fill these necklaces with lifeforce."

Abbey grinned maliciously at Grace. "I've got to get Josh to my lab. Ciao." She winked.

"What are you doing with him?"

Abbey's smile turned nasty. "Nothing he'd object to I'm sure, even if he had a choice." She blew Grace a kiss and left, taking Kylie with her.

Grace met Catherina's eyes. "If you let that minx hurt him I swear I'll bring you the most painful death I possibly can," Grace said after Abbey closed the door.

Catherina gave Grace a quizzical look as if she was on the cusp of figuring something out. And then she smiled. "Honey, she's not in the least bit interested in harming him. You've really got no idea what's going on, do you?"

"So inform me," Grace said coldly.

Her smile broadened. "I don't think so, but you are going to tell me how to make these necklaces and how to use them. How do you attune yourselves to them?"

If Grace survived, she'd have to make a necklace for Sandra. It was her duty as a mother, although mother wasn't quite the right term. Sire. Sister. Creator. Maria had pre-prepared one for Grace before she'd made her, so she'd obviously known what she'd intended when she came across the sinking Titanic. Maria may not have known the time or place, but she'd been prepared.

Grace, on the other hand, hadn't. She'd never considered creating a daughter. To make a necklace for Sandra she'd need pearls, an unflawed jewel of any sort, and some gold, all easy enough to get in the ocean.

Despite what Catherina might believe, there wasn't any magic involved. It wasn't the jewel that attuned to the mermaid, but the lifeforce as she took it from her victim. The jewel was the repository, while the pearls created the connection to the ocean and the mermaid. The gold could be replaced with anything that would hold the two together, even twine.

Catherina picked up the scalpel, Grace's blood already drying on it. "Call it a ghoul's intuition, but I suspect you're being quiet because you don't want to tell me." She wheeled Grace back to the middle of the room and positioned herself between Grace and Maria, leaning over Grace. "Shall we play the scalpel game Brenda started?"

"Sure," said Grace, preparing for more pain. Catherina gave her a hard look, turned to Maria and stabbed Maria's stomach.

Maria screamed.

"Okay! Okay," Grace yelled at the ghoul. "I'll tell you whatever you want."

Catherina pulled the scalpel free. Maria gasped, but was in too much pain to speak.

"Unfortunately little mermaid, I don't yet believe you." She stabbed Maria's again, drawing another scream.

"I said I'd tell you!" Grace cried, thrashing to try and free herself.

Catherina yanked the scalpel free. "Now I believe you."

Maria moaned, head lolling to the side. She was pale, but her eyes still begged Grace not to say anything.

"I'm sorry," she whispered to Maria before meeting Catherina's eyes. "It's just jewellery." Grace said. "It's the lifeforce that's special. I honestly don't know if it would work for you."

"Why not?"

"Because the lifeforce attunes to us when we take it."

"Grace, no," Talithia whispered, though there was no force in her voice at all.

"When we drown someone we can steal their lifeforce. If there's more than we need we can store the difference for later use."

"How do you store it?"

Grace shrugged. "It's like pouring water into a jar." She honestly hadn't thought about it. "The jewel's just the repository."

Catherina frowned, probably trying to figure out how to convert the process to her own species. "And how do you… draw on it?"

"It's just there, like a glass of water. We draw on it at need."

Catherina looked thoughtful. "Are there other uses?"

Grace wanted to shove her necklace down Catherina's throat and watch her choke on it. "No."

Catherina returned to the bench and threw the scalpel in a bin. She held Grace and Maria's necklaces toward the room's lights, examining them critically. The concrete roof was low and the lights only just out of reach. Grace had no idea what she was expecting to see.

"Brenda, come here," Catherina said.

Brenda moved from her position by the door, looking like a sulking child wishing she hadn't been sent to her room. Catherina handed her both necklaces. "Can you feel the lifeforce in them?"

Brenda held them for a moment before shrugging. "Nothing." She handed them back, totally disinterested.

Catherina examined the necklaces again. She mustn't have found whatever she was looking for, because she crossed back to Grace. "Siphon off some energy. Let me see how it's done."

She forced Grace's necklace over her head, the jewel resting in the hollow of her throat. Grace wondered what the ghoul would do when Grace failed. "There's almost nothing enough to draw on. Just residual resonance."

Catherina went back to the bench, picked up another scalpel, and returned. She held it to Grace's neck and leaned in close. "Do it, or I'll kill you."

Grace leaned away as far as the restraints would allow. "I really can't. There's nothing left in it. Surely you can feel it?"

Catherina glanced at Talithia, no pity on her face. "You've still got your necklace," she said as she walked around the gurneys. She shoved Talithia's gurney against Grace's. "Use yours to heal her."

Talithia swallowed, her voice pleading for understanding. "It doesn't work that way, but I am drawing down on it to heal my hip. Perhaps you can sense it? It'll take a few hours though."

Catherina stared for a long moment, touched Talithia's necklace and frowned. She returned to her workbench and began making notes.

"Grace," Talithia whispered. "Grace, you've got to be strong. You need to get you back to the water and tell our sisters what's going on here. If I can find a way to get you free, you must leave us behind."

Grace grimaced. "You know I can't do that," she whispered. Maria had no chance without her, and Grace may not even be able to stand up even if she could get free.

"Do whatever it takes," Talithia said. "Promise me." Talithia was close enough to be able to grasp Grace's hand, and did so. It was comforting having the physical contact.

Maria spoke, her face deathly pale and blood all over her stomach. "Please Grace. Make the promise. Talithia, do the same. One of us has to get out of here, and it's not likely to be me."

"Even if I make it to the ocean, I don't have enough lifeforce to heal myself," Grace said.

"Then drown someone," Maria said, pain edging her voice. "Do whatever it takes. If you get to the ocean you can heal. You promised to survive, remember?"

She could live a thousand years and never get used to the idea that drowning people was the only way she could survive.

Talithia squeezed Grace's hand. "Protecting our sisters is my responsibility, and if I have to die to make it happen, I'm fine with that. I think I can help."

Grace felt a fresh trickle of blood seep over her thigh. "I honestly doubt any of us will survive, but I do have a dying wish," Grace began. "Will you honour it?"

"There's no need," Talithia said, the lie clear in her voice. "You're going to survive this."

"I want you to forgive Maria for killing your daughter. Forgive her, and welcome her into your heart as you're supposed to do."

Talithia's expression hardened.

"Please," Grace said. "She gave your sister the only mercy she could. Please, forgive her. She has more reason to hate you than you her."

Talithia took a long, deep breath, closing her eyes. She gave a slight nod. "Maria, I welcome you back into our lives. You are no longer shunned, no longer an outcast. You are loved and cherished.

You are my sister and my daughter." She swallowed as if her throat had dried and tried to close against the words. "I don't expect you to forgive me, but I hope you accept I regret what I did to you and your family."

With Talithia's hand still in hers, Grace felt the truth of the words. If they ever got back to the ocean Maria would no longer be shunned. It was a small victory considering it was unlikely, but a victory nevertheless.

"That's very touching," Catherina said, her back still turned to them as she examined Maria's necklace under a lens. "Now shut up. I'm working."

"Yeah, shut up," Brenda said. She pushed off from her position near the door and wandered to the other side of the room for no apparent reason other than boredom. She hopped onto the bench in the far corner and sat there, legs crossed underneath herself, obviously wishing she could be somewhere else.

Grace offered her sister a weak smile. "Thank you."

Maria focused on Talithia, her face so pale she looked ghostly. "I'll forgive you, but only if Grace gets back to the ocean alive."

"Whatever it takes," Talithia agreed, staring at the concrete roof. "At least one of us must survive and tell our sisters." She glanced at Grace's leg wound, and there was nearly as much pain in her expression as Grace felt. "I'm so sorry, Grace. You're the one that least deserves to be here. That only makes this harder."

"Harder? What are you talking about?" asked Maria.

"It's time for you to go home Grace," Talithia said. "I'm very sorry for what I'm about to do."

[28]

"TALITHIA?" Grace asked. "What do you mean?"

Catherina turned, possibly picking up on Talithia's fatalistic tone, though she looked more curious than concerned.

"What happens when sunlight falls on a tree?" Talithia asked.

Grace watched her with concern. "The tree uses it for photosynthesis. To grow."

"And when you burn the wood and leaves?"

Grace shrugged. "The energy gets released as heat and light."

"Which can be used for all kinds of things. We're a lot like trees in that way." Talithia's grip on Grace's hand tightened. "I'm so sorry Grace. I wish there was another way."

Through their touch, Grace felt something ignite deep within Talithia, a smouldering heat at first. A moment later that heat erupted and surged through Grace's hand into her body, burning through her like a hot iron cauterising a wound. Grace screamed and arched her back.

Heat seared her nerves, her body going rigid as burning lifeforce, distilled over millennia, reforged her. Grace didn't know how, but Talithia had somehow tapped into the lifeforce distilled within her body, destroying herself so she could change Grace.

"Stop," Grace whispered, but it was already too late, her own distilled lifeforce igniting in response.

"You're killing her!" Maria screamed.

Grace's claws bit into Talithia's flesh as if electricity were coursing through her, preventing any chance of release. "Please," Grace gasped. "Stop."

Talithia tried to speak, but her face was agony even as her eyes begged for forgiveness. She took a deep breath, braced herself, and whispered a word. "Shatter."

Grace felt as much as saw the jewel at Talithia's throat explode, tiny pieces embedding in the roof as its stolen lifeforce erupted and passed through Talithia and then into Grace, much as it had when Maria had made her a century ago. It was like rain quenching a forest fire.

Grace tried to scream, her mouth open, but the air tasted like death. Her own. The mermaid she'd once been was dying. What was emerging she couldn't guess.

She felt as much as sensed Talithia's heart stop beating, and despite the pain she couldn't help feeling regret as she watched Talithia's head loll to the side, eyes staring. She'd utterly spent everything she had to ignite something deep within herself, and used to reforge Grace and give her a chance to save Maria. Together, they needed to bring news of what had happened to their other sisters.

After that, it would kill Grace as well. The lifeforce from the jewel wouldn't sustain her for long.

"Talithia," Grace whispered as the physical bond between them broke and Talithia's slack hand slipped from her own, bloody puncture marks from Grace's claws still leaking red. Grace could feel the lifeforce from the gem burning up at an incredible rate, its loss creating a powerful need for more. Much more. Like any newly born mermaid she could sense the nearest source of lifeforce.

She turned toward the corner of the room where Brenda sat, her body leaching lifeforce into the room as a human would. Grace wanted it. As she met Brenda's eyes, the werewolf frowned as if she recognised something far more amiss than a mermaid screaming in pain and another dying.

"Fascinating," Catherina said, but as she radiated no lifeforce the ghoul held no interest for Grace.

Grace heard Maria's pleading attempts to get her attention. She slowly turned her head.

"Grace? What did she do to you? Can you hear me Grace? Grace?"

Grace drew in a breath, less painful this time, and directed some of the lifeforce Talithia had given her to the wound in her leg. It healed over in seconds as if never there. Energy coursed through her veins, both as uplifting and joyous as it was painful and devastating. She was using lifeforce too fast and doubted she would last a day or two without more. Talithia had given her a gift, but it came at a terrible price.

Grace wasn't sure if she was still even a mermaid, or at least she no longer felt like the mermaid she used to be. She felt more dangerous. More powerful. More hungry for lifeforce.

She noticed her free hand was gripping the gurney so hard her claws had punched through the steel. It felt as if her body had been drawn fresh from the forge and been dropped into water to quench.

She moaned with residual pain even as she suppressed anger at Talithia. It wasn't Talithia she should be angry with, but Abbey and Catherina who'd forced the situation. Talithia hadn't expected any of them to survive, so this was her only option.

Grace wouldn't survive this transformation, but at least she could try and make sure Maria, Sandra and her sisters were safe before she burned out. Fear of failure felt like a thorn in her soul.

"Grace? What happened to you? You're glowing. You're frigging glowing!"

"I'm different," she whispered hoarsely, the only explanation that made sense. As the tidal wave of burned lifeforce reforged her body, the afterglow came at a price. She needed more lifeforce. Craved it.

She turned toward Catherina, eyes narrowed. "You're going to regret not playing nice."

Grace clenched her fists and pulled her wrists toward her chest, straining until she snapped the ropes.

"Holy shit," Maria whispered. "How did you do that?"

Grace pulled the loose ends from her wrists before ripping her feet free. The braided rope snapped loudly.

She could sense the water all around as if it were a part of her. She reached out to it and the fire sprinklers in the ceiling exploded, raining water into the room.

Catherina, who'd been watching with greed and a desperate desire in her expression, backed toward the door as she finally realised the danger she was in.

As the water sprayed down Maria shifted form, but Grace denied herself the same luxury. With three millennia of burned lifeforce still cooling within her body she had no need to change.

She drew water to her and flung daggers of ice at Catherina, but the ice shattered on the door frame as Catherina ducked out. Brenda, however, cowered in the corner while trying to avoid the water spraying into the room. She stared at Grace in fear, her hair and clothes soaked already. The nonchalance, boredom and disdain were gone. So was the malice. She looked ready to mess herself, and with good reason.

"Please," Brenda whispered.

Grace pursed her lips in disgust. "Did you say *please* when you tried to kill me after I left Josh's house?"

Barely able to control her anger, Grace commanded water and flung it at Brenda. The werewolf tried to scream, but Grace forced water into her nose and mouth, choking the sound off. Brenda thrashed, trying to cough it out, but it only allowed Grace to force more water in.

The werewolf fell from the bench to the soaked concrete floor, reaching out with one hand for mercy. Grace narrowed her eyes as she remembered the vindictive pleasure the werewolf had taken in hurting her.

Brenda shuddered like a rag doll as Grace turned the water in the werewolf's lungs into piercing ice. Drowning wouldn't kill a werewolf and neither would the internal wounds Grace inflicted, but the trauma was enough to knock her unconscious. She couldn't leave Brenda alive though. Not after what she'd just seen. Grace reached for a scalpel to sever the werewolf's spine, but paused. Something was very different.

Despite the fact Brenda was a Creature, the trauma Grace had inflicted gave her access to the werewolf's lifeforce. Grace dropped the scalpel and used the water as a conduit to draw the lifeforce out of the werewolf's flesh. Moments later Brenda's body slumped, dead.

"How did you do that?" Maria asked. "I felt what you did." She stared at Grace, mouth open in shock.

Grace crossed the room and snapped the ropes holding Maria wrists to the gurney. "No idea."

She found Maria's necklace and handed it to her as Maria got rid of the rest of the ropes. She had to get Maria back to the ocean before dark or they'd both be dead regardless of her new strength. After that she could return and finish the fight with the ghouls.

If she didn't destroy Catherina and everyone who knew about the necklaces, the conflict would spread like a disease among Creatures. They'd all want a piece of her kind's ability to store lifeforce. If ghouls discovered how to store lifeforce in gems and use it at will, they could become the dominant species in the world.

Such power, unchecked by morals and fuelled by greed, would ignite a war between Creatures, one that mermaids could never win. They didn't have the numbers or easy access to humans.

Ghouls could starve out mermaids by preventing humans from entering the ocean if it got that far, and that would be the end for mermaids.

Grace placed a hand on Talithia's forehead, knowing it was already too late for the ancient mermaid. Talithia was dead, her lifeforce expended to put Grace on the path to whatever she was now, but there was one gift she could still give to her creator's maker.

Grace gently let her hand slide to Talithia's cheek before kissing her forehead. "Thank you for helping me save Maria," she whispered. "You have my forgiveness for the cost."

Grace reached inside herself and let a blast of lifeforce surge through her hand and into Talithia's body. The mermaid had been a part of the ocean for three thousand years. The least she could do for her was ensure the ghouls could learn nothing more from her body.

The lifeforce broke down and transformed Talithia's body into water which spilled from the gurney in a rush, leaving nothing but her dress and her shattered necklace behind. "Be at peace," she whispered as she picked up the remains of Talithia's necklace. She didn't want to risk the ghouls learning from it.

Maria stared at Grace, mouth gaping like a landed fish. Her stare slowly went from Grace's face to her hair, widening in shock. "You're hair, its silvery now. Platinum. And your eyes, they're as blue as the ocean. What did she do to you?" She looked Grace up and down as if only just noticing how different she'd become. "I think you're taller, too."

Grace tried to smile, but she could feel the sadness in it. Talithia killed me, she wanted to say.

She didn't know much about the path she'd been set on, but it was a path she'd never be able to complete without killing hundreds of people a year judging by the way her body was burning through lifeforce. What remained from Talithia's necklace wouldn't last her more than a day or two, even considering Brenda's lifeforce, and Grace wasn't going to allow herself to become a Creature that killed so often.

She couldn't bear to tell Maria the truth though. "I'll get you back to the ocean, and tonight I'll return and finish this with Catherina and Abbey." Grace reached under Maria and picked her up like she was a child.

Maria stiffened with pain, but her expression suggested she'd sensed the fatality in Grace's voice. "No," she said, growing more sure of her conclusion. "They'll kill you, and I can't lose you. I'd rather die."

Grace regretted her emotions were so open to her sister. She gave Maria a sad smile. "Sandra's your responsibility now. Promise me you'll look after her."

Maria shook her head as if the act could completely erase the facts. "You can't do this. You're my sister! My daughter! I've already lost one family."

Grace pulled Maria closer, squeezing just a little. "Sandra's your family now. Promise me that if I don't return you'll look after her."

"Grace, you need to listen to me," Maria said, her tone pleading now, but there was little she could do to change Grace's mind. "We'll find another way."

Ignoring the plea, Grace walked toward the door under a shower of water from the burst sprinklers. Water splashed under her feet, although most of it was flowing toward a drain at the far end of the room.

Grace reached the door and, while holding Maria's transformed body in one arm, pulled it open.

A bullet punched into the wall beside her. With supernatural speed she dodged back just before three more hit the doorframe, sending shrapnel at her.

Maria cursed in Italian, but with her tail and wounds she couldn't even stand let alone help.

Using her new senses Grace reached out and exploded the water pipes in the corridor's roof outside the room, the artificial rain flooding the area. She held some of the water in the air, driving the heat out of it until it was a thick and cold mist, dense enough to slow bullets. She stepped out, bursting more water pipes ahead of her.

"What now?" Maria asked, fear in her voice. "We're trapped."

Several more shots tore into the water-thick air, but all fell short. Grace forced the water on the ground to spread ahead of them until it reached the end of the corridor where she felt a werewolf's tainted lifeforce.

Kylie. The bottle-blond werewolf was either too arrogant or stupid to realise the danger she was in, and Grace took advantage of it, directing the water to flow over Kylie's body like a living thing.

Kylie yelled defiantly and fired randomly as Grace dragged her to the ground, bullets tearing through the water-thick air until Grace took a tighter control of the water and used it to rip the gun free.

"Let me go!" Kylie yelled as Grace used water to drag the werewolf to her. She screamed the entire length of the corridor, her fingernails scraping against the floor and walls, but Grace's control of the water was far stronger.

Grace tried not to think about the beating that Kylie and Brenda had given her after she'd visited Josh's house, but when Kylie stopped at her feet she froze the water around the werewolf, binding her to the ground. The werewolf gasped with the cold, eyes going wider in fear as she realised just how dangerous her predicament was.

"Where's Josh?" Grace asked.

"W-with Abbey," Kylie stammered, eyes terrified as Grace directed more water to creep over her body and freeze her harder in place, strengthening her bonds. Kylie's teeth started chattering as the cold bit. "They left for the clinic."

"Where's the clinic?"

She held on for a few seconds, but Grace hardened the ice by drawing more heat from it. "Okay! It's part of the Eris building."

"Thank you Kylie."

Kylie began to beg, but Grace forced water into her mouth and froze it, stopping another scream. With Kylie's eyes wide and begging, Grace knelt and punched her sharp claws through the ice and into the werewolf's neck, drawing Kylie's lifeforce out. Kylie jerked, a portion of ice cracking with the violence of it, and then she lay still, eyes staring. She wouldn't regenerate from that.

Like the lifeforce she'd received from Talithia's gem, Grace absorbed Kylie's energy, enough to prolong her life for another a day at best. The energy from the gem would have lasted much longer, maybe weeks, if she hadn't used it to transform Talithia's body to water.

"Grace, I felt you steal the lifeforce from the werewolf," Maria whispered, even though she'd felt the same thing with Brenda. "That's not possible. Werewolves are supernatural Creatures."

"Not supernatural enough, apparently." Grace melted the water holding Kylie's body and sent it ahead of her, but Catherina had left the area and there was no one around.

"Any idea where the Eris building is?

"None."

Grace sheeted the moisture from Maria and her sister's body

instantly shifted back to human form. The wounds in Maria's stomach had closed over with contact from the water and Grace could sense the lifeforce being drawn from her sister's necklace and beginning to heal her, but it would be days before she would fully heal. The fact it was happening already was a relief. "Come on, we have to get back to the ocean before more of them turn up."

"Grace," Maria said, grabbing Grace's hand and trying to stop her, but Grace was too strong now. She dragged Maria along, ignoring the pain she sensed in her sister from the partially healed wounds.

"Grace. Wait. At least promise me you won't come back here," Maria said as Grace continued to drag her. "We can hide in the ocean for centuries, all of us. The ghouls will give up on the necklaces."

"They're immortal Maria, and technology is advancing rapidly. They'll find a means to come for us if I don't end this tonight."

Maria gave up trying to stop Grace. "Then I'm returning with you."

They reached the end of the corridor and Grace directed mist ahead of them, using it to ensure the area remained clear. Nobody. "No. They'll kill you."

"They'll kill you too."

Grace tried not to let Maria read her face or sense her emotions. "I'm much stronger and faster than them, even out of the water."

"Then we'll return with force. We'll gather our sisters-"

"Tomorrow will be too late. They'll have gone to ground. It's in their nature to survive by hiding. Besides, the lifeforce from Talithia's necklace will run out soon. It has to be tonight."

"And what happens then?"

It was a question Grace didn't want to answer, but she couldn't hold anything back from Maria. "Then I kill people or I die."

Someone ran into her mist with a cry of surprise. Two people. Three. They were all human judging by the amount of lifeforce they had in their bodies. It wouldn't take much for Grace to use the fog to suck it out of them, but instead she shrouded herself and Maria in it, filling the entire corridor. The humans slowed and stopped and began feeling their way along the walls.

"What the hell's this shit?" one asked. "I was expecting smoke, not fog."

"Just get down there. We need to figure out what happened with the sprinklers."

Grace guided Maria past them, sending tendrils of mist along the ground well ahead of them until she found an exit from the building. They left via a fire door and had to climb concrete stairs to get to ground level, moving past rubbish skips and a chain fence in the far corner holding building materials.

Grace glanced into a sky half filled with fluffy clouds. "I make it early afternoon." Outside the building and connected directly to the earth, she could feel the ocean even from this distance. She could feel the oceans all around the world.

A distant siren was drawing nearer, though Grace had no idea if it was the police, fire brigade or an ambulance.

"Better go," Grace said, touching Maria's shirt which was covered in her blood, not to mention the hole from the scalpel. "I really don't want to have to answer questions." She pulled her leather jacket off and put it around Maria, and together they began walking.

$$[\ 29 \ ]$$

GRACE AND MARIA made their way off the hospital grounds, but they'd come out of the building on the opposite side to the ocean. It was only a few hundred metres down the hill to the Bay, but they'd have to walk around the front of the hospital to get there, and more than likely they'd be seen by Catherina's Creature friends.

"Let's take the backstreets," Grace said. The day was hot and the sun biting, but it wasn't too far if they took the next side street up.

"Down the street's the fastest way," Maria said, clearly still hurting from their captivity and torture. No matter what Maria wanted, she wasn't going fast no matter which route they took.

"If they're half as organised as I think they are, Catherina will be preparing for us to head straight for the water. Uphill to the right there's a water garden which is closer, but let's not get cornered there."

"I still think it's worth risking the direct route."

"You can't run." She steered Maria up the hill, away from the ocean and left onto Leigh Street. Grace could smell and feel water all around them, but in taps or small quantities at the bottoms of pot plants or in bird baths. The small amounts might help if she got desperate, but although her reach was far greater now she couldn't match a gun.

"I can make it," Maria said stubbornly.

"Catherina saw what Talithia did to me. She's not going to let that get away from her, and she's probably counting on us going straight for the ocean," Grace said. "If I was them, I'd snatch us from the street just beyond the hospital grounds."

As they got to Bavarde Ave Grace noticed a man down the street between them and the ocean. Dressed in a business suit and looking like a bouncer, he watched them without moving. She'd been right about the hospital then. Catherina was prepared.

The Creature kept his distance for now, but once Catherina had the numbers that would change.

"Let's cut across the golf course and through the clubhouse car park. The creek on the other side of Beach Road leads straight into the marina and safety."

It was a nervous walk. All Catherina, Abbey or another Creature had to do was get ahead of them and Grace wouldn't be able to protect Maria. If she were the betting kind, she'd put money on a trap being set already.

"At least there's a few water holes here," Maria said as they passed a large pond.

It was comforting, but not as helpful as she'd like. Nothing but the ocean would ensure their safety. "It'll just delay them. We can't shield with ice and move at the same time. Keep walking."

They'd barely walked a fairway before Maria began leaning on her, her injuries telling.

"Want me to carry you?" Grace said as they passed an elderly man with an electric golf buggy. He eyed them with curiosity and more than a little suspicion. "Where's fairway three?" Grace asked him, as if a couple of girls meandering through a golf course was normal. He pointed, clearly mystified.

"Thanks," Maria said with a bright smile. The man just frowned harder.

"Didn't you have shoes at some point?" Grace asked softly.

"Lost them, along with my respect for your decisions."

Grace sighed. "You know why I have to go back."

"You don't. We don't."

"Maria, I'm burning through too much lifeforce. I might as well do some good before I run out of it."

"You are not going to die!" Maria sounded angry. "And even if you were, I won't let you. I'd drown a thousand people a day to keep you safe."

"Is that why you stepped in front of that car?"

"That was different." Maria stumbled. "Ow, shit. I stepped on a stick."

"How exactly is it different? You wanted me to be alone for the rest of my life?"

"I did it so you didn't have to share my isolation," Maria said defensively.

"Keep up the spin," Grace said, feeling the hurt again. "Maybe you'll convince the old man back there."

Maria narrowed her eyes, a sure sign of an epic fight in the making. "This is about you running off to get slaughtered, not my stupidity. How would you feel if it were Sandra in your shoes? That's what you're planning."

Grace gave her a look but didn't stop walking as they crossed another fairway, passing an overweight woman dragging a golf buggy and sweating profusely. Grace guessed exercise was a new thing for her. She should have played earlier when it was cool.

Trees shaded them, but it was still hot for a couple of mermaids so long out of the water. Maria was limping badly now, leaving traces of blood on the grass. "You could have told me you cut your foot."

"Oh sorry, my foot's cut. Surprise."

"Shut up." When they got within sight of the clubhouse and car park, she saw Abbey's convertible there, though Grace couldn't see the succubus. "They're herding us. Turning us away from the water."

"At least we have shade," Maria muttered with false brightness.

"A church would be handy about now. I've never seen another Creature in a church or chapel."

"Handy for you," Maria said. "Not me."

Grace gave her a look.

"I tried to follow you in once. It was like entering someone's home. I couldn't do it."

Grace didn't recall being invited into a church, but maybe she had and didn't remember it.

Maria glanced back and stiffened. Three women dressed in casual street clothes were walking across the course behind them. "Werewolves or ghouls?" she wondered aloud.

"What difference would it make?"

"Ghouls die if they run out of lifeforce, same as us. Do enough damage and they're done for. Werewolves don't."

"Then I say we risk a run-in with Abbey. Dash through the car park, cross Beach Road and dive into the creek."

Grace considered it. "I don't think the creek's deep enough, and if Abbey's in the car park we'll be in trouble. Let's go around the building and make for the boat ramp. It's further away and the area's more open, but it's a straight sprint once we cross the road."

Maria nervously glanced at the Creatures behind them. "I think they've got guns. They'll shoot us as soon as we're in the open, if not before."

"Better to be killed by a bullet than become a science experiment." She grabbed Maria's shoulders and steered her into motion, but her sister stumbled, her injuries telling.

"Go." Maria tried to push her away. "Leave me."

"Shark bait?" Grace asked with as much sarcasm as she could muster. Before Maria could protest, she grabbed her by the waist, picked her up and ran with as much of a sprint as she could manage, rounding the clubhouse and crossing the road amid blasting horns. She didn't need to look back to know they were being followed. "You're heavier than you look," she muttered over several exhaled breaths.

"Then drop me and save yourself!"

Grace ran down Catlin Ave, and was about half way to the volunteer boat rescue building when she heard the first shot. They'd crossed the road behind her, but there was nothing she could do but run.

Knowing it would hurt Maria, she hauled her up and over her

shoulders in a fireman's carry so she could run faster. Maria cried in pain as Grace heard another shot. A hundred metres to go before a sharp left down the ramp to the water. Another shot, and then another. People ahead scattered in all directions, a couple of cars driving off amid flying gravel.

She weaved left and right as the people ahead scattered or ducked for cover. One boat already in the water cleared out of the launch area as another shot grazed Grace's shoulder.

"Almost there," she said breathlessly to Maria.

As she got level with the boat rescue building she left the road, rounding the trees at the corner and barely keeping her feet as she crossed gravel. As she hit the concrete of the boat ramp she threw Maria toward the water with all her strength.

A bullet punched through Grace's back and she stumbled, slamming shoulder-first into the ground. The joint popped under the impact and she cried out as her body twisted and half flipped. The pain took her breath away.

Half on her back and facing the building, she saw three women pull up short at the top of the ramp, guns pointed at her. Taking in a shuddering breath Grace reached out her good hand toward the salty water.

"We got her," one said into a microphone at her wrist.

"Come and get me," Grace said through gritted teeth. The concrete was wet where boats had been towed out of the water, giving her a direct connection to the ocean, though she no longer needed it. She called to the ocean, and water responded as if it were part of her.

"Oh fuck!" one of her attackers said.

Grace's wave surged past her as three bullets punched into her chest. Pain broke her concentration and she struggled to catch the three in her attack. Using what little energy she had left she dragged them all into the ocean, her own body washing in as well.

She needed to heal before she could do anything about the Creatures, and sucked the lifeforce from the lone werewolf before she drove the other two, both ghouls, through the narrow opening of the sheltered boat launch and deep out into the Bay. They struggled and flailed against her control of the water, but with the werewolf dead she used its lifeforce to expel the bullets, heal herself and stay focused on the ghouls.

The lack of oxygen wasn't going to be enough to kill ghouls though, and their lifeforce was so foreign she couldn't steal it. She needed to kill them another way.

She wouldn't make it to dawn after the damage she'd taken, but it didn't matter. Maria was safe. She controlled the water around her and swept the struggling ghouls further out, taking them well past the Tollgates and into deep water. When she was certain she was far enough from the coast that their bodies wouldn't wash ashore, she forced the salt from the surrounding water and froze it into blades, dismembering them. There was a surprising lack of blood.

Fire would be better to kill them, but she wasn't a dragon and this was the ocean.

She drove their destroyed bodies to the ocean floor and buried them under a heavy layer of silt. They might come loose, but she doubted it.

That's when she noticed the stillness. Throughout the ocean she sensed surprise, shock and even fear from her sisters around the world.

Worse, she could sense their lifeforce now, and it was even more appealing than a human's.

$$[\ \ 30\ \ ]$$

MERMAIDS all around the world stopped what they were doing and focused their emotions and attention on Grace. The sense of community, the bond between them all, now seemed a thousand times stronger to Grace, yet there was a newer, darker undertone. She felt dominant, predatory, and the inclusiveness she'd known was gone. Although she could sense them all much more strongly, she felt totally alone.

And they all held distilled lifeforce in their bodies, just as Talithia had. Worse, she knew she could take it now. Wanted to.

She closed herself off to them, recognising she was no longer the same as they were, even if Talithia had bound her far more tightly to them than she'd ever felt before. Talithia had made her responsible for ensuring their safety, and she felt that responsibility to the depths of her being, but that dark undertone frightened her and set her apart.

She was a danger to her own sisters now.

There wasn't another Creature on the planet quite like her, and she had a very limited lifespan to ensure they all remained safe, yet even if she did she wasn't sure they'd be safe from her.

"First problems first," she muttered to herself.

If the ghouls decided to hunt down mermaids, there was only so much ocean to hide in. Sooner or later they'd catch one of her sisters ashore desperate for human lifeforce, and if they could catch one mermaid they could catch more.

She looked around, remiss to realise Maria's presence was missing. Despite casting about for her maker's emotions, she found nothing. She'd never felt a complete lack of Maria's presence before, even when Maria had been on land. They'd always shared a bond. Fear ate at her heart as she tried to find Maria again. She wouldn't have returned to land, at least not voluntarily, which left only one conclusion. She'd been caught and isolated. Calling water to help, she let it caress her like a lover as she propelled herself into the Bay, slowing only when she closed on the marina.

If they'd harmed Maria, she was going to tear them limb from limb. Her fears grew into abject panic the moment she sensed a body in the water, and not the dead werewolf.

"Please no," she whispered the moment she saw the long dark hair drifting on the surface. She rushed in and caught Maria in her arms. "No, no, no," she cried, pulling Maria close, crushing her as if she could hold whatever lifeforce remained within her body. Traces of blood seeped from a wound at the back of Maria's head.

"Maria? Maria? Wake up Maria. Maria?"

SHE MUST HAVE HELD Maria's body for an hour or more before she noticed an insistent grip on her shoulders. She looked up into an unfamiliar face.

"Grace? It's Sandra."

Grace turned her attention back to Maria as if her sister might wake up and say 'boo', like it was all some big practical joke.

Sandra. Her daughter?

"I didn't know she'd been shot," Grace said so softly she doubted anyone could have heard. She touched Maria's necklace, still full of lifeforce, but the magic it held wasn't enough to bring her back from a headshot.

"Grace?" Sandra whispered.

"I felt bullets hit me, but I thought they'd missed her. I thought..." She thought it would take more to kill a mermaid. A severed spine, at least. Not a headshot.

"Grace? You need to let me help you."

Grace frowned, trying to makes sense of the words, but as she held Maria's body close nothing made sense.

"Talithia wanted us all to be safe. What she did to me was the only way."

"Grace, let me take care of Maria for you. Please?" She reached out, but Grace protectively pulled Maria's body away.

Hurt showed in Sandra's eyes. "What exactly did Talithia do to you? You're different. Even I can tell."

Grace's anger fell away when she realised she'd hurt her daughter. "I'm sorry Sandra." In contrition, she gently held out Maria's body, and when Sandra tentatively accepted the burden Grace drifted away, unable to look anymore. If she couldn't see or touch Maria, it might not be real.

"I'll look after her," Sandra said, freeing Maria's necklace and holding it out to Grace. "Why don't you rest for now? We can... do everything that needs to be done another time." She caught Grace's hand and wrapped her fingers around Maria's necklace. "You should have this."

An old human instinct overcame Grace and she wiped her eyes as if they were blurred by tears. She took a deep breath, trying to get her thoughts and emotions under control. "I have to go back to the hospital," she said as she put Maria's necklace around her neck.

"Grace," Sandra said gently. "You need rest. Josh can wait." Clearly her mermaid instincts were beginning to take priority over her previous human life.

Grace could feel the need to fix things like a knife twisting in her soul, however. "It's not only about Josh." She glanced at Maria's lifeless body and away just as quickly. Grace finally found the courage to meet Sandra's eyes, steadfastly not looking at the body her daughter held so dearly. "Sandra, I'm not coming back no matter what happens.

Surely even you can sense I need more lifeforce now than I can justify taking?"

Sandra met her stare. "If you're going ashore I'm coming with you, even if I have to choke on air."

Grace let the water take her close. She cupped Sandra's cheek. "Talithia sacrificed her life to give me the chance to save you and all our sisters. Whatever you do for Maria, make it special, and make sure all our sisters are there. She and Talithia mended things before they passed and we need to keep that legacy and make sure nothing like it ever happens again. We're weak when divided. Strong together. Never forget that."

Despite the fact Grace couldn't see tears, she was sure Sandra was crying. "I don't want you to die. I can't be... this, without you. I won't, not even for Josh and Mikey. I'd rather die too."

She really was becoming a mermaid. Grace would have said the same thing. Only the comforting presence of the water around them gave Grace the courage to face her own fears. "If I stay I'll be a natural disaster. Humans would stop entering the water I'd kill so many, and that would be a problem for everyone." Worse, she might start killing mermaids.

"We'll find a way," Sandra said, nodding her head as if mere belief could make a difference. "We will. I'm not letting you out of my sight until we do."

If she wasn't already heartbroken, Grace might have smiled at that. "I'm only good for keeping you safe now."

"But-"

Unable to talk further, Grace swam away far faster than Sandra could follow, her tears washing into her wake as fast as they appeared.

She emerged from the ocean at the south end of Casey's Beach, as far from swimmers as she could manage. She changed to human form while still in the water, stood and walked out as if fully-clothed women did that all the time.

She left her clothes and hair wet as she emerged, but by the time she reached the road she'd dried them. Her soft, un-calloused feet felt every pebble and stick on the hot bitumen. That hadn't changed. She nabbed a pair of sandals sitting atop a bin, the sole off one, but they'd do.

She followed the road to St Bernard's Church where she'd been attending mass at for the last few years, and found the nearby school grounds being set up for night-markets, a monthly fund-raising event to help both the church and school.

"Grace?" asked one of ladies as she put out cupcakes and craftwork on her stall table, a white cloth covering it. "What did you do to your hair? It was so pretty before."

"Sorry Maise, I can't talk now. How about we catch up over a cup of tea?"

"That would be lovely dear. Tomorrow?"

"Perhaps," Grace said as she moved on, dodging around a young family who had stopped to look at trendy crystals on the next table.

Crystals. Grace went cold as she realised who stood behind the cheap jewellery. The woman was different again, but when her eyes met Grace's she knew it was Kimbriel.

"Rough day at the office?" Kimbriel asked. "I see you've still got my bracelet."

Grace glanced at her wrist. She'd forgotten about that.

"Your sisters are in danger, Grace. We need to talk."

Grace stiffened, clenching her fists. "Are you threatening us?"

"I don't need to. You can feel it coming now, can't you?"

"I swear-"

"Promises aren't a good attribute to wear when we're both immortal. You might want to consider your next words very carefully."

Grace pursed her lips. "What do you want?"

"A promise, of course. The right one."

"Shove it," Grace muttered, walking off. She wasn't in the mood for games.

The rest of the stall-holders seemed to be a mix of artists, church-goers, people looking to make a few dollars from useless junk, and a selection of hard-core sales people selling cheap imported sunglasses, t-shirts, games and the like. They all rented stalls, the money benefiting the school and church.

Grace threaded her way past a honey-seller and a lean old man offering second-hand books, making her way to the church. As she entered the smell of old incense wrapped around her like a comforting blanket.

Inside, the junior choir were assembling for practice, some of the kids still in swimmers. She found the priest, Father Sumare, in his office at the back of the church. She knocked.

"Yes?" Young for a priest, he was short and dark-skinned with thick curly hair. She thought he might be from Papua New Guinea, but had never asked.

"It's Grace Harpeden, Father."

He looked up, eyes widening in shock. "Grace?" he asked as he glanced at her hair. If he'd once had an accent he'd lost it. She couldn't tell. "I'm sorry Grace, I didn't recognise you."

She smiled. "I'd like to make a confession, Father."

"I'm really busy Grace, can you come before mass on Sunday?"

She'd be dead by then. She tried to keep her smile, regardless. "I can't Father. It has to be now. Please?"

He must have seen the desperation in her face because he smiled and led the way to the confessionals. She entered hers and closed the door, kneeling while he said a brief prayer and prepared. She watched through the grate as he readied himself.

Finally she crossed herself and spoke the ritual words. "In the name of the Father, and of the Son, and of the Holy Spirit," Grace began. "My last real confession was over a hundred years ago."

There was silence for a long moment. "I'm sorry," Father Somare said. "Can you repeat that last part?"

"My last full confession was over a hundred years ago. On the Titanic." Hadn't he ever noticed she'd never once taken the Eucharist? She didn't feel right about it considering she'd never told him or any priest all of her sins.

Another long silence. "Go on," he said, obvious doubt in the words. He was probably wondering if she'd lost her sanity.

"Over the last century or so I've drowned dozens of people. I took fourteen as the Titanic went down before they could die of cold or go under themselves. Since then… too many. Almost one a year. More recently I drowned two nurses, both good women who didn't deserve it, and three werewolves and two ghouls. I'm hoping the ghouls don't count because they're not human, but I suspect the werewolves do."

"Grace," Father Sumare began hesitantly. "I don't believe I'm the right person to help you just now. Perhaps I could give you a recommendation-"

"Father, do you believe in God?" Grace asked, cutting him off before realising what she'd said. "Stupid question. Of course you do."

"Even if it wasn't my job."

"And by necessity, you also believe in... otherworldly things. Miracles? Divine intervention?"

"Yes." There was curiosity in his voice now. "Grace, are you all right?"

"Do you also believe in the supernatural, Father?"

"Spirits?"

"No. Creatures. Mermaids, vampires, succubi, ghouls, dryads, werewolves, harpies and the like. Supernatural Creatures."

"I can't say I've given it much thought."

She sighed. "I'm not human Father, though I was once, and I have to kill to survive. Can you forgive me?"

"Grace," he began hesitantly. "Can I suggest we meet with a friend of mine? Perhaps tomorrow?"

"Father, I just want to confess my sins, and the sins I'm about to commit."

[31]

"GRACE, it's my duty to counsel you-"

"I understand, Father, I really do, but it's also your duty to pray for me. Oh, and I've also stolen things. Clothes mostly. Sorry about that too." He wasn't likely to believe her, or at least not everything, so she was wasting her time, and his. With a sigh she crossed herself and left the confessional without waiting for penance.

"Grace," Father Sumare began as he left his confessional and followed her, but she didn't stay to hear him out. There were undead to slay and werewolves to murder. Throwing off regrets she couldn't do anything about, she left the church. Outside, the air had taken on the refreshing coolness of evening.

She took the footpath in the direction of the hospital on the assumption the Eris building wasn't too far from it. She didn't know what she'd do when she got to the hospital or the Eris building, but she'd figure it out on the way.

She hadn't quite made the end of the block before two youths in a wreck of a car pulled up beside her, windows down. "Hey," said the pimply-faced passenger, his voice slurry. He had a beer in his hand and looked all of about sixteen, with angry red acne scars on his cheeks.

Just what she needed, two boys hoping to get lucky. She could sense their lifeforce, but as it didn't have the taint of a werewolf she kept walking.

"Aww, come on. Hear us out," the passenger said as the driver moved the car forward at her pace.

She stopped and leaned on the open window when the car stopped, hoping to convince them not to shadow her through the streets. The driver was built like an athlete, unlike his friend who probably ate too much junk food, judging by his soft form. "I'm heading for the hospital," she said. "I had a sex-change about a year ago and the doctor wants to do a check-up."

The passenger got a goofy look on his face while the driver chuckled. "If you weren't so hot I might believe you. C'mon, we're keen for a party. Hop in." He looked hopeful.

It was a fair hike to the hospital. What the heck. She was more than strong enough to kick their butts if they tried anything.

"Heading for a party myself," Grace said. A murder party, and quite likely her own. She opened the back door and slid in. "You're not werewolves come to spoil it, are you?" she asked, trying to hold onto her natural humour, even though it didn't feel right. Anything to distract herself from thinking about Maria. She blinked tears away.

The passenger nearly choked on a mouthful of beer. "Not today!" he said with a laugh. "Let's go, Tim."

Tim stepped hard on the accelerator and pulled out with squealing tires. What was it about boys and cars and burning rubber?

"Want a drink?" the passenger asked, holding up a fresh beer. "I'm Jon," he said.

Tim and Jon? Better than Dick and Harry. "No thanks," Grace said as they sped through the next intersection without giving way. "Hey, you might want to watch the road Tim."

Instead of going straight at the next intersection he turned left.

"Hospital's the other way," Grace said, trying not to let her suspicions creep into her voice. They may not be werewolves, but she didn't want to have to hurt them if they tried anything.

"This way's faster," said Jon.

She leaned forward, her head between them. "You know guys, I think you mistook my intentions. I really am going to the hospital."

Jon turned, his acne scars clear this close. "Oh, come on! We can pay."

Grace raised her eyebrows. They thought she was a prostitute? She looked down at herself and considered her hair and clothes.

"Thanks, but I really do need to see someone at the hospital."

Tim grinned, his eyes leaving the road for a moment. "I'll take you there for a kiss, and not a peck-on-the cheek type sisterly kiss either. A real, full-on tongue-wrestle."

"Are you really that desperate for someone to pop your cherry?"

"What? Of course not," he said defensively. "I've been with girls. Like, lots of girls. Dozens."

Grace smiled and sat back. "You wouldn't like the way I kiss. Take me to the hospital please."

"I can handle it," he said with youthful cockiness.

She wondered if she really was going to have to do something violent. They were just a couple of horny kids though, and she didn't want to hurt them. "Please?"

Tim slowed down. "Fine," he muttered and turned the car around. "I really thought you were a... never mind. Can I at least say you're frigging hot, or is that no longer PC?"

She offered a genuine smile. "How about I do you a favour? If you see me around you can brag to your friends about what a fantastic night we had. I'll be happy to lie to them and say you were the hottest guys I've ever slept with."

"Holy shit!" said Jon. "You'd really do that?"

"Of course."

"Hell yeah! Donno's going to be *so* jealous!"

They sped off toward the hospital, the car making an ominous clunking noise whenever they veered to the right. She half expected to see one of the tires shoot past them. Josh's car looked little better, but it purred like a tiger.

Jon finished his beer and opened another before the hospital came into view. Grace felt dread at the sight. She had no idea how many ghouls or werewolves were in there, and it was dusk already. They'd all be stronger. If they were ready for her she doubted even her extraordinary strength or control of water would even the odds, but she had to try, and she had to convince one of them to take her to Josh, probably with violence.

"Out the front okay?" Tim asked as they slowed.

"Where's the Eris building?" she asked.

Tim hit the brakes, almost skidding to a stop and throwing Grace against the front seat. "What the hell?" she asked.

"You're having an abortion?" Jon asked.

The Eris building was an abortion clinic? "There's no way I'd ever do that," she said.

"So why are you going there?" asked Jon with his youthful lack of alcohol-infused tact. He was beginning to look more than a little drunk.

"Rave party." It was the first thing that came to mind.

Tim gave her a look. She considered getting out and walking, but they'd been pretty nice considering, and she wasn't sure where the building was anyway.

"A friend got into some trouble," she lied. "I'm the moral support."

Tim turned back. "Why didn't you just say so?" He put the clunky car into gear and drove off, and after half a dozen turns through the nearby industrial estate he drove into the rear car park of the Eris building. The three-storey building was about a mile from the main hospital, and the park was very private with high screening fences. Intentional, no doubt.

There were a dozen cars in the secluded car park, but no one was about. "Thanks for the ride," she said.

"Hey, you going to need a lift later?" Tim asked. "You know, save you legging it home?"

"Still hoping to get lucky, huh?" she asked.

He looked mortified. "That's not-"

"Good night, Tim."

The windows shattered and Grace cried out. Glass shrapnel stung her arms and face and then something punched into her shoulder, throwing her back. She rolled to the floor between the front and back seats as bullets struck her legs.

When the gunfire stopped it was agony to move, and worse when she found Tim's head leaning back against his seat, blood leaking from his temple. She tried to move, but her muscles were torn and her body bleeding.

She couldn't see Jon at all. Despite the pain, she tried to get to the front seat where she could at least shield Jon with her body, assuming he was still alive. A bullet punched through her neck and another through her chest, the second like a hammer, throwing her back. Struggling to breathe, she began choking on her own blood.

Another bullet thumped into her leg as she coughed up blood, but she was past reacting. She tried to expel the bullets, but she needed a fresh surge of lifeforce to do it. She was barely conscious as it was.

How had they even known she'd be coming?

[32]

Agony!

Grace tried to scream as a power saw cut through her sternum. A man in a white coat and protective eyewear stood beside her, electric saw in hand. The device looked like an angle grinder.

The man stared at her in shock. "Bullshit!" he said, the device almost slipping from his hand. "You're dead. Gavin! This thing is still alive!"

"I'm not falling for that crap again," came a bored voice from across the room.

"No shit this time! She's looking at me."

"Whatever."

She tried to breathe in, causing agony from a bleeding gash down the middle of her chest, the cut almost completely dividing her ribs.

She managed to get a hand to her chest in an insane attempt to fix it, as if she could make the cut disappear at a touch.

"I ain't shitting you Gav," the guy said, still staring at Grace. "I swear, even a vampire wouldn't be conscious after the damage she took in the car, and I've cut her open since."

In too much pain to do more than try and breathe, Grace heard footsteps and another person appeared beside her, a finger tentatively poking her bicep. Shock and surprise were clear on the man's face. "Nothing recovers that quickly. I didn't even know mermaids could regenerate." They stood on each side of her, staring like she was a living corpse.

This close, she could smell their lifeforce. Werewolves.

An insatiable need overcame her and she lashed out with both hands, fingers splayed as her claws punched through their clothes and into their sides.

She gripped tight as the first guy screamed, but the second appeared too shocked to react. Like a starving human desperate for food, she sucked their lifeforce out despite the lack of water.

With gasps they collapsed to the ground in union. Dead.

Grace used the stolen energy to repair her body, her bone and skin re-joining like a zipper, while she worked the bullets from her flesh, the holes closing over as she expelled them. She took a pain-free breath, letting it out slowly. She still hurt, but it was much better than before.

Where had they taken her? The air had a chemical smell to it. Sterility. But it was clean air, not a damp subterranean smell. She figured she was in an open area in a basement somewhere.

As she sat up something slammed into the side of her head, knocking her from the makeshift autopsy table. Another blow struck her ribs, but this time she saw it coming and lashed out, claws biting in. She heard a feminine scream as she sucked the lifeforce out of her attacker, and moments later a steel bar clattered to the ground followed by a werewolf's dead body in human form. Struggling to stand after the blow to the head, the sound of more Creatures running toward her suggested things were about to get a lot worse.

Staggering, she almost made it to the door before the first Creature burst through. It was Abbey.

The succubus ran into the room and swore in surprise as she saw Grace. It was the opening Grace needed. She slammed her fist into the succubus, knocking her into the wall beside the door as another Creature came through.

Grace barely recovered in time to catch the Creature in a last-minute embrace, but her momentum knocked Grace off her feet and they hit the ground together. "Oof!"

She dug her claws into the Creature's back, a female werewolf. The woman cried out in pain and bit her shoulder in return. Grace swore, clenching her teeth as she forced her claws deeper in and clenched them, cutting. The werewolf cried out and arched her head back, mouth and lips bloody from where she'd bitten Grace. As blood pooled against Grace's fingertips, she drew the werewolf's lifeforce out.

The woman gasped, shuddered and died atop her.

"That was bloody impressive," said a female voice.

Swearing in surprise and a thrill of panic, Grace shoved the dead werewolf aside and stood, staggering slightly and a little winded from the fall. Abbey was doing her best to push herself up the wall, a large bruise already on her cheek. If she hadn't been a Creature Grace would probably have broken her jaw.

"Abbey," Grace said with a growl.

The red-headed succubus offered a pain-filled smile as if she had the situation under control, but she was unsteady on her feet and the smile held no trace of her regular self-assurance. "You remember me? How sweet."

Grace's claws dripped werewolf blood as she stalked over to the succubus and punched her again, knocking her back to the ground. Abbey moaned.

She tore strips from the werewolf's jacket and used them as a makeshift rope to bind Abbey's hands behind her back.

As she hauled the succubus to her feet Grace reached out, trying to sense nearby water, but there was nothing nearby. As far as she could tell she was in a concrete bunker in what had once been a huge storeroom. The walls showed signs there'd been shelves against them before it had been converted to a temporary morgue.

"Nothing to say, Ariel?" Abbey said with a lopsided grin, though her knees buckled. "You know this place is full of Creatures, right? Dozens. And Josh. You should probably think about Josh before doing anything fun, like torturing me. You wouldn't want him to suffer."

Grace hauled Abbey into the middle of the room and shoved, sending her sprawling to the concrete floor. "Where's Josh?"

After a couple of wincing breaths Abbey blew hair out of her eyes as if the situation were to her liking, twisting sideways to smile up at Grace. "You kill werewolves with little more than a scratch now. How do you manage that?"

"They died from clumsiness."

Abbey's expression changed, the vindictive anger finally returning. "Some friends of ours who were following you earlier disappeared. I take it you did that?"

"They couldn't swim."

"Ghouls can't drown."

"It's a headless thing."

A snarl escaped Abbey's lips. "One of those ghouls was once my human mother," she said, her tone cold and deadly.

Grace stared in surprise. Her mother had been made a ghoul, while Abbey had been made a succubus? How had that happened?

Grace finally realised she was naked and stole the clothes from the dead female werewolf, claw-punched holes in the back of the top. "I'll be happy to take you to her," she said as she put them on. They were too small, but better than nothing. "Where's Josh?" she asked. "And Rick."

"Just kill me," Abbey said, closing her eyes and exposing her neck in a mocking dare. "I ain't telling you, and if you let me go I'll be the one making you headless, so you might as well do it now."

"Is that a promise?" Grace asked. "Because if it is, you can be sure you'll be dead before I leave the room."

Abbey glanced up, her bluff called. She certainly didn't want to die if the fear in her eyes told the truth, yet for a moment Grace was almost certain Abbey was going to make the promise anyway.

Abbey swore. "You've got no idea how badly I want to kill you, but no. No promise. So how to you do it? Even a good autopsy doesn't do the trick and kill you. Perhaps we need to go with cremation the next time we put you down? Perhaps a good old fashioned witch-burning?"

Grace narrowed her eyes. "We won't know until you try, but I doubt you'll get the chance."

As if she were the one in control, she glared up at Grace. "Why are you here, Ariel?"

"Ariel? You're the redhead."

Abbey rolled her eyes. "Why are you here, Grace? It's more than Josh, isn't it?"

"Actually, no. I figured you had some nasty things lined up for him."

Abbey gave her a smile and gave a soft laugh. "Your concern is misplaced. He's the last person I want to hurt. Any of us."

Grace tried to hold her temper at the half-truths and misdirection, though she really wanted to give Abbey a matching bruise on the other side of her face. "If you turned him-"

"Oh please! He's too valuable to turn. Far too much lifeforce. It's probably why you're attracted to him too."

She'd felt it, certainly. Felt it in Sandra as well, which only left one option she could think of. "You're siphoning his blood to sell to vampires?"

Abbey gave her a look which suggested Grace was an idiot. "Not even that, sister. Mind if I stand?" She got her feet under her and stood, showing no obvious fear as she moved closer, but not close enough to touch. She smiled, leaning forward to whisper. "He's helping us make babies. Ghouls go nuts over foetal tissue, particularly when the lifeforce that created it is so strong."

Grace's stomach turned and she stepped back. Staggered, really. "You're using him to get unsuspecting girls pregnant, and when they come in for an abortion...?"

Abbey smiled as if the pain on Grace's face was all the joy she could ever want. "Like I said, we don't want to hurt him. Not at all."

"But the babies..." Grace whispered.

"We're not playing God, mer-bitch. We're just as happy to let the girls keep their babies. Some will have Josh's strong lifeforce, and that's good in the long-term. We're not stupid. We're farmers with a long-term view."

"But-"

"You just don't get it, do you? We're reaping the harvest *and* planting more seeds. Creatures now and in the future will thank us, and all it takes is treating humans like farm animals. Getting girls involved without their knowledge is the trick, but we've got doctors and programs for that. It doesn't take much to get them in for a free check-up, inseminate them, and a few months later the ghouls get a meal paid for by the nice taxpayers." She smiled in a way that was probably designed to infuriate Grace.

"I want to throw up. On you." Grace turned away, certain she'd want to rip the succubus's head off if she didn't. The silence stretched as she tried to get her roiling emotions under control. She couldn't believe they'd treat people that way.

When Grace turned back she found the succubus watching her with a frown. "You know, your lifeforce smelled foul before, but it's even worse now."

That didn't make a lot of sense. Grace could barely detect other Creatures by their lifeforce. It was usually the lack of lifeforce that gave them away. "What did you say?"

"What did that other mermaid do to you before she died?"

"How do you even detect-"

Abbey swung at Grace's head, narrowly missing with her claws. She must have slipped Grace's makeshift bindings. "I'm going to tear your frigging head off!"

"Careful now," Grace said, fingers splayed and ready to retaliate. "If that was a promise I'm going to have to dice you up real small and feed the bits to the fish. Can't have something as powerful as a succubus making promises I don't want kept." She couldn't afford to kill her, at least until she led Grace to Josh and Rick.

Abbey narrowed her eyes. "Why is your lifeforce like poison to me?"

Grace moved between Abbey and the only door out. "How should I know?" She really had no idea.

Abbey pulled a small knife from the back of her belt, holding it between them as if it were more deadly than either of their claws. "I don't know either," Abbey muttered, knuckles going white around the grip. She pressed gentle fingers to her cheek, wincing. "Nice punch," she muttered.

"Where's Josh?" Grace asked.

"In the room across the hall. Why don't you go get him? I'll hold the fort here."

Grace sighed, just wanting the whole thing over. "Sure. Just as soon as you're unconscious." She lashed out with her left hand, but Abbey blocked, nicking Grace's forearm with the knife. It was worth it though, because Grace caught the succubus with another blow across her injured cheek, knocking her sprawling and opening her cheek with her claws.

Before Abbey could recover Grace was on her, and another punch knocked her out cold. Although tempted to rip the succubus's head off, getting Josh out was more important, and there was a good chance he wasn't where Abbey said he was. Hopefully Rick was with him.

She found the door across the hall and opened it, relief coursing through her when she found Josh there, sitting against the opposite wall. Blood crusted his swollen bottom lip and he looked ready to pass out, but he was alive.

"You okay?" she asked him, rushing in and helping him to his feet.

"I'll recover." His hands were bound behind his back.

"Show me your hands."

Josh turned. Handcuffs. Grace grabbed the chain and snapped the links with only a little grunt. Josh turned back, staring. "How the heck?"

"Where's Rick?"

He looked even more concerned at his friend's name. "No idea. Why is he involved?"

[33]

"HE WAS HELPING US," Grace said. "I've got to get you out of this place first, then I can do something about Rick. I can't protect you both." She wasn't sure she could protect even one, but she had to try. Better to even the odds a little with Josh getting to safety.

She turned to find a woman standing in the doorway, shotgun pointed at Grace's chest. Grace heard the explosion and felt the impact as if they were two disconnected events. The next moment she was on her back, her chest an agony of pain. She used stolen lifeforce to expel the pellets and heal herself, but the next shot would put her back down and she doubted she had enough lifeforce to keep her conscious again.

No shot came.

She sat up, surprised, and found the woman on the ground, unconscious, and Josh standing over her.

"Nice work! Damsel in distress duly saved. Feel like a man yet?"

He turned toward her and went to speak, but didn't seem to be able to find the words as he opened and closed his fist as if it hurt.

Grace stood and moved to the woman, crouching and jabbing a claw into her forearm. "She's a ghoul," she said, glancing up at Josh. "You don't want to look." Before he could respond she snapped the Creature's neck.

He stared, mouth open.

"Come on," Grace said. "That blast will attract attention. Let's go." She picked up the shotgun, grabbed his hand and dragged him from the room, handing him the weapon once they were in the corridor. The gun looked awkward in his hands.

"I finally remembered what they did to me," he said as they headed toward the stairs. "And others." A muted peal of thunder rolled across the sky outside, almost ominous considering his words. The storm must have been close if they could hear it. In the basement though, she couldn't sense it at all.

Ahead she heard footsteps and ducked into another room, dragging Josh with her before closing the door.

She was nearly sick at the sight that confronted her. Glass-front fridges and freezers. Vacuum-sealed clear plastic bags hung on racks, each one holding body parts or an aborted foetus.

"I want to vomit," Josh whispered.

"That's absolutely wrong," Grace said in agreement. There must have been a dozen foetuses packed for shipping, and hundreds of organs including kidneys, livers and hearts. The ghouls were raiding corpses, taking what they could get away with, and shipping the parts for profit.

"Why would they do this?" Josh asked. "I mean, you can't transplant these organs now, and..." he glanced at the foetuses. "What's going on here Grace? It's not making any sense."

She had no intention of explaining ghouls and their appetites to him. She didn't really know enough herself.

Almost against her own will, she opened a fridge door and gingerly took a plastic bag from a rack. She couldn't tell what was inside other than the fact it had to be human flesh.

Sickened, she pierced the bag with a claw, her fingertip tingling at the rush of lifeforce it still held. She dropped the bag with a soft sound and backed away. It was human flesh.

"We have to stop them," Josh whispered. "This is sick." His face was deathly pale, his horrified expression probably a reflection of Grace's.

"We will," she whispered, meaning it. "We'll destroy every last one of the Creatures." She was almost ashamed at the sound of hatred in her own voice. "Come on."

When they opened the door she found the corridor empty. They ran to the concrete stairs at the end and slunk up as quietly as possible, Grace's bare feet making no sound. There was a short landing and a heavy fire door at the first level, while the fire stairs continued up. She could hear indistinct voices beyond the door. At least three. Very carefully she pulled it open a crack, but couldn't see anyone.

The voices stopped.

Grace had no idea whether she'd drawn their attention or if it was coincidence. She quietly closed it and indicated up. Josh dashed ahead, Grace following. They'd just made it past the first landing where the stairs doubled back when the fire door burst opened. Grace froze, but Josh took another couple of steps before stopping.

Heavy booted footsteps entered, two sets coming up, two going down. Grace sprang up the next flight, grabbing Josh by the shirt and half hauling him up with her. They reached the next door and Grace pulled it open, shoving Josh through as the pursuers reached the landing below. Just as quickly she pulled it shut with a solid thump.

She stepped back as the door swung open, and without thinking Grace kicked hard. She caught a rangy, red-bearded man in the chest, knocking him off his feet and directly back into the woman behind him.

"Run!" Grace screamed to Josh.

He was already moving. Grace caught up toward the other end of the corridor, office doorways on one side and an open plan area the other.

A man burst out of the last office. Grace shoved Josh aside and caught her attacker's arm, her claws biting in but sensing a lack of lifeforce as she twisted and broke his elbow. The ghoul grunted in pain but didn't fall.

He tried to bite her with sharp-looking canines, but despite the Creature's supernatural speed Grace was faster. She spun and pulled on the broken arm, throwing him into the office wall, the impact hard enough to put his head and shoulders through the wall.

She caught him by the throat as he pulled free, unsheathing her claws as she twisted with both hands. She felt the Creature's neck snap before the ghoul dropped like a rag. She didn't dare look at Josh. She didn't want to know what he might be thinking. He may not remember he was in the midst of Creatures later, but he'd remember seeing her kill people. He wouldn't forget that.

She could sense the water in the plumbing now, but just as she reached out to it a massive werewolf in wolf form slammed into her, throwing her back twenty feet. She tumbled until they hit a wall, the Creature supernaturally strong in its animal form, as strong as any vampire or succubus at night. Stronger.

It bit her arm and she cried out in pain, trying to pull it away. It held on as she tried to punch her claws into its neck, but it picked her up and shook her, trying to tear her arm off.

She cried out as it slammed her against the ground, its teeth crushing her flesh and trying to snap the bone. She could feel its lifeforce through its bite, and desperate to try anything, she drew on it, pulling lifeforce through the connection it had made with her own blood.

The werewolf realised what was happening too late and released her, but she sunk her free claws through its thick fur. It struggled, bucked and tore at her arm, but in moments it collapsed.

Gushing blood from a severed artery, Grace covered the wound with her free hand as she staggered to her feet. Three more werewolves burst out of the fire escape at the other end of the corridor, all in wolf form.

"What the hell is going on?" Josh asked, staring in horror at Grace's bloody claws and pumping blood. "How are you even alive after that?" He backed toward the wall.

"Just shoot the bloody werewolves," she yelled, backing away from the threatening pack as they stalked nearer, spreading out. Grace's canines had extended, which probably didn't add any serenity to her bloody appearance. As they cautiously neared she directed lifeforce to her arm, staunching the blood and knitting the flesh back together.

One stopped and sniffed the body she'd left, and when it raised its eyes she saw hatred.

To her right a sweeping flight of stairs led down towards the lobby, while a narrower set of stairs went upward, probably to the offices above them.

"There she is!" someone yelled from the lobby. The werewolves seemed to take it as a signal to attack.

Grace grabbed Josh and sprinted for the stairs up.

A bullet punched into the wall just ahead of her and another grazed her shoulder in a sharp burst of pain. She reached the landing and dodged around it, bouncing off the wall and shoving Josh toward the next level.

"Find a way out," Grace said, panting now as she made the corridor just behind him. She might be able to take a few bullets and bites, but anything like that would kill him. The layout of the corridor they spilled into mostly mirrored the one below, office doors to the left and right, open plan making up the remainder of the offices. The surgery rooms must have been on the ground floor.

Grace shoved through the first door they came to just as someone with a gun charged up the stairs behind them. She dragged Josh to the ground as bullets threw splinters of shrapnel. Grace rolled right, grabbed an office chair and threw it backwards at the door she'd come through, smashing the back off as it struck the open doorframe and went through. Someone grunted as Grace got to her feet, following the chair and diving through to crash-tackle the Creature, a huge ghoul.

A bullet burst through her stomach while another punched through her chest. She staggered back but snapped the ghoul's neck as she fell.

Gasping and laying still to pretend she was down for good, she expelled the bullets from her body. She'd need more lifeforce if she took any more.

A hard ball of muscle and fur struck her. Teeth bit her side as it used its momentum to throw her bodily through the air. She hit the ground hard and the werewolf followed, landing atop her and doing its best to tear her throat out.

Panicking a little, she cried out and drove her knee into its the stomach, giving herself enough room to shove it aside as another crashed into her, teeth ripping into her forearm. She yelled in pain as she grabbed it, sinking her claws into its ribs. She barely drained any of its lifeforce before the first one struck, tearing her hand free of its companion's ribs.

The other one twisted and savaged her leg. Despite the pain she tried to drain its lifeforce while punching at the other one. Taking advantage of the distraction, it let go of her leg and lunged for her throat, but as the Creature's teeth sunk into her neck she heard a shotgun fire and the werewolf fell on top of her.

With silent thanks to Josh, Grace used the contact to drain the lifeforce from the werewolf, enough to let her heal her arm and neck. She grabbed the last werewolf, claws punching through its fur and skin, and drained its lifeforce too. Still in pain, she shoved the bodies aside and clambered to her feet. Breathing hard, she looked around at the shattered walls and furniture, some of which she didn't even remember hitting.

A dozen werewolves gathered at the stairs now. Although moving as if wary of her, they were all in wolf form. If they attacked at once there was no chance she'd survive even if she killed a couple.

Beyond the werewolves, ghouls waited. Among them was Abbey, her pretty face still bruised. She was the lone succubus as far as Grace could tell.

Grace turned as she sensed someone closer, and found a ghoul with a gun to Josh's temple. Very slowly, Josh let the tip of his shotgun point at the floor.

"Maybe it's time to give up," Abbey said with a smile, and then she winced, touching her cheek with her fingertips. "Fuck. I think you broke a tooth."

[34]

GRACE SHIFTED her weight toward Josh while desperately trying to
figure a way out where at least he might survive, but three werewolves
snarled and moved as she did. She doubted she'd be able to save him if
it came to a fight, let alone herself. She'd failed Sandra and all her
sisters.

A black werewolf with white feet padded forward and nudged the
biggest of the fallen werewolves with its nose, whimpering when the
dead Creature didn't move. It raised its head and snarled at Grace, dark
red eyes narrowed and body tensing to spring.

She swore. Even if she killed it the rest would tear her apart, and
Josh too, no doubt.

Catherina shoved between the other ghouls and snapped her
fingers, making the black werewolf pause. "Back off, Monique," she
told the Creature. The werewolf gave her a brief glare but did as told.

"Good doggy," Grace said provocatively. "I'll see if I can find you a
treat later."

Catherina glared at Grace. "They don't understand language in
animal form," she said. "Just commands and tone. Similarly, they
always follow the strongest Creature. Me."

"I'll arm wrestle you for the title."

Catherina smiled thinly. "Let's talk about you, Grace."

"Thanks, but I'm on my way to the beach, but don't feel too bad. I was only leaving because I didn't like the accommodations. You should sack your staff."

Catherina narrowed her eyes. "I'll make you a deal Grace. I'll let you and Josh go if you show me how to use this." She held up Maria's necklace.

Grace reached for her throat. She wanted to snatch it from the Creature's hands. "Great. Now I have to boil it in hot water to disinfect it."

Judging by Catherina's expression, Grace was getting to her, and people who thought with their emotions made mistakes. It was her only weapon at the moment, though she could sense water in the building's plumbing. Unfortunately it wasn't close, and it would take time to draw enough to use as a weapon. The roof didn't have a sprinkler system, unfortunately.

"Promises are binding. I want a promise from you," Catherina said.

Thunder rolled across the sky again as Grace glanced at Josh. He gave her a tiny nod, agreeing to whatever she decided to do. She turned back to Catherina, not really caring what that promise might be. She didn't have any intentions of making one.

"I have a couple of conditions. First, you leave Josh out of this. He walks free, never to be troubled by another ghoul or werewolf as long as you can help it. Second, you leave all mermaids alone as well. Forever." Depending on what Catherina wanted, she might even agree if her terms were met.

Catherina smiled, but there was no kindness in it. "Show me how you make and use these necklaces and I won't need to trouble you or your mermaid... friends. Deal? Except for Josh of course. He stays."

"No deal," Grace said automatically. She wouldn't betray Sandra like that. Josh was as much Grace's grandson as he was Sandra's son.

"Then we have a problem. His lifeforce is strong. A very valuable asset."

"He's Sandra's son, and that puts him under my protection. Sandra is now a mermaid."

Catherina shrugged. "Then we kill you, take him, and find another mermaid to help us. Do you like that option better?" Her tone was soft, but forceful and uncompromising. She'd do it without a doubt.

Grace couldn't think of another way out of this that didn't involve her dying or her sisters in conflict. If they kept Josh he may not be physically harmed, but she didn't know what else they might do. They could keep him in a cage. "And the necklaces? What if you can't use them?"

Catherina smiled, and like before, there was no warmth in it. "Then that would be a problem for you and your kind. I'm sure that with enough experimentation we could find a way though. Might have to go through a few mermaids first."

Insults crept into Grace's thoughts, but she didn't want to put Josh at any further risk. "And if you can use them, but can't make them? Making them requires a certain control of lifeforce." A straight lie, but Catherina didn't know that. Without lifeforce they were just simple necklaces.

Catherina shrugged. "We can trade."

"You have nothing we want." Except Josh. And peace.

Abbey stepped forward. "Gems. You need cut gems for your necklaces. We'll supply two per necklace. One for you. One for us."

Grace bit her lip, considering. Being forced to make necklaces was far better than any mermaid's death. "I want a promise up front that you'll never harm a mermaid, or let any of your Creatures harm one. And Josh goes free."

Catherina snapped her fingers and a big ghoul came up the stairs and dumped Rick's unconscious body on the ground, and none too gently. "Rick?" Josh asked.

"How about you do it my way?" Catherina aimed her gun at Rick.

"Don't you-"

The explosion was shockingly loud.

"No!" Grace cried as Rick's body jerked and lay still. "Oh God, no." Who was going to look after his mother now?

Catherina pointed her gun at Josh. "Josh is replaceable too. Inconvenience is just a price I'm willing to pay."

Impotent anger welled up, but she held her hands up to stave off the next shot, palms outward. Regardless of whether or not Catherina was bluffing, Grace wasn't going to take the chance. "Okay! Just don't hurt him."

Catherina lowered her gun, a satisfied smile on her thin lips. "Then we have a deal?"

"Yes. Deal. Go, Josh. Get out of here."

Catherina held up her hand. "After you show me how to use the necklace."

Grace shook her head. If she could avoid risking Josh, she would. "You control a pack of werewolves. It's not like you won't be able to hunt him down if I go back on my word."

Catherina considered it for a moment, and then shrugged. "You know what, I'm going to run with it." She nodded toward Josh. "Let's play it Grace's way. But just remember Josh, you have a son, and I'm sure I can track down your extended family, friends, and anyone else you care about too. I'll be in touch if I need you."

Josh glanced at Grace, shock, doubt and fear apparent. She didn't need to feel his emotions to see them in his eyes. "Grace?" It was more than a question.

Grace nodded. "Go Josh. I'll make sure you and Mikey are safe."

His eyes went to his dead friend before he lifted his hurt gaze to Catherina, his fists clenching.

"Josh!" Grace said with enough force to catch his attention. When he glanced her way she indicated the way out. "Please. You can't help if you're dead." Or being used as a hostage. "Go."

He gave her one last look, but finally nodded.

Grace stayed where she was, listening until she heard him leave the building through the main entrance below. As the doors opened she could hear rain beginning to hit the ground outside. The air was humid with it despite the building's air conditioners. Thunder pealed overhead, though the rain was well beyond her reach.

The trickles of water in the gutters and downpipes would be close enough to control if she could get to an external wall, but by the time she could do anything with it she'd be torn to pieces or full of bullets.

Complying was the best option she had.

"Show me how to use the necklace," Catherina said after Josh was safely gone. "I want access to its lifeforce."

Grace held her hand out. "Give it to me."

Catherina approached despite the protective snarls of her werewolves. The ability to understand the difference between language and danger appeared to be two entirely different things.

Catherina held Maria's necklace out to Grace on a fingertip, but as Grace moved to take it, Catherina pulled back slightly. "I know you can use this yourself, but like you, we can sense the lifeforce in it. If you draw any of it, we'll kill you."

Grace tried to appear as if that hadn't been her intention. "I won't take any unless it's part of the demonstration, and you give me permission first. Fair?"

Catherina gave a nearly imperceptible nod.

There was enough lifeforce in the necklace to keep Maria alive for years, and Grace ached to take it. It was all she had left of Maria now. Grace doubted there'd be enough to keep her going for more than a day or two, even if she'd been attuned to it.

"Hold out your hand."

With only a hint of hesitation, Catherina complied.

"The necklace is attuned to Maria. It means she'd have been able to draw energy from it even if unconscious. If I focus on it, I could draw on the lifeforce too, but it takes effort and a lot of it would bleed away, wasted. Maybe you can do the same. Focus on it."

Catherina's fist closed over the jewel and pearls. "I sense it there, but it's completely unnatural to me. I can't reach it."

"The gem holds the lifeforce, but the pearls act as a bridge to the gem. Perhaps you need a different bridge."

"Flesh? Blood?"

Catherina was a ghoul, so it made sense. What would make more sense would be for Grace to kill her and every other Creature here, ending the threat to her kind. She had no doubt that as soon as Catherina found a way to access the gem's stored lifeforce she'd kill Grace and renege on their deal. She certainly hadn't tried to force a reciprocal promise, which suggested betrayal. "Perhaps." Grace extended a claw to spike her finger and draw blood.

"Wait," called Abbey. "Her lifeforce is toxic to me, which probably means her blood is toxic to you. Better use your own."

Grace gave the succubus a long look, considering. "She might be right," Grace said, except that wasn't quite what she was thinking. Her eyes returned to Maria's gem. The lifeforce in it might be toxic to Catherina or any Creature, except for a mermaid. Otherwise, if they could steal each other's lifeforce, Creatures would have been at war with each other since the dawn of time.

Did she dare say anything? What would happen if Catherina could draw on the necklace's stores and it didn't kill her? Would it at least make her sick enough for Grace to take advantage of?

Watching intently to make sure the ghoul didn't reach the same conclusion, she held the jewel out as Catherina pricked her finger on a sharp canine and touched it to the gem. Her eyes widened. "I can feel it much more strongly now." She frowned as she focused on it. "But it's still out of reach. It's… wrong. Not attuned to me? Perhaps I need more blood to alter it enough so I can take it."

She took the necklace from Grace, staring at it as if Grace no longer posed any threat.

Half a dozen of the ghouls were beginning to look greedy now too, clearly seeing the potential in stored lifeforce. Grace held her breath, hoping they took the bait and her gamble paid off. The ability to draw on it would probably make them considerably more powerful if it worked though, but if it didn't it could destroy Catherina. Grace hoped it went her way and didn't tip the balance of power towards ghouls.

"Human blood might work better," Abbey said. She turned to a ghoul. "Go get a bag of it."

Thankfully she seemed to have forgotten about Rick's body, still seeping blood into the carpet. The ghoul returned in half a minute with blood in a labelled plastic medical bag. He tossed it to Catherina.

Catherina pricked a tiny hole in it with a tooth, squeezed a drop onto her finger, and tentatively touched it to the gem. "Oh, oh wow! That's incredible. I could live for a century on this."

"A century?" Grace asked in surprise, her hopes beginning to shatter at the thought her gamble wasn't going to pay off. "There's only enough for about five years for a mermaid."

"It's still not attuned to me, like it's tainted somehow, but I can touch it regardless."

"Be cautious," Grace warned with false concern. She hoped Catherina completely ignored her warning, but if things went badly at least Grace could say she'd tried.

Catherina locked eyes with Grace. "I'll take the risk." She closed her eyes, and Grace could sense a trickle of the lifeforce leaving the gem. When Catherina opened her eyes again, she looked faintly sick. "It's like tasting a mermaid's blood, foul, yet it's incredibly powerful and I can absorb it."

"Careful," Abbey said. "I threw up after kissing Grace."

Catherina turned to Abbey, her bloody finger still touching the gem. "I can feel the lifeforce coursing through me already. My body is adjusting." She looked excited. "The energy is incredible!"

"That's probably enough," Abbey insisted. "We know we can access it. Let's study the effects."

Her eyes alight with power, Catherina shook her head. "You saw what an entire gem's worth of lifeforce did to Grace. It made her faster, stronger. You've got no idea how powerful this will make me."

Grace backed away. The distilled lifeforce from Talithia's body had reforged her, not the lifeforce stored in the gem. It was like comparing a burning leaf to rocket fuel. The gem's stored lifeforce had merely kept Grace alive afterward. Grace wasn't going to enlighten her however. There was already enough danger if she could figure out how to store and access lifeforce.

There was madness in the ghoul's eyes now, well beyond a hunger for power.

"Catherina?" Abbey said, hesitantly moving forward. "We need to assess the risks."

"There are none," Catherina said with gritted teeth as she drew on Maria's stored lifeforce. Grace felt the lifeforce surge out of the necklace and into the ghoul in a sudden rush, and wasn't sure whether to cheer or back away in fear.

The gem broke in two with a loud crack.

Light flared through Catherina's fingers and she gasped, almost falling to her knees. Grace squinted and turned away, but when she turned back Catherina merely stood there, the spent necklace and remains of the shattered gem in her hand. The chain slipped through her fingers and fell to the carpet.

"Oh," Catherina whispered, staring at her bloody fingers. "That's... incredible. So much power!"

Oh crap. Her gamble had backfired. She'd just made a ghoul very powerful.

Catherina's hand shimmered, the energy visibly spreading up her arm to the rest of her body. She spun, a crazy half smile on her lips. "Can you sense it?" she asked. "I'm full of life's energy." She spun again, but it was slow, as if she were delirious. "Did you see that?" she asked, a slight slur in her voice. "I moved so fast the world blurred. This is going to change everything."

"Something's wrong," Abbey said, backing away as she glared at Grace. "What did you do?"

"What?" Grace protested. "You heard me warn her! You warned her yourself!"

Catherina stared at the onlookers, staggering slightly. "With power like this I can rule... world." She didn't seem to be able to focus her eyes.

"The mermaid did something to her!" one of the ghouls yelled.

Grace took a step away. "I tried to warn her!"

Catherina fell to her knees like a drunk, an insane grin on her face. "I'm changing," she whispered. "Can... can you see?" Her skin was becoming darker. Blood red.

"Kill the mermaid," another ghoul said, pointing her gun at Grace. "She did this."

"What?" Grace protested at the unfairness of the accusation. "She did it to herself!" If they turned on Grace now she'd be dead in moments. She could heal a few bullet wounds, but that would use up the rest of her lifeforce and then they'd tear her apart.

The werewolves began backing away from Catherina as if instinct warned them of danger. One snarled at Grace, huge teeth barred.

"Oh, blame me for Catherina's stupidity," she said, backing away herself now, hands up to show she was unarmed, her claws sheathed.

A shot rang out and Grace felt a thump in her chest. She staggered back, unable to breathe as blood began filling her lungs and the pain hit. She drew on her lifeforce and expelled the bullet, healing only what was necessary to stop the blood seeping into her lungs, but it drained her.

She fell to her hands and knees and coughed blood. The taste was still on her lips as she raised her head. If she could get her claws into one of the werewolves...

"I'm amazing," Catherina slurred. Her hands were almost blue-black now, her face a mottled red. Veins stood out at her temples, dark and tight, her skin stretched. She stiffened with a gasp, her back arching, and like Grace's final gift to Talithia, Catherina dissolved.

Ghouls cried out in shock and jumped back as blood washed over Grace's hands and knees, carrying with it all the wasted lifeforce Catherina hadn't been able to contain. People had died to give Maria that lifeforce, and now it was soaking into the carpet.

"She couldn't hold it," Grace whispered. Perhaps she had no way to evolve as Grace had.

"Kill the mermaid!" cried a ghoul. "And all of her kind."

"No," Grace whispered, holding her hands up, palms out. Not for herself, but her sisters. She looked up to see every gun already pointed at her. Several of the werewolves snarled, preparing to attack.

"Please," Grace pleaded as gunfire broke the silence and dozens of bullets ripped into her.

Flesh tore, bone shattered and her lungs filled with her own blood. She collapsed to the ground, her face in Catherina's bloody remains, and she didn't have enough lifeforce left to heal.

$$[\ 35 \ ]$$

GRACE STRUGGLED to breathe as she coughed and then vomited up her own blood. She dribbled bloody saliva as she tried to breathe, sensing more than seeing a werewolf before her, the Creature's whiskers brushing her cheek as it sniffed her face to make sure she was dead. She wasn't, but she might as well be.

Blood bubbles escaped her lips as she choked on her own blood, a death gurgle in her chest.

Fear of failing to protect her sisters spiked as painfully as the bullets that had torn through her. Even so, her heart kept defying the damage, pumping what was left of her blood to the floor where it mixed with Catherina's sticky remains.

Grace forced another agonising breath in and tried to reach out to the werewolf, but the Creature moved away, wary and for good reason. Her hand and face remained on the bloody carpet, the floor still alive with the stolen lifeforce of Maria's necklace and Catherina's liquefied body. She could feel the wasted energy distilling into Catherina's drying blood and gore, soon to be thrown out and dumped with the wrecked carpet. So much power at her fingertips, and it was all inaccessible, even to her.

She was going to die and leave her sisters in danger. Not just her sisters. Josh and his son Mikey, and everyone they cared about. Despair filled her and wouldn't let go. When she died her sisters would be hunted to extinction for what had happened here, and they wouldn't even know until it began.

Her chest spasmed and she coughed more blood, dribbling it to the carpet. She had too many bullet wounds to heal despite almost swimming in the lifeforce distilled in Catherina's blood and ruptured body.

Desperate to try anything, Grace bit her claws into the carpet, but even though she could feel the lifeforce there, it was foreign to her now. It had changed Catherina, and in the process been changed itself.

More than likely many Creatures had been born of such corruptions in the past instead of dying as Catherina had. Perhaps tainted blood like this was the reason vampires had been created. More than just vampires. Ghouls ate rotting flesh to access the distilled lifeforce it held. It wasn't that corruption that called to her blood however, it was the fresh and nearly pure lifeforce of the werewolves around her. Her blood connected her to Catherina's blood and the lifeforce Maria had once stored in her gem, and she realised it was why she could sense the werewolves standing in it.

A thrill of hope filled her as she drove her senses through the blood. The werewolves stood in it, and like wiring up a battery to a motor she made the connection. Three of them crashed to the sticky carpet without a sound of protest, kicking spasmodically before finally laying still.

"What the...?" someone asked as Grace coughed blood from her lungs, a thrill of energy surging through her. She expelled bullets from her chest and abdomen, took a deep breath and coughed up more blood. She directed the lifeforce to the worst of the wounds, stopping the bleeding and healing the damage.

As the ghouls looked around for some new threat, Grace expanded her senses to the plumbing in the building. The water wasn't close enough to rip it through steel, but concentrating, she forced the water there to freeze and expand. With loud tearing sounds, the pipes finally ruptured. Ghouls and werewolves spun defensively, weapons aimed at the walls.

Grace unfroze the water and it spewed into the building's walls and cavities, the sound of it like heaven. She heard someone turn towards her, finally putting the puzzle together. She wasn't going to let them shoot her again.

She called to the water in the walls as she leapt to her feet, making it spear through the wall and spray the hallway.

Ghouls yelled in surprise, protecting their eyes as Grace turned the water into a blizzard of stinging ice.

"It's the mermaid!" A gun half deafened her and a bullet grazed her shoulder.

Grace pulled on all the water she could, the walls exploding with the force of it, knocking ghouls and werewolves in every direction and piercing their flesh with frozen shrapnel. In the aftermath, those not too hurt ran for cover.

Grace gathered all the water she could and smashed out an office wall with it, throwing the nearest ghoul into the office beyond. She forced the water into the office and used it to shatter its windows. Glass rained to the concrete outside the building, but it was the water outside she wanted. She expanded her senses into the storm and drew as much of the storm inside as possible. Hail, sleet and stinging rain burst through the windows, shredding a ghoul as he tried to stand.

Guns fired, some bullets even hit her, but she ignored the pain, using the stormwater and broken plumbing to smash the weapons aside. Ghouls fell to the ground, some ran, but two managed to stand their ground and shoot at her.

She flung hail as hard as bullets at them, pulping their bodies and pounding several werewolves into a mess. She drew the werewolves' lifeforce back through the water and healed her wounds before reaching out to the storm again.

Through it she felt lightning flicker in the clouds. She called and it arced downward, exploding the roof in an avalanche of concrete and steel shrapnel. Electricity lit up the building and exploded lights and appliances in showers of sparks.

Ghouls and werewolves screamed as they were thrown from their feet, some with horrific burns, but Grace was beyond any empathy she might have for them.

She reached through the shattered roof to the storm and funnelled more water into the building. It cascaded through the opening like a waterfall. She directed it down the corridors, blowing the circuits in the walls and shattering doors and windows. Electricity arced through the water and the entire building shorted out.

Behind her a werewolf took a chance and leapt at her back, but there was more than enough water in the building to sense it. She leapt, twisting as she moved, and grasped a hanging cable from the shattered roof with one clawed hand as she lifted her legs out of the way.

The werewolf snapped at her, trying to catch a hold as Grace lashed out with her free hand and opened its side, her claws cutting through its ribs. It crashed to the wet carpet with a splatting sound and a high-pitched whimper. Grace didn't let it suffer, reaching out through the water and drawing its lifeforce into her.

A bullet shattered her shoulder and she fell with a cry to the ground. She rolled, pulling up water to attack as bullets tore up the bloody carpet before her face. She jerked backwards, launching herself through a drywall and crashing over bookshelves to hit the ground hard. She rolled as more bullets sent shrapnel into the room, ducking behind the desk as automatic fire shattered the walls and ripped furniture apart.

The window behind her broke and she took advantage of the damage to freeze the rain outside and pull it through as hail. Ice bullets ricocheted off the walls and furniture, a good portion pelting through the hole she'd made coming through to hit someone beyond. The gunfire stopped and Grace turned the hail into a storm of water, pulling icy slush into the building through every opening she'd made.

She reached out with water to grasp the four ghouls remaining in the corridor and pin them down. Using the water like an extension of herself, she drove it into their mouths and lungs where she froze it solid, destroying from the inside. Determined to end the threat they posed to her sisters, she froze water into sharp blades and severed their heads, ensuring they stayed dead.

Staggering to her knees, she expelled the bullets she'd taken and healed the damage, but it took most of the lifeforce she'd stolen from the werewolves to do it. She had to finish this before they shot her again. She wasn't sure she had enough energy to heal herself unless she killed more werewolves.

She reached out to the storm yet again, wishing she could control the winds as well as the water, and directed as much rain as she could at the building. She staggered to the shattered window, placing her hands on the wall outside, and froze the water all over the building to seal the doors and windows shut as quickly as she could. She had to trap them all or this would never end. With every second the rain added to her coating of ice, making it thicker and thicker.

She drew more water from the gutters and rooftop and pulled a miniature tsunami into the building through the roof. Somewhere below she heard cries of shock and horror, and howls of rage as the ghouls and werewolves found themselves trapped.

More water than she'd ever controlled before rushed into the building via the storm, gushing into offices and freezing solid against doors and windows. She directed as much as she could into the stairwells until it began filling the basement, forcing ghouls and werewolves who'd taken shelter there to flee upwards.

Grace froze water against every window and door in the building, reinforcing her ice as ghouls emptied their guns against it in desperate attempts to escape. She couldn't allow even one out.

Sensing them all through her water, she pulled more into the building, freezing it in the air outside and bringing down hail with thundering devastation.

Entire sections of the roof collapsed under the weight. She directed more water downstairs until it began to rise beyond the basement, using the connection of water to burst every tap in the building, bringing more water in.

When she was sure she had all the werewolves and ghouls trapped, she drove icy water to them, freezing them in place like a macabre ice-age display. The water responded to her thoughts like a lover keen to please, and she used it to swallow them under and tear them apart. She stole all the lifeforce she could from the werewolves, letting it buoy her, but didn't stop there. The ghouls weren't dead yet.

She drew more water in until the first floor was filled to the roof, leaving no space untouched as she forced out all the trapped air she could find, determined not to let any of them slip past her notice.

She sensed one ghoul hiding inside a chest freezer. She filled the container with icy water and tore the Creature apart with it.

It wasn't enough. She had to be sure. She continued drawing more and more water into the building, flooding the next level and then her own, using the water to seek them all out in whatever hiding place they'd found. As she trapped each one she formed knives of ice to behead the ghouls, one at a time. All died without a scream, water already filling their lungs.

Reaching out through the water she drew the last ghoul to her, the woman's long black hair streaming in the freezing water as she struggled and kicked and tried to grab anything that might help.

Grace pinned her to the floor with ice and created a large air bubble for her. The ghoul vomited water from her lungs, sucking in air as if she actually needed it to survive.

"Please!" she begged, eyes desperate. Grace didn't recognise her, but there was one Creature missing from her kill count. Abbey. She had to find the succubus too.

"Please?" Grace queried. She diverted more water over the ghoul, freezing everything below her neck. "Your kind started this, not me. Who else have you told about mermaids and our necklaces?"

There was absolute fear on the ghoul's face. "Nobody! I swear. Please don't kill me. I'll do anything! I promise. Please, just let me live."

Grace crouched beside the trapped ghoul and drew water into her hand, forming a thick blade. "Our promises are binding." She touched the sharp edge of her frozen knife to the Creature's throat. "Why don't you beg me to drive this through your heart? You promised me you'd do anything, after all."

Trapped by her own promise, the ghoul's eyes widened. "Please drive that blade through my heart," she said, but as soon as the words were finished she screamed. "No! No! No! Please don't!"

"Where would Abbey go?"

"I have no idea."

"And no one else knows about any of this except Abbey?"

"Only Josh. I promise."

Grace pursed her lips, regretting what she had to do to finish this. "Sometimes you have to kill to survive," she whispered, and drove the blade through the Creature's heart. She might have offered the ghoul some mercy if she wasn't likely to die when her own stolen lifeforce ran out, but she had to ensure her sisters were safe.

She used frozen water to sever the ghoul's head, turning away as she did it.

With the last of them gone, she released her hold on the water in and around the building. Windows and doors shattered outward in a gushing flood from the vast majority of water that had remained unfrozen, carrying bodies, blood, office supplies and even furniture with it.

Grace had no idea what the authorities would make of it afterward, but they were hardly likely to blame a war between ghouls and mermaids despite the dismembered bodies they'd find. She trudged through the sodden building, searching for Abbey despite being sure she was gone, but hoping to find her anyway.

The succubus must have escaped before Grace had sealed the building. Hopefully no one else had gotten out.

Outside, Grace circled the building as quickly as she could while the comforting storm pounded her head and shoulders, doing little to shift the mess she'd made. Streams still flooded from windows and doors toward drains, many blocked by the debris she'd created. The sound of a lone siren in the distance suggested someone had noticed. No doubt more humans would follow.

Surprisingly, the threat humans posed didn't bother her. Abbey was out there somewhere, and Abbey was a much greater threat.

Grace placed her palms on wet concrete, letting herself sense the entire town through the rain the storm had brought. There were more people out and about than she'd have expected, including Josh, trudging toward his house. He was safe, at least.

She concentrated, searching for the tell-tale signs of a Creature. Unless Abbey had managed to get inside and dry, Grace might still be able to find her.

And if she couldn't? To protect her sisters Grace was prepared to bring ruin to the entire bayside town even if it meant using the storm to smash every building and flush out the red-headed succubus.

[36]

Closer than she'd expected, Grace found a presence with barely any noticeable lifeforce. It was entirely different to the ghouls and werewolves she recognised, and hoped it was Abbey. The presence disappeared for a moment, but then reappeared, almost as if the Creature had stepped under shelter from the rain and back into it. It happened again. Whoever it was, they were avoiding water, a good sign for Grace. Even better, she couldn't sense any other Creatures nearby.

Grace began running, her bare feet splashing and keeping her connected to the wet town. She hurtled through the streets south of the hospital and across the golf course at supernatural speeds, a sickly feeling beginning to grow inside her. Grace was heading toward Josh's home.

She almost stumbled as she tried to keep a vague map of the suburbs in her head, but all she knew was the direction and rough distance. If she was right, Abbey was already there, which put Josh in incredible danger, though she didn't actually know where he was now.

Risking speed over certainty, she stopped tracking and ran faster, almost collapsing when she got to Josh's house. The place was dark and quiet, and as far as she could tell no one was home. The front and back doors were locked, and no one responded to her pounding on the doors or windows. Belatedly, she remembered the storm and the fact everything was wet, and sent out her senses through the water. Abbey had been here, but left alone. There was no trace of Josh. Instead, found him close to the town centre.

She focused on Abbey then and sprinted down street after street until she got to the same church grounds where she'd recently confessed her sins.

Her quarry was nearby, probably hoping holy ground would put Grace off. Big mistake. She concentrated, placing her palms on the ground. She sensed the succubus on the grounds on the far side.

Was she trying to break into a church? Was that even possible?

Careful not to be seen despite the dark and rain concealing her, Grace darted across the open ground and moved close to the wall of the building. She could hear a church service of some kind inside, and people singing a hymn. Could Abbey enter churches too?

She ran to the back of the church, but as she rounded the corner something punched her in the chest. She staggered back as another bullet hit her in the shoulder, the weapon. A third bullet barely missed her temple as she scrambled back around the corner. Summoning some of her stolen lifeforce, she expelled the bullets and healed herself, but she didn't dare risk rushing around the corner again. Every bit of lifeforce she used meant an earlier death, and despite her desire to kill Abbey, she had no death wish.

Abbey rounded the corner at a distance, the gun pointed at Grace's head. She smiled in victory. Her sodden hair was stuck to her head and face, but she didn't push it aside. "I'm pretty sure a bullet in your brain will put you down long enough for me to make it really hard for you to regenerate," Abbey said.

Grace held still. "Shall we discuss options over tea and bickies?"

Abbey's grin widened. "You messed up a really sweet operation here. I think you've killed every ghoul in the town."

"Considering you went to Josh's house on the way here, I'm thinking you're next."

"I'm thinking not. I haven't seen you move fast enough to dodge a bullet, so that gives me the advantage. And don't try any of that ice crap either. I'll shoot you first. We underestimated you, that's all."

"So what then? Planning on making me dig my own grave before you shoot and dismember me?" Grace wished she was fast enough to take the gun and stuff it sideways up Abbey's arse.

Abbey gave a wicked laugh as if the comment delighted her. "I'm honestly not sure that will work, but I'm willing to try."

Grace dodged as Abbey shot. The bullet shattered her left cheek even as Grace moved forward and knocked the gun out of Abbey's hand. Abbey punched, pain from her shattered cheekbone almost sending her to the ground. She stumbled against the brick wall, a downpipe at her back, and for a good half second she saw nothing but black.

Abbey swore and dived for the gun which had landed near the retaining wall while Grace drew the weakening rain to her and pummelled Abbey with it. It was enough to distract her. As the succubus staggered Grace sprinted around the corner of the building. A bullet ricocheted from the brick just as she rounded the corner.

Desperate to avoid more damage, Grace jumped and drove her claws into the wall, breaking away shards of brick as she pulled her feet up and sprang for the roof. She grabbed the eve just as Abbey rounded the corner and took a bullet in the leg as she hauled herself up.

Wincing, Grace drew on her precious stores of lifeforce to heal both her face and leg, but at least the second bullet had gone through. She'd barely finished as Abbey reached the roof and hauled herself up with supernatural strength, landing lightly on the slippery metal. Grace kicked hard, knocking Abbey sprawling across the roof, her claws tearing up the sheet metal to stop herself falling from the edge.

Grace leapt onto the steep slope of the upper roof, claws punching into the sheet metal as she went for the cross at the top, using the high point for cover as Abbey got to her feet and shot again. Sliding down a couple of feet on the other side, Grace sat on the metal overhang sheltering one of the high windows.

Taking a breather, she swore. She should have brought a gun too. There'd been plenty of them at the Eris building.

People had begun running out of the building after hearing the fight on the roof. Tearing up the roof with her claws probably hadn't helped keep them calm. If she slid down she could make a run for it, but that would still leave a problem. Abbey.

"You're trapped!" Abbey called. "Only option is down and I'll put a bullet in you the moment you try."

Thunder rumbled in the distance, the bulk of the storm having passed, but rain still sprinkled down, pattering lightly on the roof. She ignored the familiar desire to change form, focusing instead on Abbey's voice as she placed her palms against the roof. As always, the water was keen to do as she wanted, almost like it had a mind of its own yet still part of her. What she wanted was ice, and it spread out from her fingertips and became slick and hard.

Abbey swore. "An icy roof can't hurt me," the succubus called. "And I'm not likely to slip like a human. It's an inconvenience."

Grace used the falling rain to thicken the ice, but there really wasn't much. Ice formed on Abbey too, but not enough to hurt the succubus. What's more, Abbey simply moved and it shattered and fell.

Grace needed more water. Much more.

Grace sensed Abbey moving around the roof to her right. The succubus wasn't stupid enough to get too close, but it was enough to force Grace to move too. The ice under Grace's bare feet melted slightly and moulded to her step, keeping her from slipping, which gave her an idea. There wasn't enough water on the roof to draw and freeze into a shield good enough to defend herself, but maybe she didn't need a shield. She was on a church after all, and most magical Creatures weren't able to enter a holy place any more than a human home. She had no idea why she was an exception, but she'd take it.

She drew as much water as she could and worked it between the metal sheeting and into the roof under Abbey's feet.

"You can't hide forever," Abbey called. "And I've got more clips to empty into you. I want to know how many bullets you can take before you die for real. You wouldn't be hiding if they didn't have some effect."

Grace kept low while directing as much water as she could into the roof cavity and among the supporting timbers under Abbey, not easy considering roof was designed to prevent that and Abbey was on the far side. She punched the tips of her claws through to make it easier. When she was sure she had enough water within the roof cavity under Abbey's feet, she froze and expanded it between the roofing supports. They blew out with the sound of an explosion, and the succubus cried as a huge hole appeared under her and she fell.

Grace broke from cover, crossed the roof and jumped for the hole, hoping to catch the succubus and disarm her.

She slammed feet first into Abbey who was suspended in the air, the rest of the roof having fallen through to the pews below. Grace almost tumbled off the succubus toward the church's floor, but dug her claws into her leg as she fell past.

Abbey screamed in pain and swung the gun at Grace, but Grace caught the weapon with her free hand, wrenched it free and threw it back out of the hole above them and onto the roof.

"I am not dying today," Abbey swore, trying to reach for a broken spar, but it was almost as if she were laying on a sinking sheet of plastic suspended over a hole. She kept slipping deeper toward the sagging centre, and further away from freedom.

Below them, the church had completely emptied, a small mercy.

Grace dug her claws deeper into Abbey's leg, wishing she could suck out whatever lifeforce her body contained.

"Aahh!" Abbey screamed in rage more than pain, twisting enough that Grace fell, crashing hard over the back of a timber pew and shattering it.

"Ooh," she whimpered among the broken timbers, the only word she could say as she tried to breathe. Her whole left side felt bruised. She directed some lifeforce to the area and flushed away the swelling and bruising, thankfully finding her hip okay. It hurt worse than a bullet, though.

"How the..." Abbey whispered in surprise, staring down at Grace. She remained suspended by whatever magic protected homes and holy sites from Creatures.

Grace winced as pain shot through her neck. Abbey still seemed to be stuck as if she were trapped inside a giant slippery bubble, the bubble bending further and further toward the floor with her weight.

"How can you enter a church?" Abbey asked. She pushed herself up to her hands and knees, the barrier protecting the church almost solid under her. She slipped and only her supernatural reflexes helped her maintain her balance.

She was too high for Grace to reach, even jumping. She had to be fifteen feet above the ground or more. Grace would have to go outside the church and climb back up to the roof to get at the succubus. Or...

"I invite you in," she said, tensing to strike in the anticipation that Abbey would fall.

Nothing. Abbey remained suspended.

"Not your church, water wench. Guess you'll have to build a tower." Abbey glanced at the roof, plotting some sort of escape. As she twisted she slipped like she was on some sort of a water slide. "Frag it," Abbey swore, her face squished against the invisible barrier like a sheet of clear plastic. She carefully pushed herself back to her hands and knees.

It was a standoff, at least until Grace could get to the roof again.

"I invite you in," called a male voice from the church's altar.

[37]

"No!" Abbey screamed as she fell into the church, slamming into shards of the broken pew Grace had already shattered.

Grace reached toward Abbey as the succubus drew another gun from her ankle holster and shot Grace square in her chest, knocking her backwards.

"What does it take to kill you?" Abbey asked as she stood.

Grace collapsed with the gun pointed at her. Grace clutched at a bit of broken pew, desperate for any weapon, but another bullet punched into her side.

She doubled up with a grunt, and without looking hurled the wood as hard as she could, sensing Abbey through her wet clothing and hair.

The broken timber struck with enough force to punch through Abbey's side, throwing her back over a pew. The succubus crashed to the ground with a cry of pain.

Grace had to finish it. Now. Clenching her teeth in pain, she pushed herself to her feet and staggered toward Abbey, determined to twist the succubus's head off if necessary.

"Wait!" Abbey cried as Grace approached, and stupidly, Grace hesitated. Abbey raised her gun and fired again, the bullet slamming into Grace's chest. She staggered as another three quickly followed.

She collapsed to her knees, choking on her own blood again as she called on her precious store of lifeforce to force the bullets out.

Holy water. She could sense it in the two fonts at the front of the church. She pulled the water to her and then sprayed frozen droplets at Abbey with all the force she could.

The succubus cried out and dropped her gun.

"Bitch," Grace whispered as Abbey writhed from the pain of having her face torn up. Gingerly, Grace got to her feet. If she healed much more than she already had she'd most likely die from a lack of lifeforce.

She didn't like the situation, but for the safety of her sisters she'd do anything, including murdering a succubus in a church. "Time to die," Grace whispered.

"Please," Abbey said, grasping the wood skewering her as if she hoped to pull it free and crawl away. "I'll leave you all alone. I promise, no bargaining. A simple promise."

Father Sumare approached, his dark skin pale after what he saw. "I realise this is none of my business, but this is still my church. Please Grace, there has to be another way."

He didn't understand the danger Abbey represented. Abbey may have to abide by any promise, but there was a lot of damage she could still do. Talking to other Creatures, for one. Grace didn't want to kill again, but it had to be done.

"I'm sorry, Father," Grace whispered. "It's for the best."

"I know you Grace, and I know you don't come from a place of anger and hatred. Find another way. Please."

Abbey abruptly cried out, both hands clutching the wood through her stomach. She'd managed to pull it out about three inches, dark red blood smeared on the surface.

Her hands slipped away as a tear escaped her right eye and ran down her face. "Just kill me then," she whispered. "You're going to anyway. Make it quick."

Father Sumare put a hand on Grace's shoulder. "You don't have to."

Grace reluctantly turned to Abbey. The succubus had one hand on the wood impaling her, but she wasn't trying to remove it, or at least trying to find the courage to.

"Well," Abbey muttered. "What else do you want? Another promise? Or are you still planning to kill me?"

"You want to die?"

"Of course I don't want to die. If you expect me to kiss your arse though... well, I guess... maybe I could." She grimaced in pain. "Yeah, I'm willing to do that. I did it for Catherina often enough. I guess I got too greedy."

Grace raised her eyebrows. "You'd kiss my arse?"

"Well… not literally." She hesitated. "Well, maybe literally. Would it help?"

"I can't have you as a threat to my kind."

"What do you want me to say? That I'll be your faithful lapdog and obey your every word? That I'll never betray you or your secrets?"

It was better than anything Grace had considered. Considering she was in a church and she should give Father Sumare a say in this, she shrugged. "That'd about do it, but not if you're going to try for loopholes. Make it an honest promise."

Abbey gave the wood in her stomach an experimental tug, and winced. When the pain passed, she sighed.

"I promise to be your faithful servant and willingly obey you. I promise never to betray you, your secrets, or the secrets of your kind. Happy?" She put out a bloody hand, as if shaking on it would make some kind of a difference.

Grace shook the offered hand. "Happy," she said, sensing the full weight of Abbey's promise settle into the Creature's flesh.

She couldn't help riling Abbey up though, just a little. "My own pet succubus. What the hell am I supposed to do with you now?"

"How about unimpaling me?"

"Now you're giving me orders?"

"You asked."

"Here's what's going to happen," Grace began. "You're never going to reveal what happened. Never a word."

Abbey rolled her eyes. "Of course. I promised, remember?"

"Next, you'll obey my daughter Sandra under the same conditions as you would with me, keeping all her secrets too. For the rest of your life."

Abbey glared. "As you command."

"Say it as a promise."

She sighed dramatically. "I promise to obey your daughter Sandra under the same conditions I promised you, and to keep her secrets as I would for you."

Relief washed through Grace. Abbey's promise to Grace would die with Grace, but Sandra would remain. Her sisters would be safe. "You'll also look out for Josh and protect him from Creatures if necessary. I want him to lead a normal human life, free from our complications."

"Fine. I promise to look after Josh. He won't even know I'm around."

"I also want you to buy a house near the water, close enough so mermaids can leave the ocean and find a sanctuary there, with plenty of clothes to dress in. Any mermaid will be welcome to use it, and I'll expect you to provide the clothes and anything else they need."

"Why don't you just bankrupt me?"

Grace narrowed her eyes.

"Okay! Okay! I will, of course. I'll find the money and get it organised as soon as possible."

"And you'll never harm a human again. Is that clear?"

"But I need lifeforce-"

"Then you'll need to get it without harming anyone."

"Fine!" She might have promised to obey, but the promise hadn't removed her attitude. "I promise not to harm humans."

Grace gripped the wood and Abbey tensed. With a sharp pull, Grace ripped it free. Abbey cried out softly and slumped, eyes closed and tearing as she curled in on herself. "Oh God that hurts."

"Go. Start organising the beach house first. Stand with your feet in the water every dawn in case I or Sandra wish to give you further instruction."

Abbey painfully got to her feet as Grace dropped the bloody wood to the ground. "You could be more polite about it," Abbey muttered as she slowly limped from the church.

Outside Grace heard distant thunder, the storm moving out to sea.

She guessed she had enough lifeforce to last to dawn. She'd be able to witness another sunrise, at least.

Grace was beginning to feel every ache she'd somehow missed before. She could have used lifeforce to properly heal herself, but that would only reduce the time she had left.

"Thanks for looking after my soul," Grace murmured. She gave Father Sumare one brief nod before staggering out of his church, trying not to look at the disaster she'd caused. What would the humans make of everything that had happened tonight? She was surprised the cops hadn't turned up here, but they were probably busy at the abortion clinic. Whatever supernatural force protected Creatures from discovery would no doubt force a logical explanation, though they'd have to get very creative.

Outside, every step brought Grace the sensation of water covering the town. All she had to do now was find somewhere nice and quiet to die.

She figured she'd been born on land yet lived in the ocean, so dying by the sea seemed appropriate. Perhaps she'd dangle her feet in the water as she died. That would be nice.

[38]

THE ROAD GLISTENED WETLY under the streetlights as Grace slowly walked downhill toward the ocean, the occasional car pulling up spray as it passed. From the church the view to the water was normally beautiful, but now she could only sense the ocean at a distance.

With all the excitement over she could feel her body using up the remains of her stolen lifeforce at an incredible pace. What she burned in hours would give life to any mermaid for a year. She couldn't justify living with the cost of maintaining that.

When she arrived at the ocean she strode into the waves and dived under, calling to Sandra. Within minutes her daughter slammed into her with a fierce hug, her fears for her son carried on the water and through their touch.

"Josh is safe," Grace whispered. That drew another hug.

It took Grace a while to tell the full story, leaving out only the part about her impending death. "And Abbey will obey us? No tricks?"

"No tricks, though expect some attitude," Grace said. "Go back to our sisters now. I have one more thing to do."

It almost broke her heart to see Sandra leave. It was the last time they'd ever see each other. The sky was brightening over the ocean when she eventually strode out of the water and onto a secluded beach a good distance down the coast.

She reached out and gently calmed the stormy waves around the headland as she followed the rocks to its point. Through the water on the rocks she sensed Sandra out deep, a few miles away already and awkwardly making her way toward the company of her new sisters.

Grace still half expected ghouls or werewolves to jump out at her. She was sure she hadn't missed any. All her sisters were safe. It had cost Maria, Rick and Talithia their lives, and it would soon claim her own, but it was better than igniting a war her sisters couldn't hope to finish without devastating losses on both sides. She felt oddly content with that, as if her life had meaning and been worth it.

She stopped where a flat rock met water, and feeling the agitation of the storm-tossed ocean she reached out and calmed the surrounding water once more. The surface became quiet again, only small waves lapping against the rocks with gentle splashing sounds. She had a strong desire to be touching the ocean when she died, so Grace sat and dangled her feet over the edge and let the water tease her feet and ankles.

And then cold fear overcame her. She'd forgotten her promise to Maria to do everything she could to survive. Despite the fact Maria was gone the promise wasn't reliant on Maria's life or presence.

"Oh no," she whispered as the first stirrings of an urge to kill began growing inside her. Worse, it was one of her sisters she wanted to kill so she could take not only the lifeforce contained in her necklace, but the distilled lifeforce in her body.

Grace's lifeforce was almost gone now, fuelling her promise to Maria. She fought it off even as she felt it like a clock winding down, only each second was a measure of her remaining life and a rising need to kill.

If she could resist it long enough though, she might be able to ensure she didn't kill in time to save herself.

She had minutes left, hopefully enough to see the sun rise. Gritting her teeth she closed her eyes and tilted her head skyward, eyes closed to the brightening horizon as she tried to focus on the sounds of the ocean meeting the land. She was a Creature of both worlds, land and sea, so it was fitting that she should die straddling the two, if she could.

"You look like you're feeling unhappy with yourself," a woman said.

"What the-" Grace twisted with surprise to find Kimbriel standing on the rock behind her. Unconcerned by her reaction, the small blonde woman sat beside her, though she wasn't tall enough for her feet to reach the ocean.

"How did you do that?" Grace asked. "I never heard you." Waves washed over the woman's bare feet in reaction to Grace's agitation, letting Grace know the woman's lifeforce was as human as her own must have once been. And yet, Kimbriel wasn't. She couldn't be. "What are you?"

Kimbriel laughed merrily. "You've made the ocean very peaceful here." She pushed her long blonde hair over a shoulder and gave a quick shake of her head to settle it. "I'm one of the few people in the world that understands the true nature of magic, or lifeforce as you think of it, and I know it's fading in you even if I can't sense it myself. Your body has needs far greater than you can absorb through natural means, but then, I suppose that's true of all mermaids." She met Grace's eyes with a flat stare. "I also know about your promise to Maria."

Grace wasn't sure if that was some kind of a threat, or merely an astute observation. Why else speak of it?

A cold shiver of fear passed through Grace, along with exhaustion and regret. Her claws began to extend in response. She could smell the woman's lifeforce this close, her body beginning to crave it. In another minute or two she'd be lucky to be able to control herself.

The woman glanced at Grace's claws as if reading her mind, a hint of a smile quirking a corner of her mouth. "I'm not here to threaten you or your kind, Grace, and you'll find that taking my lifeforce is a little more difficult than you'd like. I just thought you might like some company."

"If I wanted company I'd have sought out someone I love. You should go. I'm dangerous to everyone right now." It's why she'd come to a secluded headland. That, and she had no doubt she'd attack the woman soon. She'd made a promise to survive after all. Grace sat straighter. "What do you want?"

Kimbriel stared at the impending sunrise without squinting, ignoring any threat Grace may represent. "You have no idea what's happening to you, do you Grace? You don't even know what you are. Not really."

"What I am?" Was Kimbriel taunting her, or was it an honest question? "I'm a mermaid. What do you want?"

Kimbriel met her gaze, and it was unsettling. "Do you really want to die, Grace? More to the point, do you really want to regularly kill your sisters, or a human every day, just to meet your promise to Maria?"

"No."

"Very good answer. We've reached an understanding then."

"What? We've done no such thing."

"Ahh, but we have. I'm prepared to share a secret with you, but only on the understanding it's not to be shared with anyone else. We have to keep it between you and me. Want to play?"

Grace was not about to bind herself into any deals without knowing the risks. "No." Out on the water, perhaps a mile away, she could see a boat. A boat meant people, and she needed to kill. She should have gone inland, away from people, not to the ocean. She could feel herself beginning to tremble with need.

The woman returned her gaze to the sunrise as if the answer bothered her. "There's not enough magic in this world to sustain you, Grace. Not easily. I assume you understand that?"

"Of course. It's why I'm trying to die." God, how much did this woman know about Creatures?

"You're evolving, not dying, but your body requires more magic than it used to. Much more. The distilled magic your sisters contain within their bodies would at best slake your needs."

"Speak plainly or bugger off. I'm over riddles."

Kimbriel smiled. "Lifeforce is the magical energy derived from living creatures, including you. Those necklaces of yours are surprisingly innovative, which brings us to the next point."

Grace gritted her teeth. Either she was about to attack Kimbriel or she was going to go for the boat. All she wanted was a little peace and quiet, and to die before she could do anything bad. "Please hurry."

"Talithia kicked off a reaction in your body. An awakening, if you like. You're evolving, but your body needs a more abundant supply of magic to complete the transition."

"You've covered that."

"I've been waiting for you for a long time Grace, and I'm loath to let you die. Yet I'm sure you'll find a way to top yourself despite your promise."

She touched one of the white crystals on Grace's wrist, her fingertip caressing it.

Hesitantly, Grace held her arm up, wondering if the touch was a hint. "Are you telling me there's another way?" she asked, indicating the crystals. Her lifeforce was burning up so rapidly she doubted she had more than a few more minutes. She dug the claws of her other hand against the stone, chipping a shell off. Perhaps if she held on tightly enough.

"Promise to keep the secret I'm going to give to you, and I'll explain how you can survive without having to kill another human or any of your sisters."

Grace swallowed. "But-"

"Promise you'll keep the secret or I won't share."

"But Sandra and my other sisters, they'll still have to kill humans. There's no deal without them."

Kimbriel shrugged. "I'm sorry we couldn't do business, Grace. I'll leave you to your..." she glanced across the water to the distant boat. "Murder."

"Wait!" Grace said, grasping the woman's hand in both of hers. She could feel the last of her reserves burning up like ignited oxygen, and the urgency to kill consumed her thoughts. "Okay. I promise to keep your secret. I won't share it." She felt the promise settle on her like a suffocating smog.

Kimbriel smiled. "Give me the bracelet."

Grace still felt nothing from it. "Why?" she asked as she removed it, growing desperate now she had some hope. "There's nothing there." She could already feel the last traces of her lifeforce burning out, and it was all she could do to avoid attacking Kimbriel. Even if there was magic in the crystals, she only had moments left.

Kimbriel turned Grace's hand flat and positioned one of the crystals on her palm, placing her own hand over Grace's. "Don't do this more than once every two years, and certainly not until the last measure of what you gain has settled into your body. You want to feel like you're starving before doing it again. Absolutely starving, as you are now. You won't like the consequences otherwise."

The woman concentrated and energy surged into Grace through the crystal. She jolted as if hit by lightning.

Lifeforce, distilled into its purest form, rushed into her body. It was an impossible amount. A couple of years' worth for her, and centuries for any other mermaid. Perhaps more. It was fire and ice, love and ecstasy and everything she'd ever needed. Her hand clenched around Kimbriel's smaller one, crushing. Her claws distended but failed to damage the woman's skin. She felt like exploding. Her heart stopped beating.

She collapsed, falling backwards to hit the hard rock. It was too much magic. Kimbriel had killed her.

And then her heart thumped, alive with the thrill of untainted lifeforce. Not stolen. Given after being distilled into the crystal.

She drew in a breath, and the air that rushed into her lungs felt fresher than she'd ever known. It was cool and salty and perfect, clean off the ocean.

Blood pounded noisily through her ears while salty air filled her lungs, carrying with it the full joy of the ocean and the sense of her sisters within it. The water lapping against her feet seemed far softer than water should be. Even the stone she lay on, water-smooth as it was, had developed an entirely new texture. She tried to raise her head but didn't have the energy to lift it, while the cool stone pressed gently against her free palm.

She hadn't made love to anyone in more than a century, but making love had felt something like that. Joy and desire, all of it wrapped into one tiny crystal. And still she couldn't move.

Magic filled her. Pure, incredible, and joyous. It thrummed through every cell of her body like the perfect note struck from a crystal glass, resonating like music.

Kimbriel knelt beside her. "Mermaids are tadpoles in the greater scheme of things. Unfortunately, this world doesn't have the magic your kind needs to evolve. Your sisters barely survive as it is. What I just gave you is a way around that. This world will need you one day, and you'll want to ensure your sisters survive. When the conditions are right, magic will return and they can evolve in their own time."

Grace struggled to raise her head. All over the world she could sense water. In the clouds, the rivers, the lakes. She could feel mermaids everywhere. Her sisters. *Her daughters*. Her charges.

And she wanted to kill them all. "What the hell?"

Kimbriel smiled sadly. "Three thousand years ago I brought a friend to this world in preparation for someone like you. She created the first endemic mermaids here. You're the first since then to begin evolving."

Kimbriel folded Grace's fingers over the crystals. "Can you feel the magic in the crystals now?"

Grace nodded. She wanted it. It called to her now, as did the distilled magic she could feel in the flesh of her sisters. They were different types of magic, but they were all accessible to her now. "What did you do?"

"You may burn the lifeforce stored in a crystal no more than once every two years, and only ever one at a time," Kimbriel said. "Avoid your sisters if you can. They represent temptation now."

"But… it's like we're all sharks in a womb, and I'm the only egg that's hatched."

"It'll pass in a few dozen millennia. Focus on the crystals. It takes them a solid decade to recharge even if conditions are favourable, and you only have five. Use them to avoid turning on your sisters. Don't burn the magic in them until you're desperate, no matter how tempting, or you'll turn on your sisters if you come up short. If you absorb magic from the crystals more often than once every two years you'll also start to crave and need it more often, and you don't have enough to sustain a faster rate of evolution. Your sisters will suffer for it."

Grace sat up, still breathing hard. "I'll do as you say," she said softly. Anything for her sisters.

"Let's see if you're still thanking me when I call on your help."

"Help?"

Kimbriel stared toward the horizon, the sun just beginning to appear. "There's a war coming Grace. With you we have a slim chance. Goodbye." With a smile, Kimbriel faded away as if she'd never been there.

Grace stared at the empty space. Kimbriel had just... vanished. Again. Only the crystals in her palm gave Grace any indication she'd ever truly been there. At least now she could sense the distilled magic in them.

"What war?" she wondered aloud.

[39]

It took Grace a while to get motivated, but she left the question of what she'd got into alone for now. She dived into the ocean, relishing the water's embrace as her body changed. She kicked her stolen clothes free and collected them, pinning them to the ocean floor with a rock, and then called to her sisters through the bond of water.

She felt fear from them. On some instinctive level they recognised she'd changed, and that they were in danger from her. Regardless, as many who could make it at short notice began gathering in the depths of the Pacific Ocean.

She shot through the water like a bolt of lightning, easily defying any speed she'd previously achieved by a hundred-fold, shooting up the coast and past the Great Barrier Reef, and then deep into the crushing ocean. She dove miles under the surface where sparse creatures resembled nothing like those near the surface. Giant squid and blind fish were briefly sucked into her wake, but she left them all behind before they could recover.

Ahead, a dozen mermaids had already gathered for a Council, the Council Grace had called. She could sense their curiosity growing at her impossibly rapid approach, but they'd already been curious to begin with. It was the undercurrent of fear she'd never sensed before. Fear of Grace.

She slowed to a speed only the oldest of the mermaids could achieve, those like Talithia, and then slowed again as she approached. The group formed themselves into a semi-circle, warily watching her. Many reacted with shock at the sight of her - her hair, at least, was now platinum-coloured and short, but it would grow, though she doubted its natural colour would ever return.

She settled into the centre of them, turning slowly so they could all see her clearly. Her tail was longer now, tipped by thin needle-like spines, and it had a long spine trailing from the end like a stingray's. The back of her tail and lower spine had a dorsal fin too, also spined and dangerous. She sensed their love and curiosity as well as their dread and concern. They couldn't help but love her, and she them, even if they'd began to fear her. "Sisters," she began. "Thank you for coming."

One of the older mermaids left the circle and approached her, a patronising smile on her face. Asumi, one of the original twelve sisters, and around Talithia's age. Her glorious jet-black hair streamed out behind her as she moved gracefully through the water. "Your unnatural ability to swim beyond normal limits offers no seniority," she said. "However, we are curious how you achieved it."

Asumi reached out to place her hands on Grace's temples, but Grace caught Asumi's wrists. Asumi's eyes widened in surprise and then anger. Asumi attempted to push past Grace's hold. Under normal circumstances, she should have been able to.

"Grace?" Asumi asked with a hint of fear in her voice. "How can you do that?"

"You may not read my thoughts and memories," Grace said, gently releasing Asumi's wrists. She'd promised Kimbriel she wouldn't share her secret, after all.

"But-"

"I'm here to formally announce that Talithia forgave Maria. She absolved Maria of all punishment, and accepted that no punishment should ever have been meted out. Both are gone now, but Maria was our sister and is to be remembered only as our sister, not our sister's killer."

Asumi narrowed her eyes. "Talithia was not our mistress. She had no right to revoke Maria's punishment."

Grace looked around the Council. "Then as a Council, you will formally agree to Talithia's final words and put the matter to rest," Grace said, the words more a command than a request. "I'll not have the same thing happen ever again."

"Maria killed our sister!" someone called from the circle. Uma, a mermaid nearly as old as the original twelve. "I don't believe Talithia would ever forgive Maria for that."

Grace couldn't afford any more conflict if Kimbriel's words came to pass. War. They had to be united. Grace didn't have any idea how powerful Kimbriel was, but didn't doubt she was far more dangerous than Grace understood. "Will you accept select memories?" she asked formally.

Looking around for some sort of assent from her sisters, Asumi nodded reluctantly.

Grace took Asumi's hands and placed them on her face before allowing Asumi to rest her forehead against Grace's. Most of the memories of the last few days flowed through her and into Asumi, focusing on the conversation Maria and Talithia had while captured in the hospital. She held back her conversations with Kimbriel.

Asumi gasped. "The truth," Asumi said. "How could it be otherwise? I'm sorry Grace, we've believed differently for so long. We should have sought the truth from Maria centuries ago, only no one wanted to accept her after committing so horrible a crime. She has my forgiveness, and I hope one day she'll give me hers." She stiffened. "I'm sorry. I didn't mean to say that." She turned toward those holding the circle. "I declare Maria innocent of any wrongdoing, and I'm happy to share Grace's memories to confirm it."

Uma looked from Grace to Asumi. "Of course. You can share the knowledge later, Asumi."

Grace finally had justice for her sister, even if it was too late. "Thank you. Until we meet again," she said formally.

"Go in peace."

When Grace returned to the coast off Batemans Bay, it didn't take long to find Sandra. "I think I might know how you can see your son really soon," she said. "Do you think you can avoid drowning him if he's in the water with you? Scuba diving?"

Sandra's sudden joy was tinged with fear. "Maybe, if you're there to keep me calm."

Grace smiled. "I'll stay close. And I'm sure that as long as you see him every couple of days he'll never forget what happened to you."

"Can we see him today?"

"I can try to arrange it." She took Sandra's hand, grinning. "Let's go home, daughter. And later, there's a whole ocean I want to show you."

PLEASE LEAVE A REVIEW

Thank you for reading Epicentre.

If you enjoyed the story as much as I loved writing it, I would consider it a personal favour if you left a review wherever you buy good books.

Thank you.
Chris Andrews

ALSO BY CHRIS ANDREWS

Fiction

Divine Prey: Normagaell Saga #1 - A Veil of Gods Novel

Moonlit Genesis - A stand-alone Veil of Gods Novel

Urban Magic and Other Tales

Non-Fiction

Character and Structure: An Unholy Alliance

ABOUT THE AUTHOR

Chris Andrews is an author of science fiction, fantasy and horror.

Find him at - http://chrisandrews.me

Stay in Touch
Subscribe to Chris's Newsletter

 facebook.com/chrisandrewsau

 twitter.com/ChrisAndrewsAU

 instagram.com/chrisandrews.me

 amazon.com/author/chrisandrews